THE ARROWS OF TIME

Orthogonal Book Three

GREG EGAN

The right of Greg Egan to be identified as the author
of this work has been asserted by him in accordance with
the Copyright, Designs and Patents Act 1988.

First published in Great Britain in 2013 by
Gollancz
An imprint of the Orion Publishing Group
Orion House, 5 Upper St Martin's Lane,
London WC2H 9EA
An Hachette UK Company

This edition published in Great Britain in 2014 by Gollancz

1 3 5 7 9 10 8 6 4 2

A CIP catalogue record for this book
is available from the British Library

ISBN 978 0 575 10577 5

Typeset at The Spartan Press Ltd,
Lymington, Hants

Printed and bound by CPI Group (UK) Ltd,
Croydon, CR0 4YY

The Orion Publishing Group's policy is to use papers that
are natural, renewable and recyclable products and made
from wood grown in sustainable forests. The logging and
manufacturing processes are expected to conform to the
environmental regulations of the country of origin.

www.gregegan.net
www.orionbooks.co.uk
www.gollancz.co.uk

Note to Readers

The Arrows of Time is the third volume of a trilogy set in a universe with laws of physics that are very different from our own. The protagonists belong to a species whose biology, history, politics and technology – as revealed in the previous books – bear crucially on everything that follows. Accordingly, anyone approaching this volume is strongly advised to read the preceding volumes first.

Contents

Contents

1

From her hilltop post, Valeria swept the telescope's field of view methodically across the barren plain. The grey rock showed few features in the starlight, but so long as she didn't rush the task and left no gaps in her search, the kind of change she was looking for would be hard to miss.

She knew she was done when she'd made a full circle around the scope's mount, bringing her feet back to a patch of rough ground that she could recognise by texture alone. Done and ready to begin again.

Two bells into her shift, Valeria could feel her concentration faltering, but whenever she was tempted to abandon the mind-numbing routine she thought of the incident outside Red Towers. The watcher there had seen a speck of light in the distance, small but growing steadily brighter. His team had reached the fire within a chime or two, and by drawing out its heat into three truckloads of calmstone sand they'd succeeded in extinguishing it. The Hurtler that struck must have been microscopic, the point of ignition shallow, the field of flame relatively small – and some scoffers had gone so far as to insist that there must have been similar strikes before, unobserved and untreated, that had come to nothing. But Valeria was sure that between the spot fires that would fizzle out on their own and the kind of unstoppable conflagration that would simply vaporise everyone in sight, there was room for the watchers to make a difference. If a planet-killer struck, it struck, but it wasn't futile for people to try their best to fend off disaster for as long as possible.

The clock beside her rang out the last bell before dawn. Valeria gave herself a break, rolling her neck and taking in the view untrammelled by the scope's restrictions. At the foot of the hill the response team, her co among them, were napping in their sand trucks. Gemma had risen now, bright enough to hide most of the stars, but seven Hurtlers shone in the grey half-light: seven streaks of colour, scattered but parallel, each one displaying perfect mirror-symmetry across its dark centre. These ghostly spikes were lengthening slowly, their violet tips just perceptibly in motion, proof that they hadn't even been near misses. If a planet-killer was on its way, there'd be no elegant pyrotechnic warning.

But nor would the opposite fate come with portents: if a real solution to the Hurtlers was imminent, the moment of salvation would pass without distinction. If such a feat was possible at all then it was due to be achieved any day now, but there would be no signal from the travellers on the *Peerless*, no manifestation in the sky, no evidence of any kind.

Still, Valeria took the Hurtlers themselves as proof that the travellers' first goal was attainable: one object really could possess an infinite velocity relative to another. The history of each Hurtler was orthogonal to her own: the tiny rock's eons of ancient darkness and its fiery passage through the thin gas between the planets all came and went for her in an instant, with nothing but the time lag for the light to reach her prolonging the spectacle. If the *Peerless* really had been accelerating steadily for the past year, its engines firing without mishap, its relationship to her would soon be the same as the Hurtlers'. Having entered that state, the travellers could maintain their course for as long as they needed, and whether the need was measured in generations or in eras, from her point of view they would live out their lives in the same blink of her eye, regardless.

Valeria stepped away from the telescope and followed the lines of the Hurtlers to their notional vanishing point. Watching from Zeugma, she'd seen the blaze of flaming sunstone as the mountain sped away in exactly this direction. She held up her thumb, blotting out the point in the sky where the *Peerless* had been heading – blotting out a line that stretched away from her for an immeasurable distance. At the moment of orthogonality, that line would contain the entire history of the travellers from the day they shut off the engines to the day they had reason to return.

In that instant, Yalda would struggle to give the whole endeavour the best foundations she could; in that instant, her time would come and she'd divide or die. In that instant, generations would follow her who had never seen the home world, and knew they never would. But they'd strive to gain the knowledge that their distant cousins needed, because they'd understand that it was the only way their own descendants could thrive. And in that instant, the journey, however long it had continued, would have to reach some kind of turning point. Hard-won triumph or abject failure, the same moment would encompass it all.

Valeria kept her arm stretched out to the sky, humming softly as she mourned the woman who'd helped raise her. But Yalda would leave behind a powerful legacy. Among her successors in that cloistered mountain, free to spend their lives in unhurried rumination, someone would find a way to spare the world from the Hurtlers.

Valeria was done with asking when. With nothing in the sky to prove her right or wrong, she was free to name the moment when the story of those generations finally unfurled, and the fate of the planet was settled in the blink of an eye, behind her thumb.

Everything that happens, she decided, *happens now*.

2

'Let the ancestors burn!' Pio declaimed. 'Why should we risk our children's lives to save those barbarians? We need to stop talking about "the home world" and start looking for ways to make a home for ourselves, right where we are.'

Agata was shocked. She turned to her mother and whispered, 'Did you know he was planning to go this far?'

'It's a debate,' Cira replied calmly. 'The speakers should put both sides as strongly as possible; that's the whole point.'

In the meeting room's near-weightlessness the audience was spread out in three dimensions, and the hubbub evoked by her brother's opening statement came at Agata from all directions. It sounded very much as if the people around her had taken Pio's words to be more than a rhetorical flourish – and, alarmingly, she could hear a few chirps of approval mixed in with the murmurs of disquiet.

Pio waited a few more pauses for the crowd to settle before he continued. 'People talk about estimating the risks and making some kind of trade-off. People talk about weighing the gross-to-the-fourth living on the home world against our own numbers: less than a gross squared. People do their best to convince us that it would be an abominable act of selfishness and treason to contemplate sacrificing so many lives for the sake of so few. But to sacrifice *ourselves* in some misguided attempt to rescue the ancestors would benefit no one. It would simply be the end of the species.'

This bleak conclusion relied on at least two false premises, but Agata restrained herself from offering a running commentary. Pio's official opponent would soon have a chance to rebut him in front of the whole audience; all Agata could do was irritate her mother and a few hapless bystanders.

'So what's the alternative?' Pio asked. 'We have the means to go on living in this mountain for at least a dozen more generations – and in that time, surely, we can find a way to make the orthogonal worlds our home.'

An amused voice interjected loudly, 'How?'

'I can't answer that,' Pio admitted. 'Perhaps a physicist will find a way to transform our positive luxagens into negative ones, letting us walk safely on the Object before we move on to a larger orthogonal world. Perhaps a biologist will find a way for us to sculpt orthogonal matter into a new generation of children, who bear our traits without being shed directly from our own flesh.' Agata's neighbours in the crowd were reacting with equal parts hilarity and incredulity now. 'Did the ancestors know that we'd learn to make an Eternal Flame?' Pio persisted. 'Of course not! They merely trusted that, with time and dedication, we'd solve the fuel problem one way or another. We need to respect our descendants' abilities to deal with a problem of their own.'

The debate timer rang. Pio flipped the lever to silence and restarted it, then moved back along the guide rope, allowing his opponent to take centre stage.

'Who knows what our descendants will achieve?' Lila began. 'I'm not going to try to refute Pio's speculations. But it does seem clear to me that any attempt to migrate into orthogonal matter would be perilous – and beyond the danger to the actual pioneers aspiring to set foot on the Object, everyone on the *Peerless* would be hostage to the need to complete the process in a limited time. Over the generations, as their resources dwindled, they'd be forced to keep wondering whether they needed to cut their losses and try to head home after all. But the longer they put it off, the longer that return journey would be, and eventually any misjudgement of the time they had left would be fatal.

'Why should we subject our descendants to that kind of torture? We can turn the *Peerless* around right now, confident that it will support us long enough to complete the trip.'

Lila brought an image onto her chest; the room's camera picked it up and displayed it on the giant screen behind her. 'This is the plan,' she said. 'This was always the plan, from the day Eusebio broached it with Yalda.' The sight was enough for Agata to feel a latent impression of the same familiar curve, ready to rise up on her own skin. This was

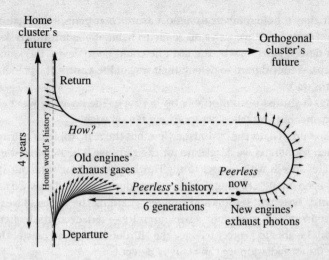

Home cluster's future

Orthogonal cluster's future

Return

How?

Home world's history

4 years

Old engines' exhaust gases

Peerless's history

Peerless now

6 generations

New engines' exhaust photons

Departure

the map of her life's purpose; she'd understood that since the day she'd first seen it.

'We know we can make the turn,' Lila said. 'All the way around that semicircle, the acceleration we need can be produced with the engines sending photons into the future of *either* the home cluster or the orthogonal cluster. Only the last stage of the journey presents a problem: it's not clear how we can begin to decelerate in the approach to the home world. But we'll have six more generations to address that, and I can't believe it will prove insurmountable.'

Lila glanced at the timer. 'To describe this plan as "dangerous" is absurd. Dangerous compared to trying to give birth to *children made of negative luxagens?* I don't think so!'

The timer rang. Most of the crowd cheered; Agata ignored her mother's look of lofty amusement and joined in. Lila deserved the encouragement. Pio's ideas weren't likely to get much traction, but with the vote less than a stint away they needed to be refuted decisively for the sake of everyone's morale.

Pio dragged himself forward again. 'What dangers would the return pose?' he asked. 'Let's start with a wildly optimistic view, and suppose that the entire journey could be completed safely. Once we reach the home world and deal with the Hurtlers, the barbarians are sure to be grateful – for a while. But could we really live among them, after so much time apart? I can't see them approving of our ideas about governance, let alone our reproductive methods, and my guess is that they'd hold Starvers in almost as much contempt as Shedders. Then again . . . since we've made such a habit of bequeathing tasks to our descendants, maybe the last one could be to devise the kind of weapons they'd need to defend their way of life against the planetary status quo.'

Agata shifted uncomfortably on her rope. She knew he was being sarcastic, but any talk of weapons put her on edge.

Pio said, 'That's the optimistic view, but the real problems will arise much sooner. As we decelerate for the turn, we'll be moving at ever greater speeds with respect to the Hurtlers. For a long time our spin has been enough to fling these specks of dust away, and now we have a fancy system of sensors and coherers guarding the slopes so we can spin-down the mountain with impunity – but even the coherers won't be able to protect us once the Hurtlers are moving faster than the fastest radiation we can actually detect.'

The audience fidgeted, underwhelmed. Everyone knew that the *Peerless* was a small target, and though it was true that the mountain's defences would be useless once the Hurtlers crossed a certain threshold velocity, the period of vulnerability would be brief.

Pio inclined his head slightly, acknowledging the weakness of the point and moving on. 'Lila assures us that the engines won't need to violate any thermodynamic laws as we turn the *Peerless* around. But how certain can we be that they really will keep functioning? And even if the turnaround itself proves uneventful, keep in mind that *the entire return journey* entails our own arrow of time pointing against the arrow of the orthogonal cluster – a configuration we've never experienced before.'

Agata couldn't contain an exasperated hum. The most dramatic effect she expected from the reversal was for the orthogonal stars to vanish from the sky.

'Beyond those disturbing uncertainties, no one has the slightest idea how we could commence the final deceleration. Lila herself admits as much!' Pio paused to let the audience dwell on this – despite his own cheerful confession that he had no idea how a viable migration scheme would work. 'Imagine what it would mean to be trapped in this mountain, heading back into a region full of ordinary matter but unable to slow down and match speeds with it. Every grain of interstellar dust we encountered would strike us with infinite velocity – rendering it as lethal to us as a Hurtler would be to the ancestors. Astronomers in Yalda's day searched the sky for years to find the safe corridor we're moving through now. We should take their gift and make the most of it: we should remain on this trajectory for as long as it's clear, and use the time to prepare ourselves to step away from all of these colliding worlds and find a home that will be safe for eons to come.'

As Pio reached down to reset the timer there were a few scattered cheers.

Lila took his place. 'If migrating to the orthogonal worlds would be so much easier than slowing the *Peerless* for the final approach,' she said, 'then let people ponder both questions while we're travelling back towards the home world. When one problem or the other is actually solved, we'll be in a position to make an informed choice. What's more, sticking to the plan and reversing the *Peerless* would actually make migration easier: all those negative luxagens in the orthogonal worlds will become positive to us! The thermodynamic arrow of the orthogonal stars will be pointing against us, but between coping with *that* and trying to walk on antimatter, I know which challenge I'd prefer.'

Agata turned to her mother and whispered, 'The woman just won. It's over!' Diehard migrationists might have their reasons to remain committed to the more difficult route, but whatever allure the idea held for wavering voters, Lila had just offered them a vastly less terrifying way to go on thinking about deserting the ancestors, without burning any bridges until their own safety was guaranteed.

Cira made a non-committal noise.

'It's a dangerous cosmos,' Lila declared. 'For us, for the ancestors – and for our descendants, whatever choices we make. But thanks to the efforts of the people who launched the *Peerless*, we've had six generations of thought and experiment to ameliorate that danger, and the prospect of six more to come. Pio calls those people barbarians, but what would be barbaric would be turning our backs on them for no other reason than a lack of certainty. If we're ever confronted with proof that trying to return to the home world would be suicidal, then of course we should change our plans. Until then, why would we not do our best to save the lives of the people to whom we owe our existence? And why would we not all wish our own descendants to be present at that glorious reunion, when the generation who flung a

9

mountain into the sky learn of the extraordinary things we've done with the time that they stole for us?'

Agata clung to a rope outside the voting hall, watching the bars of the histogram slowly rising on the news screen beside the entrance.

'Agata!' Her friend Medoro approached, the amiable look of recognition on his face giving way to one of amusement. 'How long have you been here?'

'A while,' she admitted. 'I voted early, and then I thought I'd stay and watch the turnout.'

'So you've been here since the first bell?'

'I've got nothing else to do,' she said defensively.

'If I'd known you were holding a vigil, I would have brought you supplies.'

'Go and vote,' she suggested, shooing him towards the entrance.

Medoro leant towards her in a conspiratorial pose. 'How much are you paying?' he whispered. 'I took a dozen pieces from your brother's side, but you still have a chance to buy me back.'

'That's not funny.'

He swayed back on the rope. 'Seriously, what's wrong with you? When I come out we should get something to eat.' Agata saw him lift his rear gaze towards the screen. 'I can barely even see that sliver for the no vote.'

'I'm not afraid that we might lose,' she said. 'What worries me is that we had to ask the question at all.'

'So we should just be happy cogs in Eusebio's machine?' Medoro goaded her. 'Born into the mountain with no say in anything?'

'You make it sound as if *Eusebio* had a choice,' Agata retorted. 'If there'd been no launch, you wouldn't have been born anywhere.'

'Of course,' Medoro agreed. 'The builders did the right thing, and I'm grateful. But that doesn't mean we should be enslaved to them. What we owe the ancestors isn't blind allegiance, it's constant scrutiny of the actual possibilities. Your brother's wrong because his arguments are wrong – not because the mere idea of deviating from the plan should be unthinkable.'

Agata was unimpressed by his euphemism: 'deviating from the plan' was a phrase befitting a bold rebellion against pernickety bureaucracy, not a calculated act that amounted to mass murder. But she wasn't in the mood to pick a fight. 'Pio's had his chance to be heard, so maybe that will get it out of his system.'

Medoro said, 'Sure – but it's not just Pio and the people who'll vote with him who needed this. Every one of us knows that the outcome was always a foregone conclusion . . . but it still matters that it's only a foregone conclusion because we'll judge it to be the best choice on offer.'

'Hmm.'

Medoro headed into the hall. Agata watched as the tally on the screen reached one third of the enrolled population. The 'yes' count now outnumbered the 'no' by more than a dozen to one. In principle the result remained undecided, but the truth was that her side was heading for an overwhelming victory.

Medoro emerged, and approached her with a guilty demeanour. 'Don't be angry with me,' he pleaded. 'But I thought it would only be fair to even things out a little—'

Agata took a swipe at him; he twisted away. She was almost certain that he was joking, but if he wasn't she didn't want to know.

'Come and eat,' Medoro said. 'Assuming you're not turning into a Starver.'

'Hardly.' Agata followed him down the corridor towards the food hall. 'I'm not turning into a Shedder, either.' The idea of giving birth terrified her – whether or not she had to live through the process – but beyond her own fears the last thing she'd wish on any child was to be raised by her idiot brother.

3

Greta turned to Ramiro. 'Start the spin-down,' she said.

Unaccountably, Ramiro hesitated. He'd been anxious for days that, at this very moment, some obscure detail that he'd failed to allow for would make itself known by undermining everything – but an unplanned hiatus wouldn't so much forestall the risk of humiliation as turn his fears into a self-fulfilling prophecy.

Just as Greta's expression of controlled anticipation was on the verge of faltering – and revealing to every onlooker that the delay was not just unexpected but incomprehensible – his paralysis ended and he threw the switch. A single tiny coherer in the panel in front of him sent its light into the maze of photonics below, and the system that Ramiro had spent the last six years building, testing and refining began, very slowly, to move the mountain.

The entire Council had crowded into the control room, and now they turned to watch the main navigation screen mounted high on the wall. At Greta's insistence, Ramiro had programmed an elaborate animation that made it look as if the sensor readings confirming the successful firing of the counter-rotation engines were only arriving gradually, piece by piece. 'Not so slowly that they start to get worried,' she'd suggested, 'but not so fast that it's an anticlimax.'

'And if something fails?' he'd asked. 'How do you want that paced?'

Greta had given this careful thought. 'Delay it long enough that it looks as if things were going perfectly, up to a point. But not so long that anyone could say that we were hiding it.'

Ramiro's own unobtrusive display was feeding him news in real time; so far it was all encouraging. Not only were the engines reporting a flawless performance, the accelerometers and the star trackers showed that the *Peerless* really had begun shedding its spin. If all went well, in less than three days the mountain would be perfectly still.

For the first time in six generations, chambers at the rim of the *Peerless* would be as weightless as those on the axis, and for a stint, the farmers and an army of helpers would work to reconfigure the fields, shifting soil from the useless centrifugal floors to surfaces once seen as walls. When they were done, the mountain would be slowly flipped, base over apex, ready for the main event.

The catalogue of triumphs unfurling on the navigation screen finally reached the same conclusion as the real-time reports. 'Congratulations!' Councillor Marina offered effusively. 'We couldn't have hoped for a smoother start.' Ramiro glanced towards her with his rear gaze, but she was addressing herself solely to Greta.

Greta inclined her head graciously.

'This is promising,' Councillor Prisca conceded, 'but the real test is yet to come.'

'Of course,' Greta concurred, though Ramiro could see her struggling not to add a few words in favour of the present achievement. The mountain had gained its spin from giant slabs of sunstone spewing flame into the void, controlled by compressed air and clockwork. Now it was losing it through nothing but light – light flowing through the switches and sensors as much as the engines themselves. If that didn't count as a *real test*, they should all just stay silent and humble until the home world itself had been shifted from its course.

An inset opened in the navigation screen and Tarquinia spoke from the observatory on the peak. 'I've made sightings of six beacons and estimated the rate of change of the *Peerless*'s spin. Everything's within the expected range.'

Ramiro thanked her and she closed the link. For all the built-in redundancy in his own system, an independent manual check was a welcome proof that the software was faithfully reporting reality.

The Councillors filed out, with Greta following. Ramiro leant back in his harness and stretched his shoulders, chirping softly with relief. In principle, the program controlling the photonics could do everything now without further intervention: kill the spin, turn the mountain so the giant engines at the base were aimed in the right direction, then start those engines and keep them glowing with exactly the right power and frequency, until they'd fully reversed the travellers' original velocity with respect to the home world. Ramiro could see himself sitting at his console watching the script playing out day by day. But if it was too much to hope that the

Peerless really would drive itself for the next three years, he'd be satisfied if the program managed to detect and describe any problems it was unable to circumvent.

'Ramiro?'

He looked up; Tarquinia had reappeared on the navigation screen.

'What's happening?' he asked, surprised that she'd have anything more to report so soon.

'Don't panic,' she said. 'The spin-down's going perfectly.'

'But?'

'I just saw the latest snapshot of the halo.'

Ramiro's anxiety deepened. The navigators used ultraviolet images of the region around the Object as a way of measuring the density of interstellar gas, traces of which could be seen being annihilated as it struck the orthogonal asteroid's dust halo.

Tarquinia read the look on his face and buzzed softly. 'The gas is as rarefied as ever; the corridor should still be safe to traverse. But there was something unexpected on the image. I think it was a gnat moving away from the Station.'

Ramiro struggled to make sense of this claim. 'I heard there was a gnat left behind; the last shift didn't have enough pilots to fly them all back. It should have been tied up, but I suppose it could have sprouted some kind of air leak that pushed it away—'

'I don't mean *drifting*,' Tarquinia interjected. 'It was firing its engines. Some of the flare came our way – that's the only reason it showed up on the snapshot.'

'But the Station's empty. Everyone's been evacuated.'

Tarquinia knew what she'd seen. 'Do you think someone could have automated the gnat?' she asked. 'To start flying on its own, after they'd left the Station?'

'It's possible,' Ramiro conceded. 'But why would they?'

'I have no idea. But it's either that, or someone's managed to stay behind.'

'What are you suggesting? Some disappointed voters from Pio's faction have decided that they're going to get their way after all . . . *at the Station*?' Ramiro didn't know whether he should be amused or horrified. The ambition was comical, but if there really were hold-outs who'd concluded that the safest life they could make for their children lay in an abandoned research habitat, there'd be nothing funny when they starved to death.

'This image shows a gnat using its engines,' Tarquinia replied. 'I'm not going to try to guess if there are people inside, let alone what their motives could be.'

'Do you want me to chase down the Councillors?' Ramiro didn't know whose job it had been to ensure that every last traveller was inside the *Peerless* before the spin-down commenced, but he was glad it fell entirely outside his own domain.

Tarquinia said, 'You'd better do that.'

Ramiro loosened his harness. 'If we had cameras in all the corridors,' he mused, 'and programs for recognising invariant anatomy . . .'

'We could have done an automated census before starting up the engines?' Tarquinia suggested.

'Ah, good idea.' Ramiro hadn't been thinking on quite that scale. 'I was just picturing a way of getting messages to people when they were wandering around the mountain.' But Greta and her guests would not have gone far. 'Are you certain this isn't a false alarm?'

'No,' Tarquinia admitted. 'But if we fire the main engines and there are people left behind, do you want to be the one who takes responsibility?'

Ramiro said, 'I'll find the Councillors.'

Ramiro was roused by a discordant clanging of his own design, impossible to mistake for anything else. It was not a pleasant way to wake, but experience had shown him that no gentler sound could penetrate his sleep. He dragged himself out from beneath the tarpaulin of his sand bed and over to the communications link. The walls' red moss-light had been gentle on his eyes, but when he switched on the display the sudden brightness was painful.

'I'm going to need you to go outside,' Greta said.

'Why?' Ramiro asked, baffled. 'Is someone waiting in the corridor?'

'I'm not talking about your apartment.'

Ramiro massaged his skull, hoping to conjure up a third interpretation.

'The census results are in,' Greta said. 'There's no one missing from the *Peerless*.'

'Good! We can fire the main engines with a clear conscience.'

Greta hummed impatiently. 'The observatories are tracking the gnat, but we still have no idea what it's doing.'

'Why should we care?' Ramiro was mildly curious, but chasing a moving target across the void when no one's life was at stake, and the environs in which the whole strange prank was playing out would soon be left far behind, struck him as a little disproportionate.

Greta said, 'Who understands automation better than you do?'

'Appeals to my vanity will get you nowhere.'

'That wasn't a rhetorical question,' she retorted. 'The gnats aren't meant to be able to do this. But it looks as if someone else knows your field well enough to make it happen.'

'It's a trivial modification,' Ramiro stated flatly. 'If you want to get me interested you're going to have to do better than that.'

Greta fell silent.

'What?' he pressed her. 'You can trust me to automate the turn-around, but you can't tell me the Council's paranoid theory about a self-driving gnat?'

'We think the intention might be to exploit the Object as some kind of weapon,' she confessed.

Ramiro's skin tingled strangely. He had never even been close to the Object, but since childhood he'd heard stories of Carla and Ivo's near-fatal first approach, when even the faint wind leaking from their cooling bags had set the rock below them on fire.

'We could always start the main engines ahead of schedule,' he suggested. 'Before this gnat can finish doing whatever it's trying to do.'

'And what about the farms?'

'Some soil spills down the walls, to the place we were moving it anyway.'

Greta said, 'It's only the wheat fields that have been left fallow for the changeover. There are timber plantations, medicinal gardens and a dozen different crops we use for fibres and resins that all need careful transplantation.'

Ramiro doubted that anyone would have cared about a few up-ended trees if it had been clear that the whole mountain was at stake. But if the cost to agriculture seemed too great in the face of an undetermined threat, there were other routes to certainty.

'Why not just destroy the gnat?' he suggested. 'How hard could that be?'

'The Council wants it intercepted, undamaged,' Greta insisted. 'We need to inspect the navigation system and find out exactly what the plan was.'

'Then send your best pilot to bring it back, and I'll happily dissect the whole system in the comfort of a suitably equipped workshop.'

'That would be ideal,' Greta conceded. 'But it might not be possible.'

Ramiro hummed derisively. 'This is just a gnat with a modified navigation system. There's no one inside to defend it. Once your pilot gets on board and cuts a few photonic cables, it will be no different from any other kind of cargo. They can attach a rope to it and tow it back.'

Greta said, 'When the Station was vacated there were dozens of samples from the Object left in its workshops. If someone gained access to the gnat at a time when they could move around the Station with next to no scrutiny, who knows what else they might have done besides reprogramming the navigation system?'

Ramiro stared at her for a moment, then he understood that there really was no squirming out of this. The one thing he couldn't ask any pilot to bring back to the *Peerless* was a machine potentially booby-trapped with fragments of antimatter.

'Strap yourself in,' Tarquinia suggested. 'It's going to be a bumpy ride.'

Ramiro took her advice, fumbling at the harness with hands fitting loosely in the gloves of his cooling bag. While their gnat hung suspended from the outside of the *Peerless* the long flat couch against his back was vertical, like some kind of recuperative splint to help him stand upright.

He'd flown in a gnat before, but this was a different design, with space for just the pilot and one passenger and a storage hold between the couches and the cooling system. The clearstone dome that stretched over their heads was close enough to touch. 'Did they let you talk to your family?' he asked Tarquinia. Though he didn't doubt her skills as a pilot, he suspected that one reason she'd been chosen for the job had been to limit the number of people who knew about the situation.

'Greta made the case for secrecy,' she said. 'But I told my brother anyway.'

'Good for you.' Ramiro had resented the pressure to keep quiet, but then welcomed the excuse to say nothing. He wouldn't have known how to explain the task he was facing without alarming his family, and the last thing he needed right now was a lecture from his uncle about his duty to the children his sister was yet to shed. If everything went well he'd be back long before he was missed.

He pointed to the navigation console. 'Have you updated the local maps?' No one had been expecting to go flying once the spin-down had begun, and apart from the altered velocity of the slopes there was the small matter of steering clear of the beams from the counter-rotation engines.

'No, I just thought I'd leave everything unchanged and see what happened,' Tarquinia replied sarcastically.

Ramiro was unrepentant. 'If you're going to take offence every time I nag you about something that could get us killed—'

'All right!' Tarquinia's expression softened. 'I'm all in favour of some mutual irritation anyway. Better than falling asleep on the job.'

'Don't tempt me with that.'

'Ready,' she said. It wasn't a question. She threw a switch on her panel and the gnat fell away from the mountain.

Ramiro's queasiness at the sudden loss of weight soon changed to elation. He'd forgotten how beautiful the outside could be; after six years of moss-light and display screens, the muted shades of starlit rock spreading out above him felt like liberation. As the mountain retreated, he looked down to the bright line of jumbled colours that divided the sky. To his right, the long trails of the home cluster's stars reached their greatest luminance along this border, then vanished completely. To see any further would have meant seeing these stars' futures – and they weren't sending light backwards in time against their own thermodynamic arrows. To his left, the orthogonal cluster had the sky to itself, sprinkling its domain with small, neat colour trails.

'Firing engines,' Tarquinia warned.

Ramiro was thrust abruptly back against the couch, ridding him of any notion that he was standing. He'd been expecting the change of vertical, but the pressure on his body was distinctly more uncomfortable than he remembered. After a few pauses wondering whether he was going to be able to hold down his last few meals, he managed to ossify parts of his torso, giving it better support against the un-accustomed weight so that it no longer threatened to squeeze out the contents of his digestive tract.

As the gnat sped away from the mountain, the sky's stark asymmetry made it easy to maintain a sense of direction, but Ramiro still needed to check the navigation console to gauge their progress. When he finally looked back towards the *Peerless* again it was a pale grey triangle, a dwindling near-silhouette against the star trails. The engines labouring to end its spin produced no visible trace at all; even if the sparse dust rising out from the slopes was scattering the beams a little, they were far into the ultraviolet.

'It should take about three and a half bells to reach the Station,' Tarquinia predicted.

Ramiro said, 'Isn't it usually six?' No wonder he felt so much heavier than on his last flight.

'This gnat was designed for towing cargo,' Tarquinia explained. 'I flew it myself, the last time they upgraded the Station. I was carrying a whole prefabricated living unit, but coming back, with no external load—' She brought six gloved fingertips together, then flung her hand forward as she spread them.

Ramiro didn't want to risk insulting her again, so he fought back the urge to ask her exactly how much cooling air they'd brought. Carla's glorious optical rebounders required no fuel, with the gnat's gain in kinetic energy coming solely from the creation of light, but the frequency-shifting mirrors that enabled that trick still generated waste heat. The more powerful the engines, the more air it took to carry heat away into the void.

Tarquinia panned across the console's map to show a featureless marker far from the Station itself. The rogue gnat had travelled a long way from its starting point – away from the Object too, with no apparent destination in sight – though in the latest observations it had been decelerating. With its engines now aimed in the opposite direction to their initial orientation there was no spillage from them reaching the *Peerless*; if the astronomers hadn't known the gnat's earlier trajectory they would never have been able to locate it. Ramiro would have enjoyed the challenge of instructing a second unoccupied gnat to seek out the first for a mutually destructive collision at the greatest possible velocity, but the gentler approach was going to be much trickier to achieve, and from his present perspective a great deal less enjoyable.

'What were they thinking?' he asked wearily.

'Who?'

'Pio's group. We get all those earnest speeches about their fears for our descendants, and then suddenly they're trying . . . what? Some kind of feint involving the Object?'

'Feint?' Tarquinia pondered the idea. 'Whatever they've programmed the gnat to do, I don't see how they could call it off now, even if they wanted to.'

Ramiro took her point: the kind of communications system that could connect to such a distant target wasn't something a disgruntled minority could have set up in secret out on the slopes. 'They might still have a shutdown code that they could offer us,' he said. 'Something we'd have to transmit on their behalf.'

'That's possible,' Tarquinia agreed. 'Or they might just offer us the flight plan itself. It was pure luck that we spotted the thing at all; they might have thought they'd still have that to bargain with.'

Ramiro buzzed disdainfully. 'Some people are very bad losers.'

Tarquinia said, 'I don't think it's that. It's not just pride; I think they're genuinely afraid. I don't know what I'd do, myself, if I honestly believed that everyone around me had just voted for a literally suicidal folly.'

'If you honestly believed it, you'd have a good reason,' Ramiro countered. 'You'd try to talk the rest of us around, while staying open to the chance that you might be mistaken. There'd be no need for extortion.'

Tarquinia wasn't convinced. 'It's a strange situation that we're in. We have a whole range of ideas about the interaction of thermodynamic arrows, some of them better supported than others, but none of them conclusive. And if we can't reconcile everyone's intuitions, what counts as a perfect solution? Even if we've all listened to each other's arguments in good faith, it's always possible that someone's going to end up believing that we're heading for annihilation – and that by the time the evidence is indisputable, it will be far too late to retreat.'

Greta said, 'We have a theory.'

Ramiro strained to hear her; the UV link to the *Peerless* was noisier than anything he'd experienced before.

'So far, the rogue's just followed a straight line,' she said. 'Maximum acceleration away from the Station, then maximum deceleration, without veering at all. If it keeps this up, we know exactly where it's going to come to a halt – and there's nothing there. It's not a destination. It's a staging point.'

'So then it turns and heads for the *Peerless*?' Tarquinia suggested. 'The rogue's instructors are planning to announce that a gnat loaded with antimatter is on its way – but they've offset it far enough from the Station that they think we'll have no idea where to look for it.'

'That's a possibility,' Greta replied. 'But they might not be trying to bargain at all. Why enter into negotiations if they can get what they want directly?'

Ramiro felt sick. 'You think they'll try to destroy the engines, without warning?' Crashing a gnat into the base of the mountain – with either enough antimatter or enough sheer kinetic energy to do the job – would probably kill half the population in the process.

Greta's voice crackled.

'Say again,' Tarquinia requested.

'Not the engines. The corridor.'

Ramiro struggled to hear what followed, but eventually Greta's theory became clear. She believed the rogue was doing nothing more than giving itself a run-up: travelling away from the Station in order to turn around and come back – with as much velocity as possible. Its target wasn't the *Peerless*. It was the Station.

Given the angle of arrival, the collision would set the Station on a grazing trajectory towards the Object. When all those empty workshops and living quarters skidded across the surface of the asteroid, the explosion would send a plume of antimatter far out into the void – and the geometry of the impact would guarantee that the plume polluted a region that the *Peerless* needed to traverse if it was to commence the turnaround.

The hazard would take a generation to disperse. If they tried to steer the mountain through the debris, the system that protected the slopes from the usual smattering of tiny specks of antimatter would be utterly overwhelmed – and the failures would not be embarrassing spot fires, they'd be blasts that tore cavernous holes in the mountainside and risked setting everything ablaze.

'Can we move the Station?' Ramiro asked. The habitat's own engines were weak things, intended to do no more than stabilise it in orbit around the Object, but if the rogue gnat could shift it with a few bells' worth of accumulated power, surely their own benign craft could spend the same time gently towing it out of harm's way?

'Not quickly enough,' Tarquinia replied. 'With a load as massive as that, the limiting factor's not our engines, it's the strength of the tow ropes.'

'Right.' Ramiro had been wondering why the rogue wasn't simply dragging the Station to its demise, but apart from the question of which approach would be the easiest to automate, the least conspicuous and the hardest to prevent, the go-away-come-back-and-crash method would actually deliver a faster result.

Greta said, 'The only choice is to intercept the rogue.'

'You couldn't have worked all this out before we left?' Ramiro complained. If the rogue came straight back towards the Station, there'd be nothing more to learn from its navigation system. They should have just tried to destroy it from the start.

The console emitted Gretaesque noises, then the link cut out completely.

Tarquinia turned to Ramiro. 'Don't worry,' she said. 'If it's as predictable as they're saying, we'll match trajectories easily.'

'You're not the one who'll have to climb on board and shut it down.'

'If there's any problem, we do have other options.' Tarquinia gestured to the hold behind their couches. 'Timed explosives. All we have to do is attach one of these and get out of the way.'

Ramiro could not have been less comforted. 'High-velocity debris in the void – possibly spiced with antimatter. Do you really want to fly through that?'

'If we give ourselves enough time, the risk will be negligible.'

'And how much time is ours to give?'

Tarquinia turned to the navigation console, instructing it through the photonic corset that wrapped her torso beneath the cooling bag. When she'd finished, a flight plan appeared on the screen.

'If Greta's theory is right,' Tarquinia said, 'we'll be able to match trajectories with the rogue in slightly more than five bells – about half a bell before the impact. If we set the explosive's timer for three chimes, that will leave another three chimes for the debris to spread out – enough for the bulk of it to miss the Station. And in three chimes, we can put almost three severances between ourselves and the explosion. The rogue will still be accelerating as fast as it can towards the Station, so if we scarper in the opposite direction we'll get the benefit of both engines.'

23

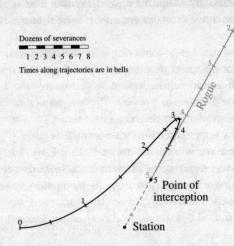

Dozens of severances

1 2 3 4 5 6 7 8

Times along trajectories are in bells

Rogue

Point of interception

Station

Ramiro was slightly mollified. Three severances wasn't much on the scale of this map, but it was more than six gross times the height of the *Peerless*. The shrapnel they were fleeing would never slow down, but it would grow ever sparser.

'So is Greta right or not?' he asked. They'd lost the link with the *Peerless*, so they'd had no updates on the rogue's actual behaviour.

Tarquinia flicked a switch on the console; a moment later the link was restored.

'What did you do?' Ramiro demanded.

'I vented some air through an outlet next to the photoreceptor,' Tarquinia explained. 'Sometimes it just gets dusty.'

Greta asked anxiously, 'Can you hear me?'

'Loud and clear,' Tarquinia replied.

'The rogue came to a halt three lapses ago, and reversed without a pause. It's headed straight back to the Station.'

'Understood,' Tarquinia said cheerfully. She made no move Ramiro could see, but she must have sent a command through her corset because the flight plan on the screen changed from grey to red – transformed from a hypothetical doodle to a set of firm instructions. The sky through the dome rotated a quarter-turn as the gnat swung around to redirect the engines.

'We're really going to do this?' Ramiro asked numbly. He'd been half-hoping that the rogue would set out for the *Peerless* instead; forewarned, the mountain's defenders could have launched any number of pilotless gnats against it, so the risk of it actually striking its target would have been vanishingly small. 'What if we programmed a collision instead?' he suggested. 'Then we can climb out here and wait to be rescued.' That would mean half a day in the void, but they had locator beacons on their cooling bags and they could take a couple of extra air tanks from the gnat.

Greta said, 'Absolutely not!'

Tarquinia gave the idea some thought. 'We don't know the rogue's trajectory with enough precision to ensure that we'd hit it, but I suppose we could use the explosives to make a near miss almost as good. The only trouble is . . . it wouldn't take much of a course change by the rogue to ruin the whole plan. Even if you reprogrammed our navigation system so they could tweak the trajectory from the *Peerless*, the explosive isn't that sophisticated: once we set the time delay, it would be impossible to change it remotely.'

Ramiro was prepared to accept this argument, but Greta felt obliged to add her own reasons. 'The Council still wants the rogue's navigation system analysed,' she said. 'The trajectory might be obvious now, but there could be other information about the perpetrators that can be gleaned by studying what they've done.'

'Yeah, I'm sure they signed their names in the software.' Ramiro didn't doubt that there was such a thing as programming style, but the idea of identifying a saboteur on the basis of anything so vague was ludicrous. 'I'll be happy if we manage to keep the Station from being hit, but once that's guaranteed I'm not risking my life humouring the Councillors.'

Greta didn't reply; she knew better than to push him now.

'So . . . we're going ahead with the interception?' Tarquinia asked tactfully.

Ramiro stared at the flight plan: the map of their future for the next five bells. As far as he knew, on every other occasion when two gnats had come together in the void they'd had cooperating pilots, and their main engines had been shut off for the approach. But here were the trajectories, meeting up perfectly right before his eyes.

'Why not?' he said. 'What could possibly go wrong?'

At Ramiro's request, Tarquinia showed him a version of the flight plan with their acceleration marked. Translating between the standard maps and the starry emptiness around her might have been second nature to Tarquinia, but the only way Ramiro could hope to stay oriented was by knowing which direction would feel like 'up' to him for the various stages along the route.

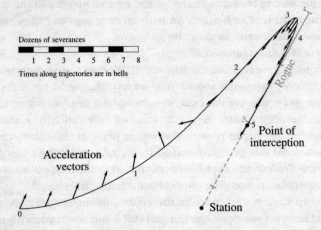

Dozens of severances

1 2 3 4 5 6 7 8

Times along trajectories are in bells

Acceleration vectors

Point of interception

Station

They'd already acquired a substantial velocity towards the Station on their way from the *Peerless*, and now they were veering sideways, bringing them closer to the rogue's trajectory. But in a bell and a quarter they'd begin to swing the engines around, until they were using all their power to reverse. Ramiro found it utterly perverse that they could have caught up with the rogue much sooner if it had been fleeing from them, rather than heading their way: the need to match velocities wouldn't have forced them to waste time going backwards.

'Do you have a tuneable coherer in your toolbox?' he asked Tarquinia.

'Of course. Why?'

'I think we'll need to burn the proximity sensors, before we get too close.' For long-range navigation the gnats relied on beacons, but to dock they picked up the reflections of their surroundings in infrared. The rogue had no hope of seeing them coming from afar, but once they tried to sidle up to it, it would know that it had company.

Tarquinia said, 'It won't have a lot of freedom for evasive action; if it delays its arrival too much, the Station will have moved around in its orbit. And it can't make up lost time later; the engines are running at full power as it is.'

'It could still shift sideways with the manoeuvring engines,' Ramiro suggested. 'There'd be nothing to stop it recovering from that – and it would be enough to make our job impossible.' Once they were beside the rogue any sudden change in the main engines' thrust would see it plummet out of sight, but it would only take the tiniest swerve to snap a boarding rope slung between the vehicles.

'True enough,' Tarquinia conceded. 'But we'll need to combine the coherer with some kind of sighting scope.'

She unplugged the photonic cable from her corset, then clambered down into the hold. As she rummaged around for the parts she needed, Ramiro contemplated her empty couch and unattended console. He'd happily imagined the *Peerless* driving itself for years – but in this fragile craft, rushing towards a near-collision, even the briefest absence of the pilot was enough to unsettle him.

'How about this?' Tarquinia handed him a scope, three clamps and a coherer. 'The range of the sensors would be about a saunter. Through this, you should be able to see them at twice that distance.'

Ramiro said, 'We'll need to calibrate the alignment.'

'Of course. Put it together, then I'll get the optics workbench.'

'You have an *optics workbench*?'

'A small one.'

The bench was half the size of Ramiro's torso, but it let them measure the angle between the scope's axis and the coherer's beam. By the time he had the crude weapon aligned, he looked out through the dome to see that the gnat had rotated again without him even noticing. The engines were dragging them backwards now, giving them a trajectory much like the parabola of a ball thrown under gravity – albeit in some very strange game where the skill lay more in controlling the direction of the ongoing force than in the initial toss.

'Do you have children?' he asked Tarquinia.

'No.'

'So what did your brother say, when you told him about this?'

'He wished me a safe journey,' Tarquinia replied.

Ramiro said, 'If I'd told my uncle, I probably wouldn't be here at all.'

'Hmm.' Tarquinia sounded sympathetic, but reluctant to take sides. 'So let's neither of us do anything reckless,' she said. 'If we play this right, your family need never even know that you were out here.'

*

The gnat reached the top of its parabola and started falling back towards the Station. Ramiro glanced up from the navigation console, unable to dismiss a stubborn intuition that the event ought to be visible somehow, but nothing in the view through the dome had changed.

The *Peerless* was still tracking the rogue and sending updates; the thing was five dozen severances away, off to Ramiro's left and 'below' him – in the sense of 'down' rammed into his body by the engines, the opposite of that in his tossed-ball analogy. He slid his head past the edge of the couch and examined the sky with his rear gaze, knowing full well that there was nothing he could hope to see. Even if he'd slipped on the ultraviolet goggles that Tarquinia had given him from her trove of gadgets, the rogue's engines were pointed away from him. A similarly equipped passenger on the rogue might have seen the UV flare from the gnat ahead of them, but Ramiro was hoping that the saboteurs had had no chance to augment the vehicle with extra hardware.

'We need to eat now,' Tarquinia declared, tugging at the lid on the store beside her couch.

'I don't have much appetite,' Ramiro protested.

'That's not the point,' Tarquinia said flatly. 'You've only had half a night's sleep, and you're going to need to be alert for this. It'll take a bell for the loaves to be digested, so this is mealtime.'

Ramiro buzzed at her presumptuousness. 'Yes, Uncle.'

'I'm your pilot, that's worse. Can your uncle toss you out into the void?'

He took the loaf that she handed him and bit into it dutifully. It was a struggle to force the chewed food down his oesophagus; half the flesh that usually helped him to swallow had been ossified.

When he'd finished, Ramiro brushed the crumbs from his gloves. 'What happens if we get this wrong?' he asked. 'If we scare the rogue into some kind of evasive manoeuvre that changes its trajectory, but it's still not enough to stop it hitting the Station . . . could that skew things so that the plume ends up aimed at the *Peerless*?'

Tarquinia had already thought it through. 'Any collision at this speed is going to give the Station so much energy that it will be oblivious to the Object's gravity: it will be travelling on a virtually straight line, not whipping around in an eccentric orbit. So even if the impact's skewed, either the Station will crash on the side where it was meant to crash, or it will miss the Object completely and fly off into the void.'

'So the worst that can happen is that the saboteurs get what they want: a delay in the turnaround.' Worse was possible for the two of them, but Ramiro was trying to calm himself for the task ahead, not give himself a reason to back out completely.

Tarquinia said, 'As far as I can see. But the problem then is how people will respond.'

'You mean . . . retribution?' Ramiro hadn't been thinking that far ahead. 'The migrationists will be in trouble just for trying this stunt, whether or not we manage to stop it.'

'I think a lot of travellers will be a great deal more displeased if the turnaround is actually postponed for a generation than they would have been by the mere effrontery of the attempt.' Tarquinia sounded bemused: hadn't Ramiro invested a third of his life preparing for the event?

'I'd be disappointed,' he confessed. 'But it's not as if everything I've done will have been wasted. Even if the delay is so long that they decide to replace the whole system with something more modern, they'll still end up using a lot of my ideas.'

'Hmm.' Tarquinia was surprised, but she wasn't going to try to argue him out of his position. 'Most people have been looking forward to this for a long time, though – and for someone who hasn't directly contributed to it, it's living through the turnaround that would make all the difference. You get to take some pleasure in having made it possible, whenever it happens. The rest of us will just be robbed of the biggest thing we hoped to see in our lives.'

'Three years of arduous gravity, and some changes in the appearance of the stars?'

'It's not the novelty, or the spectacle,' Tarquinia replied. 'It's the proof that what we've been through might be worth it. It's seeing the mountain heading back towards the home world – seeing the plan finally enacted, not just promised. We can't take part in the reunion, but a whole generation's been clinging to the hope that at least we'd be here for the turnaround.'

'That's all a bit teleological for me.' Ramiro had no wish to offend her, but the idea of anyone's sense of worth being reduced to their role as witness to the Great Project just dismayed him. 'I hope our descendants can help the ancestors. But why should everything we do derive its meaning from that?'

Tarquinia buzzed incredulously. 'So you don't care *why* we're turning around?'

'I never said that,' Ramiro protested. 'I think the turnaround will be a good thing for everyone. If I felt otherwise, I would have joined the migrationists. But day to day? I just like solving problems and doing my job well. That's enough. There's no need for all this grandiose posturing.'

Tarquinia fell silent. Ramiro felt a twinge of guilt: 'grandiose posturing' might have been a bit too strong.

'Anyway, forget it,' he said. 'We're not going to mess this up, so any consequences are hypothetical.'

'One kind are hypothetical,' Tarquinia allowed. 'But don't forget the rest.'

'The rest?'

'Most travellers will be happy if we succeed,' she said, 'and I hope they'll forgive the migrationists, out of sheer relief at their ineffectuality.'

'But?' Ramiro shifted uneasily in his cooling bag, hoping his meal was going to stay down.

Tarquinia said, 'Whoever did this, they're not going to give up. If they're certain that the *Peerless* is heading for oblivion, what else can they do but keep on trying to save us?'

Half a chime before the expected encounter, Ramiro slipped on the ultraviolet goggles. It was impossible for the astronomers on the *Peerless* to measure the rogue's position down to the last saunter, so Tarquinia had decided that the only reliable way to synchronise the next stage of the process was to allow the rogue to overtake them. The goggles didn't leave Ramiro blind – the photonics aimed to overlay an image of any incident UV on an ordinary view – but the result was an imperfect compromise and he could understand why Tarquinia didn't want to try to read the navigation console while wearing the things herself.

'After this, every new gnat will have UV cameras built in,' he predicted.

'Then we're lucky no one thought it was worth it before.' Tarquinia gave a curt hum of displeasure. 'What next? Weapons built in? Everything we make from now on designed with the worst in mind?'

Ramiro adjusted the straps on his goggles. He wasn't going to fret about some hypothetical escalation of the conflict. There was a problem right in front of them; they had to focus on it completely now.

'Three lapses to go,' Tarquinia announced.

Ramiro tensed, willing himself to vigilance. He turned slightly to the left. If the rogue arrived later than they'd anticipated, sticking rigidly to the flight plan would leave them perpetually ahead of it. Only by cutting their engines completely could they guarantee that the rogue would pass them, revealing itself through its flare.

'Two lapses.'

Ramiro fixed the pattern of the stars in his mind, noting each trail's extension in artificial white beyond the usual violet. The rogue might pass them in the distance, and he did not want to be confused about the significance of some pale white streak.

'One lapse.' Tarquinia waited, then counted down the last pauses. 'Five. Four. Three. Two. One.'

Ramiro said, 'Nothing.' He was weightless now; the engines had cut off automatically. He strained his eyes, wondering if the trajectories could have been so misaligned that the rogue had already passed them by, completely out of sight.

Something moved in the corner of his vision; before he could turn towards it there was a light in front of him, vanishing into the distance. 'Now!' he shouted. Tarquinia restarted the engines, at a lower thrust intended to match the rogue's acceleration.

Magically, the white speck stopped fading.

'It's stable,' Ramiro marvelled. In all these cubic severances of void – and the further three dimensions of velocity in which they might have gone astray – they'd actually succeeded in crossing paths with their foe and keeping pace with it.

Tarquinia raised the acceleration slightly; the speck grew brighter and slid off-centre. 'It's going left,' Ramiro warned her. Tarquinia eased the thrust down, turned the gnat fractionally for a few pauses, then turned it back again. As far as Ramiro could tell, the rogue was dead ahead now.

By trial and error they whittled away the distance between the two gnats. Tarquinia advanced cautiously; if they overshot the rogue its engines would become invisible. Instead, the light grew gratifyingly intense, to the point where Ramiro had to lower the gain on the goggles.

Tarquinia said, 'I can see the hull now.'

Ramiro took off the goggles and waited for his eyes to adjust. Ahead of them and slightly to the left, the rogue gnat's dome glistened in the starlight above its grey hardstone shell. In visible light, the blazing beacon he'd been following was reduced to a black patch at the rear of the hull.

Tarquinia brought them closer. 'I'm going to depressurise,' she said. As the air hissed out of the cabin, Ramiro opened the valve on the tank attached to his cooling bag. Tarquinia put on her helmet, but Ramiro deferred; it would be awkward trying to aim the coherer with his face covered, and with the heat being drawn off most of his body he'd be comfortable for a while yet.

When the rogue was suspended a couple of saunters away, he unstrapped his harness, found the release handle under the dome on his left and pulled open the exit hatch. He slithered around on the couch until he was facing out. Tarquinia handed him the coherer. He held the scope to his eye; there was nothing between him and the rogue but void now. He searched the hull for the two dark circles of the proximity sensors; he knew more or less where they had to be, but it still took three sweeps to find them.

Ramiro reached up and set the coherer to blue – far enough from infrared that it wouldn't trigger the sensors – and checked that the spot was falling on his first target. Then he slid the tuner further along, to a point he'd marked earlier with a speck of adhesive resin: an ultraviolet frequency that would permanently damage the lattice structure of the photodetector.

The dark circle showed no visible change, but he'd expected none. He'd just have to trust the physics. He shifted his attention to the second sensor.

When he was done, Ramiro righted himself on the couch. The navigation console was predicting an impact with the Station in less than four chimes.

He put on his helmet. 'We're too late to use the explosives, aren't we?'

Tarquinia's voice came through the link, but he could hear a muffled version through the couch as well. 'I'm sorry,' she said. 'It took me longer to catch up than I thought it would.'

'Don't worry about it.' On balance, Ramiro was relieved; the whole idea had sounded like a dangerous gamble.

The rogue was drawing closer now; Tarquinia was using the manoeuvring engines to ease the gnat sideways. Ramiro waited for the rogue to turn skittish, but their presence had no effect on it at all. Either he really had killed the proximity sensors, or the saboteurs hadn't even tried to make use of them.

Ramiro slid into a safety harness attached to a short rope. Tarquinia had brought the two gnats to within about three stretches of each other; Ramiro could see right through the rogue's dome now, into its empty cabin. If he'd been weightless he would happily have attempted to jump straight for the rogue's hull, but under this much acceleration he doubted that he would have made it a quarter of the way.

He poked his legs out through the hatch and reached around with his right foot for the panel that covered the boarding rope. He slid it aside and groped for the hook on the end of the rope. He'd chosen a cooling bag that left his feet uncovered, allowing him to re-form them easily into hands. He took hold of the hook, released the brake on the reel, then unwound what he judged to be a little more rope than he'd need.

Seated on the rim of the hatch with his legs dangling down into the void, leaning a little so he could watch himself through the dome, Ramiro tossed the hook. When it struck the other gnat's dome he cringed, expecting the worst; if the rogue's software was monitoring sound in the cabin, this would be the time for it to scupper the attempted boarding.

The rogue stayed put. Ramiro was puzzled, but he was beginning to suspect that the saboteurs had baulked at the idea of trying to automate a response to every contingency. Their overriding aim would have been to keep the rogue on course and on schedule; with the Station deserted and the *Peerless* so far away they had hardly been guaranteed visitors, and any extra layers of complexity in the software aimed at dealing with that possibility would have carried some risk of jumping at shadows. It was just bad luck for them that their plan had been detected so early; if he and Tarquinia had left the *Peerless* half a bell later, this whole encounter would have been impossible.

Ramiro gathered up the rope and tried again. On his fourth

attempt, the hook passed through the ring beside the rogue's hatch. The boarding rope hung down into the void; he didn't want to tighten it so much that any jitter in the engines would snap it, but as it was the catenary looked dauntingly steep. He wound some rope back onto the reel, until the dip at the centre was no more than a couple of strides.

'How long have we got?' he asked Tarquinia.

'A bit more than three chimes.'

Ramiro removed his safety harness. The rope that tied it to the cabin's interior was too short for the crossing, but if he'd substituted a longer rope that would have put him in danger of swinging down into the gnat's ultraviolet exhaust. Having had no training in using a jetpack, he'd decided that the bulky device would just be a dangerous encumbrance. If he lost his grip, or if the boarding rope snapped or came loose, the safest outcome would be for him to plummet straight down away from both vehicles and await rescue.

Tarquinia said, 'Be careful.'

'I intend to.' Ramiro clambered out of the hatch and took hold of the boarding rope, swinging his legs up to share the load. He was more used to dealing with ropes in low gravity – as antidotes to drift rather than weight-bearing structures – but with four limbs in play he had no trouble supporting himself. With his rear eyes he gazed down at the stars beneath him; if he was going to react badly to the infinite drop it would be better to do it now than when he was halfway across. But though the sight was discomfiting, he didn't panic or seize up. A long fall could only harm him if there was something below on which to dash open his skull. Nothing made for a softer landing than the absence of any land at all.

As he dragged himself out along the rope, Ramiro's confidence increased. He wasn't going to lose his grip for no reason, and the two gnats remained in perfect lockstep, their engines running as smoothly as he could have wished. His thoughts turned from the mechanics of the approach to the task ahead. With only three chimes remaining, it had passed the point where all he'd have to do to spare the Station was shut off the rogue's engines. Its sheer momentum now would be enough to carry it to the impact point with only a few pauses' delay – not long enough for the Station's orbit to move it out of harm's way. But the saboteurs might have made it difficult to change the flight plan quickly, so his best bet would be to plug his corset directly into the engine controller. That was not a smart way to try to fly a gnat to a specific destination, but all he had to do was swerve sharply enough to avoid both the Station and the Object. Once he was clear of both, he could kill the engines and Tarquinia would come and find him.

Ramiro felt the rope tilting disconcertingly as he approached the rogue feet first. He'd been looking up into the star trails, but now he raised his head; the hatch was just a few strides away. Clambering upside down into the cabin was going to be awkward, but he didn't think it was worth trying to turn his body around. When the hatch came within reach, he took his right foot from the rope and stretched it towards the handle.

His leg jerked back before he was aware of the reason, then the pain arrived, driving everything else from his mind. He was seared flesh and a bellowing tympanum, skewered to an endless, unbearable present, begging for relief that never came.

'Ramiro?' Tarquinia repeated his name half a dozen times before he could form a reply.

'I'm burnt,' he said.

Tarquinia was silent for a moment. 'They must have sabotaged the cooling system,' she concluded. 'Do you want me to come and get you?'

Ramiro had closed his eyes; he opened them now, and realised that he'd managed to hang onto the rope despite the shock. 'No.' His damaged foot was useless, but he still had three good limbs. 'Can we pump some of our own air through?'

'There isn't time,' Tarquinia said flatly.

'No.' It would take at least a chime just to set up the hoses, let alone for the air to have any effect.

'I'm going to try pushing the rogue, hull to hull,' Tarquinia announced. 'How quickly can you get back here?'

'I don't know. Let me try.'

Ramiro braced himself and began. Even with his injured foot touching nothing, his body complained about the effort and the motion; it wanted to curl up where it was. He tried bribing it with images of the safety of the cabin: the rogue was fatal, and the rope was precarious, but once he was in the cabin he could rest.

Halfway back, Ramiro felt his foot growing mercifully numb. He looked down to see a swarm of tiny yellow globules spilling from the ruined flesh, glowing like the sparks from an old-fashioned lamp as they fell into the void.

'Tarquinia?'

'Do you need help?'

He could ask her to bring out a knife and amputate his foot, but that would take too long. 'The wound isn't stable,' he said. 'I'd better not come back into the cabin.'

'What do you mean, it isn't stable?'

'The burn's denatured the tissue to the point where it might be explosive. You'd better start the manoeuvre, and I'll drop out here.'

'You can't drop, Ramiro.' Tarquinia presented the verdict as if she'd brook no contradiction.

'I trust you,' he said. 'If I survive this, I know you'll come and get me.'

'If we were clear of obstacles, you can be sure I would,' Tarquinia replied. 'But if you let go of that rope now, I won't have time to deal with the rogue and pick you up before you come to grief.'

Ramiro felt himself scowling in disbelief; his pain-addled brain was proffering an image of him tumbling away into the safety of the void. With no rock beneath him, what was there to fear? But if he insisted on taking the gnats' frame of reference and its fictitious gravity seriously, to complete the description he'd need to include the two things above him: the Station and the Object, falling straight down. Letting himself fall, too, wouldn't protect him: those giant battering rams had already gained too much velocity. Turning his air tank into an improvised jet to push himself sideways might just get him clear of the Station in time, but the Object was too large, his aim too unreliable.

He stared down at the sparks escaping from his foot. 'Maybe this won't go off – but if it does I don't want us both dying.'

'Then stay where you are!' Tarquinia insisted. 'It's the shock wave in air that kills bystanders; if anything happens, the dome and the void will protect me. Look, we don't have time for a debate! I'm going to start the manoeuvre now. If you get into trouble, shout.'

Ramiro said, 'All right.'

He adjusted his grip on the rope, taking the opportunity to rest one arm for a lapse. He didn't think it would be wise to try to mess with the cooling bag to let him extrude a fresh pair of limbs, but if fatigue really did start to threaten his hold he could try tying his corset's photonic cable in a loop around the rope.

As the gnats drew closer together, the centre of the rope dropped lower, nearer to the engines. Ramiro began climbing towards Tarquinia's side, alarmed at how much harder it was to make progress with the rope at a steeper angle. Tarquinia poked her head out through the hatch, then reached down and began winding the rope in; Ramiro could see her straining to shift his weight, but she was doing much more than sparing him the effort of the climb. With the rope shortened the angle improved, and Tarquinia kept winding until it was nearly horizontal again.

Then she disappeared back into the cabin, and the gnats moved closer still.

Ramiro clung on, trying to ignore the revived throbbing of his foot. Everyone had imagined the rogue defending itself with antimatter, or elaborate software to deal with would-be intruders. But the measure that had actually defeated him might not even have been a deliberate strategy: in those last days at the Station, whoever had reprogrammed the navigation system might simply never have had an opportunity to restock the decommissioned gnat with cooling air. At this very moment, they might be fretting over the possibility that their weapon had overheated to the point where every photonic lattice had cracked and the rebounders' mirrors had split into shards.

Tarquinia turned the gnat so that its flat belly faced the rogue's. Ramiro scrambled to keep himself away from both the engines below and the approaching slab of hot rock. As Tarquinia eased the gnats' bases together he found himself suspended half a dozen strides below the hatch through which he'd left the cabin. With the side of his body resting against the polished grey stone of the hull, he could feel the surface growing warmer as heat spread into it from the rogue. But before he could panic, he registered a quickening flow of air from the cooling channels. Tarquinia's gnat was built to run at three times its current power; the extra burden would not overwhelm it.

'How long to the impact?' Ramiro asked.

'A chime and a half,' Tarquinia replied evenly. 'I'm going to start applying force now; this might get rough, but don't let it shake you.'

'I'll do my best.'

Ramiro hugged the rope. The immediate effect of Tarquinia's shoving was imperceptible, but it wouldn't take long before the rogue sensed itself drifting off course – and no tampering by the saboteurs was needed to ensure a response. The navigation system would adjust the power in the individual rebounders, skewing the direction of the main engines' thrust to try to compensate for the deviation.

Above, still, there was nothing but stars. How hard could it be to miss a target too small to discern? Ramiro flinched suddenly, his teeth aching with a hideous vibration. It was over in an instant, but his skull kept ringing. One gnat must have suffered a brief drop in thrust, scraping hull against hull.

He steadied himself and tightened his grip. He still had no real sense of motion; if he closed his eyes, he might have been clinging to the side of a wall back in the *Peerless*, somewhere out near the rim. But now that Tarquinia had gone beyond simply matching the rogue's trajectory, there could be no more placid mimicry: the instruments that were detecting her provocations were not so perfect and standardised that their response could be predicted and allowed for in advance. The rogue wasn't even trying to shake them off – with the proximity sensors dead, it thought it was moving untrammelled through the void, in battle with nothing but its own errors.

Ramiro cried out in shock before he knew why: the hulls were moving apart. Tarquinia said, 'I've got it, I've got it!' The gap began to shrink, then the surfaces made contact again with an ugly grinding sound.

Ramiro was shivering. If the gnats separated and the rope snapped on the wrong side, he needed to be ready to release his hold to stop his body being slammed against the overheated hull. Better to end up dashed against the walls of the Station than be flayed by heat from head to toe.

He looked down at his ruined foot. It had grown numb again, but the luminous discharge was unabated. In all the years since the launch, only three people had gone to light in the *Peerless*; Ramiro had never paid much attention to the accounts he'd read of the phenomenon, other than fixing in his mind the importance of fleeing if he ever saw a glowing liquid seeping from someone else's wound. All he could do was wait for the manoeuvre to be finished so Tarquinia could bring him a knife. He looked to the zenith and finally spotted a tiny pale oval against the star trails.

'How's our course?' he asked. They'd pushed gently against the rogue – not gently enough to remain unopposed, but there had to be some small chance that the net result had ended up in their favour.

'Not good,' Tarquinia admitted. 'We're still aimed at the Station.'

Ramiro tried to accept the news calmly. 'What more can you do? Give me a couple of lapses with a knife, then we can fly away.' He could still survive this: he just had to cut through the rope on the rogue's side before starting work on his leg.

Tarquinia said, 'I'm going to unbalance the main engines.'

Ramiro's shivering grew worse. *'Manually?'*

'Yes,' she confirmed.

The manoeuvring engines delivered a modest push that any trained pilot could use manually, for docking. Severing the main engines from the feedback loop of accelerometers and gyroscopes that aimed to keep their thrust perfectly symmetrical, and then imposing a deliberate asymmetry to try to push their neighbour off course, would escalate the speed and violence of the interaction between the gnats by an order of magnitude. Tarquinia had the stronger engines – but the gnats could easily smash each other into rubble without anyone winning.

Ramiro said, 'Automate it.'

'We have eight lapses to impact, Ramiro. We don't have time to rewrite the navigation system.'

'What I'm thinking of would take a very small change.'

'We don't have time!' Tarquinia repeated.

Ramiro struggled to find the words to sway her. 'Do you trust what I did for the *Peerless*? Most of the tricks I used there were things I learnt from the woman who programmed the gnats. I know their navigation software backwards – and I've been revisiting it in my head from the moment Greta sent me out here.'

'You don't think I can do this myself?'

'I'd trust my life to you as a pilot,' Ramiro promised her, 'but no one has the reaction time they'd need to make this work. All we have to do is poke a skewed target value into one register, and instead of disabling all the guidance sensors we'll have enlisted them: we'll force them to deliver a measured push, whatever the rogue does, no more and no less. Everything you usually rely on to keep you flying straight will be working towards this new goal. Can you really do better than that by gut alone?'

In the silence, Ramiro glanced up at the Object. It still looked absurdly small, but in another few lapses he'd see how big a target it made. Tarquinia seemed paralysed with indecision; if he let himself drop now he could take his chances with his air tank, while hoping that she came to her senses and simply flew away from the rogue in time.

Tarquinia said, 'How do we do this?'

Ramiro was confused. 'Do what?' Settle the argument before they were dead?

'How do we *automate the push?*' she asked impatiently. She'd accepted his plan.

Ramiro described the commands for the navigation system, raising the glyphs on his own skin as he spoke, picturing them repeated on Tarquinia's body under her own corset's empowering gaze.

As Tarquinia echoed the last command back to him, the opposing hulls began to screech and shudder. The shaking cost Ramiro's good foot its grip on the rope; the other one fell back against the hull. He barely felt the knock, but when he looked down there was a swarm of brilliant yellow specks dropping away into the void, endlessly replenished from his disintegrating flesh. The balance of energies that tamed his body's chemistry was coming to an end; the damaged tissue was making ever more light, wrecking all the finely honed systems that had held the process in check. His only chance to survive would be to part from it, but in this juddering chaos he doubted he could take a knife from Tarquinia's hand, let alone use it.

The rogue shifted suddenly, its hull scraping backwards like a boulder sliding down an incline. Ramiro watched the slack part of the rope stretching out below him and readied himself for the void – but then the motion stopped abruptly.

He understood what was happening: as the rogue fought to stay true – with no extra power to spend on the task – it could only shift its balance by throttling some of its rebounders, decreasing its forward thrust. Tarquinia was doing her best to fall back alongside their neighbour – and at least his clumsy fix had spared her from having to micromanage the sideways shove at the same time – but the whole encounter was too complicated to be rendered truly stable, and their luck couldn't last much longer.

Ramiro placed his injured leg against the rope and managed to work a full turn around it. But the loop was too low, barely above his ankle. He brought his hands down a span to lower his body while kicking out with his leg, until the rope rode up to encircle his knee. He made a second loop, then a third.

He looked up to see the Object looming ahead, its red and grey rock mottled with craters and crevices limned with shadows in the starlight. Then in the foreground, far smaller for an instant but growing in no time to obscure the whole asteroid, he saw the Station: a cluster of stone boxes, rooms and workshops pieced together in weightless anarchy, rushing forward greedily towards the duelling gnats.

Instinctively, Ramiro released his hold on the rope, convinced for a moment that this would save him. He fell upside down, hanging by his knee, his face to the sky as a featureless shadow flickered across the stars and was gone.

He braced himself for the second, greater threat: a cratered landscape of antimatter rushing past near enough to touch – or rising up to meet him in extinction. The vision of it hung in his mind's eye, stark and terrible. But the thing itself failed to appear.

Ramiro lacked the strength to right his body but he raised his head sufficiently to stare up at the zenith. There was nothing ahead of the gnats now but the long, gaudy star trails of the home cluster. The shadow he'd mistaken for the Station passing by had been the Object; the first missed target had come and gone too rapidly to be perceived at all.

He was still chirping with elation at the near miss when he noticed the yellow sparks falling around him. His whole lower leg was radiant now, filled to bursting with light.

'Pull away!' he begged Tarquinia.

He saw her helmet poke out of the hatch.

'Wait,' she said. She was gone for a moment but then she reappeared with the safety harness.

'There isn't time!' Ramiro protested. But he understood why she was taking the risk: if he ended up falling alongside his amputated leg, it could still kill him.

Tarquinia dropped the harness. Ramiro reached out to accept it, but the rope wasn't long enough; the harness hung suspended beside his bad knee. He tried to raise his torso, but the effort merely set him swaying.

'Grab it with your other foot,' Tarquinia urged him.

Ramiro tried, but some earlier knock against the hardstone must have damaged his foot, robbing it of its power to grip. He poked it

41

between two of the harness's straps, pushed his leg through and bent his knee.

'Now!' he pleaded redundantly: the gnats were already separating. He could see starlight between the hulls.

As Tarquinia retreated into the cabin, Ramiro felt the rope tightening, until he lost all sensation in the constricted flesh. Viscid yellow fire sprayed from the stump of his foot. The glow became too painful to watch; he threw his arms up in front of his helmet.

Suddenly all his weight shifted to his good knee, almost pulling him free from the harness. The light from above was gone; Ramiro lowered his rear gaze and saw his severed leg tumbling through the void, part of the snapped boarding rope beside it. As he watched, the flesh liquefied completely then swelled into a ball of flame, lifting the rogue's form out of the darkness. A moment later he felt a faint gust of warmth penetrate his cooling bag, then a single sharp sting to his shoulder. He groped at the wound with a gloved hand; it was painful to touch, but any break in the skin was too small to discern. Maybe he'd been hit by a fragment of bone.

When the fireball had faded, Tarquinia shut off her engines. The rogue shot forward, passing the gnat, making no attempt to recover from its failure. But even if this was a ruse – and even if the rogue didn't overheat and shatter from a lack of cooling air – it would need eleven bells just to slow and come back, and twice that to make a fresh stab at the original plan. That left time for half a dozen more gnats to come from the *Peerless* and start towing the Station away.

Weightless, Ramiro reached up and took the safety harness in his hands. He clung to it for a while, too weak to go any further, then Tarquinia began drawing the rope back into the cabin.

4

'Happy Ancestors' Day!' Agata greeted her mother. 'Are you coming to the celebration?'

Cira regarded her with undisguised pity. 'I came here to ask if you'd visit your brother with me.'

Agata dropped clear of the doorway to allow Cira to clamber down the entrance ladder. 'Mind the bookcase.' A year and a half into the deceleration, Agata had kept the changes to her apartment messy and proudly provisional. 'Why would I want to see Pio?'

'Common decency.'

Agata felt a twinge of guilt, but she remained unpersuaded. 'All we ever did when he was free was argue, so I doubt he spends his time now yearning for my company.'

'You need to mend things with your brother,' Cira insisted. 'If you think Medoro's going to do Pio's job for you, his sister might have another opinion.'

Agata grimaced. 'Medoro's a friend! Is there anything going on in your head that isn't about *reproductive strategies*?'

'Someone has to think about these things.' Cira peered suspiciously at Agata's console, as if the images of phase-space flows on display might reveal the true source of her daughter's intransigence. 'If you value your work, you should value your brother.'

'Really?'

'Why do you think I had a son at all? It was for your benefit, not mine.'

Agata was chilled. 'Whatever my differences with Pio, at least I don't think of him as some kind of *useful machine*.'

'You can take all the holin you like, and it will never give you certainty,' Cira said bluntly. 'But no woman who's shed a child has ever divided afterwards. If you try to raise a child on your own, it will

43

cost you years away from your research. This is what men are for. Argue politics with Pio as much as you like, but to alienate him completely would be self-defeating.'

Agata said, 'He tried to stop the turnaround. It's gone beyond arguing politics.'

Cira spread her hands in a gesture of agnosticism. 'There was no evidence connecting him to that. And I would have thought you'd be troubled by this whole notion of "preventative detention".'

In truth, Agata was divided. That the Council had empowered itself to imprison people without trial disturbed her, but she'd almost convinced herself that the *Peerless*'s vulnerable transition state justified the move. Pio and the other migrationist leaders were being treated well enough; three years in comfortable accommodation, free to read and study, wasn't exactly torture.

'If you won't visit him, you can still do right by him,' Cira suggested.

'What do you mean?'

'If you had a child, I don't believe they'd keep her from her uncle.'

Agata was appalled. 'Now you want my daughter to be raised in prison?'

'Only for a couple of stints,' Cira assured her. 'After that, we'd have grounds to ask for his early release. If he's looking after a child, what harm can he do? They can still monitor him, but it would be absurd to keep him locked up.'

Agata's head was throbbing. 'You're unbelievable!'

'Do this for him now,' Cira replied, 'and he's sure to be so grateful that he'll happily raise a son as well. Then the next generation will be complete. You owe that to your daughter: to give her the opportunities I gave you.'

Agata said, 'I'm going to the party. You're welcome to join me—'

'To commune with the ancestors?' Cira hummed contemptuously.

'To remember what we're here for,' Agata countered.

Cira said, 'We're here to survive, and to strengthen our position.'

'You mean manipulate each other, and preserve the status quo?'

'Your grandmother lived under the old rules,' Cira reminded her. 'Starving wasn't an eccentric choice then; it was forced on every woman in the mountain. If you'd listened to her more, you might not be so complacent.'

Agata said, 'If you're so terrified of the old ways returning, why did

44

you have a son at all? You got by without a brother. Why not wipe out your enemy completely and be done with it?'

'Far better to keep them alive and weak,' Cira replied, 'than to turn against ourselves and reduce some women to playing the role of men.'

Agata arrived at the celebration later than she'd intended. It was easy enough to make allowances for the time it took to climb the rope ladders between the levels she frequented day to day, but when a journey took her up or down the old helical staircases she found it impossible not to dawdle. For six generations these elaborately carved grooves had been nothing more than peculiar decorations wrapping the walls of horizontal tunnels, but to traverse them now meant treading on stone that had last been used this way when Yalda was alive. If Agata spotted a blemish in the rock she had to stop and inspect it in the moss-light, hoping that someone who had walked on the home world – famous or obscure, she didn't care – might have carved their name into these steps.

As she entered the observation chamber, she saw that at least six dozen people had shown up. The space couldn't have held many more, but there were similar festivities taking place up and down the mountain's rim. She squeezed her way through the crowd, moving aimlessly until someone called out to her.

'Agata! Over here!' It was Medoro's sister, Serena. The whole family was gathered around a table by the edge of the dome.

Agata approached, trying not to be distracted by the view before she'd greeted everyone. The lighting in the chamber was subdued, but she still needed to stare out at the sky to convince herself that she really was seeing it – that her vision wasn't being blocked by reflections from the interior. All the long, orderly star trails she'd grown up with, the great meridional arcs that together filled half the sky, had shrunk into the kind of tiny, random lines of colour that she'd only ever known before as the signature of the orthogonal cluster. This was the ancestors' sky. In less than a chime, the mountain would be at rest with respect to the home world. Apart from the effect of the *Peerless*'s displacement on the arrangement of the nearest stars, and apart from the absence of Hurtlers and the sister-world-turned-sun, Gemma, *this* was the view that anyone on the night side of the planet would be seeing right now.

'Cira didn't come?' Medoro asked, feigning puzzlement.

Agata wasn't in the mood for jokes about her family – and apparently Medoro's own relatives felt the same way: Gineto reached over and gave his nephew an admonitory thump on the arm, to Serena's amusement. 'Feel free to do that yourself whenever he annoys you,' she suggested to Agata. 'It's the only way we manage to put up with him.'

Vala said, 'Agata and her mother have been through enough. Just let her enjoy the party.'

Medoro cast Agata an imploring glance, as if he expected her to defend him.

She said, 'Don't worry, nothing could spoil this day for me.'

'Not even a Hurtler strike?' he joked.

Agata spread her arms and turned to face the sky. 'Here we are, come and get us!' For a day or two they'd be as vulnerable as the ancestors – but that felt more like a gesture of solidarity than a real source of danger.

'Not even engine failure?' Medoro persisted.

'Our exhaust will be heading into the home cluster's future,' Agata replied. 'That's no different from the ancestors lighting a lamp, or the stars in the home cluster shining. There is no magical thermodynamic curse that can stop us making the turnaround. Or do you think Yalda and her friends couldn't walk east when the Hurtlers' arrow of time pointed west?'

'And yet they were careful not to launch against the arrow,' Medoro noted.

'For which we should be grateful,' Agata declared. 'That let us observe the orthogonal cluster for six generations before losing sight of it. Better that than getting a surprise on the turn.'

'Hmm.' Medoro had run out of ways to needle her.

Serena gestured at the food in front of them. 'We've all been stuffing ourselves, so don't be shy about catching up.' Agata took a spiced loaf from the table. She hadn't been able to eat with Cira in the apartment; every bite she took in her mother's presence made her feel as if she were betraying her starving dead grandmother – who hadn't actually starved for long, and whose co had helped her raise her machine-fathered daughter.

Vala asked Agata how her research was progressing.

'Still slowly,' Agata confessed.

Gineto hummed sympathetically. 'What is it exactly that you're doing? Medoro's tried to describe it to us, but I'm not sure he really understands it himself.'

'I'm just a humble instrument builder,' Medoro said. 'You can't expect me to begin to comprehend Agata's work.'

Agata ignored his teasing, but Gineto seemed genuinely curious. And if he wasn't, he was being too polite to be brushed off with 'it's complicated'.

She said, 'Do you know about Lila's work?'

'Vaguely,' Gineto replied. 'Didn't she find a way to make gravity compatible with rotational physics?'

'Exactly. Vittorio's law of gravity assumed absolute time. Yalda must have known that it wasn't rotationally invariant, but in those days the discrepancy wasn't seen as important. People were busy enough trying to understand light.'

'So . . . what changes?' Gineto asked. 'What does Vittorio's inverse square law become?'

'It's trickier than that,' Agata warned him. 'In Lila's theory, gravity isn't a force at all, in the traditional sense: it's a result of four-space being curved. You know how lines of longitude on a globe come together? Even though they start out parallel at the equator, they don't remain the same distance apart.'

'Right,' Gineto agreed tentatively. There was nothing esoteric in the geometry she'd described, but he couldn't quite see the connection.

Agata said, 'In Lila's theory, gravitational attraction is the same kind of effect. When two massive bodies start out at rest with respect to each other – that is, with their histories parallel – they don't stay the same distance apart, they accelerate towards each other. But you don't need a force for that; all you need is curvature.'

Gineto buzzed: he got it now. 'That's an elegant idea. Have the astronomers tested it?'

'That's the hardest part,' Agata admitted. 'The mathematics is beautiful, but we're so far from any truly massive bodies that it's almost impossible to devise a test.'

'The ideal thing to study would be a planet orbiting close to its star,' Medoro interjected. 'Like the innermost planet in the home system. What was that called? Paolo? Peleo? I can never quite remember it.'

Agata said, 'Lila's theory predicts that a close elliptical orbit would undergo "apsidal precession": the near and far points of the orbit should move around the star, instead of staying fixed in space. So careful observations of a system like that could distinguish her theory from Vittorio's.' She sketched an example on her chest.

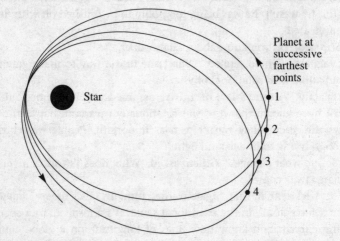

Planet at
successive
farthest
points

Star

1

2

3

4

'If there are other planets in the system it's more complicated,' she added. 'The way they tug on each other will cause precession, too, so you have to separate out the various contributions. If we had copies of all the ancestors' astronomical measurements we could hunt for some sign of Lila's precession, but nobody thought to include that kind of thing in the library.'

'And where does your own work fit into all this?' Gineto pressed her.

'My work's about trying to understand entropy in the context of Lila's theory,' Agata replied. 'According to Lila, the curvature of four-space depends on both the amount of matter present and the way it's moving. If all the particles' trajectories are neatly lined up, the curvature is different than when they're moving around at random.'

'Different how?'

Agata said, 'Ordered matter creates positive curvature along its time axis, so objects that start out at rest are drawn together. But sufficiently disordered matter produces negative curvature, with parallel histories spreading apart.' She drew an illustration.

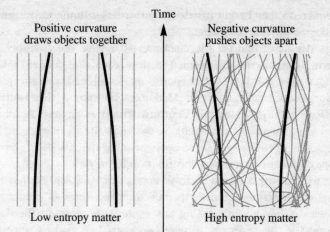

Time

Positive curvature
draws objects together

Negative curvature
pushes objects apart

Low entropy matter

High entropy matter

'But when would the second case actually apply?' Gineto wondered. 'If you're talking about a hot gas, won't that always spread out into the void and become too thin to make any difference? Doesn't the gravitational pull of a star come mostly from the rock beneath the fire – the solid part that actually stays put?'

'That's true, of course.' Agata had underestimated him when she'd thought he might have just been making conversation. 'In fact, Lila proved that a positive-temperature gas can't be gravitationally bound – if the stars weren't mostly rock, they couldn't hold together at all! But on a large enough scale there might still be a disordered state that's gravitationally significant. Our cluster moves one way, the orthogonal cluster another . . . and if you could step back far enough, you might see clusters moving in every direction in four-space. So it's possible that something analogous to a giant hot gas – with clusters of stars playing the role of particles – determines the overall curvature of the cosmos.'

Serena said, 'It's getting close to the time.'

All the partygoers were turning to face a screen mounted high on the chamber's inside wall, showing an animation of an old-fashioned mechanical clock with its dials approaching the sixth bell. Hanging in the darkness behind the clock was an artist's rendering of the home world. Medoro caught Agata's eye, and he didn't need to say a word for her to read his cynical mind: this was just the Council playing on their emotions. No doubt that was true, though to give them credit they hadn't inserted any Hurtlers into the scene, poised to skewer the beloved planet.

As the pause-dial on the clock neared twelve the chamber fell silent. To Agata the dial seemed to slow, each click forward taking longer than the last. But then the marks aligned and the room erupted with exuberant cheers. Medoro's whole family were emitting deafening chirps – Medoro as enthusiastically as anyone. Agata felt her own tympanum thrumming, so she knew she was joining in, but the sound of the crowd was so overwhelming that she didn't have a hope of discerning her own contribution to the din.

After crossing a dozen vasto-severances of void, the *Peerless* had reached the farthest point in its trajectory, halted for an instant and reversed. They weren't fleeing any more; they were on their way home. For the ancestors, a mere two years had elapsed since the launch, and with luck the travellers would return in two more.

They would not be too late, Agata believed; they would not find a world in flames. The journey would fulfil its purpose – and the generations who'd endured the isolation of the mountain, who'd suffered through famine and turmoil, who'd struggled and died with no reward, would not have lived in vain.

Overcome, she sank to the floor on folded legs, her face down-turned, her rear eyes closed. She'd seen the ancestors' sky, she'd stood motionless beside them. What more could she have hoped for in her lifetime?

But these moments of connection would never be repeated. All she had left was the distant promise of the reunion, as remote to her now as the launch.

Someone touched her shoulder. Agata looked up, expecting Medoro's hand, but it was his mother's. The noise was still too great for there to be any point in speaking, but Vala's face was eloquent: she shared the same bitter-sweet feeling.

Agata rose to her feet, hoping that she hadn't embarrassed her friends too much, but the whole room was full of distraught people, torn between celebration and loss.

Medoro approached and put an arm around her. 'It's enough,' he said. 'It has to be enough.'

'Of course.' Agata willed herself to accept that.

'I know you don't want grandchildren,' he teased her, 'but you can always tell your stories to my niece's kids.'

Stories of the spin-down, the exotic gravity, the shrunken stars. All her life, she'd ached to live through these tangible signs that the voyage really would have an end. But now that ache felt worse than ever. When her apartment's floor was horizontal again, when the giant stairwells were tunnels and the star trails had stretched out into coloured threads that squeezed into half the sky, what could she look forward to?

Serena joined them, standing beside her brother. 'How are you feeling?' Agata asked her.

'I couldn't be happier!' Serena spread her arms. 'I know, everyone's emotional, everyone's confused . . . but what can I say? Octofurcate me: *we're headed home!*'

Agata was ashamed. How many people had kept up the struggle when there'd been no end in sight? She still had her work, she still had her friends, and she'd always have her memories of this day. What more did she want?

'We're headed home,' she agreed. 'That's enough.'

5

Seated at his console in the main control room, Ramiro watched the image feed from the camera out on the slopes. At his behest, a small tethered engine ran through a series of moves, tugging on a set of restraining springs and force gauges that allowed its thrust to be measured.

To his astonishment, the rules that the test rig was obeying remained as simple and intuitive as he could have wished: he could point the engine's outlet any way he liked, and when he powered up the engine it generated thrust in the opposite direction. No exceptions, no complications – and no dependence at all on the disposition of distant worlds.

'That's disturbing,' he told Tarquinia. An inset showed her in her office near the summit; she'd carried out the tests herself before inviting Ramiro to repeat them.

'What did you expect?' she asked. She wasn't mocking him; it was a serious question.

'I don't know,' Ramiro replied. 'Maybe part of me always imagined this outcome, but I shouted it down as naïve.'

'I never knew what to think,' Tarquinia admitted. 'My gut feeling – when I was looking at the engine in isolation – was that there'd be thrust in all directions. But all I had to do to change my mind was picture the consequences of that: all the specks of dust and gas out in the void that would need to conspire to make it happen.' She sent Ramiro a sketch via her corset; it appeared in miniature in a second inset. 'But then all I had to do to change my mind again,' she added, 'was to think of the engine magically "knowing" that it wasn't meant to work when it was pointed towards the wrong part of the sky. That was just as hard to swallow as the alternative.'

Ramiro said, 'Well, now you've settled it. Either way, something had to offend our intuition – so we should be grateful that the chosen offence happens far away and out of sight.' He enlarged Tarquinia's sketch, which drove home the point: eerie as it would have been to watch the engine selectively fail, if they could have witnessed the actual results in every detail that would have been at least as unsettling.

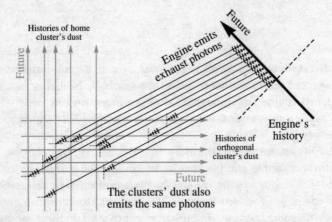

Histories of home cluster's dust

Future

Engine emits exhaust photons

Future

Histories of orthogonal cluster's dust

Engine's history

Future

The clusters' dust also emits the same photons

Unless the engine's outlet was aimed at the *Peerless* itself, every photon it pumped out would eventually strike some distant object: usually just a particle of gas or dust belonging to one of the clusters. Given the present motion of the *Peerless*, it was easy to arrange the geometry so that the light would be arriving from the dust's future – which meant that according to its own arrow of time, the dust would be emitting the light, not receiving it. By that account, the engine's whole exhaust beam was being spontaneously emitted by countless tiny sources scattered across the void, just as much as it was being emitted by the engine's own rebounders.

'So the final slowdown shouldn't be a problem,' Ramiro realised belatedly.

'If this holds up – no, it shouldn't,' Tarquinia agreed.

Ramiro leant back from the console, pondering the political consequences. Even the staunchest reunionists had assumed that they'd be leaving their descendants with the burden of finding a way to start decelerating on the approach to the home world. But the tiny engine Tarquinia had set straining against its springs had had no difficulty achieving thrust in exactly the direction that the *Peerless* itself would need for that last manoeuvre. The migrationists had lost their most powerful scare story.

But physics had lost a story of its own. From the point of view of the ultimate recipients of the engine's exhaust, its successful firing was the kind of absurd picture that came from imagining time running in reverse, with the fragments of some shattered object reassembling themselves into the whole.

'So much for the law of increasing entropy,' Ramiro said.

Tarquinia was unfazed. 'That was never going to last.'

'No.' If the cosmos really did loop back on itself in all four dimensions, nothing could increase for ever. 'But what do we put in its place?'

'Observation.' Tarquinia nodded towards the image of the test rig.

'So everything becomes empirical?' Ramiro was happy to be guided by experiments, so long as some prospect remained that they could yield the same result twice in a row.

'The cosmos is what it is,' Tarquinia replied. 'The laws of optics and mechanics and gravity are simple and elegant and universal . . . but a detailed description of all the things on which those laws play out seems to be nothing but a set of brute facts that need to be discovered individually. I mean, a "typical" cosmos, in statistical terms, would be a gas in thermal equilibrium filling the void, with no solid objects at all. There certainly wouldn't be steep entropy gradients. We've only been treating the existence of one such gradient as a "law" because it was the most prominent fact in our lives: time came with an arrow distinguishing the past from the future.'

Ramiro said, 'But isn't there still a question of how brutish the brute facts are? We know that the home cluster's entropy was much lower in its distant past, and the same was true of the orthogonal cluster. The most economical explanation is that both clusters shared a common past.'

Tarquinia said, 'So you want to cling to the notion of parsimony? A single region of low entropy is already stupendously unlikely, but even if we have no choice about that, you want to hold the line and refuse to allow two?'

'You don't think that's reasonable?'

Tarquinia thought it over. 'I don't know what's reasonable any more,' she said.

Ramiro closed his eyes for a moment, raising some crude scrawls on his chest based on Tarquinia's diagram, but keeping them private. 'Forget about whether or not the clusters have a common past; forget about the orthogonal cluster entirely. Suppose the only thing we rely on is the fact that the home cluster had vastly lower entropy in the past.'

'All right.'

'So the state of the home cluster long ago is already "special",' he said, 'compared to a random gas made of the same constituents. But now if we take it for granted that this state could, potentially, give rise to all kinds of situations analogous to the experiment we just did with the engine, which result would require the most "unlikely" original state? The result where *none* of those situations ever actually arise: no fast-moving object ever emits a burst of light in such a way that the light would need to be emitted, as well, by other objects scattered around the cluster? Or the result where such events do occur, with the original state guaranteeing coordinated action by all the different emitters? And you can't say "neither"; it has to be one or the other.'

Tarquinia buzzed wryly. 'When you put it that way, I'd bet on a lack of restrictions, not a lack of conspiracies. I mean, consistency comes for free; we're not entitled to say that it's freakishly unlikely when the cosmos does whatever needs to be done to avoid contradicting itself. What's unlikely would be for the requirements of consistency to go out of their way to avoid offending our usual notions of cause and effect.'

'Yeah.' Ramiro buzzed. Though they'd reached a consensus of sorts, his own argument didn't really silence his disquiet. A part of him would never be able to accept that distant dust particles were creating the engine's exhaust as much as the engine itself was.

'I'd better spread the good news,' Tarquinia said.

'Not so good for Pio's gang.'

'Don't be so cynical,' Tarquinia chided him. 'They have one less thing to fear now, like all of us. Why shouldn't they be happy?'

Ramiro said, 'Wait and see. By the time they're out of prison I'm sure they'll have thought of some new reason to give up on the home world.'

Tarquinia wasn't in the mood for an argument about the migrationists. 'Thanks for talking this through with me. I'll feel a lot less rattled now when I report to the Councillors.'

'Any time.'

Her feed vanished from the console, replaced by the status display for the main engines.

As he contemplated the results of the test, Ramiro couldn't help feeling a twinge of disappointment. If every engine working in the void had been selectively inhibited, excursions by the gnats away from the *Peerless* would have become extraordinarily challenging. He'd seen some elaborate proposals from the instrument builders that aimed to get around the problem – most of them requiring high-powered beams passing between the *Peerless* and the gnat, though a couple had sought to exploit the mountain's weak gravity as the controlling force, and one had involved extremely long ropes.

Automating any of those outlandish schemes would have made an exciting project after the turnaround. But now gnats would just be gnats, and it was beginning to look as if he'd soon have nothing new to work on at all.

'Corrado?' Ramiro swayed sideways so he could open the door fully without banging his head. 'You should have warned me, I would have prepared a meal—'

'I'm not here for your cooking,' his uncle replied brusquely. He glared at Ramiro impatiently, waiting for him to move down the ladder so he could pass through the hatch.

When they were both on the floor, Ramiro gestured towards the couch. He knew the gravity was hard on his uncle; before the engines had started up, Corrado's apartment had been in near-weightlessness.

Corrado made himself comfortable, but then wasted no time on pleasantries. 'In three days, your sister will be a dozen and nine years old,' he announced.

'It's that soon, really? I lost track.'

'I understand that you need to supervise the turnaround to the end,' Corrado conceded. 'So you won't be free of that commitment for more than a year. But this is the right time for you to come to an agreement with Rosita. You need to tell her that as soon as the *Peerless* is spinning again, she can shed a daughter and you'll be promised to the child.'

Ramiro examined the floor beside the couch. There was a hole that had once held a peg supporting a bookshelf; he'd left it empty in the hope of reusing it, but it was filling up with dust and food crumbs.

'We should wait and see what happens,' he suggested. 'There might be some kind of technical problem that will prolong the turnaround. I don't want to make any promises I can't keep.'

'Your sister's too easy on you,' Corrado replied flatly. 'That's the only reason I'm here: someone has to speak up on her behalf.'

'What makes you so sure that she's desperate to start shedding?' Ramiro countered.

'She's been fertile for a long time,' Corrado said. 'If she divides, do you want that on your conscience?'

'Of course not,' Ramiro said. 'But the holin is so pure now, and they take such high doses—'

Corrado cut him off. 'That's no guarantee. Imagine your sister gone, and four children to feed. Do you want to be the one who kills two of them?'

Ramiro covered his face – unmoved by the preposterous scenario, but unwilling to reveal just how angry he felt at being cornered this way. For as long as he could remember, his uncle had been assuring him that it was in his nature to want to raise a child. That lesson had come second only to the other glorious message about manhood: if he ever succumbed to his urge to touch a woman in the wrong way – as the Starvers did – it would annihilate her. His duty as he approached maturity was to quash that terrible, lingering compulsion – while also joyously coveting a role that, in nature, could only have followed his failure at the first task.

When the turnaround was finished he'd have no more excuses, no more reasons to delay. The only tactic left was honesty.

He looked up. 'I don't think I can do it.'

'Do what? Kill two children?' Corrado was still lost in his own cautionary fable. 'Of course you can't! The idea is to stop it coming to that.'

Ramiro said, 'I don't think I can raise a child. It's not in me.'

Corrado stood up and approached him, stony faced. Ramiro stepped back, but refused to recant. 'I can't do it,' he said.

'Do you want this family to die out entirely?'

'Die out?' Ramiro lost interest in feigning respect. 'I wish you'd make up your mind what you're threatening me with: is it four children, or none?'

Corrado raised his hand, but then stayed it. He'd probably worn himself out already in the high gravity. 'If you don't do this—' he snarled.

'If I don't do this,' Ramiro replied, 'and Rosita actually wants a child . . . she'll find a man whose sister died, or whose sister wasn't interested in shedding. Or she might even raise the child on her own. Who knows? I want her to be happy, whatever she chooses – but I'm entitled to make my own choices too.'

Corrado stood in front of him, silent for a while. 'If you don't do this, why would she ever have a son? Why would she go through all that pain and trouble a second time, if you've proved to her that it will be wasted?'

Ramiro said, 'I have no idea what her plans will be. Why don't you ask her, if it's so important?'

'But you don't care? Nephew, no nephew – it's all the same to you?'

Ramiro buzzed humourlessly. 'Absolutely. So long as I don't have to coddle the brat.'

Corrado struck him hard across the face. Ramiro staggered back, and had to squat down to regain his balance.

'We're barely clinging on,' Corrado said. 'One family in three has no son. But I didn't know I'd raised a self-hater: the kind who wants to see us wiped out entirely.'

Ramiro was shivering. 'You don't know the first thing about me. But if you were such a great champion for the male sex, why didn't you turn my mother into a Starver and take her right out of the picture? That would have done wonders for your census counts.'

Corrado walked over to the ladder and ascended, leaving the apartment without another word.

Ramiro knelt on the floor, humming to himself. Part of him was jubilant: he'd finally punctured the old man's presumptuous fantasies of an endless chain of obedient nephews, all living out their lives in exactly the same fashion as the family's First Shed Son. And he felt a glorious, self-righteous glow at having provoked Corrado into assaulting him without raising a hand in retaliation.

But another part of him looked back on the confrontation with dismay. All he'd really wanted was more time to consider his choices, a chance to talk honestly with Rosita, an end to being taken for granted. Now it would be impossible to change his mind without humiliating himself completely.

6

On the day that the mountain's centrifugal gravity returned to full strength, Agata spent the morning tidying her apartment.

Her intention had always been to keep as much of the layout as possible fixed across the changes of vertical, and though the demands of safety and comfort had forced various compromises she'd managed to leave one large corner-mounted cupboard unopened for the whole three years, in the hope that a strict refusal to meddle with its contents might allow every item to return of its own accord to its original position.

This proved to have been excessively optimistic. In retrospect, she realised that it was probably the brief interludes of weightlessness, rather than the long exposure to sideways gravity, that had wreaked the most havoc, allowing the effects of small bumps and vibrations to accumulate, feeding entropy into the jostling mass of books, papers and knick-knacks. If there'd been any prospect of the turnaround being repeated, she would have started by tying a few more items together with string, cutting down the number of degrees of freedom.

Agata had a meeting with Lila in the afternoon, but she'd run out of food so she left the apartment early to give herself time to eat on the way. Striding down the corridor, using a guide rope to help her maintain traction, she ran her free hand over the dusty footprints still clinging to the wall on her left.

'Agata!'

She raised her rear gaze. She hadn't been mistaken about the voice: the man approaching behind her was her brother.

Pio caught up with her. 'I almost missed you.'

'I have an appointment,' Agata said curtly.

'Can I walk with you? I won't slow you down.'

Agata hummed indifference.

'They let me out yesterday,' Pio explained, moving beside her and taking the same guide rope. 'Cira came to meet me, but she said you were still angry.'

'Why would I be angry?'

'I had nothing to do with the gnat at the Station,' Pio declared. 'That was a dangerous stunt, and if I'd known anything about it I would have tried to stop it myself.'

Agata didn't believe him, but she knew she'd only make a fool of herself if she started arguing about the migrationists' internal power structures with someone who actually knew what they were.

'Well, there'll never be a chance to repeat it,' she said. The *Peerless*'s reversal had rendered every cousin of the Object into ordinary matter, and turned the Hurtlers into nothing but slowly drifting sand. 'We're in for six generations of cosmic tranquillity.'

'Good,' Pio replied.

'And you know there are no restrictions on the engines?' Agata added.

'I heard that at the time,' he said. 'They let us watch the news.'

A woman walked past them, looking twice when she recognised Pio, then hurrying on. Agata felt herself soften a little. She'd had visions of her brother emerging from prison ranting denials against every unwelcome new fact. 'If cooling air escapes from the mountain now,' she said, 'it will end up mingling with the orthogonal cluster, violating its arrow of time. And yet—' She stopped and spread her arms. 'I don't feel myself burning up.'

Pio buzzed. 'I don't think you blame me for the gnat; I think you're still punishing me for my debate with Lila. There *might* have been a problem for us with the arrows clashing. At the time nobody had proved that there wouldn't be, and I was right to point that out.'

'So you'd say we've been lucky,' Agata pressed him, 'but you're satisfied now that there's no reason not to forge ahead, all the way to the reunion?'

'That's a weighty demand,' Pio replied lightly. 'If you're asking me whether I'm going to advocate any kind of change in course in the immediate future, the answer is no. There's nothing we could do at this moment that would make the *Peerless* any safer, and no risk that we urgently need to avoid.'

He gestured towards the floor – towards the rim, out into the void. 'But as Lila said in the debate, the orthogonal worlds are still out there, and they can't annihilate us any more. So don't ask me to renounce the possibilities they offer. All I'm calling on people to do right now is to keep an open mind. Is that so terrible?'

Agata said, 'You've forgotten your own slogan: "Let the ancestors burn." Why should anyone open their mind to that?'

'Let them burn *if necessary*,' Pio replied. 'If the alternative is even worse.'

Agata stopped walking. 'You know, you almost sound convincing sometimes. But you were ready to give up on the home world before on much weaker grounds than *necessity*.'

Pio raised his hands contritely. 'I got carried away in the debate. I know it offended you, and I'm sorry.'

They'd almost reached the turn-off to Lila's office. Agata didn't want to detour for a meal now in case Pio insisted on joining her.

'I have to go,' she said. 'You can tell Cira that you tried your best, to no avail.'

'What are you talking about?' But Pio's baffled demeanour was a bit too self-conscious to be believable.

'You should find something useful to do,' Agata suggested. 'I'm sure they still need help re-bedding the medicinal gardens.'

'And your work's useful?' he retorted. 'Try some gardening yourself!'

'Goodbye, Pio.' Agata strode towards the intersection, glancing at her brother with her rear gaze in the hope that he'd set off back down the corridor so she could get to the food hall after all. But he must have been hungry too, because he headed for the hall himself.

Agata muttered imprecations against her family and readied herself for a bell or two of higher mathematics through the eyes of a Starver.

'Are you eating for four now?' Medoro joked.

Agata looked up. 'We can share if you want to. I might have ordered too much.'

Medoro sat on the floor, facing her, and helped himself to a loaf. The food hall was quiet, and Agata had been lost in thought.

'How's work?' he asked.

'I finished proving an interesting result today,' she said. 'Lila and I had been fairly sure that it was true, but it took a while to clear up all the technicalities.'

'Ah. Would I understand it?'

'Maybe not the proof,' Agata admitted, 'but the result itself is simple.'

Medoro buzzed sceptically. 'Try me, then. But be warned: if I can't explain it properly afterwards you'll be hearing from Gineto.'

'Suppose the topology of the cosmos is that of a four-dimensional sphere,' Agata began. 'Not the shape, just the topology: the way it all connects up.'

'I thought the cosmos was a torus,' Medoro protested.

'A torus was Yalda's preferred model.' Agata had nothing but respect for Yalda, but she wished the schools would stop treating this favoured model as an established fact. 'It makes for a nice, concrete example that's simple to work with – but the truth is, we don't know the real topology. It might be a torus, it might be a sphere, it might be something else entirely. The only thing we know for sure is that it has to be finite in all four dimensions.'

Medoro said, 'All right. So you hypothesise that the cosmos is a sphere. Then what?'

'Then you ask what kind of curvature it might have.'

'The curvature of a sphere?' Medoro ventured.

'Ha!' To her amusement, Agata realised that her own intuition now filtered out this eminently sensible guess so rapidly that she hadn't even thought of mentioning it. 'Well, you might think so: why shouldn't the cosmos have the curvature of a perfectly symmetrical four-dimensional sphere? The trouble is, a perfect sphere has equal positive curvature in all dimensions: no direction is different from any other. But in Lila's theory of gravity, if the disposition of matter is like that – with no direction favoured – what you get is uniform *negative* curvature. You could only get uniform positive curvature if the energy density were negative, and we have no reason to believe that that's the case.'

Medoro thought for a while, chewing on a second loaf. 'So can you have something with the topology of a sphere, but with uniform *negative* curvature?'

'You can't,' Agata said. 'In fact that's what we just proved. A four-sphere with positive curvature is possible geometrically but impossible physically, while a four-sphere with negative curvature would make sense physically, but it's impossible geometrically.'

'Hmm.' Medoro brushed crumbs from his tympanum. 'Which

leaves you with what? That the cosmos can't really be a four-sphere at all?'

'No, that doesn't follow,' Agata replied. 'It just means that if the cosmos *is* a four-sphere, topologically, then it can't be perfectly uniform: it must differ from place to place.'

'Aha!' Medoro chirped appreciatively. 'So it goes some way towards explaining the entropy gradient?'

'Some way.' Agata was pleased with the result, but she didn't want to oversell it. 'If we had a reason to believe that the topology *had to be* a four-sphere, then we could say that the cosmos would need to contain some regions of lower entropy in order to meet the geometrical constraints.'

'And do you have a reason?'

'No,' Agata admitted. 'As far as anyone knows, the cosmos might just as easily be a torus, in which case our theorem can't be applied and the entropy gradient is as inexplicable as ever.'

'Never mind,' Medoro counselled consolingly. 'I'm sure someone will work it all out eventually.'

Agata was about to retort that she had every intention of being that 'someone', but she caught herself; he was just goading her. 'That's enough cosmology,' she said. 'How's the camera business?'

'Cosmological,' Medoro replied. 'Actually, that's why I came looking for you. I'm starting a new project, and I wanted to hear your thoughts on it.'

Agata was intrigued. Medoro made cameras for the astronomers from time to time, but he'd never felt the need to consult with her before. 'What are you building?' she asked.

'A new imaging chip,' he said. 'One that can visualise the orthogonal cluster.'

'Visualise it?' Agata scrutinised his face, half suspecting that she was being set up for a joke, but either way she couldn't resist the bait. 'How?'

Medoro said, 'Instead of polling the array of pixels on the chip and counting how many photons have struck each of them, it will count how many photons each pixel has *emitted*. Point the camera at the sky . . . and when it emits light towards the orthogonal stars, you can read off the details.'

Before the turnaround Agata would have been sceptical, but now she could see that the possibility of a camera like this had been implicit in the results of the very first engine tests after the reversal. Just as the engines had happily given off light that the ultimate recipients would consider to be arriving from their future, the orthogonal stars were – presumably – still shining down on the *Peerless*, despite being rendered invisible by the very same property. People's eyes had not evolved to know when they were the joint authors of a beam of light, as responsible for creating it as the distant star at the other end. But a camera could be made to catch its own strange radiance in the act.

'Who commissioned this?' she asked.

'Do you know Greta?'

'No.' Agata knew all the astronomers, and there was no Greta among them.

'She's a technical adviser to the Council,' Medoro explained. 'She supervised the turnaround, but now that it's over she's been given this new thing.'

'Which is . . . ?'

Medoro leant forward as if to share some delicate confidence. 'I was told that the camera would be part of a general upgrade of the navigation systems. The rationale being that the old maps are fine for most purposes, but if we can find a way to keep getting real-time images of the orthogonal stars, so much the better.'

'Except that this is better than real-time,' Agata joked. 'Instead of seeing where the star was, we'll know where it will be.'

Medoro said, 'That, and a great deal more.'

'I'm sorry?'

He buzzed impatiently. 'Come on, you're the physicist! Do I have to spell it out?'

Agata stared at him, bemused. Knowing the future positions of the orthogonal stars would not be a momentous revelation: their trajectories were already predictable over a time-span of eons. And in fact, these stars' 'future' positions would be positions in which they'd already been observed, earlier in the *Peerless*'s own twisted history. Telescopes had improved since then, but there were unlikely to be any spectacular, collision-avoiding surprises.

'You've lost me,' she confessed.

'Suppose something occults an orthogonal star that I've been watching with this camera,' Medoro said. 'What happens then?'

'The occulting object will take the place of the camera as the second source of the light.'

'So we'll know about the occultation?' he pressed her.

Agata said, 'Of course! If there's no light passing between camera and star, the "image" of the star will disappear, just as an ordinary image would.'

'And when will we know about it?'

'When? The exact time will depend on the geometry: the location of the object that blocks the light, and the speed of light for the part of the star trail that's obscured.'

Medoro said, 'Now suppose that we *arrange* a sequence of occultations – of the slowest detectable light, with the blocking taking place as far from the telescope as possible.'

Agata thought she knew where he was headed. 'Then the image of the star will blink out before the blocking object is actually in place. But you know, even the slowest detectable infrared is quite hard to outpace. So unless you build some massive engines, these flying shutters of yours would need to be launched long before you see their effect on the star.'

But Medoro wasn't finished with his thought experiment. 'Now add a pair of mirrors and fold up the light path, so we can achieve the same effect while manipulating an object that's much closer.'

Agata raised a quick sketch of the proposal.

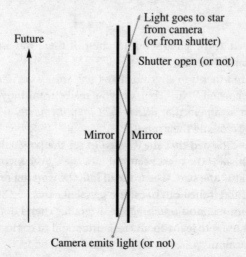

'Depending on the dimensions of the system and the number of bounces before the loss to the mirrors is too great,' she said, 'you'll be able to make observations that reveal the shutter's position some time into the future. I'm no expert on practical optics, but I'd guess that a realistic time-span would be measured in flickers at most.'

Medoro said, 'Maybe. But suppose it's more than twice the response time of an automated signal booster. You might only be able to receive the message from a short way into the future, but so long as you can resend it to a time when the booster will be free to handle it "again" – without any overlap with the later boost – the process can go on indefinitely.'

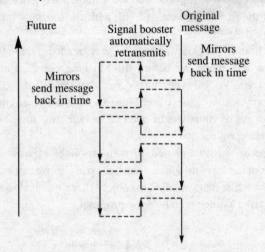

Agata gazed at the picture on his chest. If there was a flaw in his plan, she couldn't see it.

'Greta didn't mention anything like this?' she asked.

Medoro scowled. 'No – but do you really think anyone could commission a camera that *detects light from the future*, without this sort of thing crossing their mind?'

Agata was ashamed that she'd failed to see the possibilities herself long ago. This was the most beautiful idea she'd ever encountered.

'You're right,' she said. 'The Council must be working on a messaging system. And if they can boost the signal like this . . .' She reached over to Medoro, almost touching the diagram. 'Then I don't see why we couldn't use it to learn about the journey still to come, all the way up to the reunion.'

7

'Have you lost your mind?' Ramiro had come to the interview with high hopes, but within a few lapses his mood had been transformed from anticipation to bemusement to horror. 'That's the most deranged thing you've ever asked me to do – which is not an easy contest to win.'

Greta motioned with her hand on her tympanum, imploring him to keep his voice down.

Ramiro said, 'If you're going to keep raising this subject with people, you might want to think about soundproofing your office.'

He began drawing himself out of the harness facing her desk. 'Where are you going?' Greta asked anxiously.

'Relax,' he said. 'I'm not going to tell anyone. Though next time you ask me to keep something between us, I'll take that as a sign that I should turn and run. And when you put this to a referendum, I promise you I'll be campaigning very noisily—' Ramiro caught a flicker of discomfort on her face. 'There is going to be a vote, before you actually build this?'

'That's up to the Council,' Greta replied. 'But there's not much point voting on a system whose feasibility is entirely hypothetical.'

Ramiro slipped back into the harness. 'So you were thinking of building it first? And then what? Hope you can learn something in advance that will guarantee the outcome of the vote? But how would that work? What if the message from next year's Council is simply that whatever they tried, failed?'

Greta said stiffly, 'It's not about *vote rigging*. It's about security. You of all people should appreciate that.'

'Me of all people?' Ramiro stared back at her in disgust. 'If we're being frank, I blame you for the farce with the gnat just as much as I blame the migrationists.' As the words emerged he wondered if he was letting his anger get the better of him. But Greta showed no sign that she was wounded, let alone contrite.

'I don't understand why you're so vehemently against this,' she said. 'You should take a few days to think it over.'

Ramiro buzzed. 'What's funny is that you've been planning this for a year – but you still can't see that your last remark should answer the preceding question.'

Greta spent a pause or two struggling to parse that, but it seemed to be beyond her. Ramiro said, 'You're inviting me to take my time to ponder all the pros and cons before reaching a decision – but the answer you want from me would eradicate my ability ever to go through the same process again.'

'That's nonsense,' Greta said amiably. 'No one's asking you to surrender your free will.'

'And that's not how I'd put it, myself,' Ramiro replied. 'But I'm not going to start debating terminology. The simple fact is that anyone who knows their own actions in advance will be living a different kind of life than someone who doesn't.'

'What makes you think that you'd be forced to know anything about your own actions? The Council will use this facility for planning and security purposes. Any other applications will be carefully controlled – and exposure to information is hardly going to be compulsory.'

Ramiro said, 'That's naïve: information would spread through third parties. You could never come close to promising me that I wouldn't end up hearing things I didn't want to hear.'

'What if we'd known the rogue gnat's trajectory in advance?' Greta demanded. 'Are you honestly telling me that it wouldn't have been worth it?'

Ramiro wasn't going to let her use the rogue to bludgeon him into submission. Perfect knowledge of the future might have spared him the dangerous encounter, but the whole mountain shouldn't have to pay the price for the way the threat had been mishandled from the start. 'I'm sorry I blamed you for that débâcle,' he said sarcastically. 'The fault was mine: I should have just let the gnat hit the Object.'

He struggled out of the harness.

'Are you going to keep your word?' Greta asked. 'I knew I was taking a risk, but I thought I could trust you.'

Ramiro freed himself and clung to the guide rope leading to the doorway. If he said the wrong thing, could she have him imprisoned until the messaging system was complete? They'd set a precedent with the migrationists, and if he vanished from sight he wasn't sure that anyone would come looking for him.

'I'll keep my word,' he said. 'I don't break promises.' He contemplated adding that he trusted the Council to ensure that the matter was put to a vote, but even Greta was likely to pick up the sarcasm.

Outside the office, Ramiro still felt rattled by the confrontation, but as he set off down the corridor he began to regain his composure. It was never exactly prudent to hurl abuse at potential employers, but Greta had a thick skin and he doubted that he'd be thrown in prison for refusing a job. So long as he kept quiet about the offer he'd be left alone.

He reached an intersection and turned into a busy corridor. People strode by, purposeful, intent on their various plans, shaping the minutiae of the unfolding morning. But every child knew that, to the ancestors, the sequence of events that a traveller perceived as evolving over time was no different from the fixed pattern in a tapestry. From the right perspective, each life was a completed picture from birth to death, there to be taken in at a glance.

Every child was also taught that this incontestable fact did nothing to rob them of their freedom. The laws of physics bound people's choices to their actions, as firmly as they bound a tumbling rock's positions from moment to moment into a single, coherent history. Though no one ruled unchallenged over their own flesh – no one could be immune to coercion or injury, no woman to spontaneous division – the exceptions only made it clearer that most acts were acts of will. An omniscient observer who could read the fine details of the tapestry would see that woven into the pattern: deliberation beside resolve, resolve beside deed. Each choice would have its own complex antecedents, inside the body and beyond it – but who would wish to sit in isolation, churning out decisions that came from nowhere?

Ramiro had long ago reconciled himself to this picture of time and choice, and though he couldn't claim to perceive his own life in these terms from day to day, he felt no disquiet at all at the prospect of the timeless point of view growing more compelling.

But Greta's system would do far more than confront the travellers with a stark confirmation of abstract principles that most of them

71

already acknowledged. The one thing a message from the future couldn't tell a person was what they *would have* decided in the absence of that message – it would not be as if the ordinary deliberation really had taken place elsewhere, and was now being delivered to them as a kind of executive summary to spare them from needlessly repeating the effort. The old process wouldn't merely be rendered more efficient, so it reached the same endpoint with less uncertainty or stress. The endpoint itself could be completely different.

And even if it wasn't, was that all that mattered? Ramiro stopped walking and moved to the side of the corridor so he wasn't blocking the guide rope. If he heard from the future that he'd raised Rosita's child, then in the end he would choose to make that happen. If he heard that he hadn't, he would choose differently. He couldn't claim that this would turn him into some kind of hollow puppet, when both outcomes were already possible in the ordinary course of events.

But the nature of the decision would still be utterly different if he reached it with foreknowledge. All that the need for consistency could impose was the requirement that he actually went along with the choice – however reluctantly, resignedly or apathetically he closed the loop. The revelation wouldn't need to ring true, or fill him with joy, or cast any light on the dilemma it resolved. He merely had to be capable of acceding to it – of muttering 'Yeah, that'll do.'

He couldn't live like that – and he couldn't stand by and let the Council force it on everyone else for the next six generations. Greta's promise that the information would be contained was just wishful thinking; that would certainly make the technology more useful to its owners, but Ramiro had no doubt that the content of the messages would still leak out.

And the sooner he broke his own promise, the safer he'd be. He called out to a woman approaching on his left, 'Excuse me!'

She stopped. 'Yes?'

'My name's Ramiro, I'm an automation engineer.'

The woman looked puzzled, but she introduced herself. 'I'm Livia, I'm a shedding technician. Didn't you—?'

'Lose an exploding leg near the Station? Yes, I'm that idiot.'

Livia paused expectantly. Famous or not, his claim on her time was strictly limited.

Ramiro said, 'I've just heard that the Council is planning a new messaging system; they invited me to work on it, but I declined. If they build it, it will affect all of us, so if you can spare a couple of lapses I'd like to tell you about it.'

By the time he was halfway through his account there were six more people listening. Ramiro confined his message to the science itself; people could ponder the implications at their leisure, and if he started philosophising that would only encourage disputatious onlookers.

When he'd finished, Livia thanked him and walked away, but some of the others gathered nearby in heated discussion. Ramiro left them to it; it was more important to keep spreading the word than to try to influence one small debate. He raised a schematic on his chest and spread his arms. 'New messaging system! Hear all about it!'

A dozen people walked past him, bemused or embarrassed, but then a woman stopped. 'What new system?'

'The one that uses light from the orthogonal cluster to bring information from the future.'

'You're joking?'

Ramiro said, 'Hear me out, then decide for yourself.'

As he started speaking, more people gathered, while the remnants of his last audience dispersed. In a chime or two there'd be no hope at all of tracking down everyone who knew about the scheme, let alone locking them up.

8

'You should ask Pio for some debating tips,' Medoro suggested. 'He's the expert.'

Agata hummed frantically. 'Are you going to help me or not? I only have three more days to get this right.' The last time she'd sought Medoro's advice he'd fobbed her off with an excuse about the camera creating a conflict of interest. The Councillors themselves were required by law to stay out of the debates, but if every last person who had some stake in the outcome kept themselves at arm's length from the process there'd be no one left with a reason to argue the case on either side.

Medoro relented and invited her into his apartment. 'I'll do what I can. If your enemies portray you as part of my self-serving cabal, so be it – but when we're in public you'll have to call me "puppet master" and answer to "stooge".'

Agata rewarded this suggestion with silence.

He said, 'Seriously, wouldn't Lila be more use to you?'

'Lila's staying out of this. I'm not sure if she's even made up her mind how she'll be voting.' Agata hadn't pushed her on the matter, and she respected Lila's right to take a different view, but without even her long-time mentor backing her she was beginning to feel desperately isolated.

'What's your brother's position?' Medoro asked.

'Against, of course!'

'Why "of course"? What happened to protecting our descendants from unforeseen risks?'

Agata said, 'Don't ask me for his detailed rationalisation, but from what I've heard he's claiming that the messaging system *is* the unforeseen risk – unforeseen by everyone but him, since he warned us that there'd be dire consequences from the clash of arrows.'

'Fair enough,' Medoro judged. 'His message from the future told him that the rest of us would soon want messages from the future – but he couldn't tell us that until now, because otherwise we might have wanted our messages sooner.'

Agata buzzed wearily; at least she wouldn't be debating Pio. 'Have your own family taken positions?'

'Gineto against, Serena for, Vala undecided.' Medoro didn't seem too worried by the split. 'But they all gave me grief that I didn't go public.'

'That's unfair,' Agata protested. 'Ramiro had it all laid out for him. We were just guessing – it would have been irresponsible to start a rumour when we weren't even sure of the facts.'

'Hmm.' Medoro sounded unconvinced, so Agata let the subject drop.

She said, 'But now Ramiro is courage personified, and I have to stand in front of a crowd of his admirers and tell them he's wrong.'

'I'm sure you'll have admirers too,' Medoro teased her.

'For what? My theorems on sectional curvature?'

'Why not? Any idiot can set himself on fire.' Medoro rearranged himself on the guide rope. 'Anyway, you don't need to attack Ramiro. His arguments aren't unreasonable: of course there could be drawbacks if the system is abused. But that doesn't mean we can't minimise the risks.'

'I was going to start with a few practical benefits,' Agata said. 'Suppose we learn that a new crop disease shows up three years from now. We can't prevent it arising altogether – or we'd never hear about it – but we can still take early quarantine measures and ensure that the outbreak is limited.'

'Boring but sensible,' Medoro declared approvingly. 'Exactly the kind of thing people want the Council to be doing. Throw in a reference to the Great Holin Shortage, and you'll have won over half the women in the room. What about averted collisions?'

Agata said, 'No – in most realistic cases we would have had plenty of warning by conventional means.'

Medoro was disappointed. 'You don't want to go for the frisson of danger? Message: "Thanks for starting a sideways swerve when you read this, it just paid off and saved the whole mountain"?'

'I could raise it briefly,' Agata decided. 'Almost as a joke, so Ramiro can't go too hard on the implausibility.'

'What else?' Medoro pressed her.

'Next, reassurances about privacy, validation and containment. Everything can be encrypted and signed, in exactly the same way as with the ordinary network. So there'll be no chance of anyone else reading a message intended for you personally, and no chance of the sender convincing you that they're someone they're not.'

Medoro said, 'I can check a message that purports to be from you because you've published a validation key – and you're here to complain loudly if someone else tries to distribute a different key and claim that it's yours. But if I get a message from someone who claims to be my grand-niece . . . how do I authenticate *that*?'

'You just need a chain of trust,' Agata explained. 'You get a message from your niece, signed with a key that you'll give her personally when she's old enough. Her message gives you a key for authenticating her daughter's message.'

Medoro grimaced. 'So I need to have one key ready right now, and be sure that it won't get lost or stolen before I have a chance to give it to a child who hasn't been born yet?'

'Yes. But is that so much harder than keeping your own key secure?'

'I think I deleted my key,' Medoro confessed. 'That's why I never sign messages any more; I'm too embarrassed to apply for a replacement.'

Agata said, 'If Ramiro raises that kind of problem, what can I say? Nothing's perfect, we can't expect it to be, but we cope with the flaws in every other technology.'

'You mentioned containment,' Medoro reminded her. 'Suppose your neighbour hears from her son about your death; how can you stop her telling you the details, if you don't want to be told?'

'Punishment,' Agata said. 'If you violate someone's right to be future-blind, all messages addressed to you will be deleted henceforth.'

'Not that anyone would bother sending them any more,' Medoro reasoned. 'But can't we strengthen that further, and make it impossible to do the damage in the first place?'

Agata was amused. 'I doubt it. I mean, the Council could *declare* that if someone receives a message that leads to an offence, the sender will never be allowed to send it in the first place. And if their ability to follow through on that were infallible, then it would never even need to be acted on. But realistically . . . ?'

Medoro said, 'I might have been overreaching there. What's next?'

'I won't have time for much more, but I should end with something about the reunion.' Agata waited for Medoro to mock her, but he listened in silence. 'We all have stories of the launch, passed down from generation to generation. Why shouldn't it be the same with the reunion? Why shouldn't we all have that sense of completion?'

'That's reasonable,' he said. 'Don't overdo it, though; just say enough for the people who'd be swayed by it to complete the picture for themselves – without starting the cynics groaning about ancestor worship.'

'No talk of receiving photographs of our descendants strolling through Zeugma beside Eusebio?'

'I think not.'

'That's all I have,' Agata said. 'Practical benefits, rigorous safeguards, future-nostalgic finish. The rest of the time I'll need to be dealing with Ramiro's arguments. So if you can think of any downsides I haven't addressed, this would be a good time to hear them.'

Medoro took a few moments to consider the request. 'What about the idea that the system could be demoralising for innovators? You've been struggling for years to understand why the entropy gradients exist; how would you feel if you read a message from the future that handed you all of the answers, robbing you of the chance to discover them for yourself?'

Lila had expressed similar misgivings, but when Agata had thought the matter through she had not been swayed. 'Complex ideas don't come out of nowhere,' she said. 'Not because that would violate some law of physics or logic, but because it's stupendously improbable. The most probable routes to complexity involve some kind of backstory. There were no people around at the entropy minimum – it took eons for the first simple organisms to arise, and eons more for life to evolve to include a species with a complex culture.'

Medoro was confused. 'What has that got to do with some future rival stealing your glory?'

'Complexity grows in a sequence of steps,' Agata stressed. 'So far, we've never seen it appear fully formed, and we have no reason to think that the messaging system could change that. If some future researcher did send me a theorem that made all my own efforts obsolete, it would enter the scientific culture and be passed down the generations – so whoever wrote the message would merely have heard the result during their own education: they wouldn't be its discoverer.'

'In which case . . . who would?' Medoro struggled.

Agata buzzed. 'Nobody! And there'd be no contradiction in that, but it's as *unlikely* for the cosmos to contain such an isolated loop of unexplained complexity as it would be for the same idea to have popped into my mind all by itself this morning, with no prompting from any future informant.'

Medoro thought it over. 'Suppose I take your word for all that. You've still only told me what you think *won't* happen – you've given me an unlikely scenario. So what's the alternative? What's the likely story?'

Agata said, 'There'll have to be some self-censorship of the messages. People won't pass back ideas that would entail the creation of complexity out of nothing.'

Medoro hummed with frustration. 'Now you've introduced some magic cosmic censor?'

'It's not magic,' Agata insisted. 'It's not some extra premise or some new constraint. If the messaging system can be built at all and the cosmos is self-consistent, the less improbable scenario – by far – is the one that contains some limits on the content of the messages, not the one that allows whole new sciences to come into existence without a day's toil by anyone.'

Medoro plucked at the rope, dissatisfied. 'What if someone in the future decides to break this rule?'

'They can't, they don't,' Agata said flatly. 'Or to be precise: it's prodigiously unlikely. The fact that ordinarily such an act would be unexceptional is beside the point: the messaging system will put them in a situation where the prerequisite for such a disclosure is that they have something massively improbable to disclose in the first place.'

Medoro wasn't placated. 'What happened to the freedom the engine tests gave us?' he demanded.

Agata said, 'That's just the freedom to send messages in general, not some open-ended guarantee that the usual range of actions will always be possible. You didn't complain about our lack of freedom to ignore an outbreak of crop disease, if we get a message spelling out everything we *will have done* to contain it.'

'No,' Medoro admitted. He buzzed wryly, finally reconciling himself to the strangeness of it. 'Maybe you should stay clear of this in the debate. It might make people feel a bit . . . trammelled.'

'If Ramiro doesn't raise it, I'll have no reason to bring it up.' Agata felt much happier about the whole subject after arguing it out with Medoro, but she wasn't going to spread anxiety needlessly just to prove to people that she had the cure. 'It's going to be hard enough as it is.'

'You'll be fine,' Medoro assured her.

'Will I?' Agata pictured herself at the front of the packed meeting room, ready to follow in Lila's footsteps. Or possibly her brother's.

'I'd offer you an eyewitness report of your success,' Medoro said. 'But we can't quite pull that off yet.'

9

Tarquinia reached across and squeezed Ramiro's shoulder. Her hand made contact roughly, imperfectly controlled in the near-weightlessness, but that only gave the gesture more force.

'Good luck,' she whispered. Ramiro kept his rear gaze on her as he dragged himself away along the guide rope towards the stage.

The meeting room was full, and brightly lit by the beams from a dozen coherers bounced diffusely off the ceiling. People were still talking among themselves as Ramiro approached the front of the stage and reached over to start the timer. He waited a pause or two for the echoing ping to grab their attention, but he knew it would only waste time if he held out for complete silence.

'My job,' he began, 'is to automate things. There are many tasks where we already know exactly what we want to achieve, but find it too arduous to supervise the execution of our plans in detail. If I do my job well, though, the results are easy to foresee: you tell me what you want some machine to do for the next five stints, and I make that happen.

'So I'm familiar with the advantages of *control* and *predictability*, and I can understand why the Council aspires to bring those qualities to as many aspects of the running of the *Peerless* as possible. If we could receive a message from the future assuring us that the mountain had reached the home world safely, and this message was accompanied by a list of the actions we'd need to take – or in the sender's view, had already taken – to sidestep a host of potential calamities, then I'd have no complaint about that at all.'

Ramiro let himself scan a few faces in the audience; so far, he didn't seem to have offended anyone.

'The problem,' he continued, 'is that if we build the proposed system, I don't believe it would be possible to limit it to a single, clear-cut purpose like that. Whatever the Council decrees for now, they can't control the way the facility would be used in the future. In practice, what will confront us is the photonic equivalent of a vast storehouse of documents whose content will have been determined by other people, some of them very remote from us in time. Over the generations, certain documents will have been removed – another process that will be out of our hands – while others are kept and passed down to us. If we hope to reap any benefit from whatever remains, we'll have no choice but to appoint people to read and assess everything we receive. But people can't forget things on command, and even people sworn to secrecy can't ignore what they know. With all those messages and all those readers, information will spill out and reach the public, whether they want it or not.

'Stories of distant calamities averted might bring us courage and optimism, but how would we respond to details of our own personal fates? Some bad news might well come through to us that serves no useful purpose at all: who would want to hear of an early death that no warning could prevent? And some good news would surely lose its lustre if revealed at the wrong time: look back on all the joyful surprises in your own lives, and ask yourselves if you really would have wished to be confronted with a list of them, years in advance. And even if you succeeded in remaining ignorant, how would you feel if your friends and rivals knew your future history? People might be compelled to seek as much news about themselves as possible – in spite of their original wishes – simply to prevent others—'

The timer rang. Ramiro was startled; his pacing must have been slower than when he'd rehearsed with Tarquinia the night before. He flipped the lever and dragged himself back towards the rear of the stage. He'd barely registered Agata's presence before, but now he forced himself to stop fretting about his poor timing and focus all his attention on her.

'Ramiro has done me the favour of acknowledging the enormous benefits of this scheme,' Agata began. 'But he's been rather vague about the details, so let me try to make the possibilities more concrete. Imagine receiving a message from the future telling us that one of the medicinal gardens had become infested with a species of goldenrod blight that we'd never encountered before. Unwelcome news, of course, and we'd be powerless to prevent it – but now imagine that message going on to explain that, thanks to this early warning, we would isolate all the other gardens in time to keep them safe.

'I'm not saying that this system would be a panacea, but we could all make a list of dozens of tragic events where a warning would make all the difference. Imagine encountering some uncharted rock from the home cluster, crossing our path at infinite speed and wiping out a fire-watch platform – but missing the *Peerless* itself, thanks to a course correction that only a message from the future could have guided. Indeed, we could surround the mountain with expendable objects, purely for the sake of rendering near misses visible – just as that one blighted garden allowed us to save the rest.'

Ramiro thought it more likely that consistency would be achieved by the rock simply destroying the *Peerless*, leaving no one to report on the event. But since he doubted that either kind of collision would actually occur, if he quibbled about it he'd just sound desperate.

Agata had moved on. 'All this talk about information bursting from the system and spilling down the corridors is fanciful. Has Ramiro never heard of encryption? If it's good enough to protect our privacy now, why should we expect it suddenly to fail us? If there are messages from our future selves, we'll be free to use all the protocols we use now when exchanging confidences with friends to ensure that no one but our present selves can read them – and of course, we'll also be free to delete these messages unread if we choose to, strange as that would be. With the same methods, we can guarantee the privacy and authenticity of messages from our descendants, or indeed from anyone in the future who chooses to address us. So there'll be no swarm of prying clerks sifting through our private mail, gossiping about us to their friends. Matters of public interest will be sent in plain text, but everything else will be person-to-person.

'For those rare cases where some future informant and present-day recipient might act together out of spite to violate your wish not to be informed of certain events, we can discourage that with appropriate punishments. Nobody is claiming that this technology will transform us into a flawless society, but people have survived over the ages without any perfect, pre-emptive cure for hurtful gossip or malicious slander. Words can damage people, I acknowledge that, but it's nothing new. We'll find the right balance in our laws to protect against the worst kinds of harm, just as we've done in the past.'

Agata had been stealing glances at the timer with her rear gaze and adjusting her pace. Now she waited a moment for it to start ringing, then reached down to silence it.

Ramiro took her place. 'Agata has expressed a touching faith in the power of the law and technology to protect us from unwanted personal revelations,' he said. 'I don't believe that her faith is warranted, but even if it were that wouldn't be enough to make this system benign.

'As I speak, many of you – I hope – are still struggling to decide how you'll vote on this question. And when the result is declared, that will surely be a public matter. The announcement won't be an invasion of anyone's privacy, an act of libel, or anything else that could fairly or sensibly be punished. And yet if you'd known the result in advance, wouldn't you feel that your own personal decision-making process had been altered? Of course you'd still be free to vote in accordance with your wishes, but the whole sequence of contesting thoughts – all the private debates inside your own skull that led you to that final action – would be playing out in a very different context.'

Ramiro checked the timer; he was still less than halfway through his quota, but he was not going to let himself get cut off again.

'Knowing even the most mundane facts from the public record will crush our political lives, flattening our inner dialogues into a choice between impotent rage and apathetic conformity. Of course we're accustomed to being helpless *after the fact* to reverse a vote that goes against us, but remember: the results of elections and referenda that we know in advance will *not* be guaranteed to be the same as they would have been in the absence of foreknowledge. We won't be hearing about a future that would have happened regardless – as every proponent of this system will affirm, because if that were true it could never yield any benefits. Rather, we'll be reshaping the whole process by which we make decisions – at the political level without a doubt, but I believe that the same kind of distortion will afflict every aspect of our lives.'

Ramiro waited for the satisfying punctuation of the bell, but then he realised that he'd rushed through his final words too quickly and left himself with time to fill. 'For example,' he extemporised, 'decisions about births and child-rearing are as difficult as any we face, but it won't take prying clerks to disclose our final choices to us once we hear from a child whose very existence had been in doubt.' He caught a look of bafflement on one woman's face, and an expression of outright hostility on another's. 'It's not that a message like that need be unwelcome, but if we flatten the deliberation process, then just as with the vote—'

The timer interrupted him. Ramiro punched it, then slunk backwards.

Agata took centre stage, pausing just long enough to let Ramiro's awkwardness linger and become fixed in everyone's minds. 'If you don't want to read the result of some future referendum, I'm sure you won't have to,' she declared. 'And if mere rumours of the result prove to be too hard to avoid, they could always be camouflaged with competing rumours. People could choose to learn the true result in advance from some trusted informant if they wished, but those who didn't would end up hearing a range of false claims as well, with no way to distinguish between them.'

Ramiro waited for someone in the audience to ridicule this inane proposal, but they let it pass without complaint. Maybe they all liked the idea of taking advantage of their idealistic neighbours, who'd be wrapped in shrouds of scrupulously balanced, government-supplied misinformation.

'This system could vastly improve our safety,' Agata contended, 'as Ramiro and everyone else acknowledges. We can deal with the privacy issues, and the political ones: your vote will always be your own to cast, and you'll have the choice of knowing the outcome in advance or not, as you wish. But you don't need to take my word for any of this. The present vote is merely for a year's trial in which we can discover what the real problems are – and if, in the end, you find that they outweigh the advantages you'll be free to change your mind and vote to have the system dismantled.

'If we look beyond Ramiro's fear that in this maze of information we might inadvertently stumble on some unwelcome facts about our lives – most of which would be no more harmful to us than a friend's reminiscence about a youthful misadventure that we'd prefer to forget – we'll see something far less petty and mundane. Many of us have heirlooms from the day of the launch: diaries, or letters from mothers to their children, or even just stories passed down unwritten. In this mountain of photonic documents from the future we could find our descendants' stories of the reunion. Then we'll all have a chance to be part of the *Peerless*'s return, in a way that we never imagined before.'

As the timer sounded, the audience cheered – some sections more loudly than others, but it was the first real response they'd offered all evening.

Agata paused to acknowledge the applause, then exited gracefully. Ramiro was stung. How could his case not be obvious to everyone? What hadn't he said that would have made it clearer?

Tarquinia approached and drew him back into the moss-lit side room. 'You did a good job,' she said.

'They loved her,' Ramiro replied. He could barely make out Tarquinia's face as his eyes adjusted from the stage lights. 'Didn't you hear?'

'It was the end of the debate, the applause was for both of you.'

She sounded as if she almost believed that, but Ramiro remained despondent. 'What if I've lost it for us?'

Tarquinia hummed irritably. 'You didn't do as badly as you think. And for anyone you didn't convince, there are five more debates to come!'

'But if people here have made up their minds they won't want to hear it all rehashed.'

'You put a strong case,' Tarquinia insisted. 'You stumbled with the timing, that's all.'

Ramiro could tell that she was beginning to find his pessimism wearisome. 'Thanks for your help,' he said. 'I couldn't have faced that crowd without it.'

'I couldn't have faced that crowd at all,' Tarquinia replied. 'But this way I can still tell my children that I played a part.'

'A part in what, though?' Ramiro joked. 'Victory or farce?'

Tarquinia said, 'Let's not rule anything out. Last time we worked together, we managed both at once.'

10

Medoro had promised that he'd bring Agata food for her vigil, but when she spotted him approaching the voting hall she saw that he'd also brought his whole family.

Medoro and Serena left two baskets of loaves with her then everyone went in to vote. Agata felt a little foolish now, camped beside the moss-red wall with her supplies, no longer able to pass herself off as someone merely waiting for the queues to thin. She could have watched the results accumulating from anywhere in the mountain, but it was the sight of voters coming and going in the flesh that made the experience real for her. At home she would have felt as if the whole thing were some kind of simulation, with a random-number generator filling out the counts.

Gineto emerged first and squeezed his way through the crowd towards Agata. 'I can't say I just made you happy,' he warned her.

'Let's not have an argument,' Agata pleaded. 'I've voted, you've voted; there's not much point in us trying to change each other's minds now.'

'The whole thing's so unnecessary, though,' Gineto brooded. 'We got through the turnaround safely. What threat are we facing? In the home cluster's terms we're just retracing our old path, and the Hurtlers are completely tame now. We could have had a quiet life, waiting patiently to arrive back home. But no, we had to find something to argue about.'

Agata did have some sympathy for this view. 'We can't undo the whole dispute now, but at least this should settle it. Believe me, I'm not going to argue with the result.'

'Nor will I,' Gineto replied, 'but we all saw what happened last time.'

Agata glanced at the screen above the entrance; the pro-system vote was lagging by about a twelfth of the count. If Gineto wanted her to start looking for a downside to victory, she'd need to have victory itself in sight.

Serena and Vala joined them. Agata had tied the food baskets to a guide rope where it met the wall behind her, and Serena wasted no time in opening them.

'I hope this isn't rude, but I'm trying to put on mass,' she explained, biting deeply into her first loaf. 'I talked to the technician yesterday, and she said I'm still about three hefts below the ideal.'

'Oh.' Agata wasn't sure if she should say something congratulatory; Medoro hadn't told her anything about these plans.

'Daughter now, then son after a year,' Serena enthused. 'Over and done with before Medoro gets too old.' She glanced at Gineto. 'He'll thank me later – won't he, Uncle?'

Gineto was bemused. 'You think I was too old? I didn't have an uncle of my own to help me, and I still ran rings around both of you.'

'Do you want to raise these two as well, then?' Serena joked.

'I'm not going to intrude into Medoro's life,' Gineto replied. 'But I'll give him advice if he wants it.'

Agata struggled to animate the fixed expression she could feel on her face. 'It's very quick now, isn't it? The recovery?'

'I'll be mobile in a day, they said,' Serena replied. 'It's not just better drugs and better signal delivery; they really stress the target mass now.' She started on a third loaf.

Vala turned to Agata. 'I suppose you've been busy with the referendum?'

'I sat in on three of the debates, after my own,' Agata said. 'I couldn't make it to the others.' In truth, she'd found it too frustrating to keep attending; as a former participant she wasn't allowed to interject. 'There were good speakers on both sides. No one can claim that all the arguments haven't been aired.'

'I wish they'd show them on the network,' Vala complained. 'Not everyone wants to be packed into a crowd like that.'

Serena said, 'I think the traditionalists are afraid that if we start broadcasting the debates, they'll turn into two people taking turns addressing an empty room. But maybe the Council will change the rules next time.'

Agata looked up at the news screen. The vote had crossed one sixth of the roll, and her side was still behind.

Medoro approached, catching her in the act. 'Does it bother anyone else that a sharp-eyed observer might see which way you voted by watching those things?'

Agata said, 'The scale's never finer than a dozen people per pixel.'

Medoro was undeterred. 'What if I already know how eleven of those people will be voting?'

The five of them spent the next half-bell arguing about the safe-guards in the voting system. With Serena's help they managed to empty both baskets of loaves before midday; Agata had eaten her fill, but she felt like a break so she volunteered to fetch some more.

'I'll come with you,' Medoro offered.

'How will you work on the camera now?' Agata asked him as they left the voting precinct.

'Serena told you about the children?'

'Yes.'

'She's going to help look after them,' Medoro said. 'She and Gineto. I'll still have time to work.'

'You'd trust her with the job?'

Medoro buzzed, affronted. 'I can't believe you'd say that! You were raised by a woman single-handed, and you turned out all right.'

'Did I?'

'Better than the woman who raised you.' He caught himself. 'I shouldn't criticise Cira; that whole generation was confused. And it's hardly her fault that it took so long for the biologists to learn how to shed men.'

'But now they can, and everything's perfect.' Agata hadn't meant to sound bitter, but the words kept emerging that way.

'So you've given up on making Pio an uncle?' Medoro asked.

'There's nothing we agree on,' Agata said. 'It would feel like I was doing it for selfish reasons, and then the children would be stuck with all his crazy ideas.'

'And you don't want to try a Cira? Raise them yourself?'

'No. I'd probably mess them up even more than Pio would.'

'I don't believe that,' Medoro replied. 'But if you don't want a child, don't have one. Pio will survive. Cira will get over it. And despite your rude remarks about Serena, if you ever feel like babysitting you're welcome to join the roster.'

'Thanks.'

'You're just worried that I'll get more letters from the future than you,' Medoro joked. 'All that lavish praise for your theories of cosmology won't cut it; you'll be looking for mindless gossip from the descendants, just like the rest of us.'

They were approaching the food hall now. There was a news screen at the entrance; from a distance the two counts looked perfectly matched, though that impression was unlikely to survive closer scrutiny.

Agata said, 'And if we don't win today—'

Medoro reached over to thump her arm. 'If we don't win, it's not going to kill you. Stop feeling sorry for yourself.'

'Ha.' Agata felt a pang of shame, but not enough to shift her perspective. 'If we win, I'll stop being jealous of your sister's perfect life,' she said. 'How's that for a promise?'

Medoro said, 'I'm waiting to hear the second part.'

'If we lose . . . I don't know.' If she had never imagined any of the miracles the messaging system offered, she would have lived happily enough without them. But it was too late for that now.

'If we lose, you can leave behind a message for Eusebio,' Medoro suggested. 'Tell him how much you enjoyed flying in his rocket. We can carve it in an axial staircase, then no one will mess with it before it's been sanctified by age. That's contact with the ancestors, isn't it?'

Agata said, 'No, that's graffiti. It's only contact if he sends me a reply.'

11

'It was so close!' Rosita said consolingly. 'You should be proud that you made it so close.'

Ramiro forced himself not to snap at her. She'd come to his apartment unbidden, to stand beside him through the final two bells of the vote. No one else in his family had even acknowledged his efforts.

'Close isn't good enough,' he said. He wanted to switch off the console so he didn't have to keep staring at the skewed bar graph that had already burnt itself into his brain – but he knew that as soon as he did he'd feel compelled to switch the machine on again, just in case there'd been an error found, a correction issued. 'This isn't over,' he swore.

Rosita's tone became less sympathetic. 'Someone had to lose. If you don't accept the vote, what does that say? That if the other side had lost, they'd be entitled to ignore it and build the system anyway?'

'Knowing the Council, they probably would have,' Ramiro muttered.

'You got more than five votes in twelve,' she said. 'After the trial run, some people are sure to change their minds. You still might get your way in the end.'

'Once the system's in place, what will a vote mean?' Ramiro asked darkly.

Rosita scowled. 'Listen to yourself! If people don't like it, they'll vote to get rid of it. No one's cutting us out of the loop.'

'It's not that simple,' Ramiro protested. 'Suppose the Council claims that they've received an official message with the result of the referendum – before they've actually identified the real message and examined it. Just announcing a win could be enough to turn that into a self-fulfilling prophecy.'

Rosita hummed dismissively. 'Most of what you said in the debate made sense, but now you're just sounding paranoid. An official report would quote *the exact numbers* on each side, not just a win or a loss. A fake announcement of a win might raise the likelihood of a real win, but publicising a fake set of numbers would have no chance of making those precise numbers come true.'

Ramiro considered this. 'You're right,' he admitted. He was sure that the Council would still find a way to use the system to seal their victory, but he needed to think through the mechanics of it more carefully. 'You really came to the debate?'

'Yes. Why wouldn't I have? Just because you're fighting with Corrado doesn't mean there's a problem between us.' She lowered her gaze. 'He doesn't speak for me on any subject. I always thought we were going to decide those things together, and work out what suited us both. It's not his business trying to force anything.'

Ramiro was grateful for the sentiment, but her timing could not have been worse. 'I can't think about that now.'

'I understand,' Rosita said. 'I just want to make sure that Corrado doesn't stop us talking, whenever you're ready.'

'It will take them half a year to build the system,' Ramiro replied. 'Then the trial will run for a year. Maybe after that, when everything's settled, we'll be able to . . .'

'Make plans for the future?' Rosita suggested. She buzzed softly, as if the idea had already become quaint.

Ramiro said, 'You have to promise me something.'

'What?'

'Promise you won't send back any messages about this.' He would have been happier if she'd sworn to receive no messages from any-one, but she'd already made it clear that she was determined to take part in the trial.

'I know how to keep quiet,' she replied. 'I won't tell you anything you don't want to know.'

Ramiro said, 'That's not enough.'

'It's not up to you!' Rosita retorted angrily. 'You don't get to tell me what I can or can't communicate to myself.'

Ramiro was chastened, but he couldn't let the matter drop. 'Just knowing the outcome would give you something over me. That's the kind of thing I'd expect from Corrado – but if you're serious about respecting my choices, when we talk about this you'll come to it blind.'

Rosita struggled visibly to contain her response. Finally she said, 'Respecting your choices doesn't mean I have to limit my own perspective.'

'*Limit your perspective?*' Ramiro buzzed incredulously. 'You'd think I was asking you to gouge out your rear eyes. When did this toxic gimmick that you hadn't even heard of until a few stints ago become your birthright?'

'The day it was invented,' she replied.

Ramiro said, 'It might have been invented, but it hasn't been built yet. You shouldn't take anything for granted.'

'Nor should you.' Rosita headed for the door.

Ramiro didn't want them parting like this. 'I'm sorry I offended you,' he declared. 'And I'm grateful for what you said before, about Corrado.'

Rosita paused, clinging to the rope. 'We should talk again when we're both feeling calmer.'

'All right.'

Ramiro watched her leave, glad that he'd salvaged something from the encounter. Then he turned back to the console and the unchanged tallies.

Who could be satisfied with a community divided along the lines of that vote, with half the population knowing the future all the way to the reunion, while the rest battled day after day to defend the integrity of their decisions? Rosita had given him a foretaste of the kind of negotiations the two sides would be facing, and that was already bad enough.

What exactly was he free to do now? He'd had his chance to try to sway the vote, and he'd failed; he couldn't unpick the tapestry and try again. But the link between his will and his actions still shaped his own history as strongly as ever. All he could do now was keep on fighting not to be told how the fight would end.

'We should start by withdrawing our labour,' Pio suggested. 'We only lost the vote because people succumbed to a fantasy: that this system would deliver exactly what they wanted, with no disruptions or inconvenience at all. But if they can't imagine the harm the messages themselves will do, they need to be given some more tangible disincentives.'

Ramiro was only half listening as he tinkered with the cameras and checked the network feed. There were barely four dozen people gathered in the cavernous space of the meeting room – all clinging to ropes in the audience section, with the stage left bare – but so far more than a dozen times that number were following the discussion on their consoles, all around the mountain.

'But what is it that we'd be bargaining with?' Emilia asked. 'We don't have a monopoly on any skill.'

'No, but we have the numbers,' Pio replied. 'We can't make any one job in the mountain impossible to do, but if five twelfths of the population stop working we'll be doubling everyone else's load.'

'You won't get every no-voter participating,' Lena pointed out. As she started speaking, the feed switched automatically to the camera covering her, and Ramiro relaxed a little. The acoustics of the room had been confusing the software, but he seemed to have found the right way to filter out the distracting echoes and make it possible to triangulate each speaker's location.

'That's true,' Pio conceded. 'But we could encourage people to join us by focusing the effects of the strike on non-participants. What if we make a public register of everyone who's taking part? Then instead of sitting at home doing nothing, we could still help each other out.'

Lena buzzed with mirth, unimpressed. 'And then the Council takes the names and locks us all up?'

Pio said, 'At most, they could do that to about two gross; after that, they'll run short of prison space – let alone guards. We won't make the list public until it's larger than that.'

'We could set up a register that only members would have access to,' Ramiro suggested.

'And then some spy would join up, just to read it!' Lena countered.

'Hmm.' Ramiro couldn't see a way around that.

'They might not lock us up,' Diego said, 'but if we're going to make life hard for people off the list, they're going to return the favour.'

'Of course,' Pio replied. 'We have to expect to receive far worse than anything we can inflict on the majority. But for most of them, the messaging system is just a novelty that they know they can live without; once the cost becomes high enough, they'll drop their support.'

Placida said, 'And what happens when the Council passes a law that makes your entitlement void if you're not working?'

'Nobody would accept that,' Pio said flatly. 'The right to a share of the crops is in the hands of each family, not the Council. If they tried to change that, everyone would riot.'

'Not everyone,' Placida replied. 'The more we were actually hurting them, the more willing they'd be to go along with the change. If your job really has become twice as hard, why wouldn't you want the Council doing their best to starve the freeloaders into submission?'

Pio thought it over. 'It's not impossible. But if things reach that point we'll have to move beyond the strike. If they deny us food, we'll have to be prepared to take it by force.'

At the end of the meeting, everyone in the room agreed to join the strike. There was no public register of names, but anyone curious enough to access the feed – friend or enemy – had already seen their faces. Ramiro tried to tell himself that he'd been taking a greater risk on the day he broke his promise to Greta. But the truth was, many more people would have defended him for exposing her clandestine plan than would back him up now, after the system had been openly debated and approved.

As Ramiro was packing up the equipment, Pio approached him. 'Thanks for your help tonight.'

'It was nothing.' Ramiro unplugged the photonic cable from the wall socket and began winding it back onto its spool.

'What did the audience come to?'

'We peaked at a dozen and five gross,' Ramiro replied. 'But the whole thing will still be available for anyone who wants to view it later.'

'Can the Council block access to it?' Pio asked.

'Not legally. I suppose they could block access but deny that they'd done it – blame it on a technical glitch.'

'Then we need to think about ways to get around that.'

'We?' Ramiro stopped winding and regarded him quizzically.

Pio buzzed. 'All right: I have no expertise in these things. I meant you, and anyone else in the group who's studied automation.'

'All the automators I know are on the other side,' Ramiro said. 'The messaging system is too beautiful to resist: it's going to be full of problems that can only be solved with smart photonics.'

'But you've resisted the allure?'

Ramiro jammed the spool of cable into his storage box. 'I'm with you up to a point,' he said bluntly. 'But if you start turning this into a war, don't expect any kind of loyalty from me.'

Pio frowned. 'I'm not looking for violence either.'

'Would you describe crashing a gnat into the Station as an act of violence?'

'I had nothing to do with that,' Pio protested.

Ramiro said, 'All right, but I'm still interested. How would you classify it?'

Pio considered the question. 'I suppose it's a borderline case. There was no intention to harm anyone, but they still endangered your life and Tarquinia's. And if they'd managed to blast half the Object into the void, we would all have been at risk.'

'Well, there are plenty of things short of antimatter that could wipe us out,' Ramiro said. 'Enough damage to the cooling system. Enough damage to the farms.'

Pio said, 'I understand that. I'm not about to ask anyone to ransack the farms – all I said was that if the Council went so far as to starve us, we'd have to take our entitlements by force.'

Ramiro pulled the lid closed on the box. 'We need to make our opponents understand how strongly we feel. I agree with you on that. But if we lose sight of where the line is, we could all be dead very quickly.'

'I've spent my life trying to keep the *Peerless* safe,' Pio replied. 'You don't have to treat me as some kind of fanatic.'

'All right.' Ramiro didn't know what more he could say. If he was going to work with Pio at all, he had to give him the benefit of the doubt.

He unhooked the box from the rope and began dragging himself towards the exit, feeling more hopeful now than he had since the day of the debate. From what he'd seen of the resistance so far, they were committed but they weren't reckless. They could take a stand and refuse to be cowed, without burning down the only home they had.

12

'Do you want to take her for a while?' Serena offered, holding out her daughter.

Agata couldn't tear her gaze away from the stitches that criss-crossed Serena's torso, pulling the skin tight over the wound where a quarter of her flesh had assumed a life of its own and torn itself free. But at least her campaign of pre-maternal gorging had paid off: she'd managed to keep all four limbs intact. The cautious approach was to resorb them first – to make as much flesh as possible available for the child – but then it could be days after the birth before new ones could be extruded. The risk if you declined to resorb them was different: Agata had heard of women whose hips were commandeered by the blastula, severing the remainder of the legs.

'Go ahead!' Medoro urged her.

Agata regarded the child warily, but she didn't want to offend anyone. As the first visitor from outside the family to be invited into the recovery room, the least she could do was show an interest. 'She's beautiful,' she admitted. 'It's just a shame we can't grow them from the soil, like wheat.'

'Soon,' Medoro joked.

Agata reached over tentatively and Serena placed the child in her hands. Arianna had managed to sprout four limbs, but she was still having trouble forming fingers: six slender digits protruded from one hand, but the other limbs ended in round stubs. She stared up at Agata, frowning in puzzlement but showing no sign of fear.

'How long until she talks?' Agata wondered. She must have watched Pio as he was growing up, but she'd been living in a child's timeless world herself then.

'Five or six stints,' Medoro replied.

'So you have to talk to her for all that time, without getting a single reply?'

Medoro buzzed. 'It's not like being snubbed! She's already listening to every word we say.'

Agata gazed into the child's face. 'Is that true?' she asked Arianna. 'But when do you start understanding?'

Arianna was struggling with something, but it wasn't the meaning of these mysterious sounds. 'Sorry,' Medoro said, reaching out deftly to grab the cluster of dark faeces drifting down towards Agata's feet. He left the room briefly and returned brushing sand from his palms.

'And when will she learn to feed the worms directly?' Agata asked.

'That comes a little later. Eight stints, maybe.'

'Better you than me.' Agata held the child out to him; Medoro took Arianna and swung her around, eliciting chirps of delight.

Agata turned to Serena. 'You're both braver than I am, that's all I can say.'

Serena was amused. 'Brave? What's a few days' pain, compared to what our grandmothers did?'

'True enough.' Agata was tired of hearing this line from Cira, but it was hard to argue with a woman whose memory of the act was still fresh. 'And you're willing to do it all again?'

Serena replied without hesitation, 'Of course. Arianna needs a brother.'

Agata glanced at Medoro, lost in adoration of the child. After the birth, a technician would have poked a few photonic cables into his chest, then into his niece's, so the machines could fool both bodies into believing that this mere uncle had literally fathered the child. Every instinct for attachment and protection that would have arisen unaided in a natural birth had been invoked by that controlled exchange of light, and it seemed to make no difference to Medoro that he'd missed out on the once-essential prerequisites. In the sagas, bad things befell men who triggered their sisters instead of their cos, though if their brothers had died it was more or less a duty. But now that only the Starvers had cos, who did men think of when the urge arose?

'I wonder what they'll be doing in a couple more generations,' Agata said. 'Promising women?'

'You want to wipe us out?' Medoro joked. 'Men can't shed, women can't be promised. If the words still mean anything, what else can they mean?'

Agata felt a perverse stubbornness rising. 'Why shouldn't a mother be able to love her own child? I can't believe it's biologically impossible; they just have to find the right pathways. Then everyone would have the choice.'

Medoro was growing less amused. 'There won't be an "everyone" if that's how it ends up.'

'Of course women can love their children,' Serena said, trying to conciliate. 'Women have been aunts, sisters, cousins; no one's saying we have no feelings. We must have helped raise children all the time. I can love Arianna the way a woman on the home world loves her niece.'

'That wouldn't be enough for me,' Agata said. 'I don't want to wipe out men, but if I couldn't be the one who loved the child the most, I wouldn't go through with it at all.'

'That's just greedy,' Medoro said. He was keeping his face calm and happy for Arianna, with a voice to match, but Agata could tell that none of this warmth was intended for her.

'You make your choices, I'll make mine,' she said.

'And what if it's impossible?' he taunted her. 'They can pump as much light into your body as they like, but if the man you want them to wake isn't in there, he isn't in there.'

Agata said, 'Wait and see. Maybe you'll get a message from Arianna soon enough, letting us all in on the answer.'

'Spheres are simply connected,' Lila said. 'Don't you think that's the key?'

'Perhaps.' Agata let her rear gaze drift, taking in the crammed bookshelves behind her. Generations of knowledge were packed in there, revelations dating all the way back to Vittorio. She could smell the dye and the old paper – a scent that had always delighted her, promising the thrill of new ideas – but by now she'd absorbed the contents of those shelves so thoroughly that nothing from the past still had the power to astonish her.

'Any loop on a two-dimensional sphere can be deformed into any other,' Lila mused, doodling an example on her chest of an elaborate loop being transformed into a simpler one.

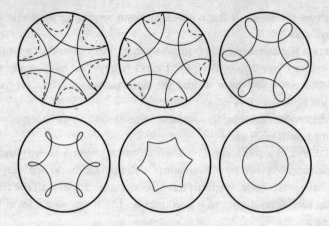

'But on a torus, you can't change the number of times the loop winds around the space in each dimension, so there are an infinite number of different classes.' She sketched examples from four of them – pairs of loops that could be transformed into each other, because they shared that distinguishing set of numbers. No amount of stretching or shrinking could take a loop from one class to another.

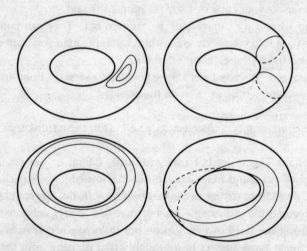

Lila hesitated, as if expecting Agata to pick up the thread, but after half a lapse she lost patience and prompted her: 'So what can we say about a four-sphere?'

Agata struggled to concentrate. 'It's the same as the two-dimensional case: there's only one class of loop.' She could wind an imaginary thread a dozen times around the four-sphere, weave and tangle it any way she liked, but if she tried removing all those complications and shrinking the loop down to a plain circle, nothing she'd done and nothing about the space itself would obstruct her.

'And is that true of the cosmos we live in?' Lila pressed her.

'How would we know?'

Lila said, 'If you can find a good reason why it has to be true, that would be the key to the entropy gradient.'

Agata couldn't argue with the logic of this claim, but she didn't have high hopes for satisfying its premise. 'I don't see how it could ever be forced on us. The solutions to Nereo's equation are just as well behaved on a torus as they are on a sphere.'

'Then perhaps we need to look farther afield. You must have some new ideas on this that you want to pursue.'

Lila gazed at her expectantly. Agata felt her skin tingling with shame, but she had no inspired suggestions with which to fill the silence. 'I've been a bit distracted by my new duties,' she said.

'I see.' Lila's tone was neutral, but the lack of sympathy made her words sound like an accusation.

'I know that's no excuse,' Agata said. 'Everyone has to help keep things running until the strike's over. But when my mind's blocked, what can I do?'

Lila adjusted herself in her harness. 'That depends on the nature of the obstruction.'

'It can't always have been easy for you,' Agata protested. 'You must have got stuck yourself, sometimes.'

'Of course,' Lila agreed. 'But I was never forced to contemplate the imminent arrival of messages from a culture that had solved all my problems so long ago that any bright three-year-old would know the answers. I doubt that would have done much for my motivation.'

Agata said, 'I'm not expecting any help from the future. That would make no sense.'

Lila inclined her head, accepting the last claim. 'You've made a good argument for that. But I'm not sure that you've convinced yourself as thoroughly as you've persuaded me.'

Agata was unsettled. 'What do you mean?'

'Ever since the messaging system was mooted, you've been like this.' Lila waited for her to object, but Agata was silent. 'Maybe it's just excitement at the prospect of the thing itself, or the distraction of all the politics. But be honest: can you really block it out of your mind that you might soon be reading the words of people who've had six more generations of prior research to call on than you've had?'

Agata said, 'What does it matter, if they can't communicate any of it?' Lila claimed to have accepted her argument: complex ideas were far more likely to remain unmentioned in the messages than to arise without clear antecedents.

'What matters is that it seems to have paralysed you.'

Agata struggled to recall some small achievement she could hold up against this claim, but since she and Lila had proved their conjecture on the curvature of four-spheres she'd really done nothing but mundane calculations. 'Everyone gets stuck,' she said. 'I'll snap out of it soon enough.'

Lila said, 'I hope so. Because once you learn whether you do or you don't, it'll be settled for good, won't it?'

Agata had set her console to wake her early. She ate quickly, then made her way to the axis and propelled herself down a long weightless shaft, touching the guide ropes lightly to keep herself centred.

She followed the shaft all the way to the bottom, emerging on a level that housed what remained of the feeds for the old sunstone engines. She dragged herself through chambers full of obsolete clockwork, the mirrorstone gears and springs tarnished and clogged with grit, but still offering up a dull sheen in the moss-light. For a year and a half after the launch, mechanical gyroscopes had tracked the mountain's orientation, and the feeds' machinery had kept the engines balanced by adjusting the flow of liberator trickling down into the sunstone fuel. Agata doubted that anyone at the time had imagined that a piece of photonics the size of her thumb would take the place of all these rooms.

As she moved further away from the axis, the chambers' erstwhile floors became walls. Descending the rope ladder that crossed the third room, she passed precariously dangling assemblies of gears and shafts spilling out of their cabinets, the pieces still loosely bound together against the long assault of centrifugal gravity. The eruptions looked almost organic, as if the neglected cogs were sprouting from exuberantly blossoming vines. There must have been people inspecting and maintaining all of this quaint machinery, up until the day when Carla finally proved that none of it would ever be needed again. Now it would only take a couple more rivets snapping for these strange sculptures to come crashing down.

Agata left the decrepit clockwork behind, and dragged herself down a narrow passage to the shabby office of her supervisor, Celia. The office itself looked as old as the *Peerless*, but Celia's networked console was a slab of bright modernity among the ruins – its roster of volunteers encrypted, for what that was worth when every strike-breaker could be seen coming and going. Celia handed her an access key and tool belt, and Agata signed for the equipment with a photonic patch, not dye.

'This must seem pretty menial to you,' Celia teased her. 'Your predecessor wasn't much into cosmology.'

'I like it,' Agata replied. 'It's meditative.'

'That'll wear off,' Celia promised.

Agata turned into a dusty corridor and followed it for a few stretches. The entrance to her section of the cooling system was easy to find: moss had eaten a great concave chunk out of the wall beside it, and the usual red glow was criss-crossed with threads of yellow. She slid the key into the access panel and strained to pull it open.

A short ladder led down into the tunnel. The breeze pulsing through the darkness chilled Agata's skin, but after the first shock it wasn't unpleasant. The ceiling of the tunnel was too low for her at her normal height, but she only had to resorb half a span from the top of her legs and she fitted comfortably. She started walking, one hand on the wall to guide her. The splotch of red light spilling in from outside shrank in her rear vision, and when it was gone she was in utter blackness.

A saunter or two down-axis, in a set of reaction chambers carved into the lode of sunstone that had once been destined to be burnt as rocket fuel, a decomposing agent was turning that fuel directly into gas – without the usual accompaniment of light and heat. The gas built up a considerable pressure, then as it forced its way out against the resistance of a spring-loaded piston, it grew colder. This was much more efficient than the old system that had used the exhaust from burning fuel as its starting point, but the moss that coated the mountain's walls grew so vigorously beneath the new kind of breeze that it threatened to clog all the cooling tunnels.

As Agata's eyes adjusted to the darkness, she began to see the small red patches of new growth around her. A shift ago, she'd left this whole section as bare rock, but it didn't take long for fresh spores to blow in and find purchase. She took the coherer from her tool belt and aimed it at the nearest colony, closing her eyes against the flash so they wouldn't lose their sensitivity.

Three stints into the strike, she still found the job absurdly satisfying. The work was vital, and she could see the results of her efforts immediately. That the moss returned so quickly didn't bother her at all, so long as she could keep it under control. Better to walk the length of the tunnels regularly, searching for these early infestations, than wait for the walls to become so encrusted that they'd need to be scraped clean with a hardstone blade.

As she advanced along the tunnel, scanning the blackness ahead for another faint speck of moss-light, Agata realised that this was exactly the kind of task during which she once would have ended up pondering the questions Lila had berated her for neglecting. She had only ever made progress on her research when the problem she was tackling rose up unbidden to occupy her mind in idle moments – whether she was walking or eating, cleaning her apartment or lying in bed waiting for sleep, her thoughts would be dragged back to the same place, to chip away at the obstructions until they yielded. At her desk, at her console, she could analyse her own earlier work in detail, or carry out a lengthy new calculation, but entirely new ideas only came to her when she was meant to be doing something else.

Now, though, when her thoughts weren't gravitating to the subject of Lila's criticism or scrutinising their own dynamics, the only thing that occupied them effortlessly was speculation on the kind of news that the messaging system would bring. It wasn't intrusive or disturbing – any more than her obsessive return to the niggling questions of curvature and entropy had been – but the entire space in which her creative work had once taken place had been thoroughly colonised by the interloper.

But the cure wasn't far away: once the system was completed she could hardly remain in the thrall of revelations still to come. And was it so terrible if she found herself distracted for a while by the prospect of learning the future of the *Peerless*? She had less than two dozen stints to wait – and, thanks to the strike, she could still do useful work in the meantime. Even if Lila was right and some part of her was refusing to accept that she could expect no help with her research, once she'd seen the actual contents of her messages any hope of impossible cheat notes would soon dissipate. In most respects her life would return to normal, but her spirits would be bolstered by the news of the mountain's safe return. She would resume her work with new energy and optimism, not because her future self had furnished her with theorems she was yet to prove, but because she'd know that her whole life, and the lives of everyone around her, were part of a great struggle whose end was in sight.

Agata felt the tremor in the rock beneath her and braced herself instinctively, her tympanum growing rigid, rendering her protectively deaf. She lost her footing and fell to the floor, disoriented, unsure if the shaking had been enough to unbalance her or whether she'd been struck down by a shock wave in the air.

She curled up against the cool stone, waiting for worse, waiting for the mountain to split open and spill her out into the void. But the rock was still, and when she forced the membrane around her throat to relax she heard nothing but distant creaking.

As she clambered to her feet the air on her skin smelt acrid. She fumbled for the coherer and flashed it briefly, averting her eyes from the dazzling spot it made on the wall; the secondary reflections lit up the rock around her and showed a fine haze hanging in the air. The breeze from the cooling chambers was as pristine as ever, so the smoke must have entered the system somewhere ahead of her, up-axis, with enough pressure to force it back against the usual flow.

Agata turned and began retracing her steps in the blackness. She had no experience with which to gauge the intensity of the blast. There'd been plenty of accidents in the workshops of which she'd been unaware at the time, but as the cooling tunnels linked every part of the mountain she had to expect to feel the effects far more strongly here. With no basis for comparison, she shouldn't rush to any wild conclusions about collisions with infinite-velocity rocks.

It was only when she reached the entrance to the tunnel and began climbing the ladder up into the moss-light that she realised how badly she was shaking. She steadied herself as she approached the office, afraid of Celia's disdain if it turned out to be a routine part of her job that every tiny bang the chemists set off would echo down the tunnels and knock her off her feet this way. The cooling air fed their ventilation hoods, where they carried out some of their most dangerous experiments. Maybe she should have been expecting this concussive initiation all along.

When Celia noticed Agata approaching, she didn't seem to be in the mood to mock her. As Agata drew closer she saw that a news inset had opened on the console's display screen, but the angle made it impossible to read.

'What happened?' she asked Celia. 'I felt it in the tunnel, but I didn't know exactly . . .'

'There's been an explosion in one of the workshops.'

'The chemists'?'

Celia said, 'The instrument builders'. The one where they were working on the cameras for the messaging system.'

13

'We can keep you locked up for as long as we like,' Maddalena told Ramiro. 'You could spend the rest of your life in that cell – with no visitors, no work, no diversions. Nothing at all to occupy your mind.'

'Is that right?' Ramiro replied. 'Yalda would be proud of you.' He glanced around the interrogation room, wondering if Greta would ever join them again. She'd sat in on the first few sessions and, as coldly as she'd treated him, the presence of even one familiar face had been enough to make him feel less isolated. But then, perhaps that was why she'd stopped coming.

'Seven deaths on your hands, and you compare yourself to Yalda?'

'Actually, it was you I was comparing to Yalda.' Ramiro drew back from the table and allowed a trace of his anger to show. 'I mourn those deaths, and I condemn the perpetrators – but I don't know who they are and I certainly didn't help them.'

'If you don't know who they are, how can you know you didn't help them?'

'I could ask you the same question,' Ramiro retorted. 'Maybe you gave directions to one of the bombers three days before the blast. Maybe you shared your lunch with one of them at school, when someone stole their loaves.'

Maddalena said, 'Is this funny to you?'

'Seven people dead isn't funny at all. But if you want your attempts to do something about it taken seriously, you're going to have to earn that.'

'Do you deny that you were giving technical advice to the anti-messager groups?'

'Not at all,' Ramiro replied. 'I helped them make their meetings public – sparing you from any need to go to the trouble of listening in on them covertly. You can still hear every word we said. No one was discussing bombs.'

'And in the private meetings?' Maddalena asked.

'You tell me. If there were private meetings, I wasn't invited, so that's when the whole spying thing would have helped.'

Maddalena reiterated his defining characteristics in her eyes. 'You violated an undertaking not to disclose the plans for the messaging system. You campaigned against it in the referendum. You used your expertise to help everyone opposed to the system—'

Ramiro said, 'Apparently not everyone.'

'You expect me to believe that with all those key roles in the movement, you knew nothing about the preparations for the bombing?'

'I made it very clear to the people I worked with that I wasn't interested in violence. That might not have been the best way to earn the confidence of any fanatics among them, but strangely enough it seemed like a perfectly ethical approach at the time.'

Maddalena paused, staring past him at the bare wall, possibly consulting some third party through her corset. There were no clocks in the room, and Ramiro had stopped trying to gauge the length of these sessions. All he could do was keep answering the questions one by one, refusing to be cowed and refusing to start fabricating the kind of replies that might satisfy his interrogator.

'You must have been frustrated with the way the strike was going,' Maddalena suggested.

Ramiro said, 'Of course I was frustrated. I wished more people had joined in. I wished it had had a greater impact.'

'So why would you continue with such an ineffectual strategy?'

'No one had any better ideas.'

'Apparently someone did,' Maddalena replied.

Ramiro hummed wearily. 'Where is this getting you? Is your boss listening in and giving you points for literal-mindedness? *No one who spoke to me proposed a better strategy.* If you're going to make me talk for three or four bells at a time, you'll have to forgive me if some of my statements are made on the understanding that you haven't ignored everything else I've said.'

'So who was the most frustrated?' Maddalena pressed him. 'Even if they didn't talk about their plans, you must have picked up on their mood.'

'We were all frustrated. If you want to make a comparative assessment, go and look at the recordings yourself.'

'People knew when they were on camera,' Maddalena pointed out. 'But you were among them when they were less guarded.'

Ramiro couldn't fault her logic there. He slumped back in his harness, wondering if he was punishing himself for nothing. It was possible that he'd spent time with the bombers without knowing it, and it wasn't absurd to think that they'd let something slip – some remark that betrayed the degree of their impatience. He wanted the killers caught and punished. If he could give the authorities a genuine clue to their identities, he'd be proud of that.

Off camera, who had ridiculed the strike most vehemently? Placida? Lena? It was hard to put one above the other, but maybe they'd conceived of the bombing together. No doubt they were both already in custody, but with Ramiro's testimony against them they might buckle and confess.

Maddalena was watching him expectantly. Ramiro felt a cold horror spreading through his gut at the thought of what he'd almost done. The women's moaning about the strike wasn't proof of anything, but he couldn't trust his jailers to accord the observation as little weight as it deserved. Anything he said, however cautiously phrased, could damage two innocent people's lives irreparably.

'Analyse the bomb site,' he said. 'Find out where the chemicals came from. I want these murderers caught as much as anyone, but I'm not a mind-reader.'

Ramiro woke in the blackness of his cell and shifted on his sand bed. With the walls around him sterilised by the harsh lights of the day cycle, at night there was no trace of moss, leaving a perfect darkness that seemed to stretch out in all directions.

If he'd kept his promise to Greta, would those seven instrument builders be alive now? And if the Council had been able to keep the messaging system secret, would its impact on ordinary people's lives have ended up being less intrusive? Maybe there would have been a violent backlash when word of its existence finally leaked out – or maybe the foreknowledge that the system granted would have been enough to prevent that.

But he'd made his choice, and now he had to take some share of responsibility for the way things had unfolded. All his feelings of shame and sadness were just useless self-indulgence, though, if he did nothing more than stare into the past and wish that everything could have been different.

The only question now was: *where did this end?* Ramiro had had no news from outside since his arrest, but he suspected that the strike had been called off, as a gesture of respect to the grieving relatives. That would be the right thing to do, but it wouldn't resolve anything. So long as the messaging system was still being built, almost half the population would remain disaffected – and the change being forced on them wasn't something they could learn to live with. It made no difference how he felt, himself; he could renounce the killers as loudly as he liked, he could give up the fight and embrace his enemies. There would never be peace in the mountain again.

And was that it? The situation was unsalvageable?

He reached out for a rope and raised his torso off the bed, the tarpaulin crinkling around him. There would never be a consensus, but that didn't mean there had to be violence. He was never going to be reconciled with Corrado, but so long as no one locked them in the same room together they weren't going to kill each other.

What if they partitioned the *Peerless* and let the messagers and anti-messagers live apart – dividing the resources of the mountain in proportion to the votes? Those who chose to live without the system need never cross paths with those who used it.

The trouble was, there'd be people on both sides who wouldn't be satisfied with their share of living space. The messagers might find ways to use their foreknowledge to manipulate their neighbours – and even if they didn't, the possibility would be enough to drive the kind of fanatics who'd bombed the camera workshop to keep on trying to destroy the whole system.

Ramiro looked out across the darkness. Maps and treaties would never be enough. Locked doors and solid stone walls couldn't separate the two groups so completely as to end their mutual fear and suspicion.

The only cure was distance.

'You want me to set you free – and then give you *your own gnat*?' Greta was incredulous. When word had reached her that Ramiro had a proposal that he would only put to her in person, she must have envisioned a deal in which he testified against a former comrade or two in exchange for a lighter punishment. 'How could you imagine anyone agreeing to that?'

Ramiro said, 'If you want to get rid of this problem, you need to get rid of the dissenters. But you can't expect people to leave the *Peerless* behind until they know that they can survive somewhere else. I'm willing to travel to the nearest substantial orthogonal body and find out if it can be made habitable.'

A flicker of amusement crossed Greta's face. 'The nearest substantial body is almost certainly the Object. Are you going to try to sell people on the idea that they were inside that rock, unnoticed, living their lives backwards — while the last three generations of their ancestors were coming and going, taking samples from the surface?'

Ramiro hadn't thought of the Object. But as satisfying as it would be to set foot on the very rock that had once threatened to annihilate him, the prospect of burrowing into it didn't sound much like liberation, even without the bizarre twist of having to stay hidden from all the earlier visitors. 'I meant something large enough to hold on to an atmosphere, so people could live on the surface. Something on the outskirts of the orthogonal cluster. I don't have access to the astronomers' catalogues, but there must be something planet-sized within reach.'

'Within reach?' Greta was doubtful; she paused to make use of her corset. 'The nearest orthogonal planet would entail a round trip of a dozen years.'

Ramiro had hoped for something closer, but he persisted. 'A dozen for the passengers,' he stressed. 'But still only four years for you. We could make it even less if it really mattered; I'm sure I could put up with the higher acceleration. But we'll need to talk to the experts as to whether the cooling system would allow that.'

Greta said, ' "We"? You might be getting a bit ahead of yourself.'

Ramiro looked down at the hardstone fetter piercing the side of his abdomen. In the room's low gravity, he hardly noticed it – unless he moved without thinking and the chain that joined it to the wall became taut. 'How else should I talk, when I know that I have no chance of doing this without you? I think we'd still make a good team.'

'Oh, I'm getting all nostalgic now,' Greta replied sardonically. 'Let's reminisce about the time you lied to my face and betrayed me.'

'You never used to take things personally,' Ramiro complained. 'All the time we worked together on the turnaround, did I ever make a fuss when you took all the credit with the Council? We both treated each other pretty shabbily, but we still managed to solve every problem that was thrown at us.'

Greta was unmoved. 'Try to be objective. You're asking me to give a gnat to an automator whose greatest claim to fame will remind anyone who might have forgotten that *automating* a gnat is just what you need to turn it into a weapon.'

'That's a very negative way of looking at it.' Ramiro thought for a moment. 'The biggest problem with the rogue gnat was that it took us by surprise. We can arrange things so that this craft has no way of doing that. And you can always send an observer from the messagers' side to keep me honest – if you can find any volunteers for the job.'

Greta said, 'Right now I'm having trouble even thinking of a pilot.'

Ramiro didn't reply. For all the help Tarquinia had given him with the debate, after the vote she'd refused to get involved with the dissenters. A dozen years away from the mountain would be too painful a sacrifice to ask from anyone with a clear conscience.

'You'd also need an agronomist,' Greta added. 'I doubt that even the diehard migrationists would take your word about the prospects for growing a crop.'

'That's fine with me.' That she'd bothered to make the suggestion at all was a sign that this might not be hopeless – that he might have snagged her mind on the rough edges of his plan.

'Do you really have no idea who the bombers are?' Greta asked.

'None at all.'

'I believe you,' she said, 'but I don't know how to prove it to the Council.'

'Whatever happened to the need to prove people guilty? Half the *Peerless* voted the same way as I did, but I doubt you've even locked up all the strikers.'

Greta pretended that she hadn't heard his last remark; he wasn't allowed to know who else had or hadn't been imprisoned.

'If I put this to the Council,' she said, 'they'll only agree to it if it comes from them. *They* have to be the peacemakers, reaching out to their enemies for the sake of the greater good.'

'Well, naturally.'

'And they might not even want you on the mission,' she warned

112

him. 'What if they go with the idea, but then pick a crew without you?'

Ramiro buzzed. 'At worst, I might have to stay in prison for the whole four years that they're away. Compared with spending twelve in something not much bigger than my cell, I don't think the disappointment would crush me.'

Greta was puzzled. 'And yet you're willing to do it, if you're asked.'

Ramiro said, 'Who else could make this work politically? If you send Pio, half the mountain will riot. You trashed his reputation as soon as you locked him up over the rogue.'

'And we haven't trashed yours?'

'Not yet, I hope.'

Greta drew herself out of her harness. 'I'll give this some thought. In the end, all I can do is take it to the Council.' She dragged herself towards the door and tapped for the guard.

'And put it to them the right way,' Ramiro pleaded.

Greta turned to face him. 'And what's the right way?'

Ramiro said, 'Forget it. It's not for me to tell you how to do your job.'

When she'd gone, he closed his eyes and pictured the scene in the Council chamber. *What would you say*, Greta the fixer would begin, *if we could find a way to inspire every troublemaker in the mountain to march, willingly, into the void, out of our lives for ever?*

14

Agata reached over and took Arianna from Gineto. The child ran her hands over Agata's face, then frowned, disappointed. A moment later she started humming in distress. Agata handed her back to her great-uncle.

Serena said, 'Don't worry, she's moody with everyone. I'm sure she'll get used to you.'

'I'm happy to look after her,' Agata declared. 'Any time you want me to.'

'That's very kind,' Gineto said, in about the same tone as Agata might have used if he'd offered to help her prove a theorem in topology.

Gineto had moved into Medoro's old apartment, so at least Arianna would still have the same surroundings. Agata didn't know what she could contribute beyond the occasional period of baby-sitting, but she needed to do something to assuage the ache she felt from Medoro's absence. If she couldn't even help with his niece, what was left to her?

Medoro's books still lined the walls of the living room: mostly specialist works on the theory of solids. He'd always teased Agata about her esoteric research, but improving the design of photonic arrays had required far more physics than she'd ever mastered. She would have needed to study for years to have any chance of taking his place in the camera team.

'What do you think of this new mission they're proposing?' Serena asked her. 'The *Surveyor*?'

'I don't know.' When she'd first heard the news, Agata had been disgusted; it had sounded like a gesture meant to appease Medoro's killers. Since then she'd grown less adamant, but she'd still been too angry to try to think through all the ramifications.

Gineto said, 'If someone's fighting to impose their will over the mountain, they're not going to give that up and walk away.'

'Not even for a planet all their own?' Serena replied.

'You think they want freedom? They just want power.' Gineto was talking in his hyper-happy baby voice, beaming down at Arianna, pulling faces to make her chirp. 'The *Peerless* is all they know. If they'd wanted to take their chances on their own, they could have asked for that any time since the turnaround.'

'Then what's the solution?' Serena demanded. 'If it were up to me I'd abandon the messaging system, but the Council's already talking about the bombing as proof of how much we need the warnings.' Her voice faltered; Agata reached over and squeezed her shoulder.

'The *Surveyor*'s not a bad idea,' Agata conceded. 'If they can grow crops on an orthogonal world, it would be one of the safest places to start a colony. There'd be a limit to the kind of collisions with home-cluster matter it could suffer in the migrants' future – since anything really catastrophic in the world's own past would have destroyed it, or lit it up like Gemma. On a cosmic timescale the entropy gradient would be a problem, but compared with the *Peerless* or the home world, a planet guaranteed to stay intact for eons would be a haven.'

'Then it's worth trying, isn't it?' Serena said.

Gineto wasn't swayed. 'You think people who don't want to know the future will migrate to a world where they can step out of their houses and see what a dozen generations of their descendants will have carved into the rocks?'

Serena said wearily, 'I just want a plan that both sides can live with. If not this, let them split the mountain in two.'

Gineto drew Arianna against his chest to hide his face from her as his expression grew grimmer. 'The war to decide the size of the pieces would kill us all. If that's the alternative, the *Surveyor* can fly with my blessing.'

'I'm very sorry about your friend,' Lila said gently.

'Thank you.' Agata shifted in her harness. 'His uncle's looking after the baby, but it's hard for the whole family.'

'Of course.' Lila offered a moment of sympathetic silence, then delicately broached a different subject. 'Have you had a chance to think about the gradient problem, since our last meeting?'

'Not really,' Agata confessed. She pictured Medoro standing in the corner of the office, the expression on his face enough to convey exactly what he thought of her laziness. It had been three stints since the bombing; she really had no excuse not to get back to work.

Lila said, 'I've had one idea myself, if you're interested.'

'Of course.' Agata leant forward attentively and tried to concentrate.

'It's possible that what we're lacking is a proper understanding of vacuum energy,' Lila suggested. 'You know the naïve version: if you look at the free light field, and assume the right kind of relationship between the mass of a photon and the dimensions of the cosmos, each mode of the field that wraps around the cosmos a whole number of times is like a simple oscillator. Wave mechanics tells us that an oscillator like that can't have an energy of zero: the lowest energy level has some non-zero value. So even if the cosmos were empty, the vacuum would have as much energy as you'd get by adding up the lowest levels of all the possible modes of the light field.'

'Plus the same kind of contributions from all the modes of the luxagen field,' Agata added.

'Yes. Which are actually negative, if you take the mathematics seriously.' Lila buzzed softly. 'When I was developing the gravitational theory, I was never sure if I should claim that this kind of energy would need to be included as a source of curvature – and then go on to insist that the very mild curvature that empty space seems to possess is proof that the two kinds of vacuum energy more or less cancel each other out.'

'Hmm.' Agata wasn't sure whether Lila was mocking this idea or trying to resurrect it, so it seemed wiser not to offer an opinion of her own.

'The thing is, though,' Lila continued, 'the naïve version is just that. We don't know if the cosmos really has the right dimensions to allow *any* free modes of either field, and we don't know how to calculate the vacuum energy under more realistic assumptions: taking account of the interaction between luxagens and photons, and taking account of the curvature of four-space.'

Agata said, 'But if the vacuum energy is a source of curvature, and the curvature itself can influence the vacuum energy . . .'

'Then it's much less clear what combinations of the two are actually possible,' Lila replied. 'That's what I'm hoping would shed some light on the gradient problem.'

'Ah.' Agata finally caught a glimmer of that illumination. 'If we take account of the way the geometry of the cosmos determines what kind of waves can exist – which governs the vacuum energy, which contributes to the curvature – we might end up showing that a uniform cosmos would be self-contradictory.'

'It's conceivable,' Lila said cautiously. 'Of course, that wouldn't help much if a tiny wrinkle in the curvature was enough to make things work out. What we'd need is for there to be no solutions without a significant entropy gradient.'

Agata understood the proposal now – and it was terrifying. To make any progress they would need to combine field theory, wave mechanics and cosmology in a manner that no one had ever achieved before.

'Can I think about this?' She didn't want to agree to the project only to find that she couldn't summon up the kind of focus and stamina that an undertaking of this scale required.

Lila said, 'Of course.'

Agata hadn't set out with any intention of going near the demolished workshop, but when her path took her to the boarded-up entrance she wasn't surprised.

The floor of the tunnel outside was still covered in a layer of fine dust; she knew it was bluish by artificial light, but in the red glow of the moss it looked almost black. The last time she'd stood here the entrance had only been covered by a curtain, and she'd peered in through a gap. A string of coherers hung across the ceiling had illuminated a team of investigators at work in the rubble. They'd been photographing everything as they sifted patiently through the debris, hoping they might find fragments of the bomb.

As far as she knew, they never had. The Council had locked up all the anti-messagers who'd argued their case most vigorously in public, but as likely as not Medoro's killers were still free. When the new team of instrument builders was assembled they'd have bodyguards around the clock, and no one would get within a stroll of the workshop without being searched. But if the bombers' first choice of target became impossible to reach, they would find another one. Even if all of the system's components could be built without another incident, when the whole thing was finally assembled it would be vulnerable to other kinds of sabotage.

The *Surveyor* mission wasn't an act of appeasement; everyone would be better off with the two factions living apart. Agata didn't know how many people would be prepared to abandon the familiar surroundings of the *Peerless*, but it was brave of Ramiro to be willing to make the journey to discover if migration was possible at all.

She leant against the wall, humming and shivering. Sometimes she missed Medoro so badly that she wanted to die, but everyone expected her life to go on as if nothing had happened. And now Lila was inviting her to spend the next few years struggling with some beautiful ideas that for all she knew might have no bearing on reality at all.

Agata stilled herself and stared down into the black dust at her feet. She felt as if she'd been waiting all her life for just one message from the future, telling her that everything would be worth it in the end – but the hungrier she grew for that scrap of comfort the further it receded, and the greater the cost. She would have given up all hope of it to get Medoro back, but no one was offering her that choice.

She couldn't spend another day sitting in her office juggling equations, with no idea if they were true or false. And she couldn't bear to be around Medoro's family if she had nothing useful to contribute to their lives. Everything on the *Peerless* was ash to her, now. She needed to find another reason to live, or she was finished.

The *Surveyor* team were still looking for volunteers. At the cost of spending twelve years cooped up in a glorified gnat, the crew would be the first travellers in six generations to set foot on anything like a planet. If they could bring peace to the mountain, all the better, but just making that trip would be extraordinary.

Agata turned away from the entrance and began retracing her steps. She'd very nearly talked herself into it – but if all she had to offer the rest of the crew was her desperation, they'd be better off leaving her behind to go insane on her own time. She could go through the motions with the vacuum energy calculations, then if the messaging system survived the saboteurs she might at least get a verdict from the future as to whether or not Lila's theory of gravity applied in the real world. There'd be nothing inconsistent with the laws of physics in being told that she'd wasted her life.

She stopped dead, her skin tingling, ashamed of her self-pity but grateful for one detail of her maudlin fantasy. A verdict on Lila's theory, *how?* She'd always imagined that such a thing would never come until after the reunion itself, once there'd been a chance for a future generation of astronomers to make observations from the home world. But the home world was no longer the only planet worth imagining.

15

Ramiro scratched the skin around his fetter; it had been itching horribly for the last three days. Despite his pleas, Greta had insisted that he remain in chains even when they were interviewing candidates. He was beginning to wonder if he'd be kept in restraints even once he was on the *Surveyor* itself.

'The planet Esilio is orbiting a massive star,' Agata enthused. 'But we'll be blind to the light of that star; it will appear to us as nothing but a pale grey disc. That combination offers the perfect conditions for the observations I want to carry out.'

Ramiro had no idea what she was talking about, but they hadn't seen anyone else with pro-messager credentials half as eager to make the journey. 'Go on,' he said.

'If gravity is really just the curvature of four-space,' Agata continued, 'then light that passes close to this star will be bent *less* than it would be under Vittorio's theory. I know that sounds strange, but in Lila's theory the curved space around the star makes centrifugal force stronger than it would be in flat space, so it's harder to bend the light's trajectory. With no glare to hamper the observations, we could measure the apparent positions of home-cluster star trails as they approach the edge of this star's disc, and see which predictions turn out to be correct.'

She summoned an illustration of the phenomenon onto her chest.

'I've exaggerated the scale of the effect here,' Agata admitted, 'but it would certainly be measurable with a small telescope.'

Ramiro thought this sounded harmless enough. The last applicant who'd claimed to be drawn to the mission by the chance to carry out a scientific project had wanted to experiment with exotic methods of pulverising Esilio's surface from orbit, in order to impose their own

Light paths (violet, blue, red) if Lila's theory holds.

Light paths if Vittorio's theory holds.

entropic arrow as firmly as possible. Listening to the woman's wish-list of weapons that she hoped to load onto the *Surveyor* had been entertaining, but a theodolite or two would probably be easier to sell to the Council than a flying armoury.

Greta, though, was as suspicious as ever. 'You'd be willing to give up twelve years of your life, just to observe this minor optical effect?'

'I would,' Agata replied. 'The precise angle by which a beam of light is deflected by a star might not sound important, but until we know for sure whether matter and energy really do curve four-space, the answers that we're struggling to find to much bigger questions – the geometry of the cosmos, the reasons for the entropy gradient – will just be guesswork.' She paused, then added, 'I also think the mission's worthwhile for its own sake. If there are people who can't live with the majority's decisions on the *Peerless* any more, we should let them leave.'

'I understand that you were close to one of the instrument builders?' Greta pressed her. 'To Medoro?'

'Yes.'

'So wouldn't you rather see his killers punished?'

'Did I miss the news where they were caught and tried?' Agata replied sarcastically. 'If it's a choice between letting them migrate to Esilio and having them around to do the same thing again, I'd rather get rid of them.'

'So you see this as protecting other travellers?'

'Other travellers,' Agata agreed, 'and the messaging system itself. I debated Ramiro in the campaign – and I still believe every word I said about the benefits of the system.'

'How old are you?' Greta asked.

'A dozen and ten.'

'You won't have many years left when you return, and you'll have aged more than all of your friends. Do you really want to spend the best years of your life inside a vehicle the size of your apartment – in the company of the man who lost that debate, but then turned around and tried to extort us into giving him his way regardless?'

Ramiro had developed a thick skin when it came to Greta's characterisations; much as she enjoyed it, her main goal seemed to be to spur his would-be travelling companions into venting their hostility now, instead of waiting until they had the opportunity to carve him up and toss the pieces into the void.

Agata gestured towards Ramiro's chains. 'I can see that you don't trust him – and nor do I, completely. But he was an honest opponent in the debate, and I don't blame him for my friend's death. This mission needs people from both factions or it isn't going to fly at all.'

'That's a nice sentiment,' Greta replied condescendingly. 'But are you sure you're ready for the cost of putting your own flesh behind it?'

In response, Agata only grew more stubborn. She said, 'The first travellers left their friends and family behind for ever. Between the chance to learn how gravity works and the chance to make the *Peerless* safer, I'm willing to put up with a few years of hardship.'

'It's coming together nicely,' Verano said, leading Ramiro and Greta across the echoing space of the workshop. Verano had the gaunt frame of a Starver, but he displayed no lack of energy or enthusiasm. Ahead, slowly descending from the ceiling's horizon, the fat disc of the *Surveyor* sat balanced on its rim within a cage of scaffolding, the polished hardstone glinting in the light of three banks of coherers angled up at it from the floor.

As they approached, it became clear that the gradual revelation would fall short of exposing the whole disc. Verano's team had had to cut a rectangular hole in the ceiling to make more room, leaving the top third of the craft poking up into that slot.

Ramiro tried to hang back, suddenly reluctant to get too close. Greta wound his chain lengthwise around her forearm a few times to take up the slack and pulled him forward. 'Come and see your new prison,' she whispered. 'This is what you asked for, isn't it?'

The *Surveyor* looked a great deal larger than his cell, but most of the interior was destined to be taken up by essential stores or machinery. The main engines were already in place – six beautiful dark panels packed with ultraviolet rebounders, symmetrically arranged around one face of the disc – but the team had yet to install the cooling system, which for a trip of this duration meant a complete sunstone gasification plant, not a few tanks of compressed air.

'Do we still get to call this a gnat?' Ramiro asked.

Verano buzzed. 'Probably not. But this is where my grandfather built the original – the one that made the first trip to the Object.'

'You're Marzio's grandson?'

'Yes.'

Ramiro felt a slight diminution of his anxiety. Marzio's skills were legendary, and though talent of that kind was unlikely to be heritable, much of its legacy could still be passed down the generations through teaching and experience.

'We adapted this from a design that a group of engineers developed a few years before the turnaround,' Verano explained. 'It was meant as a proof of concept for a shuttle running between the *Peerless* and the home world, but they still planned it down to the last detail.'

'That's what I call getting in early. What did they call the design?'

'The *Uniter*, I'm afraid,' Verano replied. 'If we do start mass-producing these things, I suppose we'll have to think of a more apt generic name.'

'*Deserters*?' Greta suggested.

Half a dozen artisans clung to the scaffolding, working with everything from chisels to coherers. Ramiro moved closer; Greta followed, letting out his chain. Verano invited him to climb a ladder leading up into the atrium so he could look down into the hull. When he reached the top he could see the living quarters through a gap in the rim: four absurdly small rectangles, delimited by a series of slots in the presently vertical floor that the masons would use to insert the walls. Off to the side was a pantry, larger than all four rooms combined. They wouldn't have the space to grow crops of their own. If one live skewer-worm got into their grain store, they'd end up starving to death.

'Twelve years in this?' Ramiro hummed softly. 'What was I thinking?' He began descending.

'It's too late to back out now,' Greta replied. 'Change your mind, and it will be twelve years with no change of scenery.'

Ramiro doubted that. There was an election approaching, and the Councillors had to be coming under pressure over the internments. The investigation into the bombing might yet drag on for years – and in some people's minds every anti-messager would have to share the guilt, regardless – but there were too many voters who had friends or relatives locked up for no good reason for the Council to remain oblivious to their anger.

He paused halfway down the ladder. 'I've always admired Eusebio. He was smart enough to sell the *Peerless* to his friends as the home world's salvation, and then stay behind while they did all the real work. Stay behind and stay young: that should be my motto, too.'

Greta was not amused. 'So who are these people that could spare you the trip? Agata's the sanest of the pro-messagers so far – and we'd better hope Azelio's family don't talk him out of it, because we're never going to find another agronomist. The two of them might just hold together as a crew, but they're not going to do this on their own. If you pull out, the whole thing will be over.'

'Ramiro?'

Ramiro turned to see a woman approaching in the distance. She was limping slightly, and tall enough that from his own elevated position her face was hidden by the curve of the workshop's ceiling. Her lower torso showed all the signs of a recent shedding, the shrunken flesh leaving her hips painfully unbalanced.

He was still struggling to recognise her voice, distorted by the strange acoustics, when her head finally cleared the horizon. 'Tarquinia?' Ramiro climbed down to the floor, holding his chain with one hand to relieve the pressure. Then he began walking towards his friend, leaving Greta to decide for herself if she wanted to accompany him. She dropped the chain and let him go.

As he drew closer, the extent of Tarquinia's depletion became clearer. Ramiro doubted that even a woman who'd been through the whole ordeal herself could look upon skin stretched and sutured over such a deep absence without flinching.

'You didn't tell me,' he complained. 'When did this happen?'

'Two days ago.'

'How's your daughter?'

'My son is fine,' Tarquinia corrected him. 'His name is Arturo.'

'You had a son first?'

'No. His sister was born three stints ago.'

Ramiro was shocked; he'd never heard of anyone choosing such a punishing schedule. He didn't want to question the wisdom of her timing, but it couldn't go completely unremarked. 'How's your brother coping?'

Tarquinia was amused. 'Men used to raise four infants at once. With his uncle to help, two is nothing.'

'That's easy for a woman to say.'

'*Easy?*' She looked down at her stitches.

'I didn't say you had an easy time inflicting it on them. So what are you doing here? You ought to be resting.'

'Someone told me you were down here,' Tarquinia explained, 'so I thought I'd try to catch you. I asked at the prison but they wouldn't let me visit there. And I wanted to take a look at the *Surveyor* anyway, before I make it official.' She staggered slightly; Ramiro stepped forward so she could rest a hand on his shoulder. 'That walk from the entrance was the hardest part,' she said. 'I forgot how high the gravity is down here.'

'I'm surprised your legs haven't snapped off.' Ramiro glanced back towards the *Surveyor*. 'Make what official?'

'My application for the pilot's position.'

Ramiro wasn't sure how to take that. 'Are you serious?'

Tarquinia gestured at her skeletal hips. 'I didn't clear myself of familial obligations for the sake of a joke.'

'*Familial obligations?*' Ramiro had never heard her talk so bluntly before.

'What – you think I'm being cold?' Tarquinia didn't sound offended, just curious as to how he viewed her actions.

'It's your brother who'll be raising them,' Ramiro conceded. 'Still, four years is a long time at that age.'

'Did the ancestors miss their mothers?' Tarquinia asked. 'Or mothers their children?'

'Why wouldn't they? The only people more perfect than the dead are the yet-to-be-born. But my mother had nothing to do with me or my sister, and that didn't bother us.'

'Mine was the same.' Tarquinia straightened her body. 'So are you going to show me this thing?'

Ramiro led her over to the hull and introduced her to Verano.

Greta caught his eye; she looked smug for some reason. But it was Ramiro who'd gained an ally, not her.

'How are we meant to navigate?' Tarquinia asked Verano. 'We're not going to have time to set up a grid of beacons far enough apart to be useful, and there's only so much positional information we'll be able to extract from home-cluster star trails.'

Verano glanced at Greta. Greta said, 'Once you've made an application and agreed to the confidentiality conditions, we can discuss whatever details you like.'

Tarquinia was taken aback for a moment, but she accepted the reply without complaint.

Verano took Tarquinia closer to the hull and the two of them began chatting with some of the masons. Greta turned to Ramiro. 'Still thinking of doing a Eusebio?' she asked. 'Letting your comrade fly alone?'

'I wasn't serious,' he protested.

'Of course not.' Greta reached down and picked up the end of his chain.

Ramiro groped for an insult, but his mental scrabbling yielded an entirely different weapon. 'You've got a working version of the camera,' he realised. 'What is it – some prototype that survived the bombing?' How else would they navigate to the edge of the orthogonal cluster, if not by imaging the time-reversed stars?

Greta said, 'You don't get to ask questions like that.'

Ramiro was sure now that he'd guessed correctly. Tarquinia had probably worked it out too. It wasn't something he'd want the whole mountain to know – lest the same deranged killers behind the bombing decided to target the *Surveyor* itself – but it was always pleasing to be a little less in the dark than his jailers wished.

'You'd better think up a good cover story,' he suggested. 'A new generation of accelerometers, maybe? I've been a bit distracted, but other people won't be so slow.'

Tarquinia was buzzing with mirth; Verano had just explained the way the *Surveyor*'s toilets would work. Ramiro was unspeakably happy at the thought of having her along on the journey – and if he was trapped now, so be it. He'd wanted to stay strong enough not to back out, and if Tarquinia's presence would shame him into honouring his commitment that was nothing to lament.

Greta said, 'All I've ever done is work to keep the *Peerless* safe. I think you can trust me to do the same for the *Surveyor*.'

'Perhaps.' Ramiro couldn't stop himself goading her when he had the chance, but she'd already proved her resolve to make the mission successful. 'And I think you can trust me not to flee custody and disappear into some anti-messager safe house.'

'Perhaps.' Greta took a key from a pocket in her thigh, then reached over and unlocked the fetter. Ramiro slid the chain free, then eased the bar out of his flesh and let the whole thing clatter to the floor.

He watched Tarquinia haltingly ascend the ladder so she could look down into the *Surveyor* for herself. Six years to Esilio, six years to come back, then six more if he joined the migration. He'd be at least three dozen and four years old by the time he was walking free across the plains of his new home – and he'd need to outlive the average male in his line by five years to get that far.

He'd managed to constrain his entire future as rigidly as any message encoded in time-reversed light could have done. But if he looked at the alternatives honestly, they were all worse.

16

'And now you're dead.'

Agata could no longer see Tarquinia in the whirl of stars and shadow around her, but this flat pronouncement came through the helmet's link as if the woman were right beside her.

'I'm sorry.'

'How did it happen?' Tarquinia demanded. For a bell and a half she'd been oppressively close, observing every tiny mistake Agata made and dispensing acerbic reprimands, but even the distance this mishap had put between them wasn't going to silence her.

'I don't know! The tank just slipped out of my hands.'

'Just slipped? Why do you think you're spinning like that?'

'I must have opened the valve too soon,' Agata confessed.

'Well . . . *don't*,' Tarquinia replied irritably.

'I'm sorry,' Agata repeated.

The point of the exercise had been to try to use her cooling bag's air tank as an improvised jet. She'd understood perfectly what the prerequisites for a successful burst would be: a tight grip on the tank and a thrust aimed straight at her centre of mass. But she'd held the tank wrongly, or slipped, or panicked.

She wasn't actually going to die of hyperthermia; she had two small emergency canisters strapped to her belt. She managed to detach one and connect it to the bag's inlet without mishap. The cool rush of air felt unearned, but then, if the *Surveyor* broke apart halfway through the mission, casting them all out into the void, she doubted that a few dextrous manoeuvres with her air tank would be enough to save her.

Agata saw a figure approaching out of the mountain's shadow, a little closer each time it spun into view. It was easy for Tarquinia: she had one of the new jetpacks strapped to her body. The six nozzles were all controlled by photonics, their thrust automatically balanced so they imposed no torque at all. Bulky as the things were, Agata decided that she was going to wear her own pack for the entire twelve years of the mission, rendering these dispiriting training exercises redundant.

Tarquinia collided with her roughly, grabbing hold of Agata's arm. Agata's gut twitched; she was tumbling in a completely different plane now, and the sudden shift in the flow of stars across her vision was more wrenching than the impact. Tarquinia seized Agata's other shoulder and embraced her, pulling the two of them into equal intimacy with the slab of equipment that covered Tarquinia's chest. Then she must have told the jetpack to kill their rotation: the torque itself was imperceptible, but it looked as if someone had slammed a giant brake against the spinning black bowl that held the stars.

When the sky had ceased turning, Tarquinia released her grip and hooked Agata's belt to the front part of the jetpack.

'Are you all right?' she asked, less brusque than usual.

'Yes.' Agata realised that she'd been shivering.

'I know it isn't easy, but you have to reach the point where things like this are just instinctive.'

'I understand.' Agata gazed past her into the dark hemisphere that had once held the orthogonal stars. They were still out there, in the blackness, but her own eyes were now emitting the light she no longer received from them. 'I don't think I can do this,' she said. 'I think I made a mistake.'

Tarquinia interposed her helmet into the view. 'You want those light-deflection measurements, don't you? I thought the fate of the cosmos hung on those fractions of an arc-flicker.'

'You're the astronomer. You could do a better job at that than I could.'

Tarquinia said, 'I'm not taking any measurements that aren't essential for navigational purposes.'

Agata doubted she was serious about that. 'If my real job is to stop Ramiro going crazy and ramming the *Peerless*, why don't they choose a pro-messager pilot to keep him in check?'

'I don't think they've been overwhelmed with applications,' Tarquinia replied. 'Anyway, that's just politics; for practical deterrence, you can bet there'll be some tamper-proof way to incinerate the *Surveyor* with the flick of a switch from the Council chambers.' She squinted at Agata through their faceplates. 'I'm not going to force you to do anything. If you want to go back to the airlock right now, that's fine with me.'

Agata was tempted, but she stopped herself. If she pulled out of the training now there'd be no chance to reconsider. 'Why did you volunteer?' she asked Tarquinia. 'Do you think there'd be a war, without the *Surveyor*?'

Tarquinia didn't reply immediately. 'I'm still hoping that we're not that suicidal, but if we are I wouldn't pin my hopes on Esilio.'

'Then why?'

'Why fly to another world?' Tarquinia frowned, as if the question were absurd: the mere grandeur of the idea was reason enough.

Agata wasn't buying it. 'If it could be easy and safe, then you're right: who wouldn't want to be on that mission? But it won't be.'

Tarquinia said, 'You want to know what swings it for me? I always thought I was doing something worthwhile just by helping to keep the mountain running smoothly. Given what was at stake for the home world, that was enough. But if the messaging system starts spitting out reports of the reunion, the entire reason for the journey will start to feel like something long past: still worthy, but faded, there to be taken for granted. If I can have a little excitement with a detour of my own – doing no one any harm, and maybe even helping slightly – I'd have to be insane to pass up the chance.'

'A little excitement?' Agata would have thought Tarquinia's encounter with the rogue gnat had given her enough for a lifetime. 'We'll be unreachable. If anything goes wrong, there'll be no one to help us.'

'Hence . . .' Tarquinia spread her arms.

'You think these exercises are going to protect us?'

'They'll nudge the odds in our favour,' Tarquinia insisted. 'If you ever start taking them seriously. But if you want certainty, feel free to tell Greta that you refuse to fly until they've built the messaging system and confirmed the *Surveyor*'s return.'

'Would that be so terrible?' Agata retorted. 'Or would the whole thing become worthless to you, if you knew you'd be safe?'

'Not at all,' Tarquinia said mildly. 'But I don't think the politics would work out. If we postponed the launch until your side achieved everything it wanted, then whatever chance the *Surveyor* had of defusing tensions would vanish.'

'That's true.' Agata glanced back towards the mountain. 'We're getting awfully far from the *Peerless*.'

Tarquinia declined the opportunity to remind her exactly how many orders of magnitude larger her comfort zone needed to be. 'So do you want to correct our drift and take us back to the slopes?'

'How?'

Tarquinia detached the tank from her own cooling bag. 'Incrementally. Small bursts, then wait and observe the effects.'

Agata accepted the tank with her left hand, then brought her arms together behind her back so she could grip it with her right hand as well.

'You'll need to hang on to me,' she told Tarquinia.

'Right.' Tarquinia complied. 'The belt hook alone leaves too much freedom, it'd be asking for trouble.'

Agata said, 'If we were doing this for real, I'd leave the whole thing up to you.'

'Pretend I've lost consciousness.'

'In that case I'd cut you loose.'

'And fly the *Surveyor* back on your own? Good luck with that.'

Agata closed her front eyes so she could concentrate on the task. She took her time estimating the position of their combined centre of mass, then she aligned the axis of the tank to pass through it while pointing more or less in opposition to the direction in which she believed they were drifting.

She opened the valve, counted one pause, then shut off the air.

The thrust was slightly off-centre, imparting a small amount of spin, but at least she hadn't lost her grip on the tank. Agata waited until she'd come full circle, then she released a second burst along a shifted axis that largely compensated for the first unwanted torque.

Tarquinia said, 'See, you're a natural.'

Agata took a moment to process the remark for traces of sarcasm. She said, 'There's only one downside if I get us back safely.'

'What's that?'

'I don't want anyone believing that they could put their life in my hands.'

'Because . . . ?'

'I think we'll all be much safer,' Agata explained, 'if everyone around me is so terrified of the prospect of relying on me in an emergency that they work twice as hard to ensure that it never comes to that.'

Tarquinia said, 'Don't worry: there's nothing you can do to rob me of my healthy respect for the possibility that your incompetence will kill me.'

The guards all knew Agata by sight, but she still had to sign a patch to enter the workshop. When she reached the *Surveyor*, Verano and half a dozen of his team were conducting inspections – shining serious-looking instruments on the polished grey stone around the edges of the rebounder panels – but he motioned to her to go inside anyway.

The airlock's safety mechanisms had been disengaged to allow people to crawl through the entry hatch unimpeded. Agata emerged in the front of the upturned cabin and slid down the tarpaulin that had been spread protectively across the long, curved clearstone window that presently faced the workshop's floor.

As she rose to her feet she heard a rustle of paper from one of the rooms above her. 'Hello?' she called up.

'It's only us!' Azelio replied. The first two faces that appeared staring down at her belonged to Azelio's niece and nephew, Luisa and Lorenzo. 'Come and join us,' Azelio suggested, squatting down to shoo the children away from the opening.

Agata climbed the rope ladder up to the doorway and clambered into the cabin. After going through the turnaround it was easy to adjust her perceptions to make everything look normal; all the vertical shelves running along the wall in front of her served as a perfect cue to define the ultimate, functional orientation of the room.

The children had a thick sheaf of pictures with them that they were in the process of pinning to the soft wooden board on which they knelt. 'This is just the start,' Luisa explained. 'There's a new one for every stint.'

'Every stint of your uncle's journey?'

'Yes.'

Agata was impressed. 'That's a lot of pictures.' All the ones she could see looked like impressions from the children's own skin – there were no photographs or artificial images. Some were obviously meant as portraits of family members, but there were more fanciful works as well: scenes with strange animals surrounded by giant flowers; Esilio suspended in the void, sprouting improbably huge mountains, the black disc of its sun covering the star trails. 'You're good at keeping the colours aligned,' she said. 'I could never do that.' It was quite a skill to raise exactly the right shapes for each dye, with enough precision that the combined result of three or four separate impressions was as sharp as this.

'I can teach you,' Luisa offered.

'I won't have time.'

'I'll teach you when you get back.' Luisa smoothed the paper beneath her hands but turned her rear gaze to Agata. 'It's not so long that I'll have forgotten how. I'll only be seven.'

'Is this the *Surveyor*?' Agata asked, pointing to a grey lenticular shape with a beam of yellow light emerging from the middle.

Lorenzo said, 'Yes. I did that one.'

'Is it going to Esilio, or coming back?'

'Coming back is at the end.' Lorenzo gestured towards the stack of images yet to reach the board. Luisa hushed him, as if he might be spoiling a secret.

'I hope we didn't keep you from something,' Azelio said.

'I was just going to look around again. Fix things in my mind.' Agata knew that sounded strange, but the more familiar she became with the craft's interior, the less anxious she felt about the prospect of seeing nothing else on their journey to Esilio for the next six years. 'I want to get accustomed to the place in small doses, and then I'll be ready for it non-stop.'

'Fair enough.'

'I never thought about bringing my own changes of scenery.' She moved aside to let Lorenzo continue with the strip of images he was attaching.

'You can share the pictures if you like,' Azelio replied. 'Believe me, I'll be asking to borrow your books.'

'Can I share them?' Agata asked Luisa.

'Of course,' Luisa replied affably.

Lorenzo said, 'Just be careful you don't smudge them.'

Agata took her leave. To reach her own cabin she had to descend and then climb a different ladder. The layout was a mirror image of Azelio's; she'd already stacked the shelves with books, the vertical piles made less precarious by restraining strings.

She knelt on the blank wooden picture board, wondering if it would seem strange to the rest of the crew if she pinned a photograph of Medoro there. Or maybe she could have a stylised print made that looked like a skin impression, and then it wouldn't stand out too much among the borrowed pictures from the children.

Agata walked over to the shallow indentation that would hold her sand bed. She leant against it and imagined waking in this spot, gazing up at the cabin's moss-free ceiling, everything around her muted grey in the safety light.

But she'd woken in the same apartment for more than six years, and that had never felt oppressive. Here, there would be a reward for her patience drawing inexorably closer – the kind of guarantee that her work had never been able to provide. To walk on a planet, to tread on open ground beneath the stars would be extraordinary. Between that, the test of Lila's theory, and the chance to rid the mountain of Medoro's killers, she ought to have more than enough to sustain her.

Agata climbed down the ladder and crawled out through the air-lock. It was time to start saying her farewells.

17

Ramiro couldn't understand why Rosita had brought Vincenzo with her to the launch party. He didn't need to spend his last few chimes before departing watching the man hovering possessively around his sister, while the two of them made small talk with the vapid dignitaries who'd descended on Verano's workshop like an infestation of mites.

It was, admittedly, good to know that there was no prospect of Corrado raising the children, but he wished Rosita had simply told him that she'd found someone to take his place without parading the substitute in front of him. He already knew that he was superfluous. Rosita might well have waited four more years before shedding, but by the time he returned he'd be far too old to play any part in the children's lives.

As Ramiro stood watching them, Greta approached, a plate of food in one hand.

'Do you think you'll have grandchildren, the next time we meet?' he asked her.

'I hope not. My son will only be ten years old.'

'Really?' Ramiro remembered her taking time off for the shedding, but it felt like a lifetime ago. 'So are you here in some official capacity, or is it just your way of saying how much you'll miss me?'

'I'm sure the pain of your absence will be bearable,' she replied. 'And brief. As soon as the system's up and running, it will be as if you're already back.'

Ramiro buzzed sceptically. 'I know the Council won't formally postpone it, but after the election I suspect they'll be willing to let things slide. Technical problems with various components, deadlines missed, new reports commissioned . . .'

'That's not going to happen,' Greta said firmly. 'Nothing's been put on hold. If we delayed completion until the *Surveyor* returned, what would that be saying? That if Esilio turns out to be uninhabitable, the whole thing is off?'

Ramiro had never expected the Council to make the fate of the messaging system hostage to the *Surveyor*'s discoveries, but to rush ahead with it now seemed like a wasted opportunity to let things cool off. Then again, if the early news about Esilio was promising, that might compensate for the way it was obtained.

'So you think you'll know exactly what we're going to find, before we've even found it?'

'Of course,' Greta replied. 'I'm sure we'll get the system built in less than two years. There's a good chance that we've locked up the bombers, and in any case our security is far better now.'

'I don't want to come back to find that you idiots have blown each other up.' Ramiro was still stealing glances at Rosita and Vincenzo; he hated the idea of Greta sensing his discomfort, but he couldn't help himself. 'Maybe I'll just stay on Esilio, and spare myself all the needless travel. I'm sure Azelio can brief you on the planet's suitability as well as I could.'

'So you'll let the agronomist return, and try to farm the new world all by yourself?'

'There might be other inhabitants there already,' Ramiro suggested. 'I don't mind if they're living backwards; it ought to make for some interesting conversations.'

Greta knew he wasn't serious, but she still insisted on crushing his fantasy. 'The astronomers did a ten-year spectral analysis, before the turnaround. If there were plants growing on Esilio, we'd know about it.'

That much was hard to dispute. Even though they hadn't been able to image the star and planet separately, over time the astronomers would have picked up any small variations in the spectrum as different regions of the planet's surface rotated in and out of view. 'What if their farms are in caves, like ours?'

'So they have agriculture underground, but there's no natural vegetation on the surface?'

Ramiro wasn't in the mood to concede anything. 'Maybe you'll know the answer before I do, but that's no guarantee that it won't surprise you.'

He looked away, and spotted Tarquinia and her family nearby.

Her brother, Sicuro, had extruded extra arms to help him hold the children but they kept trying to squirm out of his grip. Tarquinia was talking with her uncle, and the conversation appeared intense; Ramiro decided not to intrude. He checked the countdown on a display screen suspended from the ceiling; the crew would start boarding in less than three chimes.

Councillor Marina called for silence, then began delivering an oration that was less about the *Surveyor*'s actual goals than the motives of the people who'd authorised the mission. 'This conciliatory project is proof that the mountain is still governed with the interests of every traveller in mind. Only those who seek to turn us against each other will fail to be inspired by this beacon of cooperation and mutual understanding.'

As the speech was finishing, Ramiro caught Agata's eye. The testing of Lila's theory hadn't rated a mention – which was a pity, since it was the only observation they'd be making that carried no risk of disappointment. The truth about gravity would be worth knowing, whatever it turned out to be.

Tarquinia was already moving towards the airlock. Ramiro searched the crowd and finally caught sight of Rosita again; she was standing beside one of the food tables. He nodded a curt farewell to Greta, then wove his way through the obstacle course towards his sister.

Vincenzo wasn't far away, but he was talking to someone else while Rosita helped herself to the spiced loaves. She'd put on a lot of weight since Ramiro had last spoken to her.

'How soon?' he asked.

'A couple of stints,' she replied.

'I hope it goes well.'

'I'll be fine,' Rosita said. 'And the children will be fine. Don't worry about anything.'

'All right.' She hadn't brought Vincenzo here to humiliate him, he realised. The sight of her living her own chosen life, undeterred, had been meant to reassure him.

'Good luck,' she said.

'Thanks.' In his rear gaze Ramiro could see Tarquinia motioning to him impatiently. 'I'll see you when I get back.'

As he turned, he felt the weight of something like grief: the burden he'd shirked all his life but never quite renounced was utterly lost to him now.

He caught up with Tarquinia, Agata and Azelio beside the airlock. They'd rehearsed the exit half a dozen times, and as they donned their corsets, cooling bags and jetpacks, Ramiro cushioned himself with the familiarity of it all.

Agata said, 'Think of Yalda parting from Eusebio, knowing that she'd never return. This is nothing.'

'Yalda's an invention,' Ramiro told her, straight-faced. 'She's no more real than anyone from the sagas.'

Agata stared at him, appalled by this heresy, but before she could summon a reply he put on his helmet. When she finally launched into an improvised defence of the historical Yalda he just frowned apologetically and feigned incomprehension.

Verano had had to build a whole new airlock to get the *Surveyor* out into the void, but the shiny clearstone chamber in front of them covered a small portal that had been here since Marzio's time. Ramiro was the last to squeeze into the chamber; he slid the door closed and watched blue resin oozing out of the frame, taking on a green tint as it expanded and solidified to make a hermetic seal.

Tarquinia's voice came through the link in his helmet. 'Evacuating airlock.' Ramiro felt the fabric puff out around his limbs as the pressure in the chamber dropped.

Tarquinia squatted down and broke the seal on the portal, then cranked the circular aperture open. She was the first to descend, seizing hold of the short stone ladder that protruded above the opening as she placed her feet on the rungs of rope below.

Azelio followed, then Agata. Ramiro felt a twinge of annoyance; he'd made a bet with Tarquinia that Agata would pull out at the last moment – and Tarquinia had made it clear that once they were on board she'd be accepting no resignations. At the edge of the portal he hesitated; he could see the assembled guests gawking from behind the cordon. Backing out now would almost be worth it, just for the joy of telling these idiots that he wouldn't be cleaning up their mess after all.

Almost, but not quite. He grabbed the top of the ladder and began the descent.

Ramiro emerged facing the black hemisphere of empty sky. The light spilling through from above lit the way well enough, and as it tapered off his eyes adjusted to the starlight. He glanced down to see the dark disc of the *Surveyor*, enmeshed in support ropes, still standing on its rim but inverted compared with its orientation in the workshop.

Only two helmeted figures remained on the ladder below him; Tarquinia was already inside. The craft's interior had been kept pressurised for the sake of Azelio's seedlings, so it was necessary for each of them to wait their turn to cycle through the *Surveyor*'s small airlock. As Azelio opened the hatch, Ramiro pictured himself releasing his hold on the ladder, starting up his jetpack and fleeing across the slopes. If he hadn't left it so late he might have thought up a way to fake his own death out here. There were probably a few anti-messagers still walking free who would have been willing to shelter him.

Agata entered the airlock. Ramiro's pride had the better of him now: he wasn't going to hand a moral victory to any ancestor-worshipping messager. He started down the ladder slowly, timing his steps so that he wouldn't arrive too soon.

When he reached the hull he could see Tarquinia clearly through the front window, already busy at the navigator's console. A moment later the first warning light blinked out on the panel beside the airlock: the inner door was closed. He waited for the pressure to be pumped down; with a finite amount of sunstone to gasify, they weren't going to throw away any more air than was necessary.

The second warning light went out. Ramiro gripped the crank with his feet and began turning it. Once he passed through this hatch, he'd have nowhere to escape to for the next six years. But he'd been forced here by his own nature, as much as by his circumstances; he wasn't merely exchanging one prison for another. And once he'd passed through these temporary constrictions, there'd be infinitely more elbow room in the end – for himself, and for everyone who followed him to Esilio.

In the cabin, the sense of familiarity he'd gained from the re-hearsals reimposed itself. Ramiro sealed the inner hatch, then clambered down a rope ladder to the nearest of the three couches behind Tarquinia's. The couches were shaped to make more sense once the gravity was at right angles to its present direction, but for now he had to lie on his back with his legs bent and raised, his feet brushing the floor-to-be.

As he strapped himself into place, his jetpack and helmet felt like absurd encumbrances, but when he plugged his corset's cable into the console in front of him the panel lit up in acknowledgement. When the automation could read any pattern he raised on his skin, it didn't matter how mobile his limbs were.

'A full crew?' Tarquinia lamented, mock-disappointed. 'I was hoping for an increase in my rations.'

Azelio said, 'I'll see what I can do once we make planetfall.'

Ramiro glanced at Agata on the couch to his left; it was hard to read her face through her helmet. 'Agata gets first call on any extra food.'

'Why?' she demanded.

'When the *Surveyor* breaks down and we're stranded on Esilio, someone will have to populate the planet.'

Tarquinia said, 'Don't worry, Ramiro: by then, the *Peerless* will have so much knowledge from the future that they'll be able to send us detailed instructions for triggering division in males.'

Before he could think of a suitable riposte his console beeped and began displaying the countdown. Three lapses remained to the launch. Ramiro tried to relax; he trusted Verano and his team. And even if the hull broke apart they'd stand a fair chance of surviving – so long as it happened sooner rather than later.

Two lapses. As Ramiro watched the symbols flickering towards zero, his anxiety vanished. He'd already crossed the point of no return. To get under way now would be nothing but a relief.

One lapse.

Eleven pauses. Ten. Nine. Eight.

Tarquinia said, 'Commenced burning support ropes.' The cables holding them to the mountain were as thick as Ramiro's arms; even a dozen high-powered coherers couldn't slice the *Surveyor* free in an instant.

Three. Two. One.

'Released.' Tarquinia's announcement was redundant: they were weightless, and the mountain was receding.

Through the window, the *Peerless* began drifting off-centre, perversely moving to the right; they'd been flung from the rim moving right themselves, but the tiny spin they'd inherited from the mountain had at first cancelled, and was now overtaking, the effect of their changing perspective.

'Firing engines.'

The thrust from the rebounders rose up smoothly, then levelled off. Ramiro sank into the seat of the couch. He was heavier than he'd been before the ropes were cut – and the jetpack felt like more of a burden, tugging down on the narrow shoulder straps. But the acceleration itself was no different from that of the *Peerless* during the turnaround.

The mountain had disappeared from sight completely. Through the window in front of him the blazing rim of the home-cluster star trails appeared horizontal as the *Surveyor* ascended towards the dark hemisphere.

'Everyone all right?' Tarquinia enquired.

'I'm fine,' Azelio replied.

Agata said, 'Can I leave my jetpack on?'

'As long as you want to.'

'Then I'm fine, too.'

'Ramiro? Any special requests?'

He said, 'I'll be happy once we can see where we're going.'

Tarquinia buzzed curtly. 'When I agreed to the confidentiality conditions, Greta stressed that you were the last person I should let in on the secret.'

Azelio was confused. 'What secret?'

Agata said, 'We're not going to travel all the way to Esilio by dead reckoning. Accelerometers are good, but they're not that good. And the home-cluster stars aren't enough, either.'

Azelio understood. 'They finished the time-reversed camera, in secret?'

Ramiro said, 'I think they had prototypes working before the bombing.'

Tarquinia shifted uncomfortably in her seat, then made a decision. 'Since everyone knows the situation, I'm not going to treat you like fools.' An inset opened on Ramiro's console showing him a patch of sky lit up with stars. Not the home cluster's long trails; these images were brief stabs of colour, some of them piling the whole spectrum together into a white smudge. He glanced to his left and saw that Agata and Azelio were being sent the same feed.

'Behold the orthogonal stars, lighting the way into the future.' Agata sounded bitter, and Ramiro couldn't blame her: this was proof that even from the killers' point of view her friend's murder had been futile.

'This is Esilio's sun.' Tarquinia drew a red circle around a bright speck near the centre of the view.

'Greta's spyware will tell her that you've broken your agreement,' Ramiro predicted. He hadn't been allowed near the *Surveyor*'s automation while it was in development, but he was sure that the *Peerless* would be receiving a constant flow of data from the expedition, far beyond the communications they volunteered.

'I don't care,' Tarquinia replied. 'What's she going to do about it now?'

'Blow us up?' Azelio joked.

Agata said, 'Not if we keep going. They'll only kill us if we start to look threatening – if we turn around and start heading back.'

18

Agata woke in a state of joyful anticipation, but then she spent a lapse or two lying motionless, wondering if she had the day right. She could see the diurnal clock on her console's panel, but she'd made a deliberate choice to omit the date from the default display. She'd fooled herself in the past, waking with all kinds of wildly optimistic notions about the phase the mission had reached, but it was important that she settle the matter by consulting her memory, with no other aids.

Since the link with the *Peerless* had crackled its last transmission and the flow of messages from Serena and Lila had ceased, time had become a desert out of the sagas: a featureless wasteland of shimmering heat haze and treacherous mirages. But Agata was sure that she'd just passed a full day with a justified belief that the long-awaited event was imminent. If she was wrong about that then she wasn't just disoriented, she was completely delusional.

She rose from her sand bed and walked over to the console. She hadn't been mistaken about the date, but she brought up the flight plan to confirm its significance. It had been a few stints since they'd passed the one-quarter mark in the duration of their outwards journey, but that fractional accomplishment had offered nothing tangible to celebrate. Today, the *Surveyor*'s progress would finally be made manifest: its history would reach orthogonality with that of the *Peerless*, and Tarquinia would shut off the engines.

Agata left her room and walked out into the front cabin. Tarquinia wasn't up yet; Ramiro was on watch.

'Good morning,' she said.

'No, it's not.' Ramiro swivelled his seat around to face her. 'Complete weightlessness is tedious,' he complained. 'We should have found a way to avoid it.'

'You could always move in with Azelio's plants,' Agata joked.

'I shouldn't have to. If they get to swing on a tether, why not us?'

'What would you use as the counterweight? Splitting the whole vehicle in two would be too complicated.'

'Yeah, yeah,' Ramiro sulked. 'What kind of expert on gravity are you, if you can't summon it at the flick of a switch?'

Agata said, 'The kind who understands enough to be willing to bet that that's never going to happen. I'll give you a gross to one that no one will discover such a thing between now and the reunion.'

Ramiro scowled. 'To be verified how? I thought your theory was that inventors would always censor the messages they sent into the past – since that's more probable than their ideas appearing out of nowhere.'

Agata wasn't going to let these complications stand in the way of a good bet. 'I think they could tell us what they'd built. They just couldn't tell us how it worked.'

Ramiro stretched his arms and buzzed wearily. Most of the cabin lights were off, and behind him the home-cluster stars filled the view. It was Ancestors' Day all over again – only this time it would last for three years.

'The reunion could be happening right now,' Agata marvelled. 'Even as we speak, the *Peerless* could be approaching the home world.'

'It's not the first time you could have said that. Or didn't you notice?' Ramiro was wearing his corset, so he sent the sketch to the nearest console. 'About a stint before mid-turnaround, our line of simultaneity would have had just the right slope.'

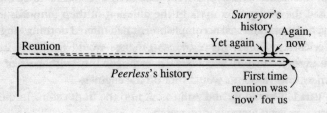

'It's the first time it's "now" by the home world's reckoning as well as our own,' Agata replied.

Ramiro was bemused. 'Name any two events in the cosmos, and there's a definition of time that makes them simultaneous. If I can't actually witness this great moment – let alone take part in it – just how excited do you want me to be?'

'I'm sure the ancestors thought about *us* at the turnaround,' Agata argued. 'What's wrong with a bit of solidarity?'

'I prefer to reserve that for people I can look in the eye.'

'All right. Forget it.' They'd exchanged their views and found nothing in common, as usual. There was no point wishing it were otherwise.

'I'm going to go strap myself down and sleep through all this nonsense.' Ramiro nodded towards the passage behind her; Tarquinia had emerged from her cabin.

Azelio joined Agata and Tarquinia for breakfast, then the three of them set about putting up the guide ropes and checking that everything inside the *Surveyor* that might drift free was secured. The tool cupboard took the most work; there were individual straps for every item, but people had grown lazy about using them. Azelio went through the pantry, checking every sack of grain for holes. The sand in their beds was already resin-coated – and hoping to contain it was a tad optimistic whatever steps they took – but Tarquinia insisted on putting tarpaulins in place before the gravity was lost.

Agata clung to a rope in the front cabin as Tarquinia finally issued the command to the engines. The end of the turnaround for the *Peerless* had taken place over three full days, out of regard for the effects on the most vulnerable travellers, but the crew of the *Surveyor* were assumed to be more robust. As Agata's weight plummeted, she was unable to dispel a conviction that the cabin was plunging down, but then the very idea of that vertical axis lost its meaning.

After a lapse or two, her body and everything around her was imbued with stillness. The view through the window was unchanged; the stars were indifferent to the sudden straightening of the *Surveyor's* history. The susurrations of the cooling system grew quieter; Agata had grown accustomed to the old sound, and the new silence made the room feel dead.

'What now?' she asked Tarquinia.

Tarquinia unplugged her corset. 'That's it. Everything's done.'

'What about the plants?'

Azelio said, 'There's no hurry. A few days without gravity isn't going to harm them. Ramiro will help me set up the tether soon.'

'All right.'

Agata dragged herself back to her cabin and harnessed herself to her desk. She looked up at the pictures she'd brought: Medoro, Serena, Gineto, Vala and Arianna, scattered among the colourful childish sketches that Azelio was sharing with her. If she'd commandeered the *Surveyor* she could have flown in a loop right back to Ancestors' Day on the *Peerless*. So far as she could tell there was nothing in the physics that would forbid it – so long as she didn't try to cut corners and make do with a semicircular route, arriving as antimatter and spoiling the party. But she hadn't seen herself anywhere else in the crowd that day, staring longingly at her friends – and if a visitor from the future really had joined them in her absence, Medoro had done a very good job of keeping it a secret.

She looked away. Nostalgia passed the time, but it needed to be rationed. And if no one else was celebrating the *Surveyor*'s parallelism with the home world, she might as well forget it and focus on her work. Though Lila had given the vacuum-energy problem to one of her students, Pelagia, Agata had decided to pursue it independently, in the hope of preventing her brain ossifying from disuse. With a wildly unfair eight-year advantage over her rival it wasn't impossible that she'd return with a worthwhile contribution of some kind, but she hadn't told Lila about her plans, sparing herself the weight of any expectations.

So far, she was still grappling with the notion of the vacuum. She'd read the definitive treatment by Romolo and Assunto, who'd adapted Carla's wave mechanics to the study of fields, but all they'd really cared about was predicting the results of particle collisions. They'd deliberately sidestepped all the distracting cosmological issues, and – apart from Yalda's insight that the cosmos had to be finite in order to prevent exponential surges in the light field – it did make sense that none of the results of any small-scale experiment should depend on whether the cosmos was a torus, a sphere, or some four-dimensional analogue of a thrice-knotted pastry.

Since all of the old-school field theorists' measurements depended on changes in energy, rather than any absolute scale, Romolo and Assunto had been free to set the vacuum energy to zero by decree. They'd certainly understood that the true value was a difficult quantity to pin down – so they'd vaguely sketched its origins, and then subtracted it out of all their other formulas so they could concentrate on the remaining parts that were more mathematically tractable and contributed to nice, tangible things like the rate at which positive and negative luxagens annihilated each other in their experiments at the Object.

But even their formal, mathematical expression for the vacuum state was a bizarre sleight of hand: they'd imagined taking the simpler vacuum of a more pristine theory – one where all particles stood aloof from each other, refusing to interact – and writing it as a sum of pieces that each corresponded to a different energy level of the true theory. If you followed that sum over a long time, you could pick out the least rapid oscillations that represented the lowest energy level. So in all of Romolo and Assunto's calculations, they'd pretended that everything happened in an infinitely old cosmos that had started – infinitely long ago – with the simple vacuum, from which a mathematical trick extracted the true vacuum before they set to work adding particles to it in the here and now.

Amazingly, all of this nonsense had worked well enough for their purposes, with the quantities they'd predicted confirmed by experiment again and again. But the real cosmos with its own real history and topology couldn't be understood by grafting on an infinitely long run-up from a state that had never actually existed.

Someone knocked on the door of the cabin. Agata dragged herself over and opened it.

'Are you busy?' Azelio asked.

'Not really.'

'Do you want to help me set up the tether?'

Agata felt a surge of excitement, but then she realised that it was premature. 'You think Tarquinia will let me do it?'

'Didn't she give you your void proficiency certificate?'

'Only because she doubted that anyone else would.'

Azelio frowned. 'Ramiro doesn't have much more experience than you. If you're willing to ask Tarquinia, I'll support you.'

The two of them approached the pilot in her couch, and Tarquinia heard them out politely.

'My job is to try to keep you all alive,' she said. 'This might not be an especially dangerous task, but Ramiro has the edge on you in confidence.'

Agata said, 'If the worst comes to the worst, I'm expendable. Ramiro isn't. If something goes seriously wrong with the automation, no one else will be able to fix it.'

'I can get us home without automation,' Tarquinia replied.

'Of course.' Agata hoped she hadn't inadvertently insulted her. 'But you have to admit that a lot of things would become more difficult if we were forced to do them manually.'

'Hmm.'

Azelio said, 'Everyone needs experience to get used to working in the void. The engines are switched off, and we'd both be wearing jetpacks; how much safer could it be? And if Agata does this now, it could make all the difference to the kind of task she can manage in an emergency.'

Tarquinia inclined her head, conceding his point. 'But she did tell me once that she'd rather not have anyone relying on her.'

'I was joking!' Agata insisted. She wasn't sure that she had been, but she certainly didn't feel that way now.

Tarquinia said, 'You can go out with Azelio and set up the tether, but that's all: install it, but leave it motionless. Ramiro will go out for the spin-up. Half the task for each of you. What could be fairer?'

Sanctified by the ancestors' gaze or not, the sky unsettled Agata. When she'd trained with Tarquinia around the *Peerless*, the contrasting hemispheres had made it easy to stay oriented. There were bright stars now that caught her eye, and constellations that she could commit to memory, but it took much more effort to seek out these relatively subtle cues than it had to distinguish between an empty black bowl and a riot of colour.

Azelio seemed to be focused on the *Surveyor* itself, so Agata followed his lead and tried to think of the disc of the hull as her horizon. Still clinging to the hand rings outside the airlock she turned her body until it was perpendicular to the disc, then she released her grip and drew a short arrow on her chest that pointed towards her head. The jetpack obliged with a gentle push in that direction; when she'd ascended half a stride above the hull she drew a stop-line that killed her velocity. The jetpack was keeping track of all the acceleration it delivered – along with any bumps and pushes she inflicted on herself – and it knew how to return her to her initial state of motion.

She followed Azelio to the rear of the hull, opposite the main cabin and its window, and halted beside him. The two agronomy pods mounted here were roughly cubical, each about as broad as Agata was tall. Azelio grasped a ring to brace himself, lit the scene with the coherer mounted on his helmet, then began turning the first of the eight wide, hollow bolts that held the first pod in place. Agata had arrived upside down for the task; she secured herself with her foot through a ring, then squatted down so she could grip another with a hand and right herself. She switched on her own coherer and squinted at the disc of brightness she'd imposed on the starlit hull; it was strange to see the sharp details summoned out of the grey shadows, as if the *Surveyor* of the void had become the *Surveyor* of the workshop again. Then she reached into the bolt closest to her and took hold of the crossbar within. The crossbar needed a twist around its own axis to disengage the spring-loaded pins that locked it in place, then it served as a handle to turn the bolt.

'My arm's tired already,' Azelio confessed. 'Why couldn't they make this a job for power tools?'

'If you want to run everything on compressed air, you'd better hope there's sunstone on Esilio.' Agata's own forearm was aching. 'Let's face it, we've all grown soft. If you asked me to harvest a crop manually, I think it would kill me.'

'Lucky you don't want to migrate, then.'

By design, the bolts could not be withdrawn entirely from their threaded holes, but once all eight had been unscrewed as far as possible the locking plates on the pod were freed from their slots in the hull.

Agata got into position on the opposite side of the pod to Azelio; the symmetry was necessary to extract the thing smoothly, but it meant they were hidden from each other. 'Move it as gently as you can,' he instructed her. 'The last thing we want to do is give it more momentum than we can control.' With their feet re-formed into hands to grip the rings on the hull, they slowly raised the pod out of its shallow bed.

When it was about a stride above the hull, Azelio called a halt. They both stood for a moment holding the thing, as if they couldn't quite believe that it would stay put when they released it. But it did.

'I'll tow this one out, and you watch over the cable,' Azelio said.

'Right.' Agata squatted against the hull and aimed her coherer at the reel. As well as tethering the pod to the pivot it shared with its companion, the cable would carry cooling air to the plants and bring data and video back to the *Surveyor*.

Azelio moved into place on the opposite side of the pod; Agata couldn't see him, so he narrated for her. 'I'm attaching the towing rope now,' he said. Then, 'I'm connected. Be patient, though, this is going to take a while.'

After a lapse in which nothing happened, Agata asked, 'Did you fire the jetpack?'

'Yes.'

'I don't think you're moving at all.' The slight tug hadn't been enough to overcome the sticking friction of the cable; it was prudent to unwind as slowly as possible, but there was a limit to how slow that could be.

'That's embarrassing.' Azelio buzzed. 'All right, a little more thrust this time.'

The reel began to turn. Agata watched the cable feeding out smoothly, the helix of the outer layer gradually shrinking. Verano's team had wound every span into place with scrupulous care, and from the flatness of the layers she could see that she wasn't expecting any hidden snags, but she focused all her attention on the process, refusing to let her mind wander.

When the cable was down to its last layer and the core of the reel was revealed, Agata advised Azelio and began counting down the remaining turns. Half a turn short of full extension, he brought the pod to a halt. Centrifugal force could complete the process; a tiny amount of slack like this wouldn't be enough to give the pod a dangerous jolt.

Agata looked up and waited for her eyes to adjust back to the starlight. The cable stretched out into the void for four or five times the diameter of the hull. With the pod's stone block hanging on the end of it, her eyes wanted to declare this direction vertical, but when she insisted on her original hull-based definition the sight became even stranger, like a conjurer's rope trick.

'When you and Ramiro do the spin-up, I want to come out and watch,' she pleaded.

'If it's up to me, absolutely,' Azelio replied. 'And since you've got Tarquinia twisted around your finger—'

'Ha! That'd be something.' Agata suspected that Tarquinia was listening in on their conversation; for safety's sake the helmets' transceivers didn't use any kind of encryption.

'I'm coming back now.'

'Have you untied the towing rope?' she asked.

Azelio was silent for a moment. 'Good idea.'

When he'd rejoined her, Agata said, 'I owe you for this. I was going insane in there.'

'You don't owe me anything,' Azelio declared. 'You sat with me after the link cut off; I haven't forgotten that.'

'I don't know if I helped much.' The children were Azelio's life; the most she'd been able to do was distract him a little, while the prospect of waiting more than ten years to hear from them again sank in.

'What will we do if Esilio isn't habitable?' he asked. They'd switched off their coherers while they talked so as not to dazzle each other, but Agata could make out Azelio's face in the starlight. She'd come out into the void to escape her dark thoughts, but the cosmic perspective seemed to have had the opposite effect on him. 'If we go back to them with nothing, it would be like the *Peerless* returning to the home world with no idea how to escape the Hurtlers.'

Agata hummed angrily. 'I don't believe that. War's not as inevitable as a Hurtler strike. Anyway . . . when we get to Esilio, we'll find what we find. No one expects you to work miracles.'

'No.'

Agata said, 'We'd better start on the second pod, before Ramiro wakes up and finds out that I've stolen half his entertainment.'

Back at her desk, Agata examined her notes. The truth was that in a year and a half she'd made almost no progress. Now she'd had her frolic beneath the stars; she'd had her Ancestors' Day celebration. And there was nothing on the calendar to break the monotony until they started up the engines again.

She could end up squandering half the journey longing for planet-fall, and half again longing to be back in the mountain. All her life, this fixation on grand turning points – from the launch of the *Peerless* to the reunion – had given her a sense of purpose, but it had also weakened and distracted her. Recapitulating the whole thing in miniature had only made the problem more acute. It was only right that the *Surveyor*'s mission came first, and that she honour Medoro, test Lila's theory, and play her part in Ramiro's peace plan. But to make any progress with her own work she had to stop thinking like a passenger: doing no more than clinging on, in the hope that someone else's flight plan would carry her to a destination worth reaching.

Agata hadn't brought a picture of Lila, but she could effortlessly summon the sound of her mentor's gentle nagging. She knew exactly what Lila's advice would have been at this juncture: Romolo and Assunto's tricks weren't suited to her purpose, and there was no point pretending that some minor variation in their methods would suffice. If she wanted to make progress, she needed to dig far deeper into the mysteries of the vacuum and come up with some new tools of her own.

19

Ramiro passed the first bell of his watch correcting the errors in a small program that he'd written the night before. It computed the shapes of two four-dimensional polyhedra, set them rotating – with different speeds and directions – then displayed a projection of the portion of the first that lay inside the second.

It was a frivolous exercise, but the endlessly mutating image was strangely soothing, and this playful tinkering did have the advantage that it kept his skills sharp. As much as he'd luxuriated in the process of ridding the *Surveyor* of its intrusive surveillance software, he'd only been able to prolong that task for about a year, and though he doubted that all the genuinely useful automation that remained would turn out to be ideal for its purpose once they reached Esilio he was still in no better position to know the true requirements than the original designers.

There was a sudden high-pitched noise from behind him, like something large and brittle being snapped. Not the ominous groan of a machine part under pressure gradually yielding – just instant surrender to an overwhelming force. It was over in a flicker or two, and though the screech itself was unforgettable the lingering impression offered no clues as to its source. Ramiro dimmed the cabin and switched on the exterior lights. Through the window he could see a trail of debris drifting off to his right, small grey rocks spinning in a haze of dust. They could only be fragments of the hull's hardstone, torn free by a collision of some kind.

An alarm sounded. The pressure in the *Surveyor* was dropping.

He grabbed his helmet and dragged himself back towards the crew's sleeping quarters. Agata emerged from her room, strapping on her jetpack, helmet in hand. Ramiro could see her tympanum moving but he couldn't hear a sound; the pressure was already too low. He put on his helmet and she did the same.

'What happened?' she asked.

'Something's hit us,' he said. 'I don't know what. Is your cabin holed?'

'No.'

Ramiro clambered past her and opened the nearest door. There was a jagged slot half a stride across missing from the far wall; the rock along the edges was shattered unevenly, but the course of the damage was unswerving. Sheets of paper were fluttering through the gash, out into the void. Azelio was motionless, tangled in his bed's twisted tarpaulin. Ramiro approached, switching on his helmet's coherer to supplement the safety lights, and saw three holes in the tarpaulin, each the width of his thumb.

Agata's voice came through the link. 'Tarquinia's gone!'

'What?'

'I'm in her cabin – she must have been blown right out.'

Ramiro stared at Azelio, imagining Tarquinia tumbling through the void in the same condition – carrying no air, insensate, her flesh pierced by splinters of rock.

'I can see sunstone spilling out,' Agata said. 'From the cooling system.'

Ramiro was paralysed. What did he do first? If they couldn't run the cooling system, they were dead.

Agata shouted, 'I can see Tarquinia! I'm going after her!'

'*No!* I'll get her!'

Agata hesitated. 'You can see her too?'

'No, but—'

'Ramiro, I can do this,' Agata insisted. She sounded impossibly calm. 'She's not that far away, and I can still see her clearly. I've got her cooling bag here, air tank and all. I'll get it to her. She'll be all right.'

'Yes,' he agreed. 'Do it.'

Agata said nothing more, but then he caught the flash of her coherer as she jetted across the trench of stars behind Azelio's wall.

Ramiro shook himself out of his stupor. Azelio's cooling bag was missing from the clamp beside the bed, but the spare was in the cupboard. He took it over to Azelio and worked it up over his limp form, then he opened the valve on the air tank and held his hand against the fabric to check that there was a flow across the skin. There were five deep wounds in Azelio's thigh and torso, but his skull seemed to be untouched. The injuries might be survivable – so long as his flesh didn't denature and ignite.

Ramiro dragged Azelio into his own cabin; abutting the opposite side of the hull, it appeared to be completely undamaged. He got Azelio under the sand bed's tarpaulin, and brought two straps across to be sure he wouldn't drift away.

'You'll be fine,' he muttered. 'You'll be fine.'

He dragged himself back into the passage and headed for the cooling system.

Whatever had grazed the side of the *Surveyor* had left a single long gash in the hull running all the way from Azelio's cabin via Tarquinia's to the gasification chamber. Looking out through the opening where the gash had breached a narrow maintenance shaft, Ramiro could now see what Agata had reported: pieces of sunstone tumbling into the void like gravel spilling from a torn sack. The feed supplying the decomposing agent should have shut off when the pressure plummeted – and if it hadn't, the result would have been spectacularly worse. But the sunstone would continue to react with the agent already present in the chamber. There was no way to render the swarm of jostling rocks perfectly motionless, so nothing would keep them in the chamber while there was a wide-open path into the void.

'Can you still see Tarquinia?' he asked Agata.

'I've nearly reached her!' Agata declared. 'How are things there? Is Azelio all right?' Once she'd moved away from the *Surveyor* she would have looked back and taken in all the damage at a glance.

'He's safe,' Ramiro assured her. 'He's got some small wounds, but I've put him in my room to recover. Please, just concentrate on Tarquinia.'

'All right.'

Ramiro leant against the side of the shaft. How was he going to seal the chamber? They had stone plugs prepared for holes up to the size of his hand, but no one had envisaged anything like this.

The repair didn't have to be airtight immediately; he just had to stop the sunstone being lost. He dragged himself to Agata's cabin and snatched the tarpaulin from her bed, then detoured to the tool cupboard and grabbed a jar of sealing resin.

If he entered the gasification chamber through the hatch he'd just drive more sunstone out as he pushed his way through it. Back in the maintenance shaft, he warily tested the rim of the gash with one fingertip. The damaged stone was still warm from the collision – with a microscopic Hurtler, most likely – but the escaping air had carried away enough heat to render it traversable. He clambered out into the void and made his way along the torn edge of the hull, hand over hand; the distance was so short that this was faster than messing around with his jetpack.

'I'm with her!' Agata announced excitedly. 'She's conscious, Ramiro. She's putting on her cooling bag now.'

Ramiro started humming with relief; embarrassed, he muted the outwards channel on the link until he'd regained his composure. 'Be careful coming back,' he managed.

Agata replied, 'Don't worry, we will.'

As Ramiro climbed into the chamber small pellets of sunstone bounced off his jetpack and faceplate; he had to force himself not to raise his arm instinctively to swat them away like insects, as that would only have added energy to the swarm. He took the jar from his tool pouch and daubed resin over the nearest part of the inner wall, then tugged the tarpaulin out of the gap under his belt and fixed one edge in place. There were no ropes or handholds in the chamber that he could use to brace himself, but he could apply pressure by closing his hand over the whole exposed thickness of the wall, clamping the fabric of the tarpaulin against the resin until it adhered.

He pushed himself off from the wall to reach the far side of the chamber; he hit it with a jolt but managed to grab the rim of the gash to keep himself from bouncing. The tarpaulin was wider than the gap he was trying to cover, and once he had it secured at both ends the pellets of sunstone were too large to work their way around the sides.

Ramiro paused to take stock. There was more sunstone in the store behind the chamber; they'd probably only lost about a twelfth of their total. If Tarquinia was safe, the next most urgent matter was checking on Azelio. Getting the gash repaired and the entire *Surveyor* airtight again would take a long time, but as an interim measure they could seal the doors to the damaged cabins and concentrate on the cooling chamber while they still had enough air in tanks to keep them from hyperthermia.

He managed to get out of the chamber through the hatch with

only a handful of sunstone escaping into the passage. Back in his cabin, he surveyed Azelio's wounds, cutting holes in the cooling bag so he wouldn't have to pull the whole thing off. At each site there was a faint yellow glow suffusing the punctured flesh, but it looked like the body's ordinary signalling rather than a runaway reaction, and the surrounding skin wasn't hot to the touch. The fragments of stone had passed right through Azelio's body, but as far as Ramiro could see his digestive tract hadn't been breached. If his skull and gut were undamaged, his chances were good.

'We're almost back,' Agata announced. 'Ah, you've closed off the chamber already!'

'Yes.' Ramiro had never expected her to prove so indomitable in the face of a calamity like this. One stride deeper into the hull and the Hurtler would have ended the mission. Maybe Agata was relishing the sense of solidarity with the ancestors, and picturing herself as a member of the most far-flung branch of Eusebio's fire watch.

The two women returned together through the same opening they'd used to make their separate exits. Ramiro was waiting for them, and he handed Tarquinia her helmet.

'Welcome back,' he said. If the ordeal had shaken her, she wasn't letting it show.

'How's Azelio?' she asked.

'He's got five wounds, but they all seem clean to me.'

'Let me take a look.'

In Ramiro's cabin, Azelio was still motionless under the tarpaulin, but even from the doorway they could see the light from the wound in his thigh, shining through the fabric.

'It wasn't like that a few lapses ago,' Ramiro declared. That meant it was deteriorating rapidly.

Tarquinia said, 'Get the medical kit.'

Agata went to fetch it.

'The hull fragments missed you?' Ramiro asked Tarquinia.

'I was lucky.' Tarquinia buzzed grimly. 'I was out in the void before I was even awake. After this, I'm going to start sleeping in my cooling bag.'

Agata returned with the box of medication and instruments. Tarquinia dragged herself over to the bed; Ramiro followed, taking off his jetpack so he could move more freely.

Agata remained by the door. 'You survived worse than this, didn't you, Ramiro?'

'Absolutely. He's going to be fine.'

Ramiro helped Tarquinia pull the tarpaulin out of the way, but they left the straps in place to keep Azelio still.

'Is there a reason the cabin lights aren't on?' Tarquinia asked irritably.

'No.' Ramiro had been relying on his helmet and the safety lights; with the cooling system dead they shouldn't be using any of the *Surveyor*'s photonics gratuitously, but well-lit surgery was hardly an indulgence. When Agata switched on the main lights, Ramiro felt a sickening disjunction between the reassuring familiarity of the room – intact and unblemished, as if nothing had happened – and the condition of his guest.

Tarquinia found a long, sharp scalpel and dusted it with astringent. 'Can you get on the other side and hold him still?' she asked Ramiro. 'The straps won't stop him wriggling, and even if he doesn't wake he might move instinctively.'

'Do you want me to hold his leg?' Agata asked.

Tarquinia said, 'Good idea.'

Agata joined them. The three of them braced themselves awkwardly over the bed, holding different parts of the same rope for support. Ramiro glanced down at the tunnel in Azelio's flesh; a luminous discharge was oozing into the hole that the fragment had made.

Tarquinia said, 'Everyone secure? I'm going to start.'

She plunged the scalpel into Azelio's thigh, a scant back from the surface of the wound, and started carving a cylinder of her own. Azelio's torso twitched under Ramiro's arm, then he opened his eyes and started bellowing. Even without air to carry the sound, the cry that passed from flesh to flesh was piteous.

Ramiro pushed harder against the rope, pinning the poor man down more firmly. **It's almost done**, he wrote on his forearm, hoping that Azelio could read the ridges through the fabric separating their skin. **Be strong, it won't be much longer.** He locked his gaze on Azelio's, trying to convey some reassuring sense that his tormentors knew what they were doing.

Azelio kept screaming, but he managed to suppress his struggling. Tarquinia completed the incision. She used a pair of forceps to pull the tube of damaged flesh out of his thigh, swabbed the spilt liquid with a cloth, then dragged herself quickly out of the room. Agata fumbled in the medical kit and found a syringe of analgesic; she injected the powder in three sites around the wound. Ramiro knew from experience that it would take a few lapses to have much effect, but Azelio responded with relief just to the sight of it being administered.

Tarquinia returned. 'Any of the other wounds need ablating?' It was lucky that Azelio couldn't hear her. Ramiro looked over the four remaining holes.

'I don't think so. But someone should stay with him to monitor them.'

Agata said, 'I'll do that.'

Tarquinia inclined her head in agreement. 'Ramiro and I will start work on the repairs.'

'Are you up to that?' Ramiro already felt guilty that he'd stood by and let her do the surgery.

'We're all in shock,' she said, 'one way or another. But no one's going to feel safe until the cooling chamber's sealed and we have pressure again.'

Tarquinia went out into the void with a camera, then used surveying software and a pre-existing map of the hull to reconstruct the precise shape and dimensions of the gash. They had enough slabs of hardstone in the stores to cover the hole in the chamber, but no single piece would do the job. Ramiro unpacked the masonry workbench and set it up in the front cabin; he'd never envisioned employing it in mid-flight, imagining it would only be useful once they'd reached the surface.

The bench's coherer could carve precision tongues and grooves into the edges of the slabs, but with no circulating air everything grew hot very quickly; the system hadn't been designed for use in a vacuum. Tarquinia rigged up an impromptu cooling system, with an air tank venting across the surface of the bench. Ramiro couldn't think of any better method, but he mentally reviewed their stock of compressed air. They had enough to deal with the crew's metabolic heat for a stint – but shaping each slab was costing them about a day of that reserve for one person.

They coated the grooves with sealing resin and clamped pairs of slabs together while the resin cured. But they couldn't assemble the whole structure outside the chamber or they'd never get it through the hatch; they'd have to carry it in as two pieces and join them there.

'We can clamp these together in the chamber,' Ramiro said, 'but how do we apply pressure to bond the whole thing to the wall?' The chamber was too large for them to brace themselves against any other surface.

'Use the force from a jetpack?' Tarquinia suggested.

'That will agitate the sunstone,' Ramiro pointed out.

'What does that matter? The assembly will already be blocking the hole.'

'But when we open the hatch there'll be residual motion – and positive air pressure – so we'll end up spilling more of the stuff.' The sunstone wouldn't be going into the void, but tracking down the small pellets even within the confines of the *Surveyor* wasn't a trivial exercise.

'That's true,' Tarquinia conceded. 'So we need to set up a tarp behind us before we go in, closing off the space around the hatch. That won't be perfect, but it should catch most of the spill.'

Ramiro had no better idea. The only alternative to the jetpack would be to try to install handholds in the chamber – again, without any easy way to apply pressure to a resin join, or to brace themselves to use a drill. He buzzed wearily. 'At least Verano will be pleased: we can bring him back a long list of suggestions for making the next version easier to repair.'

They dragged the two halves of the assembly most of the way to the chamber. Then Tarquinia fetched the largest tarp from the store-room and they tied its rim to the handholds around the hatch, enclosing themselves and the hardstone pieces in a rough sphere of fabric. When they opened the hatch white pellets began drifting out immediately like inquisitive insects, and by the time they'd man-oeuvred the two pieces into the chamber it was clear that they'd needed the tarp all along, whatever else they did.

Inside the chamber, with the hatch closed, Ramiro realised that they had another problem. 'When we put resin along the join, how do we keep the sunstone from sticking to it?' A few lumps caught under the fabric of his temporary repair hadn't made much difference, but one pellet would ruin the airtight seal between the hardstone pieces.

Tarquinia said, 'If I back myself into a corner, I can spray air over it while you're applying the resin.'

'I think we should rehearse that.'

They tried it. It didn't work. Tarquinia could keep a small part of the edge free of pellets at any time, but not the whole join.

She said, 'We need to get another big tarp in here. If we can form a kind of tent and vent air inside it while we're making the join, that should keep most of the sunstone out.'

Ramiro grew tired just listening to this plan, but he couldn't see a way to solve the problem without at least one of them leaving the chamber. 'All right,' he said. 'I'll get it.'

He took off his jetpack and left it in the chamber, opened the hatch just enough to let himself through, then untied a section of the tarp's rim and slipped past it into the passage. A few dozen pellets followed him through the gap.

When he returned with the second tarp, they wrapped themselves and the assembly in this improvised tent and struggled to drive enough of the sunstone out to be confident that they could make the join. It was impossible to make a working space entirely free of pellets, but once they'd reached a point where the density wasn't getting any lower they had no choice but to take the risk.

They manipulated the pieces so that they were almost slotted together, then Ramiro daubed resin along one half of the join. Tarquinia wound the clamp down on the assembly, then played the beam from her helmet over the edge. Everything fitted together perfectly; nothing had become trapped in the seam.

Ramiro chirped in jubilation. 'Well done.'

Tarquinia said, 'Next time we're bringing a mason.'

They waited for the join to cure, then opened up the tent. Ramiro's jetpack had ended up in a corner of the chamber; Tarquinia fetched it for him.

To fix the assembly in place they needed to use the tent again, to protect the edges of the gash they were repairing. Ramiro attached it to the wall with resin at half a dozen points, partitioning off their end of the chamber while leaving a large gap to one side through which to shoo out the pellets. But it was harder than before to drive sunstone from the enclosure, with most of the air they vented just escaping straight into the void.

They'd built the assembly with a raised rim that could sit flush against parts of the wall uncontaminated by the earlier repair. Ramiro spread resin around the whole margin of the gash, then with their jetpacks gently bracing them they manoeuvred the assembly into place.

'It's rocking a little,' Tarquinia said.

'Don't say that,' Ramiro begged her. He reached over and pushed on the spot where Tarquinia had been applying pressure, and felt the stone wobble under his fingers.

At least they'd had the foresight to put a handhold on the inner face of the assembly; Tarquinia grabbed it and pulled the whole thing back from the wall. Ramiro searched the contact region; a pellet of sunstone had stuck in the resin. He managed to wiggle it free, his body jittering as the jetpack struggled to track and counter the small changing forces.

They tried again.

'Flat, no give,' Tarquinia announced.

'Same here.' Ramiro wasn't quite ready to believe it, but all they could do now was turn up their jetpacks and push, hoping to end up with an airtight seal.

'If we'd built clamps into this thing we could have tightened them against the outside of the hull,' Tarquinia mused.

Ramiro buzzed but offered no opinion; attaching them in the first place would probably have taken more time than it saved.

'What would you have done in the old days?' he asked. 'If you'd been piloting a gnat with this kind of damage?'

'Flown it back to a workshop in the *Peerless* for repairs.'

'And if you couldn't use the engines until the repairs were completed?'

Tarquinia said, 'Then I'd call someone for a tow. See how a lifetime of experience has prepared me for this moment?'

They kept up the pressure for two chimes, the resin's nominal curing time. When they shut off their jetpacks and took their aching arms away, the assembly remained in place.

Ramiro looked over their handiwork. When the chamber was re-pressurised all the force would be pressing the glued surfaces together more closely, and the sloping side walls would also work in their favour, wedging the assembly ever more tightly into place. The whole

164

thing wasn't going to fall apart; the worst that could happen now was a small leak.

They cut the tent free of the wall and moved to the hatch, too tired now to speak. Outside, the sunstone trap seemed to have held on to most of the spillage. They took off their jetpacks and slipped them around the edge of the tarp to leave their bodies narrower, then followed them into the passage.

Together, they untied the tarp from the handholds while keeping the rim against the outer wall of the chamber. Then they brought the rim together and knotted it tight, leaving the spilt sunstone inside a large, closed sack. Tarquinia slammed the reset lever on the feed for the decomposing agent.

'That's the hard part done,' she said.

'What?' Ramiro was already picturing himself asleep.

She gestured towards the access shaft that ran between her cabin and the cooling chamber. The cabins had airtight doors, but there was still a gaping hole where this shaft met the outer hull.

'Smaller, no sunstone,' Tarquinia stressed. 'We'll be done in half a bell.'

When the shaft had been sealed, Ramiro checked in on Agata and Azelio while Tarquinia went to restart the ventilation system.

'He's sleeping,' Agata said. 'All the wounds look stable now.'

'That's a relief.' Ramiro squeezed her shoulder. 'Thanks for keeping your head, before.'

'What do you mean?' Agata sounded genuinely confused; she wasn't being modest.

'When you went after Tarquinia,' he said. 'I was a wreck – I didn't know what I was doing.'

'Really?' Agata buzzed. 'It's lucky I didn't notice, or it might have been contagious.'

Ramiro said, 'We'll have pressure soon. Do you want to sleep in here?'

'If that's all right.'

'Tarquinia's going to set the temperature low enough that we won't need beds, so just . . . make yourself comfortable any way you can.'

'Thank you.'

He left her, and dragged himself to the front cabin. Tarquinia was at the main console.

'Any problems?' he asked.

She swivelled around to face him. 'The cooling chamber's up to full operating pressure, and we'll be back to normal everywhere in four or five chimes.'

'Back to normal.' That sounded surreal.

Tarquinia said, 'We should rest for a few days before we try to repair the cabins.'

'At least. Agata's going to stay with Azelio.'

'Right. You take her cabin, then; I'll be on watch.'

'You need to rest, too.'

Tarquinia spread her arms, taking in the whole of the *Surveyor*: they could hardly leave it unmonitored in this delicate transitional state. 'You were up before this whole thing started,' she said. 'Sleep for four bells, then I'll come and wake you.'

Ramiro removed his helmet and strapped himself to Agata's bed, still wearing his cooling bag. He managed to doze off, but then he woke after half a bell, aware that the pressure was back in the cabin. He shut off the air to his bag and tried to sleep again, but then he realised how uncomfortable he was. He peeled the thing off and nestled into the sand, trying to erase the image of papers flying out of Azelio's cabin.

He was woken by Tarquinia's voice and her hand on his shoulder. 'Your turn for the watch,' she said.

Ramiro looked up at her in the dim light. 'I thought I'd lost you,' he said.

'But you didn't.'

He unstrapped himself and reached out to embrace her. She was still wearing her own cooling bag; he opened the fastening behind her neck and pulled it down over her shoulders and arms. When she was bare he pressed himself against her chest; an urgent pleasure affirmed the rightness of it, and then he felt their skin adhering.

He looked down and saw the light passing between them. He tried to pull free, but Tarquinia stopped him.

'You can't hurt me,' she said. 'After shedding two children, I can't fission.'

Ramiro wanted to believe her, but he was afraid that they'd reached the point where they could talk each other into anything. 'How do you know?'

166

'We're not the first people to put it to the test.'

Tarquinia eased them together onto the bed, then she brought the straps around them and pulled them tight. The sense of being confined in this state made Ramiro dizzy with joy; he closed his eyes and sank into the warmth suffusing their bodies.

He didn't care any more what the truth was: if the woman he loved had made him her co-stead, that was her choice. And if she went the way of women, he'd happily raise her children. He couldn't understand how he'd ever feared that. It was what he was meant for.

Tarquinia shook him awake a second time.

'Ramiro? It's been half a bell. Someone should be on watch.'

He shifted against the cool sand. She'd loosened the straps, but their bodies were still touching.

'What happened?'

She said, 'We exchanged light. And I'm still here.'

'It could have gone wrong.' Ramiro felt himself shivering. 'I could have killed you.' Leaving the *Surveyor* with no pilot, and four newborn children to care for. 'I must have been insane.'

Tarquinia said, 'I've known a dozen women who've survived this. Believe me, if I hadn't been sure I would have fought you off.'

Ramiro didn't doubt her, but it didn't change the fact that he hadn't been sure himself.

He found the catches on the straps and released himself from the bed, then he grabbed a rope and dragged himself away. In the end he'd let his instincts rule him; he'd become the contemptible animal he'd been warned of all his life.

Tarquinia watched him struggling into his cooling bag. 'People do this,' she said. 'We both enjoyed it, and no one got hurt. It's not some terrible crime.'

'If it's so ordinary,' he retorted, 'why don't they talk about it? Why isn't it in the biology course taught to every child?'

Tarquinia took the question seriously. 'I suppose they want men to concentrate on rearing their sister's children, instead of getting distracted chasing after women whose brothers are already doing the right thing.'

Ramiro turned to face her. '*I wanted you to fission.* While we were together, I didn't care if you lived or died.'

Tarquinia met his gaze, unperturbed. 'And I felt the same way,

Ramiro. I wanted exactly what you wanted. Our bodies don't hand out rewards to people who merely go through the motions. To steal the most pleasure from this, you have to come as close as you can to believing that it's the real thing.'

20

As the *Surveyor* drew closer to Esilio's sun, Agata willed the days to stop slipping away so quickly, robbing her of precious time to work.

It had taken her four years to reshape the foundations of field theory into a form that made sense to her: a kind of dissection of the behaviour of fundamental particles into a series of simple diagrams. When a photon moved from one place to another, the first diagram of the series showed this happening entirely uneventfully. But in the second diagram, the photon was shown giving up its energy to the luxagen field to create a pair of disturbances with positive and negative source strength, which travelled for a while before recombining into a replacement for the original photon.

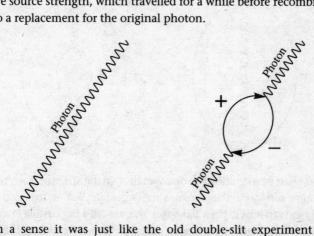

In a sense it was just like the old double-slit experiment that Yalda's teacher, Giorgio, had used to convince people that light was a wave: light couldn't be passing through one slit or the other, because the pattern of bright and dark lines it made could only be understood by adding contributions due to the light taking paths through both slits. But in Agata's version the set of 'paths' included not only a variety of routes, but all manner of transmogrifications along the way.

She had baulked at this, at first: a lone photon *couldn't* turn into a pair of luxagens – each with just a third of the photon's mass – because whatever the velocities of those luxagens, it would be impossible to satisfy the laws of conservation of energy and momentum. But she'd finally understood that each of the diagrams on its own was just a kind of fiction, expressing a narrow sliver of the true history, and any characters that came and went without being present at the start and end of each story were mere flights of fancy, subject to very different rules compared with those that endured. Every part was needed to make up the whole, but only the totality was real.

With any process the variations were endless, but the more complex the diagram the smaller its contribution, allowing the sum to remain finite. And in this scheme, the vacuum itself was simply the sum of all diagrams that started and ended with no particles at all, its energy due entirely to disturbances that came and went of their own accord, with no connection to anything persistent.

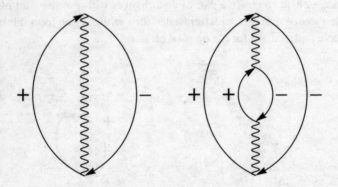

Agata had been gratified to discover that, in flat space at least, these diagrams rendered the vacuum manageable. But if the vacuum energy curved space, then flat space was actually impossible – and if curvature modified the vacuum energy, the two could only be in harmony at some elusive fixed point that remained beyond the reach of her methods.

Having come so far, she ached to complete the story. She wanted to return to the *Peerless* with everything solved: the vacuum energy tied to the curvature of space and the topology of the cosmos –

determining once and for all whether the entropy gradient that had enabled life was a stupendously improbable fluke, or simply an unavoidable consequence of a few simple principles.

When she lifted her gaze up from her desk, the prospect of the *Surveyor*'s planetfall was glorious and thrilling, the purpose of their journey finally to be fulfilled. But when she looked down at her unfinished calculations, she thought: glorious – but please, not yet.

Gathered with the rest of the crew around Tarquinia's console, Agata compared the two images on the screen. One was a grey disc faintly mottled with reds and browns, weakly but uniformly lit, grainy and poorly resolved as the photodetectors struggled at the limits of their sensitivity. The other was a disc of the same size, and two-thirds of it lay in the deepest black night, but the crescent of dayside revealed an impossibly vivid landscape of jagged grey mountains, dusty red plains and twisted brown valleys, sharp enough to touch.

Esilio by the light of the home cluster's stars, and Esilio by the light of its sun. Esilio as they'd see it with their own eyes, and Esilio through the time-reversed camera. Esilio as it had been a few chimes ago – and Esilio as it would be a few chimes in the future.

Tarquinia said, 'The good news is, the temperature looks tolerable. Hotter than we're used to, but not by much.'

Agata was surprised. 'How did you measure the temperature?'

'The density profile of the atmosphere. A hotter atmosphere will stretch up farther from the surface.'

'Is that reliable?' Agata had no problem with the general idea, but she suspected that the method would be fraught with uncertainties.

'I'm not sure,' Tarquinia confessed. 'I've never had a chance to observe a planet before.'

Ramiro said, 'If this world's come all the way around the cosmos, shouldn't it have had time to grow hotter?'

'No plants, no fires,' Azelio pointed out. 'If there's nothing making light, there's just slow geochemistry to warm it up.'

'Ah.' Ramiro turned to Agata. 'Temperature doesn't change when you swap the direction of time, does it?'

'Not as such,' Agata replied cautiously. 'Imagine reversing the motion of all the particles in a container of gas: it wouldn't make any difference.'

'But if "temperature as such" is unchanged, what about the implications?' Ramiro pressed her. 'Will heat still flow from hot to cold?'

'That depends on exactly what you're talking about.' Agata wasn't trying to be unhelpful, but the worst thing she could do was make a blanket pronouncement that ignored the subtleties of the problem. 'We ought to be able to find examples on Esilio where two lukewarm objects start out with the same temperature, but then heat flows from one to the other – making one cooler and the other hotter.'

Ramiro hummed impatiently. 'That's obvious: inasmuch as we're able to act purely as spectators, we can expect to see ordinary things happening in reverse. But when *we* touch something down there, some rock that's colder than our hands . . . ?'

Agata said, 'Why do you expect there to be a simple answer to that: a rule that will hold true in every case? We're used to predicting heat flows on the basis that entropy will increase along one direction in time — and the same principle will have held on Esilio for most of its history, for its own notion of the future. But the two arrows point in opposite directions, so each side's rule flatly contradicts the other. Those rules were never universal laws, and this is the place where we finally have to accept that.'

'But couldn't the Esilian rock pass some of its heat to us, even if it's colder?' Azelio suggested. 'Its entropy goes down, as we see it, while ours goes up. So both sides get to follow their usual rules.'

'That's not impossible,' Agata agreed. 'But we can't expect to be able to partition everything as neatly as that. While we're still far apart we can talk about the two sides and their rules . . . but deep down, matter is just matter, it doesn't come with allegiances. The real laws of physics treat all directions in time and space identically, and they're the laws that every photon and luxagen obeys — without knowing or caring about anything called entropy, let alone what side it's meant to be on in some clash of thermodynamic arrows.

'Suppose we leave a piece of equipment behind on Esilio – say, a small spyglass. Over the eons, from our point of view, we'd expect it to become pitted by dust in the wind, and eventually break up completely and turn to sand. Our spyglass, our rules: that sounds fair, doesn't it? But if that sand stays on Esilio, what origin will it have from Esilio's point of view? Most likely, some ordinary Esilian rock will have broken down to make it — which *to us*, would look like erosion running backwards. But then, in Esilian time the remnants of that rock will eventually form themselves spontaneously into a spyglass, which lies on the ground until we come along to retrieve it. So if you follow the history of the matter that makes up the spyglass far enough in both directions, it's clear that it's not committed to either side's rules.'

Ramiro said, 'That's all very fascinating, but you still haven't told me whether or not I'd burn myself by touching a cold rock.'

Tarquinia broke in. 'No one will be touching anything until we've done enough experiments to know what's safe and what isn't.'

Ramiro gave up and dragged himself away, muttering about the uselessness of theoreticians.

Azelio caught Agata's eye. 'Your story about the spyglass was unsettling,' he said, 'but I'll tell you what disturbs me more.'

'What?'

'Swap the roles of Esilio and the *Surveyor*,' he replied, 'then tell the same story again. If something from Esilio takes the place of the spyglass, it must be with us already. We must have been carrying it, or the things that will become it, from the very start. Because according to Esilio's arrow of time we've already visited the planet, and it's almost certain that something remained with us when we departed.'

'The black sun awaits your pleasure,' Tarquinia announced from the doorway.

Agata looked up, startled. 'Already?'

'It's now, or wait until we're on our way back.'

'Of course.' Agata hesitated. 'The telescope's mine, until we switch orbits?'

'Absolutely,' Tarquinia replied. 'But if you break it, you can grind a new lens.'

'From what?'

'The other part of your punishment will be hunting down suitable materials on Esilio.'

Agata could have done everything from her room, but that seemed selfish: the experiment belonged to all of them, and she wanted every member of the crew to feel free to look over her shoulder as she worked. So she dragged herself into the front cabin and strapped herself to her couch there.

Tarquinia had trained her to use the telescope's software, but Agata still felt an illicit thrill when she invoked it from her own console and began passing it instructions through her corset. Since they'd shut off the engines the *Surveyor* had been sweeping in towards Esilio's sun along a hyperbola, with the home cluster's stars behind them. But as they swung around the sun in order to help them match velocities with Esilio she'd finally have a chance to juxtapose the two kinds of stars, with the dark mass in the foreground perfectly suited to its role.

Agata used the navigation system to map out the expected path of the black disc against an ordinary-light image of the sky. Then she chose two dozen points on various star trails that were destined to pass behind the sun, and measured their current positions with as much precision as the instruments allowed. The idea that gravity might distort the appearance of these trails wasn't all that shocking – if it could bend the path of a planet into an ellipse, why wouldn't it be able to nudge a beam of light? What was astonishing was the prospect of being able to distinguish between a force tugging on the light and curving its trajectory, and the light merely following the straightest possible history through a space that was itself curved.

Azelio harnessed himself to the couch beside her. 'How do you know you won't just be measuring an optical effect from the sun's atmosphere?' he challenged her.

'I'll need to include that in the final calculations,' Agata conceded. 'But there ought to be a point where the gravitational effects are showing up clearly, while the light's still travelling far above the densest part of the atmosphere.'

'Really? You've always talked about starlight "grazing the disc," ' Azelio protested.

'I have, haven't I?' She'd been trying to stress that the lack of glare from the time-reversed sun would allow her to follow the stars right up to the moment they disappeared behind it. 'But there's nothing special about the light passing just above the surface – the effect doesn't suddenly increase there. It's the distance from the *centre* of the sun that counts, not the distance from its surface.'

Azelio inclined his head, accepting her answer. But he remained sceptical. 'And this measurement is going to tell you the shape of the cosmos?'

'No – it's necessary for that, but not sufficient. If I end up disproving Lila's theory, then I won't have much hope of working out the shape of anything. All my calculations linking energy to curvature depend on Lila being right.'

Azelio was confused. 'Why couldn't you adapt your work to Vittorio's theory?'

Agata said, 'If the results agree with Vittorio's theory then I'll have no choice but to accept that as a fact – but I'd have no idea how to integrate it into modern physics. Lila's theory makes gravity consistent with the notion that everything should work the same way when we rotate our picture of it in four-space. If gravity doesn't respect that, it would be the most shocking discovery since Yalda came down from Mount Peerless.'

'Then you should hope for that shock,' Azelio joked. 'You'd be as famous as Yalda.'

'And I'd have to throw out half a lifetime's work and start again.'

'Isn't that the price of every scientific revolution?'

'*Lila's theory* is the revolution!' Agata countered. 'It's just been a quieter one than Yalda's or Carla's, because it's been so hard to test. What the revolution will throw out isn't my work, it's Vittorio's – and he didn't live long enough to know or care that his beautiful ideas weren't perfect.'

'I won't believe that space is curved until I've seen it with my own eyes,' Azelio avowed. He wasn't usually so invested in any of Agata's purely theoretical claims, but he seemed to have found this impending empirical affront to his intuition too much to accept without protest.

Agata gestured at the screen. 'You'll see something, soon enough.'

'No, all that will show us is that the light is bent. Which Vittorio's theory predicts as well.'

Agata buzzed at his stubbornness. 'Bent by a different amount – and for some colours, *in the opposite direction!*'

Azelio said, 'Honestly, don't you think you're trying to conclude too much from such slender evidence? Even if the bending is exactly what you predicted, couldn't there be another explanation for it? Maybe the requirement for gravity to fit in with rotational physics implies certain angles of deflection for the light. But that could come from a tiny modification to Vittorio's force law, couldn't it? We've always known that gravity bends the paths of moving objects. Why not just refine that notion – instead of leaping to the conclusion that it's actually bending *space*?'

Agata didn't know how to answer him. From the point of view of everyday experience, it probably did sound grandiose to make so much of such a small effect.

She thought for a while. 'I'll tell you why I'm going to believe that space is curved, unless I find overwhelming evidence to the contrary.'

'Go ahead.' Azelio was probably unswayable, but he was still interested in understanding her position.

'If motion under gravity is due to curvature, rather than a force, it will obey an incredibly simple rule: the history of any object in free fall is just the shortest available path through four-space. In flat space, that's a straight line. In the curved space around a star, it's not.'

'That's simple in itself,' Azelio allowed. 'At the cost of making the geometry more complicated.'

'But it's more than just simple!' Agata insisted. 'It also fits perfectly with everything else we know about motion.'

'In what way?'

'When light moves from place to place,' she said, 'you need to add up contributions from different paths between its starting point and its destination. Paths where it spends about the same time travelling all add together, because the waves will have stayed more or less in step, with their peaks arriving simultaneously. Paths where the travel time varies rapidly mix up peaks and troughs, so they cancel each other out.

'Imagine a kind of mathematical valley that stretches across the landscape of all paths, where the length of each path determines the height of the landscape. The shortest path becomes the lowest point: the bottom of the valley. If you change the path there slightly, you barely change its length, because the bottom of a valley is horizontal. But if you're far up on the side of the valley instead, the path isn't just longer, it's at a point where the valley slopes much more, so any change would change the length more – making the waves slip out of phase.'

Agata sketched an example on her chest, and had the corset display it on her console.

Azelio frowned, but then he remembered something. 'We used that principle in our optics class: you can find the law of reflection by looking for the angle that light makes with a mirror that lets it arrive all in phase.'

'Right! So now apply the same logic to starlight moving past Esilio's

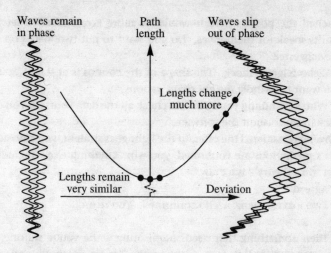

Waves remain in phase

Path length

Waves slip out of phase

Lengths change much more

Lengths remain very similar

Deviation

sun. Suppose the light does bend. If four-space is flat, then the light *won't* be following the shortest path, since in flat space that's always a straight line. It will be on a path up on the valley's slopes, where any tiny variation changes the length and throws the light out of phase. There are ways around that: we can postulate some mechanism that messes with the phase in exactly the right manner to favour the bent path – but that's complicated, because as well as explaining what happens with the light, it needs to explain the force on an orbiting planet.

'If four-space is curved, though, that does the job for everything. Light waves and luxagen waves, it makes no difference: if they're following the shortest path in four-space, they'll arrive in phase. That's enough to bend the beam, and enough to make a planet swing around in its orbit.'

Azelio pondered this, and found nothing he could object to. 'It makes more sense than I thought,' he admitted.

Agata was delighted. 'So what's your conclusion?'

'My own prediction, now,' he declared, 'is that the light won't bend at all. I can see why you think it would make things too complicated if you had to account for the bent paths of both light and matter, in flat space. So the simplest solution would be to keep space flat, but have light unaffected by gravity.'

Agata was on the verge of embarking on an account of how this would violate conservation of energy, but she stopped herself; she'd reached the point where it would be more economical to let the results speak for themselves. 'Do you want to put two loaves on it?' she suggested.

Azelio feigned shock. 'The shape of the cosmos is at stake . . . and you want to swindle me out of my rations?'

'Who's swindling you? You can check all the data yourself. You can ask Ramiro to audit the software.'

Azelio considered the offer. 'If the light goes straight, you pay me; if Lila's predictions are confirmed, you win. Anything else – including Vittorio's theory – is a draw.'

'Agreed.'

'Two loaves, then,' Azelio confirmed. 'You're on.'

'Is there something that needs monitoring while you're waiting for the stars to align?' Ramiro asked Agata. 'I'm on watch all night – it wouldn't be any trouble.'

'There's nothing like that,' she replied.

'Then why not get some rest?'

Agata looked up from her console. 'I can't just shut off my mind in the middle of this.'

Ramiro stretched his shoulders and swivelled around to face her. 'The star trails will still be there when you wake. And we'll be following the same orbit whether you're sitting here fretting, or fast asleep in bed.'

'That's true.'

'But . . . ?'

Agata said, 'Why would I wait six years for the chance to do this, and then sleep through half of it?'

Ramiro buzzed. 'Fair enough.'

'I used to hold vigils outside the voting halls,' Agata recalled. 'I'd watch the people come and go, watch the tallies rising.'

He said, 'So when you take something seriously, you try to make the most of it?'

'Yes. Is that so strange?' Agata tried to judge his mood, and decided to take a chance. 'Isn't that what you and Tarquinia are doing? Making the most of your friendship?' Ever since Azelio had confided his own suspicions about the pair's activities to her, Agata had suffered bouts of curiosity, but she'd never had the courage to ask the participants themselves about the experience.

Ramiro didn't seem angered by the question, or embarrassed. 'In a way,' he said. 'If I was back on the mountain, I'd be worried that I was doing the opposite: taking the drive to raise children and wasting it on something trivial. Here, I can tell myself that I have no chance of becoming a father, so it's not a waste at all.'

Agata said, 'Everyone but the Starvers accepts that it makes sense to have children without fission – so why not refine the process even further and select precisely the effects we want from it?'

'Why not?' Ramiro agreed. 'As an abstract proposition, it sounds as sensible as separating out the parts of a plant instead of blindly eating the whole thing. We don't have to swallow the poisonous roots when it's the stem that actually tastes good.'

'But why as an abstract proposition?' Agata pressed him.

Ramiro hesitated. 'The trouble is, even when the body can't put things back together, it never forgets how they used to be joined.'

'What do you mean?'

'It makes me want children more than ever,' he said. 'It takes that ache that might have faded with time, and reminds me, over and over again, that it's never going to be fulfilled.'

While they were in free fall the *Surveyor* could be oriented any way they liked, and Tarquinia had chosen to set the window facing the rim of the hemisphere of home-cluster star trails. As Agata's vigil stretched on, she left Ramiro in peace, ignored the clock on her console, and just stared out through the window, waiting for the first sign that something solid and invisible had moved between her and the ordinary stars.

Despite the lights of the cabin, after a few lapses her eyes began picking out a faint grey disc against the deeper blackness of the dark hemisphere. Esilio's sun scattered ordinary starlight, so she could have checked its progress through the telescope without even switching to the time-reversed camera, but she was content to let the image remain elusive, coming and going as her concentration faltered, or as Ramiro shifted in his harness and drew her focus back to the reflected interior.

When a bite appeared in the rim of the bowl, all ambiguity vanished from the scene. Agata felt a tingling of excitement, and beneath it a churning sense of disruption. When the *Surveyor* had altered its velocity the star trails themselves had stretched and shrunk, but she'd seen the same predictable deformation when the *Peerless* turned around, and in the end it amounted to little more than holding up a distorting mirror to the sky. This was different: before her eyes, an orthogonal star was leaving its hemisphere and crossing the border, obscuring the ancestors' stars behind it.

The occulted region grew larger, slowly revealing with clarity and precision the shape she'd squinted and guessed at. Agata savoured the delay still to come: she'd chosen reference points on the star trails well clear of the clutter of the rim, so it would be a bell or so before she could start making measurements.

Ramiro said, 'I wonder what the settlers will call it: that day of the year when the sun starts its passage across the stars.'

Azelio and Tarquinia joined them, and the four of them ate breakfast together as they watched the black disc become whole. Then Agata turned to her console and summoned up the image through the telescope.

She guided the software as it tracked the celestial markers she'd chosen. Some were transitions in the perceptually defined hue of a single star trail: the point where orange turned to red, easy to find by eye though there was no discontinuity in the light's actual wavelength. Others were points where two trails crossed, and were not so much fixed beacons as sites where she expected some complicated but illuminating slippage. The colours of the two trails were never the same where they met, so two beams that were initially travelling side-by-side would be bent by different amounts depending on their speed, leaving a slightly different pair of hues to meet up in their place.

Agata didn't expect any telltale distortion to leap out at her from the screen; the changes would be measured in arc-flickers. All she could do was check that the software had latched on to the correct features, and watch closely to ensure that nothing went awry as the black disc encroached on the field of view.

She did not take her eyes from the telescope's feed until the last of the markers had vanished behind the sun. Then she summoned the analysis: a plot of measurements compared to predictions.

'Azelio?' she called.

'Yes?'

'Prepare to skip lunch; I'll be eating for both of us.'

Azelio dragged himself over to take a look at the results, soon followed by Ramiro and Tarquinia. The measurements with their spread of errors wove a course that hewed closely to Lila's predictions – and ruled out Vittorio's theory entirely.

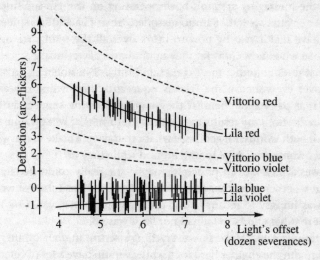

'Space is curved!' Tarquinia exclaimed delightedly. She'd taken no prior position on Lila's theory, but the sheer strangeness of the notion seemed to please her now that it could finally be justified.

'Very slightly,' Azelio conceded. 'It's barely measurable.'

'This might seem like a tiny, obscure effect now,' Tarquinia replied, 'but I guarantee that in a couple of generations, every astronomer will be making use of it somehow.'

Ramiro squeezed Agata's shoulder. 'Congratulations.'

She said, 'It was Lila's prediction, not mine.'

'And yet I don't see Lila here making the measurements.'

'When I told her I was going to be doing this,' Agata recalled, 'she said: "If the results aren't what my equations dictate, all we can do is pity the poor cosmos – because true or not, the theory will be the more beautiful of the two by far."'

'So you've proved that the cosmos is beautiful,' Azelio concluded. 'But you still can't tell us its shape.'

'The beauty is that it's comprehensible,' Agata declared. 'Even if its shape is unknown.'

'Unknown to you,' Ramiro said provocatively.

'Yes.' Agata frowned. 'But why the distinction? Have you been working with Lila's equations yourself, on all those long watches?'

'Ha! I wish I were that smart.'

'Then who . . . ?'

'If the messaging system's been operating on the *Peerless* since a year or so after we left,' Ramiro reasoned, 'then Lila and her students will have had a year by now to think over all the results we bring back. So who knows how far they might have taken things?'

'That doesn't bother me,' Agata said firmly. 'I've stolen an advantage over everyone on the *Peerless*, squeezing three years into each year that passed for them. If they end up deriving some beautiful corollaries from my results by the time I return, that will give me the best of both worlds: I'll get to see what other people make of my work – and I won't even have to wait around while they do it.'

It was a nice idea in principle; maybe she really could live up to it. But whether or not her competitors had already had the last word, she was hungry to return to her calculations, reinvigorated by this proof that her efforts so far had not been wasted.

Tarquinia said, 'Make sure everything's secure in your cabins. I'll need to run the engines hard for a while; we still have a lot of velocity to shed before we can go into orbit around the planet.'

Agata said, 'Right.' The shape of the cosmos would have to wait; there was still the small matter of Esilio.

21

While Azelio and Tarquinia debated the merits of different landing sites, Ramiro clung to a rope beside the window and gazed down at the starlit world below. How could he understand Esilio? Of all the sciences he'd studied as a child, geology had been the least developed – and at the time, he'd imagined, the least likely ever to be of use to him. Of the little that he remembered, he remained unsure what he should trust. The ancestors had had no idea what a rock was actually made of, while their successors, with all their superior knowledge, had never set eyes on a planet.

'We need to be within walking distance of four or five different kinds of soil, or what will the crop tests be worth?' Azelio said heatedly.

'I appreciate that,' Tarquinia replied. 'But if we don't come down on flat, stable ground, we could damage the *Surveyor* irreparably.'

Over the eons, Ramiro had been taught, every kind of rock exuded traces of gas, and for a body with sufficient gravity this gas would accumulate into an atmosphere. If the body also happened to orbit a star, winds driven by the temperature difference between day and night eroded the rock, and once there was airborne dust and sand that accelerated the process. The routes of the dust-flows carved out valleys and mountains, shaped as well by the differing durability of the underlying rock. But where had those various minerals come from? As far as he recalled, no one even knew for sure whether they dated all the way back to the entropy minimum, had formed over cosmic time from the sedate decay of some primordial substance, or had been forged in the core of a giant ur-world where liquid fires – contained for a while by its unimaginable gravity – thrashed and churned until the whole thing finally split apart and scattered.

Tarquinia brought an image of the next candidate onto her

console, taken in full sunlight with the time-reversed camera. Ramiro struggled to interpret it, but the combination of near-smoothness and suspiciously delicate ridges suggested a plain of wind-ruffled dust into which the *Surveyor* might sink and vanish.

'Can't we just settle for the safest-looking ground?' he proposed. 'If it turns out that there's a problem with the soil, we can always ascend and come down somewhere else.'

Azelio turned to stare at him angrily. 'I'm not spending years hopping from site to site! That's not what we agreed to!'

'All right. Forget it.' Ramiro regretted speaking so carelessly; Azelio had his niece and nephew to think of.

Tarquinia summoned another image. 'Why do we only have two probes?' she fretted. They could send one down in advance of the *Surveyor*, and the second if their first choice proved unsuitable, but that was the limit: the probes weren't sophisticated enough to explore more than one location each.

'Perhaps we could extend the survey for a few more days,' Ramiro suggested. The planet was turning beneath them as they circled from pole to pole; each successive orbit carried them over a different meridian, and though they'd sampled a wide variety of terrain they were still far short of seeing everything. 'There has to be a perfect site down there.'

'Exactly!' Azelio replied. He gestured at the console. 'None of these are acceptable.'

'We can keep looking,' Tarquinia agreed. 'A few more days is nothing.'

Azelio excused himself to check on the plants. Weightlessness wasn't good for them, but it wasn't worth setting up the tether again – not unless the selection process was going to stretch out into stints, rather than days.

Tarquinia switched to the live feed from the time-reversed camera: dawn was breaking over a red plain criss-crossed by brown fissures.

'Look at all that land!' Ramiro marvelled. If every field of wheat in the *Peerless* were laid out here side by side, they would pass by in a flicker, lost in the vastness. The sagas were full of journeys on foot that had crossed ancient empires and lasted for years, but nothing he'd read or imagined had prepared him for the scale of the world below. 'How could the first travellers ever give up so much freedom?'

'I think the Hurtlers might have helped,' Tarquinia suggested.

'Yes, but I still wouldn't have been able to do it. We never belonged cooped up in a mountain; it's a wonder we didn't all lose our minds generations ago.'

'So you're set on making this your home?' Tarquinia asked. 'Esilio's won you over already?'

Ramiro buzzed softly. 'Esilio's one thing, but twelve more years of travelling will probably finish me off.' He would have relished defying Greta and staying behind when the *Surveyor* departed – and it would not have undermined the purpose of the mission if the rest of the crew returned to the *Peerless* with the news that a colony had already been established. But he couldn't do it alone.

Tarquinia said, 'And wide-open spaces are one thing, but you can't eat dirt. Before you start picturing the flowers on your grave, let's see if anything can take root here at all.'

The probe parted from the *Surveyor*, separated by a burst of air before it fired its engines to start the descent from orbit. Ramiro peered over Tarquinia's shoulder to watch the instrumentation feed. Azelio looked on from Tarquinia's right, and even Agata had left her calculations for a while to cling to the rope beside him.

As the probe slowed to let gravity bring it down, it didn't take long to fall back behind the *Surveyor*'s horizon, cutting the link. 'Do you want to sleep for the next few chimes?' Agata teased Ramiro. 'I promise to wake you when all the results are in.'

'No thanks.' Ramiro asked Tarquinia to replay the recorded data; something unsettling had caught his eye. 'Look at how hot it was, just before we lost contact!'

Azelio said, 'We were expecting some frictional heating, weren't we?'

'Not so soon. Not at that altitude.'

Tarquinia frowned. 'We're not suffering any unexplained drag ourselves, so I don't see how we could have the density profile that wrong.'

Ramiro didn't want to argue about the cause; the fact remained that the heating was unexpected. 'If this thing burns up out of sight, we're never going to know what happened – or what we need to change when we try again. If we make the wrong guess we could lose the second probe the same way.'

Tarquinia contemplated this gloomy scenario. 'Then we'd better move quickly,' she said.

Ramiro was already strapped to his couch, but Agata and Azelio had to clamber into place as the *Surveyor* tilted then ascended rapidly. The cabin window faced the stars, but on the navigation console the land could be seen falling away as Tarquinia widened their horizon to re-establish a line of sight to the probe.

When the link was restored she cut the engines, letting them continue the upwards arc from momentum alone. Ramiro was dizzy after the unaccustomed weight, but when his head cleared he focused on the data feed. The probe's temperature was still high, but it was less than before.

'It must have been a false reading,' he decided.

The image feed was growing shaky, as if the probe was being buffeted by high winds. Greta had only provided the expedition with a single time-reversed camera, and the probe's sunless view of the landscape below was almost impossible to read. The temperature was dropping steadily now. Maybe there was something going on with the cooling air: a valve had jammed when the flow had been needed to dispose of the engine's heat, but now it had simply snapped open and was overcompensating.

As the juddering machine rushed towards the surface, Ramiro felt equal parts fear and exultation. In the history of the *Peerless*, no one had ever performed a manoeuvre that deserved to be described as a landing. But if this small, robust scout couldn't survive the process, what chance would there be for the *Surveyor*?

The image turned black. Tarquinia said, 'Side camera might be more informative now.' She sent an instruction from her corset, and the feed changed to a slanted view of an expanse of sandy ground. In the middle distance a few small grey rocks broke the flatness.

'It's down! It's safe!' Azelio chirped ecstatically, then turned to the instrument feed. 'And the temperature's fine. It's already close to Tarquinia's estimate for the surface.'

Agata said, 'In Esilio's terms, it's been there for days. What other temperature should it be?'

Ramiro struggled to accept this. On one level he understood her reasoning perfectly: according to Esilio's arrow of time, the probe was *about to ascend*, with any frictional heating yet to come. And if this was the correct perspective, the high temperature they'd seen when it was still above the atmosphere was due to its earlier heating during its ascent.

'How was it ever cool, up here?' he asked. 'Before we launched it? Or in Esilio's terms: what cooled it after it emerged from the atmosphere?'

'Any answer to that will sound strange from either perspective,' Agata replied. 'I suppose it must have happened through interactions with the cooling air – but then, from Esilio's point of view that air was rushing in from the void and striking the probe in just the right way needed to cool it, while on our terms the probe was releasing cooling air but heating up in the process.'

Ramiro clutched his skull. 'Why, though?'

'What's the alternative?' Agata replied. 'Retaining all the heat from this ascent for the next six years, while it was sitting in its bay in contact with the *Surveyor*?'

'That would have been absurd,' Ramiro conceded. 'But the fact that it heated up at all before it hit the atmosphere is absurd, too.'

'Less so,' Agata insisted. 'And "absurd" is the wrong description. If I handed you two identical-looking slabs of stone at room temperature – one of which had been heated for a while in a fire the day before – would you expect to be able to tell me which was which?'

'Of course not.'

'Now look at the same situation in reverse. Your failure to guess the stones' history becomes a failure to predict their future – but the one that would become unexpectedly hot well before it was actually in the fire would not have been doing anything absurd.'

Ramiro couldn't argue with that. 'So I should be grateful on those rare occasions when things make perfect sense from a single perspective, whether it's ours or Esilio's. But when that doesn't work . . . what are we left with?'

Agata said, 'Why should we expect a system as complex as a slab of stone to be predictable, when we don't know the detailed motion of all its constituent particles? We're used to making predictions based on nothing but a single number, like temperature or pressure, but the ability to do that depends entirely on our relationship with the entropy minimum.'

'So we'll be helpless down there,' Ramiro concluded glumly. 'Anything could happen.'

'No! Not *anything*.'

'What can we rely on, then?' Azelio asked.

'Nothing should happen that's unreasonably improbable,' Agata declared.

Azelio buzzed. 'What makes something *reasonably* improbable?'

'Cosmology.'

'I might need a little more guidance than that,' Azelio pleaded.

Agata thought for a while. 'If you took a cubic stride of air at a certain temperature and pressure,' she said, 'and chose the direction of all its particles at random, then in the vast majority of cases the entropy of that system would increase if you followed it *either* forwards or backwards in time.'

She sketched an example.

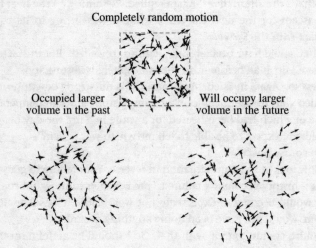

Completely random motion

Occupied larger volume in the past

Will occupy larger volume in the future

'But the air we actually deal with every day might well have been released into that large container from a smaller one, which immediately tells us that it's in an improbable state: one that would shrink of its own accord into a smaller volume if you followed it backwards in time.

'Most cubic strides of gas – in a time-blind, mathematical sense of "most" – do *not* have that property! But the entropy minimum in our past makes it entirely reasonable that we encounter air in that state. The cosmos isn't full of particles moving purely at random, or there wouldn't be an entropy minimum at all.

'But the entropy minimum is in our future as well as our past – and

Air released from smaller container

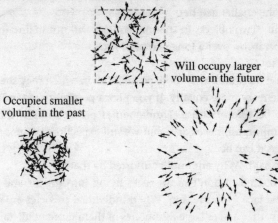

Occupied smaller
volume in the past

Will occupy larger
volume in the future

Esilio connects us to it in a way we're not accustomed to. So we're now in a situation where we might encounter a cubic stride of air that not only occupied a smaller volume in the past, but *will* occupy a smaller volume in the future.'

Midway between constraints
of entropy minimum

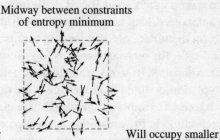

Occupied smaller
volume in the past

Will occupy smaller
volume in the future

'As a fraction of all the ways the particles could be moving, that's even more improbable than before – but given where we are and the facts of cosmology, it's not unreasonable.'

Ramiro accepted Agata's logic, but it was difficult to see what it offered them in practice. 'Tell us one thing that you're sure *won't* happen,' he challenged her.

She said, 'Two objects in thermal contact will not maintain different temperatures over a long period of time.'

'Because . . . ?'

'Because there are vastly more possibilities in which they share their thermal energy more equally. If you pick a possibility at random, it's likely to be one of those. Fundamental physics might make the entropy minimum necessary – but we still expect the cosmos to be as random as it can be.'

Ramiro said, 'Why am I not comforted by that?'

Agata buzzed. 'I don't mean rocks flying into the air and hitting you in the face for no reason. When individual particles are moving randomly, that makes large assemblies of them more predictable, not less. Most of the time, air will just be air, stone will just be stone, acting the way our instincts expect.'

'And the rest of the time?'

Agata said, 'We'll just have to be prepared for the exceptions.'

Ramiro was on watch, so he stayed in the front cabin monitoring the probe's data feed long after everyone else had gone to bed. Sitting meekly on the surface of Esilio sending back images of the surrounding landscape, the probe encountered no conspiracies of air, or rock, or heat to impair it. Its temperature remained stable – despite the heat that its photonics would be generating in the normal course of things – which seemed to imply that it was exchanging thermal energy with its surroundings in the usual way. Agata appeared to have been right about that much: the earlier, unanticipated heating had taken place for a perfectly good reason, and there was no risk of it happening again while the probe was motionless on the ground.

Tarquinia had put the *Surveyor* into a new orbit, so high that it matched Esilio's rotational period, keeping the probe permanently in their line of sight and allowing the link to remain open. Through the window, the planet itself had shrunk to an enigmatic grey disc, but as Ramiro swept the distant cameras back and forth across the starlit plain, the new world appeared as innocent and tranquil as he could have hoped it to be.

*

'I'm happy with the site,' Azelio announced. 'The probe can't verify every detail, but nothing it's shown us makes me think we were wrong about the geology of the area.'

Tarquinia turned to Agata. 'Any problems?'

'No,' she replied. 'If we're careful, I think we can do this safely.'

'Ramiro?'

Ramiro had no objection to the site, but they could at least try to deal with the one unsettling phenomenon they'd already witnessed. 'What if we lower ourselves through the atmosphere more slowly than the probe?' he proposed. 'That should keep frictional heating to a minimum, whether you look at it as an ascent or a descent.'

'It would mean more heat from the engines,' Tarquinia pointed out.

'We've had no problem with that for a year at a time,' he replied. 'I know: venting cooling air into Esilio's atmosphere might not be the same as doing it in the void. But wouldn't it be the most cautious approach: moving slowly, trying to keep our temperature constant?'

Tarquinia looked to Agata.

Agata said, 'I think Ramiro's instincts are sound. The closer we can stay to thermal equilibrium, the more predictable things should be.'

'All right then. A slow descent it is.'

Tarquinia turned to her console and began plotting their course down from orbit.

In the sunlit view through the time-reversed camera, Ramiro could see the broken ring of hills directly beneath the *Surveyor*, their eroded peaks casting long shadows to the east. Azelio had been ecstatic when he'd found this site, with the strange confluence of ancient dust flows that its peculiar topography had allowed. Ramiro didn't pretend to understand the details, but over time the central valley appeared to have trapped wind-borne detritus from at least four different sources. From on high, the variety in the soils was impossible to miss, with great splotches of competing hues laid over each other like a mess of dyes spilt from a child's paintbox. But though the colours were layered they remained distinct, which suggested that the whole arrangement was stable. The *Surveyor* was a great deal heavier than the probe, but if these deposits were prone to subsidence they ought to have shown more mixing under their own weight.

The temperature in the cabin had barely changed since they'd entered the planet's atmosphere. Ramiro didn't want to grow complacent; no one would forget the near-fatal surprise that the Object had held for its first visitors. But if a mismatch in Nereo's arrow was a guarantee of mutual annihilation, the arrows of time were more pliable. On this world of lifeless dust with its almost timeless landscape, it did not seem too much to hope for that two opposing directions could coexist.

'There's the probe!' Agata announced excitedly, pointing to a dark elliptical splotch. It was hard to distinguish the thing itself from its shadow.

The *Surveyor* was descending at a constant rate, leaving the cabin subject to Esilio's full gravity – about a third higher than the home world's. That standard was usually taken as the limit for prolonged acceleration, on the assumption that the ancestors' physiology had adapted to it over the eons. But the travellers had coped easily enough with far lower gravity than the ancestral norm, and Ramiro did not believe that the settlers would be troubled by this minor increase.

Azelio said, 'I can hear the wind.'

Ramiro strained his tympanum. It was hard to distinguish it from the sound of the cooling system, but the gusts were sharper, rising and falling less predictably.

The altitude displayed on the navigation console dropped below one saunter. As Ramiro watched the wind whipping dust across the ground, he began to discern an almost perfect dark circle with a wide penumbral ring, straight below the camera. He would have sworn it was the *Surveyor*'s shadow, but that made no sense: the sun wasn't overhead.

A warning appeared below the image: the ultraviolet glare scattered back from the ground was approaching unacceptable levels. Even though the engines' beams were splayed out to the side – and the camera was counting photons emitted, not received – too much irradiation could damage the sensor. Tarquinia closed the protective shutter and the image turned black.

The altimeter kept working, timing slow infrared pulses that were making it down and back through the dust. Half a dozen strides above the ground, Tarquinia cut the main engines and switched on the air jets to cushion their fall. Ramiro had barely registered the plummeting sensation before the impact drove him hard into his couch. The jolt left him shaken, but when he moved slightly in his harness he felt no pain.

Tarquinia swept her rear gaze across the cabin. 'Anyone hurt?'

'I'm fine,' Agata replied, and Ramiro and Azelio echoed her.

The view through the window was so dark that the pane might as well have been a mirror, reflecting back the lights of the cabin. Tarquinia redirected the time-reversed camera to a side-mounted lens; the image showed red dust swirling over the ground, darkening the sky and blotting out the horizon. The sight dragged Ramiro's attention back to the sound of the wind on the hull; he could hear the difference as the visible signs of each gust rose and fell.

'Is this just . . . weather?' he wondered. 'Like the home world?' He'd read about dust storms in the sagas, but it was hard to know which parts of those stories were real.

Agata said, 'I read a memoir by one of the first travellers, a woman named Fatima. She described the dust blowing around at the site of a rocket test, jamming all the clockwork.'

'But it shouldn't be harmful to people, should it?' Ramiro had no idea how fast the wind would need to be blowing before the dust would start abrading skin.

Tarquinia swivelled her couch around. 'I don't expect so, but no one is going out for at least two bells. I want to be certain that the ground isn't hot – and I don't care whether or not Esilio thinks we're yet to use the engines.'

Ramiro turned beseechingly to Agata, but she said, 'Good policy. In Esilio's terms, the engines' exhaust came from the environment and entered the rebounders, so that's violating the local arrow already. We should treat all these non-equilibrium situations as uncertain, and only assume that temperatures will be uniform when everything is settled.'

They passed the time checking the *Surveyor* for damage, but even the weakest points on the hull – their repairs along the Hurtler gash – seemed to have survived the landing intact. When Tarquinia ran out of things they could inspect – short of taking the engines apart and putting the rebounders under a microscope – they brought out some loaves for a celebratory meal, and Azelio took photographs to show his niece and nephew.

Two bells after they'd touched down, the instruments showed the hull's external temperature to be no different from the cabin's. No one challenged Ramiro when he finally moved towards the airlock.

He closed the inner door, then hesitated, gathering his courage. There was no need to use the pump – Tarquinia had already raised the cabin pressure to match the external atmosphere. He was wearing his helmet and cooling bag for protection from the dust; he switched on the coherer in his helmet, dazzling himself for a moment until he adjusted the brightness.

There was fine red dust covering the grey hardstone walls of the airlock. He hadn't noticed it by the dimmer illumination of the safety light. He ran a gloved finger along the seal of the outer door, trying to find the point where it had been breached, but if there was a hole it wasn't apparent.

It hardly mattered now; however the dust had entered, he was about to let in a great deal more. But as he began to turn the crank, the realisation hit him: it hadn't come from outside. They must have brought it with them all the way from the *Peerless*, scattered invisibly throughout the craft, with a little more accumulating inside the airlock each time the inner door was opened. Or in Esilio's terms: the *Surveyor*'s visit had just ended, and this residue was something they would soon take away with them.

Ramiro shivered, disoriented for a moment, but whether or not this account was correct there was nothing to be done about it. A small, stubborn part of him longed to leave the door closed and . . . what? Never open it at all, just to see if he could spite this unsurprising message from the future which claimed that, actually, he would? Every time they'd used the time-reversed camera, subtler but even stranger things had happened, as thermal fluctuations in the sensor conspired to create the orderly pattern of photons that the device needed to emit. Every image the camera had shown them had been encoded all along in the not-quite-random vibrations of various objects throughout the *Surveyor*, waiting to come together at just the right moment.

He leant against the crank and broke the door's seal; a gust of wind forced its way through the narrow gap. Dust flew into the airlock, dust flew out, erasing all distinctions between that which they'd brought and the rest. He slid the door fully open, letting the light from his helmet carve a tunnel through the storm. Amidst the chaos, sheets of darkness fluttered, where the dust piled together in mid-air for a moment before scattering again. Cautiously, Ramiro poked his head and shoulders through the portal. He felt the warm wind insinuate itself beneath the fabric of his cooling bag, but it seemed that nothing it carried was small enough, or sharp enough, to reach his skin.

He swept the beam of the coherer across the ground; the wind was raising so much dust that it was impossible to make out the surface below, but given that the *Surveyor* wasn't sinking its immediate surroundings were unlikely to prove treacherous. He slid the short boarding ladder out from the airlock; its feet vanished before it touched the ground, but a scant or two further down it encountered firm resistance.

He clambered down the ladder and stood on the surface. Even with the cooling bag encasing his feet there was an unpleasant grittiness against his soles; he took a few steps to see if he'd grow accustomed to the texture, but it remained distracting so he hardened and desensitised the skin. The wind wasn't strong enough to knock him down, but he couldn't move confidently without pausing each time it rose up, to recalibrate his efforts to compensate for the force.

'Ramiro?' Tarquinia's voice came through the link in his helmet.

'I'm fine!' he replied, shouting to be heard above the dust scraping across the surface of his helmet. He closed the outer door of the airlock, then walked around to the window and raised a hand; his crew-mates raised theirs to shield their eyes from his coherer. 'Sorry.' He swivelled the beam upwards, out of their lines of sight. 'The wind's annoying, and I can't see much. But I don't think I've started speaking backwards or ageing in reverse.'

Agata said, 'I'm coming out.'

Ramiro made a quick circuit around the *Surveyor*; he couldn't see any damage on the outside of the hull. Agata emerged, stepping gingerly across the swirling sand.

'So this is what a planet's like,' she said numbly.

'It's not exactly welcoming,' Ramiro conceded. 'But it should be more appealing once the weather improves.' He glanced up at the stars; he could just make out the arc of the rim, its usual dazzle reduced to a pale broken line. Though the wind and the dust were the most intrusive novelties, even the more familiar elements of their surroundings were juxtaposed so bizarrely that they lost their usual meaning: on the slopes of the *Peerless* strong gravity and an open sky always lay in the same direction. He wondered if he'd ever be able to sleep out here, or if he'd panic and imagine that he was falling into the stars.

'Whenever I pictured the reunion, I always thought of people meeting in a corridor,' Agata confessed. 'But it will probably be outdoors – in the countryside, where the vehicles can land safely. It might even look like this.'

'We'll recreate the centre of Zeugma for you later,' Ramiro teased her. 'To give you some better imagery for the ceremonies in the town square.'

Azelio joined them. 'I'd be happy with some gardens to break the gloom,' he said.

'Be my guest.' Ramiro gestured into the darkness.

'Once the wind dies down.' Azelio turned and swung the light from his helmet across the ground, but the exploratory oval faded into obscurity at a dozen strides.

Tarquinia stepped off the ladder. 'Given what we saw from orbit, these conditions shouldn't last long. It's coming to evening; we should get some sleep and start work in the morning, so we'll be able to use the view by sunlight if we need it.'

'Real days and nights!' Agata chirped. 'It's just a shame we couldn't put a time-reversed camera in every helmet.' She turned to Ramiro. 'So will your settlers bring a few gross of the things, or just one for navigation that they'll destroy on arrival, lest someone put it to an evil purpose?'

Ramiro had never wanted the cameras banned, but nor had he pictured the colony relying on them. 'We'll see by flowers and wheat-light,' he said. 'And I'm sure there'll be something we can use to make lamps.'

'While the sunlight itself goes to waste.'

'Did you ever see sunlight?' he countered. 'There'll be gardens, lamps, a few coherers . . . much the same as the lighting everyone's used to, with a lot less moss and a lot more starlight. We won't be trying to recreate the home world – or the mountain – but no one from the *Peerless* will find it all that strange.'

Agata was silent for a moment, then she said, 'You're right – and I should wish you luck with it. It's what we're here for, after all.'

*

Ramiro had trouble falling asleep. When he woke, the sound of the storm on the hull was gone, and the Esilian clock he'd set up on his console showed that it was more than a bell after dawn. Esilio's day was only about two-thirds as long as the home world's; he hoped Tarquinia wouldn't try to impose the new rhythm on everything they did.

In fact, when he found her at her seat in the front cabin, Tarquinia looked as if she'd been awake all night. 'The others are outside,' she said. 'The wind's died down, so we should be able to start work soon, once they stop playing around.'

'Playing?'

'Take a look for yourself,' Tarquinia suggested.

'Will I need my helmet?'

'You won't need anything,' she promised. 'We've set up some lights. Just toughen your soles.'

Ramiro felt vulnerable as he approached the airlock without even his cooling bag, but Esilian sand was just sand, and he'd probably had traces of it beneath his feet for the last six years.

When he opened the outer door he saw Agata and Azelio leaping around, buzzing like excited children for no reason he could discern, unless it was sheer joy at the stillness after the storm. A couple of coherers mounted on the hull illuminated the red soil starkly – showing up an extraordinary maze of tracks that testified to his comrades' exuberance. With the foreground so bright his eyes stood no chance of adapting to the starlight so, even with the dust haze settled, everything in the distance was lost in utter blackness.

'What are you idiots doing?' he called out.

'Trying to see which footprints are ours,' Agata replied gleefully. She jumped forward with her rear gaze fixed intently on the place where she'd been standing.

Ramiro was bemused, but then he observed her more closely as she took her next few leaps. Twice, as she jumped out of some indentation in the sand, it vanished. She and Azelio hadn't actually made all the tracks that he'd attributed to them. Or not yet, they hadn't.

'Come and join us,' Azelio said. 'Some of these must be yours.'

Ramiro stayed on the top rung of the ladder, watching. Each time Azelio lifted his feet, scattered sand unscattered itself, grains sliding in around the places where he'd stepped to settle more evenly – though not always smoothing the ground completely. After all,

Ramiro reasoned, it was possible to walk in someone else's footprints, or to step several times in your own. It would only be the last footfall on any given spot – prior to the next occasion on which the wind levelled everything – that would unmake the imprint completely.

The crew had talked over possibilities like this, dozens of times. Ramiro knew he had no right to be surprised. But having sought a world where the dissenters could escape the tyranny of fore-knowledge, what had he been given? A world where every step he was yet to take would be laid out before his eyes.

'What happens if I try to walk on pristine ground?' he asked.

'Try it and see!' Agata taunted him.

Ramiro descended to the bottom of the ladder, intending to move quickly and get the ordeal over with, but then his resolve deserted him. When he willed his foot to land on unblemished sand, what exactly would intervene to stop him? A cramp in the muscle, divert-ing his leg to its proper, predestined target? A puppet-like manipula-tion of his body by some unseen force too strong to resist, or a trance-like suspension of his whole sense of self? He wasn't sure that he wanted to know the answer. And perhaps that was the simplest resolution: he would lack the courage to walk out across the surface of Esilio for the rest of the mission. He would cower in his room, leaving the work to the others, while he waited to return to the *Peerless* in disgrace.

Agata was watching him. 'Ramiro, there's nothing to be afraid of.' She was amused, but there was no malice in her voice. 'Just step off the ladder without thinking about it. I promise you, the world won't end.'

Ramiro did as she'd asked. Then he looked down. He'd scrutinised the ground beforehand, and he was sure there'd been no footprints at all where his feet now stood.

He lifted one foot and inspected the sand below. He had created an indentation that had not been there before. That was every bit as strange to Esilio as the erasures he'd witnessed were strange to him.

'How?' he demanded, more confused than relieved.

'You really don't listen to me, do you?' Agata chided him. 'Did I ever tell you that the local arrow was inviolable?'

'No.' What she'd stressed most of all was a loss of predictability – but the sight of her and Azelio unmaking their footprints had crowded everything else out of his mind. Those disappearing marks in the sand might be unsettling, but if he could ignore them and walk wherever he pleased then they were not the shackles he'd taken them to be.

Still . . .

'What happens if there are footprints that no one gets around to before the next dust storm?' he asked Agata. 'Ones that were there straight after the last storm?'

She said, 'There can't be a footprint untouched by any foot. I don't understand the dynamics of wind and sand well enough to swear to you that there won't be hollows in the ground that come and go of their own accord – but if you're talking about a clear imprint, if we could keep our feet away from it, it simply wouldn't be there.'

Ramiro pondered this, but it seemed much less dismaying than the kind of all-encompassing trail he'd originally feared. Esilio was a world where a certain amount of noisy, partial – and predominantly trivial – information about the future would be strewn across the landscape. There had always been plenty of trivial things that could be predicted with near-certainty back on the *Peerless*, and perhaps as many of them would be lost, here, as these eerie new portents would be gained.

Emboldened, he strode out across the illuminated ground, pausing every few steps to kick at the sand. Sometimes he simply pushed the dust aside; sometimes the dust applied pressure of its own, as it moved in to occupy the space his foot vacated. But that pressure never came out of nowhere: his feet moved as and when he'd willed them to move, followed by the dust but never forced to retreat. Nor were they thrust without warning into the air by a time-reversed version of the dissipation of motion into heat that took place when they landed.

By the time he reached the point where the coherers' light gave out, he realised that the part of his brain that dealt with his gait and balance had come to terms with the ground's bizarre behaviour as if it were nothing more than an unfamiliar texture: a kind of stickiness that rendered the soil a little unpredictable. He hadn't slipped over once, or found himself rooted to the ground. On one level, he'd already taken the whole phenomenon in his stride.

Each time there was a dust storm the record of future movements would be erased, but even in a prolonged period of calm the foot-prints would overlap, conveying very little information. Compared with the crystalline certainties of the messaging system, it would be nothing: a novelty to which the settlers would soon grow accustomed.

Ramiro turned to Azelio. 'Entertaining as this is, if you want to start the planting now I'd be happy to help.'

With so little wind about, Ramiro decided that it was worth opening both doors of the airlock so they could pass the plants straight through. Standing on the ground, he was at the perfect height to accept each pot directly from Azelio, instead of climbing up and down the ladder.

'Be careful,' Azelio pleaded.

The advice was redundant, but Ramiro took no offence. Azelio had been nurturing the things for six years – and tending to them while they were spinning in their tethered pods had probably been the most arduous task that any of the crew had faced.

Azelio brought out a dozen of the plants to start with. The wheat was a miniature variety that he'd succeeded in maintaining at a staggered set of stages in its growth cycle, allowing him to compress the time needed to assess its viability in Esilian soil. Instead of waiting a year to be sure that it could survive from sowing to harvest, in one-twelfth of that time they'd watch each representative plant advance from its initial level of maturity to that from which another had started.

Ramiro looked over the collection assembled beside the airlock. 'And these are all going in the same kind of soil?'

'Yes. Just a few saunters away. I've already chosen the spot.'

Ramiro followed Azelio across the bright ground of the *Surveyor*'s domain and into the starlit valley. The two plants they were carrying put out a healthy red glow, but that didn't do much to light the way. It was soon clear that, however well their eyes adjusted, they'd need to use the coherers they'd clipped to their tool belts – sacrificing their distance vision for the sake of surer footing. Ramiro tried to balance the confidence he'd gained in dealing with the soil's peculiar forces with a suitable level of caution. There was no telling what Azelio would do to him if he stumbled and fell, crushing one of his darlings, even if 'Esilio pushed me!' was the honest excuse.

'Just here.'

Ramiro squatted and placed the pot on the ground, then swung his beam around the site. 'You already dug twelve holes!' he observed. 'And I thought you were messing around with Agata all morning.'

Azelio made a noncommittal sound. Ramiro suddenly felt queasy.

'My plan is to dig up all these plants at the end of the trial and take them back to the *Peerless* for my colleagues to analyse,' Azelio mused. 'So I guess that's when I'll see the transition between cultivated and truly pristine ground. But right now, in Esilio's terms, we've just dug the plants up – so on our terms, we're about to do that. Backwards.'

Ramiro said, 'You make it sound as if you've been practising time-reversed agronomy all your life.'

'It's not that hard to see what's going on, if you think it through,' Azelio replied lightly.

'But you don't mind following markers like this? Evidence of acts you haven't performed yet?'

'It's a little disconcerting,' Azelio conceded. 'But I can't say that it fills me with claustrophobia to know that I'll carry out the experimental protocols I always planned to carry out.'

Ramiro didn't argue; the only thing he'd gain by pressing the point was to raise his own level of disquiet again. 'Let's get to work, then.'

Azelio squatted beside one of the plants. 'The idea is to take it out of the potted soil and brush the roots clean. Pay close attention.' He leant forward and positioned his hands on either side of the stalk, but then he kept them there, motionless. After a lapse of this, Ramiro said, 'What are you doing?'

'I thought it might leap into my hands by itself,' Azelio explained, deadpan. 'Dropped in and repotted, Esilio style.'

'One more joke like that and we'll be burying more than plants here.'

Azelio took a short stone rod from his tool belt and used it to loosen the soil in the pot. Then he gently extracted the plant and applied a soft brush to the roots.

'Does it matter if there's a trace of the old soil clinging on?' Ramiro asked.

Azelio winced. 'Yes. If it's enough to keep the plant growing when it otherwise wouldn't, that would make the results meaningless. You don't want the settlers to find out after half a year that it was only contamination that made it look as if they could survive here.'

He carried the freed plant over to the row of holes he hadn't yet made. 'What happens if I try to put it in the wrong one?' he mused. 'Is that possible?'

Ramiro aimed his coherer at the nearest of the holes, then watched as Azelio knelt down, a trowel in one hand and the wheat plant in the other. He lowered the plant until its roots were in the hole, then he started adding soil from the surrounding mound. Some of the soil was scooped in with pressure from behind, in the ordinary manner. Some appeared to pursue the trowel, the way the dust sometimes pursued Ramiro's feet. *What decided between the two?* Azelio's own actions had to be consistent with the motion of the soil, but which determined which? Maybe there was no answer to that, short of the impossible act of solving in the finest detail the equations that Agata was yet to discover, revealing exactly which sequences of events were consistent with the laws of physics all the way around the cosmos.

In any case, the laws of physics seemed to allow the plant to end up firmly bedded in Esilian soil. Azelio tried to shake his trowel clean, but each time he flicked it as many specks of dirt rose up from the ground to stick to the blade as parted from it.

'I guess that's now my Esilian trowel. Do you want to do the next one?'

Ramiro said, 'I wouldn't trust myself to get the roots clean.'

'I'll deal with that,' Azelio replied. 'You can do the planting.'

'All right.'

When Azelio had prepared the second plant, Ramiro accepted it and took it to the next hole. He knelt on the ground; Azelio passed him the trowel then stood back to provide a steady light.

Ramiro gazed down at the neat mound of soil beside the hole. If he'd had a camera here during the dust storm he might have watched the mound rising up, as speck after speck fell into place from the turbulent air. But if an Esilian wind had scattered it, who had given it its shape? If he refused to do it himself, would Azelio be compelled to take his place? But why would one of them be compelled and not the other?

When he'd stomped across the sand beside the *Surveyor* each disquieting footprint had been blurred into insignificance, but he couldn't try to complicate this crucial experiment just to obfuscate the issue. He'd always told himself that he'd accepted the true nature of time and choice, and that all he'd objected to in the messaging system was the way it would flatten his deliberations. But even here, with nothing life-changing at stake, the sense of being trapped in the threads of history was more oppressive than it had ever been.

Ramiro's left arm had grown tired from holding the plant in place over the hole. He shifted it slightly to make himself more comfortable, but as he shifted it back he saw soil rising and adhering to the roots. He stared at this bizarre result for a moment, then decided to stop wasting time delaying an outcome he had no wish to oppose.

He held the trowel to the side of the mound nearest the hole, then drew it closer. The sand followed the blade – not adhering to it and needing to be brought along, but gently pushing it. He lowered the trowel into the hole then withdrew it; the sand parted from the blade and packed itself between the roots of the plant and the side of the hole.

He hesitated, groping for a clearer sense of his role in the task. But what could he actually do wrong? So long as he was committed to making whatever movements with the trowel were necessary until the plant was securely in place, that state of mind and the strictures of the environment ought to work it out between themselves.

He scooped some soil straight into the hole; like the last delivery, it clung to the roots. In Esilio's terms, this soil had spent at least a few stints packed tightly around the plant; if he could have seen the action in reverse, it would have involved nothing stranger than a clump of sand finally coming loose.

When he was done, Ramiro stood and turned to face Azelio. 'So now I have to lure half the travellers here in the name of freedom, then leave them to raise their children in a world where everything they do corrodes their sense of agency?'

Azelio said, 'That's putting it too harshly. When we get back, all you can do is give an honest account of your own experience. They'll have seen life under the messaging system, so they'll already have a better idea than we had about this kind of thing – and which way of life they'd prefer.'

'The pro-messagers should come here,' Ramiro declared bitterly. 'If they want to know the future, let them know it every step of the way. Leave the mountain to us, and we can go back to living with a single arrow.'

'That's a nice idea . . . but good luck organising the eviction.'

They walked back to the *Surveyor* to fetch two more plants. 'Can you put up some windbreaks?' Ramiro suggested. 'If that last dust storm was typical, it might not have uprooted anything, but I'd bet it would have stripped petals.'

'I have a few rolls of tight-weave fabric,' Azelio replied. 'I didn't see any stake holes nearby, but I won't let that stop me.'

Ramiro fell through the light, willing himself to move faster. He reached down to grab hold of his daughter, but as his fingers brushed her limbless form the wind shifted and tore her away.

Tarquinia grabbed his wrists, dragging his gaze back into focus. 'Ssh,' she said. 'It's all right.' She drew away from him slowly, gently separating their remaining adhesions.

'What happened?' he asked her.

'Nothing,' she said. 'Nothing's wrong.'

'No.' He had no children to lose. How many times had he told his idiot body the same beautiful lie? How stupid could it be, that it hadn't seen through him yet?

He looked past Tarquinia, to the pale grey wall of his cabin. He knew exactly where he was now. The *Surveyor* was his second prison, and outside it was the third. 'How will anyone live here?' he wondered.

'There'll be a better place than this for a city,' Tarquinia promised. 'No dust storms – just gentle winds to sweep the footprints away.'

'That's not enough.'

'Then you'll build machines to plant the wheat and harvest it. No one will ever have to touch the soil.'

Ramiro turned to her. 'Who'll build these machines?'

'You will. You and the other settlers.'

'And where will you be?'

Tarquinia said, 'I thought you didn't want to know the future.'

22

Agata pressed the broom down firmly against the floor of her cabin and tried again. 'How hard can it be?' she muttered. Dust starts off in a large area. Pressure is applied inwards along successive portions of the border. Dust ends up in a smaller area, ready to be collected and removed. On the face of it, this didn't even pose a conflict with the local arrow: Esilian dust should have been happy to have its entropy decreased as her own time advanced.

But as she moved the broom across the floor, duly concentrating the dust ahead of it, other dust began to appear *behind it* – some of it falling from the air, some sliding over the stone to pile up against the bristles. Its entropy was decreasing too, as it accumulated from whatever scattered reaches of the *Surveyor* in which it had been lurking. The net result was that the stretch of floor she'd swept remained as dusty as ever.

Azelio knocked on her open door. 'I know you're busy, but Ramiro's sleeping and Tarquinia's on watch—'

'I'm not busy,' Agata assured him. 'Do you want a hand with the measurements?'

'If you don't mind.' Azelio nodded at the broom. 'Have you found the trick to it?'

'Not really,' she admitted. 'Maybe what we need is some kind of covered system of barriers. If we can place it on the floor and then reconfigure it without opening the cover, we ought to able to manipulate the dust inside without any more arriving.'

'That sounds . . . elaborate.'

Agata put on her corset and tool belt and followed Azelio to the airlock, then waited for him to cycle through. The view through the window showed that the weather was calm, but the *Surveyor* had become so filthy that Tarquinia now insisted on the protocol, regardless. Agata was beginning to suspect that the only remedy for the dust invasion would be to ascend into the void and flush every room out with clean air – and even that depended on their arrow prevailing and the void not being ready with a conspiracy of pollutants poised to rush in the moment they opened the airlock, in a perfect reversal of the intended purge.

Outside, she caught up with Azelio at the start of the trail. It was Ramiro who'd noticed the regularly spaced indentations in the ground after the last high winds, and decided to fill them with rocks marking the way to each of the four test plots. Agata hadn't questioned him too closely on the matter, but she suspected that he'd already been contemplating doing something similar. The idea hadn't come from nowhere, inspired by nothing but the evidence of its own implementation.

'How are the calculations going?' Azelio asked her, as they started along the trail.

'Slowly.'

'Just as well. If you finish them, what will you do on the journey back?'

'There's no risk of that.' Agata had set aside her efforts to understand the curved vacuum and instead had spent the last two stints attempting to analyse their current situation, using a crude model of a field in which two opposing thermodynamic arrows met. But in the versions that were simple enough to handle, both arrows rapidly decayed away, leading almost immediately to a time-blind equilibrium state. The reality, in which countless slender fingers of opposing time interpenetrated, seemed to depend on details too subtle for her to approximate in any meaningful way.

'It's Luisa's fifth birthday today,' Azelio announced cheerfully. 'I'll show you her drawing for it when we get back.'

'Happy birthday, Luisa!' Agata played her coherer's beam over the grey stones to her left. 'You never peek, do you? You never riffle through the pile to see what's coming up?'

Azelio buzzed. 'Of course not! That would defeat the whole point.'

'I know. But that wouldn't be enough to stop me.'

When they reached the first plot the plants were all dormant, their flowers closed. Agata glanced up at the sky; she knew from the positions of the stars that the sun was well above the horizon, but she would have had to forego artificial light for a few lapses to have any chance of picking out the faint disc. 'I was hoping the petals might synchronise to the Esilian day,' she said. 'They give out photons, the sun accepts them: what could be more sensible than that?'

'Except that eons of evolution has left them with no skill but waiting for an ordinary night, not a time-reversed day.'

'Maybe the settlers could breed it into them,' Agata suggested. If detecting the dawn for themselves was too hard, the plants could still be prodded with more conventional signals into following the new cycle. For now, the Esilian sun would be getting its due regardless – from the plants, the ground, and her own skin – but not in any useful way.

'Can you do the heights and the stalk circumferences?' Azelio asked her.

'Sure.' Agata knelt by the first plant and reached into her tool belt. In a perfect world some clever instrument builder would have added a data recorder directly to the tape measure, but instead she had to aim her coherer so that she could read the tape by eye, raise the figure on her skin, and have her corset record it. 'Is one soil type racing ahead yet?' she asked Azelio. He'd started from the other end of the row, making his own inspection to record the number and condition of the flowers.

'No.'

'So there's not much difference? The settlers could farm anywhere?'

Azelio was silent. Agata regretted distracting him; she'd probably made him lose count.

As he stood to move on to the next plant, he said, 'Actually, they've all stopped growing.'

Agata was startled; nothing in Azelio's demeanour had prepared her for this news. 'All of them? Every single one?'

'Yes.' Azelio spoke calmly. 'At first it was only a few cases, and I put it down to transplantation shock. But the numbers just kept getting worse, and three days ago the last exceptions succumbed.'

Agata struggled to find the least dismaying interpretation of these facts. 'Do you think it's the wind?' They could always improve the windbreaks, or even relocate the whole experiment.

'No. They haven't lost that many petals, or had roots dislodged.'

'So it's the soil,' she concluded. 'All four kinds are inhospitable.'

'It's looking that way.'

'Have you told Ramiro?'

'The trial isn't finished yet,' Azelio stressed. 'There's still a chance that this could be a temporary hiatus.'

'Right.' Agata understood now why he'd called on her to help him with the measurements: he was trying to keep the results from Ramiro for as long as possible, in the hope that something would change.

Azelio knelt down and continued his inspection; Agata did the same. As she turned the revelation over in her mind, she was surprised at her own equanimity. After six years away from the mountain the conflict that they'd come here to remedy seemed remote and petty. If they really could rid the *Peerless* of Medoro's killers by showing that a settlement was viable, she'd certainly relish that victory – but between the light-deflection measurements and her work on the vacuum, she already found it impossible to think of her time here as wasted.

But Azelio had no such consolations; he was only here in the hope of making the mountain safer for the children he'd promised to protect.

On their way to the next plot Agata asked him, 'Is it the composition of the soil? Or is it the arrow?'

'I can't say for sure,' Azelio replied.

'Can't you guess?' Agata pressed him.

He said, 'The spectra suggest that at least two of the soil types should have had everything the wheat needed.'

'So it probably is the arrow?' There was nothing inimical to life about the mere presence of a conflicting arrow; the crew had survived it perfectly well, thanks to their store of food with its unambiguous origins and their undiminished ability to rid their bodies of excess heat. Esilio even accepted their excrement without complaint, however bizarre the material's fate would seem to a time-reversed observer. But the plants' uptake of nutrients relied on interactions between their roots and the native soil at a microscopic level, and there was no guarantee that the two systems, left to themselves, would simply sort out their differences.

Azelio wasn't ready to give up hope of a simple agronomic solution. 'We could try mixing the most promising soils,' he said. 'Or we could look for better conditions elsewhere. If it's the arrow, that's the end of it.'

Agata said, 'I'll defer to your expertise on soil chemistry – but when it comes to the arrow, let me be the judge. The problem still might not be insurmountable.'

'Really?' Azelio buzzed sceptically. 'You can't even sweep your own floor any more. How are you going to reach into the ground and persuade every speck of dust that it's mistaken about the route it's taking away from the entropy minimum?'

Agata had no answer to that. But if she couldn't change the brute facts, the cosmos wasn't taking sides in this clash: it simply had no choice but to reconcile everything it had brought together. If there had to be an accommodation between Esilio's arrow and the *Surveyor*'s, the trick would be to find a way to make the crop's failure even more improbable than its success.

Ramiro must have made a choice, Agata realised, not to seek constant updates on the state of the crops. Warned that there could be problems at the start as the plants adapted to their new conditions, he'd stepped back and left it to Azelio to monitor their health, and to offer a verdict only once it was warranted.

But Ramiro wasn't blind, and as the flowers ceased unfurling and the stalks began to wither, Agata could see that both men were losing hope.

Bell after bell, day after day, she sketched elaborate diagrams for machines to manipulate the soil's properties. Chemically, each mineral grain was no different from that of an equivalent on the *Peerless* or the home world. Physically, the distinction came down to the fact that soil on the home world had once been solid rock, while for Esilian soil, from her own point of view, that fate still lay in the future. Or in Esilio's terms, the vast bulk of the planet's soil *had* been eroded from rock . . . leaving two competing possibilities: that some small portion of it had actually been emitted from the roots of time-reversed stalks of wheat, or that those strange withered plants had failed to contribute anything before finally regaining their health and being carried away by the visitors.

Still, a plant knew nothing of the past and future of each grain of sand; the whole interaction with the roots had to make sense in the present. If she could find a way to measure the detailed distribution of thermal vibrations in the soil they'd brought with them, and then recreate that in the native soil, it would no longer be statistically reasonable for the plants to fail to absorb it.

To the naked eye, soil was just soil – and if the differences were microscopic, how hard could they be to erase? But when she took the most promising of her schemes and thought seriously about the practicalities, the measurements were close to impossible, the manipulations impractical, the computations prohibitive and the projected throughput so slow that a cubic scant of soil would have taken eons to process.

Agata deleted the sketches from her console. She peeled off her corset and lay down on her sand bed. The whole approach was a dead end: she might as well have set out to reverse the motion of every particle of air in the *Surveyor* in the hope of creating a breeze that would carry all the dust away.

Anything that sought to inscribe a new arrow into the soil at a microscopic level was doomed; the numbers would always be against her. What she needed was something infinitely less subtle.

Agata waited until she had a chance to speak to Tarquinia alone. 'Do you remember telling me once that you believed Greta had put a bomb on the *Surveyor*?'

Tarquinia replied warily, 'No, but I'll take your word for it.'

'My word that there's a bomb?'

'No, your word that I told you.'

'So it's true?'

Tarquinia struggled to reconstruct some half-forgotten chain of inferences. 'Verano dropped some hints. He was very apologetic.'

'Is there any way to be sure?' Agata pleaded. 'Greta might have put him up to the apology, as a kind of misinformation.' Even before the launch, the whole crazed-anti-messenger-rams-the-*Peerless* scenario had never struck her as very plausible, and after spending six years with Ramiro – irritating as he could be – Agata had to strive mightily to put herself inside the head of anyone who'd imagined him commandeering the *Surveyor* and turning it into a weapon.

Tarquinia was bemused. 'This is a strange time to start worrying about it,' she said. 'If an unexpected bump could set it off, we'd have been dead long ago.'

'If the Council really didn't trust Ramiro not to turn saboteur,' Agata reasoned, 'then they wouldn't have been content with a bluff, would they? They would have insisted on some genuine means to destroy the *Surveyor* if it turned rogue.'

'I suppose that's true,' Tarquinia agreed. 'Though over the last six years I've become pleasantly accustomed to not having to think about politicians at all, so I don't know what my judgement is worth now.'

'If there's a bomb, we need to find it,' Agata declared. 'We need to cut it open and extract the explosive.'

Tarquinia swivelled on her couch, assessing this suggestion. 'We need to locate the hidden, possibly tamper-proof bomb that's been obliging enough not to kill us so far, and start prodding and poking at it now . . . because?'

'Because the test plots are failing,' Agata explained. 'So we need to take the explosive up into the hills, turn some rock into soil for ourselves – against the Esilian arrow – and see if that imbues the soil with the properties that it needs to support plant growth.'

'If wheat hadn't failed to grow properly in weightlessness,' Tarquinia mused, 'then Yalda never would have ordered the spin-up. And if Yalda hadn't ordered the spin-up, the *Peerless* might well have been incinerated by antimatter. So really, I ought to be encouraged by history: anything that starts with crop failure ends well.' There was a sound of hardstone scraping against hardstone, then slipping.

'Can you see what you're doing?' Agata aimed her own coherer down into the maintenance shaft.

'Yes, I can see,' Tarquinia replied. 'It's just that none of these bolts have been turned since the engines were assembled.'

'The bomb's not going to explode just because you open that panel, is it?' Agata asked anxiously.

Tarquinia looked up at her, affronted. 'However much pressure he was under, Verano would never have done anything so perverse. We're entitled to inspect our own engines; that hardly amounts to an act of sedition.'

There was a long silence, followed by a rhythmic squeaking noise that was almost certainly one of the bolts being turned. Agata restrained herself from cheering; Ramiro was asleep.

It took Tarquinia more than a chime to loosen all six bolts and remove the access panel. Agata peered over her shoulder into the exposed cavity, where cooling pipes ran along the back of the rebounders. If one of the banks of rebounders had failed, someone could have squeezed in here to fit a replacement.

'Anything?' Agata asked hopefully.

'Nothing obvious,' Tarquinia admitted. 'I thought this was the last place we hadn't poked around in, but maybe I should sit down with the maintenance logs to confirm that.'

'Right.'

Tarquinia lingered, lowering her head partway through the hatch and turning her face sideways. 'There's a big stone beam that goes right across the top of the engines, from rim to rim.'

'Could something be attached to it?' Agata suggested. 'Out of sight from where you are?'

'I'm just wondering why it's there at all,' Tarquinia replied. 'The floors of the cabins should provide enough bracing for the engines. And why a beam that runs across one particular diameter of the disc, and not another one at right angles to it? Nothing about the stress from the engines picks out one axis like that.'

'No.'

Tarquinia said, 'If I don't come out in six lapses, send in Azelio with a rope.'

'Azelio?'

'No offence to you or Ramiro, but he's the skinniest. There's not much point in two people getting stuck.' Tarquinia climbed head first through the access hatch, slithering deeper and humming softly as the cooling pipes banged against her, until even her feet had disappeared from view.

Agata waited, listening intently for any cries of discovery or distress. She was starting to wonder if she should have kept her inspiration to herself. Tarquinia trapped in the guts of the *Surveyor* would not be a happy outcome – and if she actually located the mythical device there could be worse to follow.

Worrying silences were punctuated with thuds, pings and echoing curses. Finally, Agata heard Tarquinia returning, her steady advance eliciting a resonant hum from the maze of pipes.

'That was exhausting,' she said. 'Can you give me a hand up?'

Agata jumped down into the shaft and helped her out through the hatch. The flesh of Tarquinia's torso had become corrugated as she'd forced it between the pipes, giving her the appearance of a decoratively shaped novelty loaf on legs.

'Any luck?'

Tarquinia said, 'There's nothing hidden beside the beam.'

'Oh.'

'But the beam itself is hollow.'

'Really? How can you tell?'

'You can hear it when you tap,' Tarquinia explained.

'Couldn't that just be to save mass?'

'In principle it could be. But when I got to the far end I found something peculiar: it looks as if the cooling air is actually routed through the beam. Why do that, except to make life harder on anyone tampering with it?'

'So if there's a bomb,' Agata said, 'it might be anywhere inside a hardstone beam that spans the diameter of the *Surveyor*. And the only way we'll ever know for sure is if we cut the whole thing open – in a place where there's barely room to move, let alone the space to wield tools safely.'

Tarquinia inclined her head admiringly. 'Trust Verano to find a civilised solution.'

Agata hummed with distaste. 'Is there such a thing as a civilised bomb?'

'Well, no,' Tarquinia conceded. 'But the Council would have asked him to fit a booby trap, and at least he made that idea redundant. There's no way that Ramiro alone – or even the four of us – could have taken that hiding place apart and left the *Surveyor* functioning. A booby-trapped bomb would probably have been triggered by accident, long ago. We can thank Verano for finding a way to make the thing as good as tamper-proof, without turning it into a death sentence.'

Agata said, 'I'll send him flowers when I get back. But if we can't get the bomb out and leave the *Surveyor* functioning—'

'We couldn't have done it *in the void*,' Tarquinia interjected. 'But with an external atmosphere, there's no comparison. I think even the most paranoid Councillor would have reasoned that if Ramiro had proposed the mission merely as a cover for an attack on the *Peerless*, he would hardly have been willing to spend twelve years actually detouring all the way to Esilio just to remove this thing.'

'You really think you can go back down there and slice the beam open?' Agata gestured at the curves still imprinted into Tarquinia's body.

Tarquinia said, 'Not just like that. First we take out most of the cooling pipes. Then we drill inspection holes in the beam, to see what we can see. The whole exercise could take a while, but it's not impossible.'

'Assuming there are no other problems. Assuming there really is no booby trap.'

Tarquinia said, 'Yes.'

Agata slumped against the side of the shaft. Before she'd approached Tarquinia, she'd been picturing the bomb hidden behind a false wall at the back of the pantry, requiring nothing more to disarm it than the snip of a cable.

Tarquinia began smoothing out the kinks in her flesh. 'I'm not going to try something like this without unanimous assent. And just because you raised the idea yourself doesn't mean that you can't change your mind.'

As Agata described her plan to blast their own arrow into the Esilian soil, she could see an expression of delight growing on Azelio's face – as if she'd slipped a drawing of a flourishing garden sprouting from a bomb-shattered hillside into the stack the children had left him. There was scepticism too, but she was sure now that he would understand that it was at least worth trying.

Ramiro, though, remained as dispirited as ever. 'If we do set off this explosive,' he reasoned, 'shouldn't we be able to see some evidence of that already?'

Agata said, 'You mean a crater?'

'Yes.'

'If we found a site like that, it would be useless to us. It would imply that after we set off the bomb, the crater would be gone and the sand around it would be rock again.'

Ramiro scowled. 'Esilio doesn't care what's useful or useless, or it wouldn't have killed the plants, would it?'

'Esilio doesn't care,' Agata agreed, 'but why would *we* go ahead and set off the bomb there, knowing that it would do us no good?'

'Because the crater would prove that we did!' Ramiro replied heatedly.

'But as far as we know, there is no such crater.' Agata met his gaze openly, trying to reassure him of her sincerity: she wasn't playing some verbal game just to annoy him. 'There is no crater, because if we saw it, we wouldn't choose to make it. Esilio can't force our hand;

whatever happens has to be consistent with everything, including our motives.'

Ramiro said, 'It can't force our hand, but there could still be an accident.'

'That's true. But if we saw such a crater, we wouldn't even go near it with the explosive.' Agata would have liked to have taken comfort from the fact that there were no signs at the landing site of any future accident, but if the blast was capable of imposing its own arrow that meant nothing.

Ramiro's hostility wavered. 'I don't know how to think about any of this,' he admitted. He ran a hand over his face. 'If the plants can't bring their arrow to Esilio, why should a bomb do any better?'

'The roots of a plant aren't entirely passive,' Azelio replied, 'but they do rely on the state of the soil. I don't think the bomb going off will rely on anything like that.'

'But in Esilian time,' Ramiro protested, 'all the soil we're supposedly going to make with this bomb has to mesh perfectly with a backwards explosion in such a way that it forms a solid rock. How likely is that?'

'How likely are the alternatives?' Agata countered. 'How likely is it that the explosive will fail to detonate? How likely is it that we'll allow it to explode in an existing crater instead – just to pander to Esilio's arrow?'

'Don't ask me,' Ramiro replied bitterly. 'I only live here.' Tarquinia reached over and squeezed his shoulder.

Agata said, 'I can't predict anything with certainty either, but surely it's worth doing the experiment.'

Azelio turned to Tarquinia. 'You think you can extract the explosive safely?'

Tarquinia phrased her reply carefully. 'I'm as sure as I can be that Verano wouldn't have allowed anything on the *Surveyor* that could kill us from a bump or a broken connection. Whether I manage to set it off anyway is another question.'

They spent three more chimes talking over the details, then Tarquinia called for a vote.

Ramiro's gloom had given Agata pause. Even if the plan succeeded, he might well end up back on the *Peerless* warning his fellow anti-messagers that the crops counted for nothing when Esilio itself would rot their minds. Why should she risk her life if it would make no difference to the fate of the mountain?

Azelio said, 'I'm for it.'

Tarquinia followed him quickly. 'I am too.'

Ramiro was silent. Agata willed him to mutter a surly veto, sparing her the need to make a decision, but having advertised his confusion already he kept his resolve much longer than she could.

'I'm for it,' she said, unsure now if she had any better reason than her wish to see Azelio hopeful again.

Ramiro stared at the floor. Agata felt a twinge of sympathy for him: he'd come here with nothing but good intentions, hoping to grant both of the warring parties a chance to live exactly as they wished. It was not his fault that Esilio wasn't so accommodating.

'I'm for it,' he said finally. 'If we baulk at the risk we could still get killed by a Hurtler on the way back – but we can't go back without trying everything. If people can survive here, they need to know.'

Tarquinia said, 'Right.'

As she rose from her couch Ramiro added, 'To be honest, though, there's a better reason to do this than anything it can tell us about the crops.'

Agata was confused. 'What's that?'

Ramiro said, 'The look on Greta's face when we tell her exactly what we did with her beautiful bomb.'

Agata sat in the tent, wearing her helmet so she could hear the audio link clearly over the noise of the wind. Every chime or so the footfalls and gentle clanking echoing in the empty engine cavity gave way to the bone-shaking whine of hardstone being drilled. Tarquinia was making holes in the beam, hunting for the bomb.

Agata pictured the scene as she'd left it, with mirrors angled into the cavity to bring in as much Esilian sunlight as possible. But even the safety lights in the cabin above would be off now, leaving Tarquinia to work with nothing but the view through the time-reversed camera. Exposing the bomb to ordinary light might trigger a tamper-prevention device, but it wouldn't have made much sense to include the means to detect time-reversed light, when any act of sabotage had been expected to take place close to the *Peerless*, where the only source would have been distant starlight.

The camera could amplify the faint image obtained by a periscope inserted in each inspection hole, with sunlight introduced by a second mirrored tube. But so far, all Tarquinia had been able to report was that there were dozens of baffles inside the hollow beam, blocking the view along its length, leaving her with no way to proceed but trial and error.

Ramiro lay on the floor of the tent, one arm covering his face-plate; Azelio was crouched beside him, his head bowed in thought. They had spent eight days stripping as much as they could out of the *Surveyor*, preparing themselves for the grim contingency that an explosion might leave the hull damaged but not entirely beyond repair. Tools and medical supplies filled the tent; its three neighbours held the rebounder panels, parts of the cooling and navigation systems, and their entire stock of food. Agata understood now why there'd been so much dust around in the preceding days.

'I've found it,' Tarquinia announced calmly. 'Six strides from the rim of the hull.'

Ramiro sat up. 'What is there, exactly?'

'About what you'd expect,' Tarquinia replied. 'A UV receiver on a board with a photonic processor. And a cable leading from the processor into the explosive.' Agata felt sick. She could see the blue dust that had filled Medoro's workshop; she could picture it spilling from the broken hull to mix with the Esilian soil.

'No other components on the board?' Ramiro pressed her.

Tarquinia said, 'Remember when we shot up into a high orbit, to maintain contact with the probe? If that didn't set this thing off, nothing will. There's no accelerometer here.'

'Is the beam warm?' Ramiro asked.

Tarquinia buzzed curtly. 'Yes! I just drilled a hole in it.'

'You should leave it for a chime and see if it cools down completely,' Ramiro pleaded. Agata understood his logic: a passive system that needed an external signal to wake it would not be generating heat, but the kind of photonics required to detect an incision in the cable would have to be constantly active.

'If it gave out a heat signature, that would defeat the whole point of trying to hide it,' Tarquinia replied.

Ramiro said, 'I think they would have imagined the cooling system still running while we were doing this.'

'All right,' Tarquinia agreed reluctantly. 'I'll wait.'

Agata caught Azelio's eye and they exchanged grimaces of relief.

Tarquinia's unwavering conviction that Verano would have gone out of his way to make the bomb 'safe' was probably justified – but impugning the man's honour was quite low on everyone else's list of calamities to avoid.

Ramiro took off his helmet and rubbed his eyes. 'I should be doing this,' he muttered. Agata offered no opinion; in the end it had been Tarquinia's decision.

'Is anyone hungry?' she asked. 'I could go and bring some loaves.' She hadn't seen Ramiro eat all day.

Azelio said, 'I'll go with you.'

As they unzipped the entrance to the tent a gust of wind entered, sending the walls ballooning out and loosening the stake holding down one corner; it was only the collection of heavy tools arrayed across the floor that kept it from peeling up from the ground. Ramiro went and put a foot on the wayward corner, and Agata dashed out to fix the stake. With the wind pelting her with dust the food run seemed like more trouble than it was worth; she returned to the tent.

Tarquinia's voice came over the link. 'The beam's down to ambient temperature,' she announced. 'There's no heat coming from the bomb.'

'How's your visibility?' Ramiro asked anxiously. They could hear the wind rising; the dust had to be obscuring the sunlight entering the *Surveyor*'s window.

'Good enough,' Tarquinia assured him. 'I'm going to cut the cable.'

Ramiro said, 'You're tired now, and there's not much light. Why don't you wait for the storm to pass?'

Agata heard the drill start up again; Tarquinia would need a third hole to insert the shears.

Ramiro paced the tent. Azelio crouched in a corner, staring at the floor. The whining of the drill came to an end, replaced by a gentle scraping noise as the folded instrument was manoeuvred through the hole.

'I've got the shears around the cable,' Tarquinia announced. Agata saw Ramiro's faced contorted with fear. There was a soft click of the blades meeting.

The wind rose up, pelting the wall of the tent with dust. But one word came clearly through the link.

'Done.'

*

As Agata trudged up the rocky incline, the patch of bright ground beside the *Surveyor* remained visible in her rear gaze. But it looked so out of place against the dark valley floor that a part of her mind began to discount it, treating it as nothing but a flaw in her vision. The first few times she felt it vanish from her mental map of her surroundings she panicked, scanning the view for the comforting beacon until it snapped back into focus, acknowledged again as real. But after a while she stopped worrying and let it fade into the landscape. Tarquinia and Ramiro were not going to turn out the lights and hide from her. When the time came she'd have no trouble finding her way back.

Ahead, above the grey hills, the sky could not have marked the way more clearly. The direction along Esilio's axis that they'd chosen to call 'south' pierced the bowl of stars about a twelfth of a revolution below its bright rim, and from this valley in the southern mid-latitudes that celestial pole remained perpetually in view, with the rim twirling around it like a burning hoop and the stars in between never setting.

Azelio walked beside her, carrying two of his potted seedlings from the final dozen he'd held in reserve. He wasn't complaining, but she could see him struggling with the weight as the slope increased.

'I'd be happy to take one,' she offered.

'Thanks, but I'd rather you had nothing to distract you from your own load,' he replied.

Agata raised the bomb effortlessly above her head. 'It hardly weighs anything. And even if I drop it, it's not going to go off.' Tarquinia had assured her that the explosive could only be triggered by a bright pulse of light at a specific wavelength, and the only means of delivering that pulse was strapped securely to her tool belt.

Azelio said, 'I'm more worried that you might damage the detonator and we won't be able to set it off at all.'

'Fair enough.'

Azelio had identified a promising outcrop in the images they'd taken from orbit – a body of rock whose spectral signature suggested that it could give rise to fertile soil. No one had objected when Agata had volunteered to accompany him to the site, but she still felt slightly guilty at having wormed her way out of the tedious business of moving everything back into the *Surveyor*. Blowing up a hillside would be vastly more enjoyable than reassembling cooling pipes and restocking the pantry.

'Can we rest for a bit?' Azelio suggested.

'Of course.' Agata placed the bomb gently on the ground, then sat beside it, positioning her body so she'd be blocking its way if it began to slide. Azelio did the same with his plants.

'Do you think they already know how this ends, back on the *Peerless*?' he asked her.

'I expect so.' Unless there'd been an ongoing campaign of sabotage, it was hard to believe that the messaging system would not have been completed by now.

'In some ways that takes the sting off the separation,' Azelio mused. 'If the children are already in contact with me, that's almost like being there.'

'This from a man who voted against the system,' Agata teased him.

Azelio said, 'If the vote had gone against the system then we wouldn't have needed to be here at all.'

'Hmm.' Agata didn't want to start arguing with him over the attribution of blame.

'So long as there's peace, I don't care about the system,' Azelio admitted wearily. 'People can use it or ignore it as they wish. We managed not to go to war over shedding; we ought to be able to live with anything after that.'

'We ought to, and we will,' Agata declared. 'The fanatics who can't accept that will be free to leave.'

Azelio buzzed wryly. 'Fanatics carrying the necessary stocks of explosive?'

'Maybe we can send all the bombs they'll need in a separate craft,' Agata suggested. 'We could bundle off a whole lot of freight to Esilio in an automated vessel at high acceleration, then let the settlers follow. It's not an intractable problem; we'll think of some way to do it safely.'

'Assuming this works at all.' Azelio nodded towards their own bomb.

'It has to work.' Agata searched the dark valley for the speck of light that marked the landing site. 'If the soil is right and the arrow is right, the plants will grow. Nothing else would make sense.'

*

The rim of the star bowl was almost vertical as they came over the rise. Agata wished they could have chosen a landscape with more rock than dust from the start; it would have spared them the worst of the storms, and they could have passed the time just sitting outside, gazing at this glorious celestial clock.

'There it is,' Azelio announced, pointing ahead. Agata could barely distinguish the hue of the outcrop from that of its surroundings, but she trusted Azelio. He'd studied the image of the hills for half a day as he'd plotted their route, and he had too much at stake to be careless.

The approach was downhill, but the ground was uneven and strewn with small, loose stones. As Agata advanced the stones began jostling her feet, accelerated from a span or two away by time-reversed friction before coming to a halt against her skin. She glanced at Azelio; he was struggling to keep his footing, distracted by the bizarre bombardment.

'Can you leave the plants here?' she asked. Once they'd set the charge they'd be retreating to about this point anyway.

'Good idea.' Azelio set the pots down and they continued.

When they reached the hillside Azelio switched on his coherer and played it over the pale brown rocks. 'This is the target,' he confirmed. He gestured towards the centre of the outcrop. 'Anywhere about there should do it.'

Agata handed him the bomb and waited for him to step away to a safe distance, then she started swinging her pick into the rock face. Small chips of stone flew out from the point of impact, stinging her forearms, but the rush of power and freedom she felt at the sight of the growing excavation was more than enough to compensate. In Esilian time, the chips were rising from the ground, propelled into the air by conspiracies of time-reversed thermal diffusion, just to aid her as she rebuilt the rock. What stronger proof could there be that the cosmos had a place for her, with all her plans and choices? One day it would kill her, but until then the contract was clear: hardship and frustration and failure were all possible, but she would never be robbed of her will entirely.

She made the hole as deep as she could without widening it excessively; the idea was to confine the pressure wave within the rock as much as possible. When she stopped swinging, Azelio approached and held the bomb up against the opening. It didn't quite fit at one corner. She set to work removing the obstruction.

On the next attempt, the bomb's cubic housing entered the aperture without resistance. Azelio gently pushed it deeper, then Agata aimed her coherer into the hole. There were some small gaps around the edge of the housing, but she didn't think they'd be enough to dissipate the energy of the blast.

She took the detonator from her tool belt. Ramiro had removed most of the original components and added a timer in place of the remote trigger. She started up the photonics and it ran a self-test; a short summary on the display panel reported that everything was working as expected. She plugged the detonation cable into the bomb, and tapped the switch to start the timer. The countdown showed nine lapses and falling. She rested the detonator in the mouth of the hole, then the two of them walked away.

The loose stones harassed them again as they crossed the ground, and although the mild pressure on their skin was exactly the same as if they'd merely been dislodging the things, the timing was still disconcerting. Agata imagined the settlers' children, raised with all of these quirks of nature and entirely unconcerned by them. She could sympathise with Ramiro's discomfort, and she'd even shared it at times, but she felt no unease at the prospect of generations of innocent descendants of the anti-messagers living out their lives beneath the stars here. They'd have more comfort and freedom than anyone on the *Peerless*. So long as the crops grew.

Azelio reached the plants; he squatted protectively in front of them. Agata turned to face the hillside.

'I forgot to use my stopwatch,' she confessed.

Azelio hadn't; he glanced down at his belt. 'Still a bit more than two lapses.'

Agata groped pre-emptively for an antidote to disappointment. 'If this doesn't go off, I think we could probably smash enough rock for a test plot by hand.'

Azelio buzzed. 'Not finely enough.'

'I'm serious! We could start with a pick but then mill down the rock chips – like making flour from grain.'

'If it does come to that, I'll be reminding you that you volunteered. One lapse to go.'

Agata felt her gut clench painfully. Her body was bracing instinctively for danger, but silence would be far worse.

The hillside erupted with light. She flung an arm in front of her eyes, but with her rear gaze she saw her shadow stretched out behind her. The ground shook, and she hummed softly, remembering the blast that had taken Medoro. But this was its opposite: a force that might finally heal the mountain, as much as it could ever be healed.

A warm gust of air struck her skin, carrying dust but nothing harder or sharper. The light had died; Agata lowered her arm and waited for her eyes to adjust back to the starlight.

A great, loose mound of debris lay at the base of the hill. Azelio rose to his feet and put a hand on her shoulder; she realised that she was shivering.

'It's all right,' he said.

'Yes.' At his touch Agata ached to feel more of his skin against her, but as an internal voice started weaving a story of the only fitting coda to this triumph, she shut off the absurd fantasy quickly, less afraid of any prospect of fission than of making a fool of herself with Azelio. 'Let's go see how it looks.'

They approached the blast site cautiously. In the planning meeting Tarquinia had raised the possibility of a delayed secondary collapse, but as they drew nearer that looked less likely: the new rock face was almost vertical, but they hadn't created an unstable cave or overhang.

Azelio strode forward to inspect the mound. He knelt and picked up a handful of debris. 'It looks fine enough,' he announced warily. 'There's some coarser grit in there as well, but that shouldn't matter.' He turned to face Agata. 'I think we've got a real chance.'

Hearing the hope in his voice, Agata felt the sense of fulfilment returning more strongly, but it was stripped now of any desire to follow her instincts to the end. She had all she needed: Azelio's friendship, and the satisfaction of having played a part in this scheme. It was enough.

Azelio shone his coherer across the top of the mound. 'That could feed a lot more than twelve plants,' he said gleefully. 'I'm just glad we didn't have to do it by hand.'

'Maybe the settlers will put their first farm here.' Agata chirped, delighted by an absurd thought. 'Maybe there are traces of them around, already – a few marks that they'll unmake in the rock.'

Azelio said, 'If we can prove that they're going to be here, will I still need to go ahead with the crop tests?'

'Yes – or they'd never come!'

'What if I lied and said I'd finished the tests?'

'Then we'll find some graffiti here, cursing you as the cause of the great famine.'

'Which would shame me into doing the tests,' Azelio replied. He raised the beam of his coherer from the mound to the rock face. 'What's that?'

'Where?' Agata couldn't see anything.

'About three strides up. It looks like writing.'

Agata was sure he was joking, but she aimed her own coherer at the same spot, and the slanted light revealed the shadows of a host of narrow ridges. It really did look as if part of the stone had been carved away, leaving these lines in relief – on a surface that the blast had just exposed for the first time.

'This is too strange,' she said. She stepped onto the mound and walked across the fresh soil. She could feel herself leaving footprints, but unmaking some as well.

On a closer view, it was clear that Azelio was right: the lines on the rock face formed symbols. The sides of the ridges appeared softened and eroded, as if a generation's worth of future dust storms had left their mark. But she could still make out most of the message.

'. . . came here from the home world,' she read. 'To offer thanks and bring you . . . courage.'

Azelio said, 'Who thanks whom for what?'

Agata had never been less discouraged; she had never felt less in need of this grace. But here it was: for Ramiro in his darkness, for Azelio and Tarquinia, for everyone back on the *Peerless*, for six more generations of struggling travellers yet to be born.

'It's from the ancestors,' she said. 'They're going to come here and write this. They're going to come here to tell us that everything we've done and everything we've been through was worth it in the end.'

23

As Tarquinia stepped aside, Ramiro moved closer and took his turn examining the rock face. He hadn't doubted his crew-mates' word, but since they'd had no reason to be carrying a camera there'd been room for him to wonder if they might have over-interpreted some random pattern that had formed as the explosion fractured the hillside.

'It does look genuine,' he concluded. 'Genuinely artificial, that is; don't ask for my opinion on the authorship.' After geology, he was going to have to add time-reversed archaeology to the list of disciplines he'd sadly neglected.

'We should leave now,' Agata insisted. 'As soon as the *Surveyor*'s ready.'

Ramiro turned away from the writing. 'What about the wheat?'

'The wheat doesn't matter,' Agata declared. 'If there's nothing left to fight about, there's no reason for anyone to migrate.'

Tarquinia was sceptical. 'You really think the Council's going to switch off the messaging system on our say-so?'

'What will they need it for?' Agata was beginning to sound exasperated. 'This proves that we make it to the reunion! There's no question of the *Peerless* being struck by a meteor – or tearing itself apart in a war. How can the Council claim that they need their system for safety and security once we've shown them a message that could only be written if we're safe and secure all the way to the home world?'

'They could argue that the settlers will write it,' Azelio suggested.

'What *settlers*?' Agata fumed. 'How could the settlers write something that would undermine their whole reason for being here?'

'If the Council doesn't take it seriously, it won't undermine anything,' Azelio reasoned. Ramiro wasn't sure if that was circular logic, but as self-serving political rhetoric it did have a horribly plausible ring to it.

'You've all lost your minds!' Agata moaned. 'If you think this isn't genuine, tell me what would count as proof of authorship. A message encrypted with a key that we're supposed to prepare now and then keep secret until we deliver it to the ancestors at the reunion? Even if we found something like that, you could still claim that the key might end up in someone else's hands along the way.'

Tarquinia said, 'It's not just a question of our own doubts; we have to take a broader view of this. If you and Azelio say the writing was there as soon as the rock was exposed, then I believe you – but all we'll be able to show the Council is an image taken some time after the fact. That's not even going to establish the sequence of events.'

'My role here is as a witness for the messagers,' Agata reminded her. 'Why would I suddenly change my allegiance and start lying about something like this – just to try to get the system shut down?'

'Twelve years isn't sudden,' Tarquinia replied. 'They might think we corrupted you.'

'Then what's the point of doing anything?' Agata retorted. 'Why test the crops, when we might be lying about that, too?'

Tarquinia tried a more conciliatory tone. 'Look, I might be wrong: they might listen to all our testimony and conclude that the message really is from the ancestors. But we can't take that for granted. We need to stay long enough to assess the new soil. It's just a few more stints; what harm is there in that?'

Agata looked away; she seemed to be struggling to calm herself. 'You're right,' she said finally. 'We came here to see if Esilio was habitable. And you risked your life for this experiment; it would be foolish not to wait for the results.'

'We'll spend some time imaging the site every way we can,' Tarquinia promised. 'We'll gather as much evidence as possible to put to the Council. Then Azelio can plant his crop – and whatever the outcome, it won't take away from the significance of the message.'

'That's true,' Agata agreed.

Hearing the disillusionment in her voice, Ramiro felt a pang of guilt. She'd run all the way to the *Surveyor* in a state of ecstasy, convinced that she'd just been handed the solution to all of the *Peerless*'s problems. He couldn't fault her sincerity, or the generous spirit in which she'd brought him the news. She really had believed that it would spare him from the prospect of dying on this benighted world.

But ever since he'd seen the writing for himself, he'd been unable to stop wondering if the message suited him too well. As far as he could recall, he'd never consciously planned to commit any kind of hoax – exploiting Agata's longing to commune with the ancestors in the hope that in her innocence she'd sell the lie convincingly to the people back home.

What he didn't know was exactly what his lack of preparation meant. The words were there, Agata had seen them, nothing could change that now. But with every moment that passed it seemed more likely to him that the ancestors had nothing to do with it, and that he would find a way to write the message himself.

Ramiro winced. 'Please don't do that.'

Tarquinia ignored him and continued to palpate his abdomen. 'You definitely have some kind of mass in your gut. Maybe we should think about cutting it out.'

'Don't be so dramatic. It will pass through me soon enough.'

'Not if the wall of the gut is paralysed.'

'I think I've had something like this before,' Ramiro lied. 'When I was a child. It only lasted for a couple of days.'

Tarquinia gazed down at him, puzzled and concerned. 'I'd thought we'd passed every influence we had back and forth to each other, long ago. Where does a new disease come from, after six years in isolation?'

'Maybe I caught it from the settlers,' Ramiro joked. 'Maybe the first time-reversed influence evolves here, shortly after they arrive.'

'No eating, no work, just rest. Is that clear?'

'Yes, Uncle.'

Tarquinia gave him a stern, reappraising stare. 'If you're faking this to get out of helping with the cooling system—'

'Faking a lump in my gut?' he protested. 'Seriously, I won't eat, I promise. Last time I tried it made the pain unbearable.'

'All right.' She squeezed his shoulder. 'I'll be wearing an audio link, so if you need anything just yell.'

'Thank you.'

When she'd gone, Ramiro turned in his sand bed, trying to find a half-comfortable position. The smear of sealing resin he'd spread through the loaf had been tasteless and odourless, but the effects had exceeded his expectations. All the other substances he'd tried in similar doses had either been inert or had caused him to vomit up the meal immediately. So long as his gut did eventually regain the power of peristalsis, he'd have no qualms about sharing this 'influence' with Agata: she'd be laid low for a day or two, but the precedent of his own recovery would spare her from too much mental anguish.

All the rest would be down to timing. Azelio would want to watch over Agata, the way she'd cared for him when he'd been injured, and if he'd finished his work with the test crop there'd be no reason for him to return to the blast site.

Tarquinia would be the hardest witness to avoid. Ramiro didn't want to risk raising her suspicions by trying to manipulate her movements – let alone poisoning her – so he'd have to contrive an innocent-sounding reason to be away from the *Surveyor* for at least two bells. Either that, or tell her everything.

His gut convulsed; he rearranged himself, curling around the site of the pain, trying to take the pressure off the lump of trapped food. If he was the author of the message, nothing would intervene to prevent him from carving it before the *Surveyor* departed, but that was no guarantee that his ruse would remain undiscovered. He couldn't presume that Tarquinia would approve of the deception but, even if she did, the mere act of widening his private scheme into a conspiracy could only weaken the chance that the crew would convince their interrogators back on the *Peerless*. Agata would be the passionate advocate for her own interpretation, while Azelio and Tarquinia would be more sceptical but still able to give honest, credible testimony. Why ruin that by forcing Tarquinia to lie?

Of course, Greta would assume that he was behind the whole thing before he'd even spoken a word. But so long as the Council hadn't abolished the popular vote entirely, it was not beyond hope that the expedition's claims could sway enough travellers into changing their position. Not even a message in light from the time of the reunion could be authenticated beyond doubt, but if people were willing to give this message in stone any credence at all, it could shift the balance of their anxieties and prompt them to heal the rift that the system had created.

The strangest part was that everyone on the mountain would already know what collective decision they'd take. So the moment the *Surveyor* had re-established a link with the *Peerless* – long before the crew had been questioned in person and their individual stories tested and compared – he would discover whether or not the hoax had been in vain.

'Aren't they beautiful!' Azelio enthused.

'Well, they're not dead,' Ramiro allowed. After three stints rooted in the debris of the explosion, all twelve plants still displayed a modest selection of bright flowers – which was more than any of the earlier trials had achieved.

'They're growing,' Azelio assured him. 'Every one of them.' He knelt down near the start of the row. 'This seedling is half as tall again as it was when I put it in.' He gestured along the progression of plants. 'In fact, each one of them has come close to matching the way its neighbour appeared at the start. I know that doesn't make much of an impression: everything you see now in the first eleven specimens is something you've seen before from the second to the twelfth. It's almost as if you've just shifted your gaze slightly. But the figures bear it out: we've made the soil fertile.'

'Right.' Ramiro was trying his best to seem pleased, but short of some spectacle of agrarian bounty to summon forth an instinctive response it was hard not to take a purely calculating view.

'You wanted this to fail,' Azelio guessed. 'You thought that might put more pressure on the Council?'

'I did,' Ramiro admitted. 'Though maybe that was foolish. It might have made things worse.'

'How?'

'If we'd ended up telling them that Esilio was uninhabitable they might have thought that we were lying about everything, just to serve an agenda.' Ramiro paused for a moment to convince himself that he really had managed to rephrase the original version in his head – *lying about this, too* – before it had escaped from thought into speech. 'This way, we'll still be offering them a choice: they can accept that the system's redundant now that we know that the reunion will happen, or they can go ahead with the migration now that it's clear that the settlers needn't starve. They're not the kind of people who appreciate being told that all the evidence points the same way.'

Azelio said, 'Forget the politics for one chime. Isn't it something, just to see the plants thriving? We stamped our arrow into the soil and made wheat grow backwards in Esilian time!'

'We did.'

Azelio rose to his feet. 'At least I'll be able to tell Luisa that her picture of the wheat-flowers glowing on Esilio came true.' He walked around to the side of the row, then took the camera from his tool belt to capture a portrait. Ramiro had seen the girl's drawing, and the truth was that it made an eerily good match.

'I've been thinking of leaving half the plants here,' Azelio added. 'I'd take six back for people to study, and let the rest grow and drop their seeds. I know that sounds like some kind of vote for the migration, but it's not meant that way. I just hate the idea of ripping them all out. And if settlers do end up coming here, there'd be something welcoming about finding a crop already growing – even a token presence like this.'

'Hmm.' Ramiro had no problem with the sentiment, so long as he didn't end up harvesting the field himself. And if he was being cynical, it could only make the Council's choice seem even more open if the expedition had left Esilio with an ongoing farm of its own. Short of staying here to tend it in person, he couldn't have made the false alternative sound more genuine.

'Do you mind if I head back to the *Surveyor*?' he asked. He'd volunteered to help with the measurements, but Azelio would cope perfectly well on his own. 'I'm getting some cramps again; I thought they'd stopped, but . . .'

Azelio said, 'Of course. Will you be all right?'

'I'll be fine, don't worry.'

Ramiro clutched his abdomen and moved away slowly, but once he was out of sight he broke into a run. He'd planned the detour carefully, and with the air calm it was easy to navigate by the stars. Stones and sand fled from his feet, and sought them; he'd thought he'd grown used to that, but the speed made it stranger. His gait seemed at once more precarious and more certain; it was as if he were watching a recording of himself performing a difficult balancing act, while knowing for a fact that he hadn't actually toppled over.

Even by starlight, the probe's truncated cone stood out sharply from the haphazard shapes of the rocks around it. Ramiro paused to orient himself carefully before squatting down and embracing the thing. Just spending so much time in Esilio's gravity must have left him stronger than he had been by the standards of the mountain, but on balance the penalty it added now felt like more than enough to wipe out that advantage. He waddled across the valley floor, muttering curses, forcing himself to continue for a count of three gross steps before resting.

No one had come this way since the last of the original test plots had died off, and no one would have reason to do so again. If he could leave the probe unseen a short walk from the *Surveyor*, it would give him a chance to revisit the blast site while pretending to be retrieving the thing. That retrieval had never been part of the mission plan, but he couldn't see anyone objecting to his desire to scrutinise the probe's materials in the aftermath of its peculiar heating. They were all going to need their projects to help pass the time on the long journey back.

As Ramiro hefted the probe again, an amused voice in the back of his head demanded: *Why go to so much trouble?* If he abandoned the whole frantic scheme right now, what exactly would that change? He'd be able to look Greta in the eye and tell her honestly that he'd had nothing to do with the inscription. The true author of the words would turn out to be a settler playing along as a kind of bitter joke, or a genuine visitor from the home world six generations hence. In either case, how would he be worse off?

His arms were beginning to ache; he lowered the probe to the ground.

What he'd feared the messaging system would impose on him was an endless plateau of least resistance: every decision he learnt that he would make would strike him as acceptable – never entirely out of character, never deeply morally repugnant – but it would still be less his own than if he'd been left to ruminate on the matter without the deadening intervention of foreknowledge.

To feel alive, he needed to feel himself struggling moment by moment to shape his own history. It was not enough to look down on events from above like a biologist watching a worm in a maze, content to note that this creature's actions had never actually gone against its wishes. He desperately wanted to see the messaging system abandoned – by whatever means it took, short of war – but it was *not* all the same to him whether he played a real part in the victory, or whether he was merely an onlooker who hadn't needed to lift a finger. Why should he take the path of least resistance now, when no one was forcing it on him?

As Ramiro lifted the probe and struggled forward, he felt a rush of joy. He'd made the right choice. Agata had been overcome with bliss by the thought that the ancestors had reached across time to favour her with their beneficence – but now that he'd affirmed that he was the author of his own good fortune, Ramiro felt infinitely more blessed. Let the ancestors worry about their own problems: he didn't need their help. He could cheat the Council out of their ruinous folly entirely on his own.

Ramiro passed the last of the plants to Azelio, then scrambled through the airlock himself.

'Time to celebrate the harvest!' he said, reflexively brushing dust off his hands, though as much as he removed rose from the floor to replace it.

'Don't get any ideas!' Azelio positioned himself protectively in front of the repotted wheat.

'Don't worry; there wouldn't be enough there to feed a vole.' Ramiro called out to Agata and Tarquinia, then headed for the pantry to fetch eight loaves.

The four of them sat together in the front cabin. Tarquinia said, 'Before I plot the ascent, I thought I'd take a vote on whether we should do a few more low orbits – to see if we can spot the pre-relics of any future cities.'

'No thanks,' Ramiro replied. 'If there are going to be settlers I don't want to know about it . . . but settlers would avoid unmaking traces anyway. They'd only raise cities on what looked like untouched ground.'

'They wouldn't have to be built by settlers from the *Peerless*,' Azelio pointed out. 'If the ancestors come here after the reunion, who knows how long they'll stay?'

'It can't hurt to look,' Agata agreed. Ramiro watched as she finished her first loaf, but after raising the second one halfway to her mouth she put it back on the plate. 'Does anyone want this?'

'I'm starving,' Azelio said. 'Are you sure you've had enough?'

'Absolutely.'

Azelio reached over and took it. Ramiro forced himself to look elsewhere as he tried to decide whether or not to intervene. He might get away with a joking confiscation – protesting that he'd carried more of the plants back than Azelio – but that could only end with him eating the loaf himself. Two crew members falling ill hadn't been the plan, but did it matter? Ramiro stole a glance at Azelio's plate and saw that he no longer had a choice.

He pretended to be annoyed by the vote on the orbits and stayed out of the conversation, finishing his meal while Tarquinia was still eating. 'I might start bringing in the tents,' he said. He needed a chance to come and go from the storeroom without anyone beside him, in order to get the tools for the inscription outside.

'Relax,' Tarquinia said. 'There's no rush. We can do that later.'

'I want to get a start while it's calm,' he insisted. 'If a storm comes in it could take twice as long.'

In the storeroom he found the lever for extracting the tent stakes, but he couldn't see where the chisel had gone. With the constant gravity, people had grown careless about slotting every tool into place. He left quickly, not wanting Tarquinia to wonder what could be taking him so long.

Outside, he took the stakes and poles out of the first tent, then folded the fabric down into a square. There was no particular reason for taking the tents back with them; it almost came down to mere tidiness, a virtue that made more sense in the confined spaces of the mountain. But if leaving six of the wheat plants growing backwards in time felt apt, requiring Esilio to manufacture four tents out of dust seemed more of an affront. One day a successor to Agata might find an equation that spelt out exactly how much inexplicable junk a time-reversed world could be expected to cough up, just to cater to the whims of visitors with a different arrow. If there was a limit, that might even be the ultimate reason why there would never be settlers here: a whole city might have pushed the mathematics of consistency past its choking point. Ramiro found the idea encouraging; nothing helped a plan run more smoothly than having a law of physics on its side.

In the front cabin, the rest of the crew were still sitting and talking, digesting their meals. Ramiro carried the disassembled tent past them into the storeroom and searched again for the chisel, with no luck. It had to be somewhere, but he couldn't ask the others if they'd seen it.

As he walked back into the cabin he saw Agata beginning to sway on her couch. 'That's not right,' she muttered, pressing a fist to her chest. 'It's like a rock in my gut.'

'Sounds like what I had,' Ramiro ventured. 'You should go and lie down. If you rest straight away it might be over faster than it was for me.'

'So you're still infectious?' Tarquinia eyed him warily. 'You'd better stay in your cabin, too.'

'No, I must have spread it earlier,' Ramiro replied. 'There's probably a dormant period after the body takes it in.'

'How do you know that?' Tarquinia demanded irritably. 'Have you got some study of the aetiology at hand?'

'No, but—'

'I have to get us off this planet safely,' she said. 'What am I meant to do: wait until I've caught this disease and been through the symptoms, so I know it won't happen later when I'm in the middle of the ascent?'

'You feel well now, don't you?' Ramiro asked her.

'I don't,' Azelio said, massaging his sternum with one palm.

Tarquinia stood. 'I want all three of you in your cabins. If you need anything, call me through the link; I'll put on a cooling bag and helmet and bring it to you. But no one leaves their room.'

'I'm perfectly healthy!' Ramiro protested. 'We can stay out of each other's way – I'll finish bringing in the tents, and I'll warn you before I come through the airlock.'

'No,' Tarquinia said flatly. 'The tents aren't important, but I can get them myself. I want everyone in their cabins now. Is that understood?'

Agata rose and began limping away, bent over in pain. Azelio jumped up and went to help her. Ramiro stayed where he was; once the others had left he would have to explain his plan to Tarquinia.

'Ramiro,' she said, gesturing towards the passage. 'Please. I know you've recovered, but I can't risk catching this.'

Azelio was watching them with his rear gaze, puzzled by Ramiro's stubbornness. Ramiro struggled to think of a plausible reason to stand his ground; raising the idea of bringing in the probe now would only make it sound more suspicious.

He followed Azelio and Agata. When they'd entered their rooms and closed the doors, Ramiro closed his own from the outside.

He stood motionless for a while, trying to judge how quietly he could walk back to the front cabin, trying to think of a gesture he could make that would guarantee that Tarquinia wouldn't respond to the sight of him with an angry shout. From where he stood he could see her crossing the cabin, moving towards the airlock. She was going out to finish retrieving the tents; she had the lever he'd used in her hand.

As she disappeared from view he cursed silently. Then he started down the passage, red dust tickling his feet. He would follow her out and explain everything, confess to the poisoning, put his plan at her mercy. Maybe she'd treat his desire to create the message as a kind of empty vanity and refuse to be a part of it, lest his deceit undermined the impact of the find. But he couldn't be a helpless spectator, merely watching the mountain's history unfold. She'd understand that, surely?

He stood at the entrance to the front cabin. Tarquinia had gone out – but he suddenly remembered that he'd never brought the tent-lever back into the *Surveyor*. He'd left it by the airlock outside. She'd been carrying something else, something similar in appearance.

He heard Agata humming with pain as the spasms in her gut failed to dislodge the tainted meal. Ramiro retraced his steps and managed to get into his room, with the door emitting no more than a faint squeak while his hapless victim was at her loudest. He squatted by his bed, staring at the floor, trying to understand what was happening.

How could he carve anything into the rock face, if the idea of doing it had only come to him after he'd seen the result? Even the choice of words hadn't sounded like his own. If he'd only selected them because he'd read them, who would have made the choice? No one. Agata had told him endlessly: a loop could never contain complexity with no antecedent but itself, because the probability would be far too low. There could be no words appearing on rocks for no other reason than the fact that they'd done so.

But long before Agata had dragged the two of them to the blast site, Tarquinia had seen him falling apart. And as each new phenomenon they witnessed on Esilio made the prospect of returning with the settlers more dispiriting, she must have started searching for a way for them to stay on the mountain together – to live out their final years in a place where the dust wouldn't see them coming, where their graves had not already been dug.

Ramiro pressed his face into his hands and fought to stay silent, afraid that if he let his tympanum stir he'd shout down the walls with some confused, alarming paean to the woman that would convince the others that he'd lost his mind. He couldn't let any hint of the plan slip out – or even let Tarquinia know that he'd uncovered it. She hadn't wanted a co-conspirator any more than he had, and they'd both make more believable witnesses if they'd never spoken of what had happened, never made it real in anyone else's eyes.

He sat by the bed listening for her footsteps, wondering if he could be mistaken. It wouldn't take long to pull down a tent and bring it inside, and she'd have no reason to return quietly.

Agata hummed in misery, and Azelio called out, trying to console her. But between these exchanges, Ramiro heard nothing but the wind blowing dust across the hull.

24

'The link's open!' Tarquinia shouted.

Agata had woken just moments earlier, and for moments more she lay in a daze, astonished at her prescience. Then it occurred to her that Tarquinia must have repeated the call several times.

She rose from her bed and raced down the passage, sand still clinging to the skin of her back. The rest of the crew were already gathered around the console.

'. . . all safe and in good health,' Tarquinia was saying. 'We landed successfully on Esilio and made an assessment of its potential for settlement; we'll be sending the technical reports shortly. But as you can imagine, we're eager for news from the mountain.'

There was a perceptible delay as the ultraviolet pulses crossed the void, then a man's voice replied: 'We'll need to receive your reports first, before the channel is used for personal calls.'

Tarquinia was taken aback. 'I understand. But can't you fill us in on what's been happening?'

'What do you want to know?' the man inquired impassively.

'Is the messaging system working?' Ramiro interjected.

'Yes.'

'How long has it been in use?' Tarquinia asked.

'Almost three years.'

Agata leant forward towards the microphone. 'And how long will it remain in use?'

The signal's time in transit was fixed; the awkward pause before the reply was as unmistakable as if they'd been speaking face to face. 'My instructions are to receive your reports and then facilitate personal calls, not to engage in an open-ended dialogue.'

Agata didn't know what to make of this rebuff. But the exchange

237

would be monitored and recorded; she couldn't blame the link operator if he didn't want to break any protocol imposed from above.

Tarquinia said, 'I'll queue up the reports now, and resume contact when the transmission's complete.'

'Thank you, *Surveyor*. Audio out.'

'What a welcome!' Azelio complained. 'And it's not as if we could have caught them unprepared.'

'Oh, I'm sure they were thrilled by our safe return,' Ramiro replied. 'We're just three years late for the party.'

The console switched to a graphic showing the progress of the data transmissions. Agata squinted in disbelief at the predicted completion time, but caught herself before protesting out loud. In order to make the time lag reasonable at this distance, they needed to use very fast UV. But such high velocities also meant very low frequencies, and hence low bandwidth.

'Azelio gets the first call,' Tarquinia decided. 'Then Agata, Ramiro, myself.'

They all knew better than to argue with the pilot. Agata returned to her room and sat at her desk, skimming through the reports of her work that Lila would be receiving shortly – and then presumably sending back to herself at some time just after the system started operating. As they'd drawn closer to the *Peerless*, Agata had considered withholding her results from the transmission – hoping that she might yet complete the analysis of the curved vacuum on her own, even if it meant working in isolation in the mountain for another few years. In the end, though, that had seemed petty and mean-spirited. She'd grown tired of struggling on and on without any feedback from her peers. Now she would learn in an instant what the collective effort of the physics community had achieved over the last three years, as they argued over the significance of the diagram calculus – improving it, extending it, or maybe even refuting it entirely. She couldn't decide whether to be terrified or exhilarated, but even if her methods had been excoriated, torn apart and rebuilt entirely, they could only have been replaced by something better. Whatever the final synthesis was, it would have to be spectacular.

When Tarquinia announced that Azelio's call was coming through, instead of taking it in his own cabin he invited everyone to join him at the main console.

'Uncle?'

Agata shivered at the sound of Luisa's voice, unmistakably older but still not a woman's. It would have felt less strange if it hadn't changed at all.

Azelio said, 'I'm here! How are you, my darling?'

'I'm fine. We got your messages from after you arrived. We've played them over and over.'

'That's wonderful.' Azelio looked lost for a moment. 'Did you know we had a Hurtler scrape the side of the hull? Tarquinia went flying out into the void, and Agata had to go out and rescue her.'

'No!' Luisa was impressed, but a little miffed as well. 'Why didn't you tell us that before?'

'I didn't want you worrying. But everyone's safe – you'll see us all soon.'

'I know,' Luisa replied, mystified that he'd feel any need to point this out.

'Yes.' Azelio was struggling again: what was worth saying now, if he'd need to omit it from the great homecoming message in order to keep it from sounding stale? 'Is your brother there?'

'He didn't want to come.' This time Luisa seemed unsurprised by Azelio's ignorance.

'Tell him that's all right,' Azelio replied. 'I can understand if he didn't feel like talking this way.'

There was a long pause. 'You already told him that yourself.'

An older, male voice came over the link. 'Azelio?'

'Girardo! How are you, Uncle?'

'Everything's fine,' Girardo assured him, but he spoke with unusual vehemence. Things were fine not as a matter of course, but in defiance of some prevailing difficulty. 'We know you'll get back safely. That's enough.'

'Enough?' Azelio glanced at Agata, as if she might have some idea of what he should read into the word. 'Is Luisa still there?'

'I'm here,' Luisa replied.

'All right.' Azelio decided not to pursue an explanation in her presence. 'I'll be seeing you all very soon.'

'Of course,' Girardo agreed.

'My love to all of you,' Azelio said, forcing a tone of casual cheerfulness.

'And you,' Luisa replied.

Azelio cut the link and sat in silence.

'It looks as if there's going to be a knack to this,' Ramiro observed. 'They might have added a few tenses to the language while we were away.'

Agata squeezed Azelio's shoulder. 'Luisa sounded happy. And your uncle was probably just irritated by some political development.'

He turned to her. 'What's that a euphemism for? More people in prison, or more smoking ruins?'

'I'll sort everything out when I talk to Lila,' Agata assured him. Having witnessed Azelio stumbling she'd be better prepared to communicate across the gap.

But when her own call was connected she barely made it through the greetings before her brain seized up.

'The light bending . . . do you know about that?' she babbled.

'I read your report,' Lila replied. 'Those observations were impeccable, and you've separated the curvature theory from Vittorio's as sharply as we could have wished. It's a great achievement.' The words were warm and sincere – but Lila's excitement at hearing that her life's work had been validated was long gone. Agata had imagined the two of them dancing elatedly around her office, chanting 'Four-space is curved! Gravity is not a force!' But that was never going to happen: this was old news for both of them now.

'What did you make of the vacuum-energy work?' she asked hopefully.

'The diagram calculus is beautiful.' Lila didn't use that word lightly. 'It's the most promising approach I've seen for a long time.'

Beautiful . . . but still merely promising? Agata wasn't offended; she knew that she hadn't taken the project to completion herself. But what had Lila and her students been doing in the interim? She wasn't vain enough to imagine that they'd been hanging back, waiting for her to join them in the flesh and guide them forward.

'So how much progress has there been?' Agata pressed her. 'The effects of curvature and topology were still very sketchy in the version I sent you – but I'm sure people must have found ways to tidy up most of the loose ends by now.'

Lila hesitated. 'I'm afraid things are much where you left them.'

'Where I left them?' Agata was confused. 'When did all of this reach you?'

'Almost three years ago,' Lila replied.

Agata couldn't hide her disappointment. 'And no one's tried to take it any further?' She'd put ten years of her life into the diagram calculus, and the whole physics community had spurned the approach.

'The lack of progress isn't from a want of trying,' Lila insisted. 'And you shouldn't take it personally. It's got nothing to do with the quality of your work or the way it's been received. The problem is far more widespread than that.'

Agata was mollified, but still confused. 'What problem?'

'We've all hit a dead patch,' Lila said sadly. 'Chemists, biologists, astronomers, engineers. Since they switched on the messaging system, there hasn't been a single new idea across the mountain.'

'You mean no one's been sending back new ideas?' Agata had predicted as much – but surely that self-censorship hadn't surprised anyone.

'Oh, the messages have contained no innovations,' Lila confirmed. 'But neither has the work itself.'

'I don't understand,' Agata admitted.

Lila said, 'If people did innovate, the results would leak back to them one way or another. I know you believed that they'd be able to keep quiet, so everything would go on as usual. But everything has not gone on as usual. We've had no new ideas since the system was turned on – because if we'd had them, we would have heard of them before we'd had a chance to think of them ourselves. The barriers to information flow are so porous now that the knowledge gradient has been flattened: the past contains everything the future contains . . . which means the future contains nothing more than the past.'

Agata was stunned. If this was true, the messaging system had undermined the whole reason for the mountain's existence. Every generation before her had advanced their understanding in one field or another. What would her own generation be famous for? *Rendering the creation of new knowledge impossible.*

She dragged herself out of the dismal fantasy. To have lost three years was appalling, but the disaster would be self-limiting in the end.

'So how long does this go on?' she asked Lila.

'About a dozen more stints.'

That would be five stints after the *Surveyor* returned. 'I'm surprised people didn't act sooner.' The self-censorship hypothesis predicted an absence of news of future innovations – but news of their absence could have been sent back as soon as the dire situation was apparent. 'I suppose it's the writing we found on Esilio that tips the balance in the end?' Agata suggested. 'The system could hardly have been shut down before the *Surveyor* returned with that discovery, if it's a crucial element in swinging the vote.'

Lila said, 'The system isn't shut down by a vote.'

Agata couldn't understand why her tone was so bleak. She'd endured three frustrating years, but the dark times would soon be over. 'So the Council plans to act unilaterally?'

'There is no vote, there is no plan, there is no explanation,' Lila replied. 'All we know is that we've received no messages from any time later than a dozen stints from now. And in the run-up, there's nothing telling us why.'

'The data just cuts out?' Agata glanced up from the console; the expression on Tarquinia's face was as grim as Lila's voice.

'Yes.'

'So there's a glitch of some kind,' Agata concluded. She couldn't take all this ominous brooding seriously; she'd seen the proof with her own eyes that the *Peerless* would survive all the way to the re-union.

'No,' Lila said flatly. 'We ended up building more channels. They operate independently, so there could hardly be a glitch in all of them.'

Agata struggled to unpick the logic of that. 'You had to build a second channel, even though the first one already told you that it wouldn't help . . . because if you hadn't built it you couldn't have known that it wouldn't help. But why build a third?'

'We built a dozen.' Lila buzzed, darkly amused. 'You're forgetting the Council's paranoia. They weren't convinced that they were being honest with each other about this event, so the process couldn't stop until they each had a messaging channel of their own – built and run by people they'd vetted themselves.'

Agata was distracted for a moment by the sight of Ramiro, rocking back and forth with one hand against his tympanum, trying to contain his mirth.

'So what came of all that?' she asked. 'Putting aside our own paranoia and assuming that at least one Councillor who found the truth would let us know.'

Lila said, 'With every channel, the story's been the same: the messages cut out at exactly the same time, and nothing that's sent back while the system is still working tells us why.'

25

'I just found a picture of you in the archives,' Greta said. 'There's a banner behind you saying WELCOME HOME, but all in all it's still quite sad. You look so old and worn down that you might be that woman's uncle, not her brother. And her children don't seem happy to see you at all.'

'You sound like an actor who's over-rehearsed her lines,' Ramiro replied. 'I suppose you've studied the recording of this conversation a dozen times?'

Greta buzzed derisively. 'Don't flatter yourself.'

'No? Your first interaction with the *Surveyor*, in the middle of a political crisis? You didn't send that back to the earliest moment that the bandwidth of the oldest channel allowed?'

'I've read a summary, of course.' Greta had to make it clear that she'd done her duty. 'But I promise you, there wasn't anything worth studying.'

Ramiro suspected that she was telling the truth; the technical reports would have been more valuable. But even if this conversation had been worthless to her, it didn't follow that he'd get nothing out of it himself.

'Thank you for the bomb,' he said. 'That really came in handy.'

'Any time.'

'So are you still on the *Peerless*?' he wondered. 'Or have you evacuated already?'

'I'm where I need to be.'

'In the administrative sense, or the teleological?' He waited, but Greta didn't dignify that with a reply. 'I'm guessing that there are a dozen evacuation craft, one for each Councillor – more or less copied from the *Surveyor*'s plans. You started building them just after the system was switched on, when you learnt that Esilio was habitable and the *Peerless* might be in danger. You would have liked to improve the design or speed up the construction and make dozens more – but poor Verano found himself unable to innovate that much.'

Greta said, 'All you need to know is that the Council will continue to govern across the disruption. The system proved its worth from the start.'

'If you think that the *Peerless* is going to hit something, why not build an extra channel far away?' Ramiro mused. 'Ah – that would require some new engineering, wouldn't it? The first plan put the light path running along the axis, making use of the rigidity of the mountain to stabilise the mirrors. So all you've been able to do is repeat that. Ordinarily, the instrument builders would have found a way to keep the mirrors aligned out in the void – but if they'd managed to do that someone would have heard about it long before the event. With twelve separate teams all spying on each other, they can't even keep a secret from themselves when that's their only real hope of success.'

'You know a great deal less than you imagine,' Greta said flatly.

'Really? If only you hadn't had to know everything yourself. You didn't just turn traveller against traveller: you've turned the mere possibility of knowledge into a kind of stupefying drug.'

'There are some flaws in the system,' Greta conceded. 'We'll learn from them. After the disruption, certain things will be reorganised.'

'*Reorganised?*' Ramiro buzzed. 'Will you put all the scientists and engineers in isolation, incommunicado, in the hope that that will solve the problem?'

'Just be patient,' she said. 'You'll see how things turn out.'

'Tell me one thing, then,' Ramiro asked solemnly. 'Tell me there's a pact between the Councillors to shut down all their channels voluntarily. Tell me the disruption's nothing more than that.'

'I can't lie to you,' Greta replied. 'The disruption is not a voluntary shutdown, it's proof of a grave threat to the integrity of the *Peerless*. Knowing that it's coming will help minimise the danger and ensure the continuity of governance – but beyond that, I know no more than you do.'

Agata brought a basket of loaves from the pantry and passed it around. 'I don't know why everyone's so gloomy,' she said, breaking the silence. 'The whole idea of a collision makes no sense to me.'

Ramiro approached the subject warily. 'What if the Councillors and their entourage are prepared to travel to Esilio? They wouldn't have an easy life there, but over time they might be able to build up their resources to the point where their descendants could protect the home world. There needn't be a contradiction.'

'I'm not talking about the inscription,' Agata replied. 'Whatever hit the *Peerless* would have to be large enough to disrupt the messaging system immediately, or there'd be a message describing the initial effects of the impact: a fire on the slopes, a breach of the hull – even if people didn't have time to narrate it, there'd be instrument readings sent back automatically. But anything that large ought to be visible as it approached. Even if it was travelling at infinite speed, it would cast a shadow against the orthogonal stars that we could pick up with time-reversed cameras.'

Azelio was hanging on her words, desperate for reassurance. 'What if it comes in from the wrong direction?' he asked.

'There is no wrong direction if you deploy the cameras properly,' Agata insisted. 'Suppose this meteor is approaching with infinite speed from the home cluster side. That would render it invisible from the mountain, but if it passed a swarm of time-reversed cameras *looking back towards the mountain*, they'd see the meteor's shadow against the orthogonal stars before it was actually present.'

Ramiro wasn't persuaded. 'That all sounds good in theory, but the surveillance network certainly wasn't that sophisticated when we left. There'd be some serious technical challenges with processing the data fast enough and getting the result back to the *Peerless* before the impact. It wouldn't be trivial.'

'And that's the measure of things now?' Azelio was incredulous. 'You're saying that everything we do to protect ourselves is only possible if it's *trivial*? I thought this was all down to probabilities! How likely is it that people who desperately want to solve these problems could just sit at their desks fretting about it, while making no progress at all?'

He turned to Agata for support, but her confidence was wavering. 'I spent years in that state myself,' she admitted. 'It's not that difficult to achieve.'

Azelio lowered his gaze. 'We should start our own evacuation, then. Bring as many people as we can on board.'

'I'd have no objection to that,' Tarquinia said. 'But once we dock, whatever happens to the *Surveyor* will be out of my hands.' Ramiro had a brief fantasy of the *Surveyor* orbiting the mountain at a safe remove while evacuees jetted across the void to join them – but unless they were lugging six years' worth of food there wouldn't be much point. And even then it could only end badly, once the lucky few had to start turning the rest away.

Azelio's expression changed abruptly. He buzzed with a kind of pained relief, as if he'd just decided that his fears were not only groundless but embarrassingly naïve. 'Whatever else we're missing,' he said, 'we know the *Peerless*'s location when the disruption takes place. If we were going to be hit by something, we could avoid that just by changing course: we wouldn't happily steer straight for the meteor.'

Ramiro said, 'Maybe they will change course. Maybe they already did. Either way, the disruption still happens.'

'Exactly!' Azelio replied. 'So it can't be down to a collision. If changing the location were enough to stop it happening . . . it couldn't happen. On Esilio, we were never forced to do anything against our will, so how could a mountain full of people with no intention of dying be forced to choose a fatal trajectory? Stumbling blindly into a collision would be one thing – but how could it happen with foreknowledge?'

Agata considered this. 'I think your argument would hold if we knew the cause with certainty. But it's not so clear-cut when we're less informed – when we're not sure that the disruption will be fatal, and we're not sure that it involves a collision at all.'

Azelio scowled. 'So because we can't *know* that it's a collision . . . it's more likely that it is?'

'Is that really so strange?' Agata replied. 'If everyone on the *Peerless* was confronted with the certain knowledge that the course they were on was suicidal, then there's no way they'd persist with it – unless some freakishly unlikely set of events undermined the efficacy of their intentions. With three years' warning to achieve the necessary swerve, what could possibly stop them? The engines would need to drop off, and every last person capable of improvising any kind of substitute would need to die of some convenient affliction. I don't believe for a moment that the cosmos contains anything so unlikely.

'But taking an unknown risk is different. If we don't know exactly what would make us safe, there's no need for an endless barrage of misfortune to keep us from finding the right solution.'

Azelio abandoned the argument and the cabin fell into a despondent silence. Ramiro almost wished he hadn't argued against Agata's first, cheerful verdict. He couldn't imagine what Azelio was going through, but even his own brief, hallucinatory experiences of fatherhood offered a hint. Nothing could be more harrowing than being forced to contemplate the death of the children you'd promised to protect.

'Maybe the Councillors are going to shut down the system themselves,' he suggested. 'Just because Greta denied it doesn't mean they won't do it.'

'But why would they?' Tarquinia asked irritably.

'If it's a choice between that and the destruction of the *Peerless*,' Ramiro replied, 'then I don't believe they'd choose the latter. Whatever their flaws, they're not that deranged.'

Azelio was taking no comfort from the theory. 'But are they deranged enough to think that that's their choice? If you can't avoid a meteor by choosing your trajectory, how can you avoid it just by switching off the messaging system?'

Agata had a different objection. 'If they did shut down the system, wouldn't that be an unsupported loop? They'd only be doing it because they learnt that it was going to happen.'

'There's not much complexity to it, though,' Ramiro argued. 'It's hardly the same as learning a whole new theory of the vacuum from your future self; all they have to do is flick a switch.'

'The Council wouldn't want the mountain destroyed,' Tarquinia agreed, 'but they might well share Azelio's view about their choices. They've come into this looking for a vindication of the system – so I don't see anything inconsistent if they find themselves receiving three years' worth of reports from the future that all describe them clinging to their original position: that the whole thing's a boon, and there couldn't possibly be any reason to shut it down deliberately.'

Ramiro ran his hands over his face. 'Forget the Council, then. Let's assume that there's no chance of them causing the disruption. What's the next most benign explanation?'

'We could do it ourselves,' Tarquinia suggested.

'How?' Azelio demanded. 'What could we do that would be harder to see coming than a meteor at infinite speed?'

'I have no idea yet,' Tarquinia admitted. 'But at least we're isolated from the messaging system for a few more stints. We ought to be less vulnerable to the innovation block.'

Agata said, 'But in the end, it would only be the shutdown itself that would have driven us to find a way to cause the shutdown.'

'And that's meant to stop us?' Tarquinia was undeterred. 'If that kind of loop really is too unlikely to be true, then we'll find out eventually. But the only way to know is to try it.'

Ramiro recalled his own farcical attempt to steal the authorship of the fake inscription from her. It still seemed wisest to keep that to himself, but he didn't need to confess anything to make the case for a more robust strategy.

He said, 'There are plenty of people on the *Peerless* who could have planned this shutdown long before they heard about it.'

'You mean saboteurs?' Agata asked coldly. 'The people who murdered the camera team? You want to replace a meteor strike with a bomb?'

'Of course not.' Ramiro spoke more carefully. 'Most of the anti-messagers found those murders abhorrent, but a group of them could still be planning a way to cause the disruption without hurting anyone. And if they're intent on using explosives at all, we can try to replace that with something better.'

Tarquinia understood. 'We have seven stints to work out a plan of our own, and then we can try to sell it to these would-be saboteurs. That way it becomes a hybrid effort: their motives predate the news of the disruption, but if they've left the details too late we might be able to offer them a technological edge.'

Azelio hummed with frustration. 'What's all this talk of replacement? If a meteor is going to hit us, it's going to hit us! You can devise as many ingenious plans as you like to try to sabotage the system at the very same moment, but if there's a rock on its way, nothing you do is going to make it disappear.'

'*If* there's a rock on its way, that's true,' Ramiro conceded. 'But until we know that there is, why should we assume that? The history of the next twelve stints ends with the messaging system failing; we're about as certain of that as we can be. Some sequence of events has to fill the gap between that certainty and all the other things we know. So which snippets would you rather the cosmos had on hand to complete the story? Just one, where a meteor hits the *Peerless*? Just two: a meteor, or a bomb? Making our own preferred version possible won't rule out everything else – but if we don't even try, we'll rule out our own best hope entirely.'

Agata brought a schematic onto her chest. 'Whatever the details of the final design they used, each channel must have components something like this.'

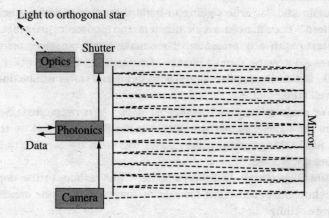

Ramiro hadn't thought about the technical aspects of the system for years, and as he reacquainted himself he was surprised by its apparent fragility. 'Disrupt the light for a flicker, and the flow of information is cut. There's no need to damage anything.' Although the messages were constantly being converted into a less transient form to be boosted and re-sent, that version of the data only endured forwards in time – it couldn't bridge a gap into the past. He'd often pictured the messages as a storehouse of documents, a kind of future-archeological find, but they were much more vulnerable than anything written on paper, or even in the energy states of a memory chip.

'Could we launch some small objects into the external light paths?' Tarquinia wondered. 'If each one starts on the mountain close to one of the channel's outlets, it could probably occult the target star without being picked up by a surveillance camera first.'

Azelio said, 'The outlets will have to be on the base of the mountain, won't they?'

'Yes,' Tarquinia replied. 'Unless they've turned everything around while we were gone.'

'We'd need to know exactly which orthogonal stars they're using,' Agata pointed out.

'Maybe our collaborators will have that information already,' Ramiro suggested. 'So if we can offer them some miniature auto-mated craft to fly up from the mountain and block those stars, why wouldn't they use them?'

Azelio said, 'So who's going to build these things without being noticed? They'll need accelerometers and photonics in order to navigate with any precision. If we make them ourselves on the *Surveyor*, we won't stand a chance of smuggling them out when we dock. But on the *Peerless*, all the workshops and stores will be under surveillance.'

'We could release them before we dock,' Agata suggested. 'Send them out to hide somewhere. If they're small enough, and we time the whole thing carefully, they could pass from the *Surveyor* to the slopes undetected.'

'And then what?' Azelio pressed her. 'They adhere to the slopes somehow, and then crawl towards the base – like insects crawling along a ceiling?'

'Yes.' Agata wasn't backing down, but the proposal was growing more ambitious by the moment.

'And then later,' Azelio said, 'since we won't know the coordinates in advance, we have to be able to instruct them, remotely, to crawl to a particular take-off point and then fly along a certain trajectory. Without the signal being detected.'

Tarquinia disagreed with his last claim. 'If a brief encrypted signal is picked up by the authorities, what can they do about it? So long as they can't pin down the exact source or destination, mere detection need not be a problem. Even if they take it as a sign that some form of attempted sabotage is under way . . . they would have had that possibility in mind for the last three years, regardless.'

Azelio hesitated. 'So why would they even try to stop us? They *know* the disruption is going to happen – so unless all this clandestine activity is irrelevant and a meteor is going to be responsible, this is a battle they know they can't win.'

'They're not going to give up, any more than we are,' Agata replied. 'Do you see any sign in what we've heard from the mountain that the

Council have resigned themselves to a state of fatalistic powerlessness?'

'No,' Azelio conceded.

'Think of it as a kind of equilibrium,' Tarquinia suggested. 'I'm sure there are limits to how far the Council would go to try to stop the inevitable, but there must be limits, too, on how supine they'll become: they're not going to shut down the system themselves, or release all the anti-messagers and let them go on a rampage with mallets. They've taken a stance and they're going to pursue it as far as they can. When this is over they'll be looking for a political advantage in the details of the fight, as much as in the outcome.'

Azelio was looking disoriented. 'I want this to work,' he said haltingly. 'But every time I stop and think about it, it feels as if all we're doing is playing some kind of game. Shouldn't we be trying to build better meteor detectors? If we really are the only people left with any hope of innovating, why not design a device that could actually save the mountain – instead of one for faking its death?'

Agata said, 'If we saved the mountain from a meteor, don't you think we'd know about it?'

'I have no idea.' Azelio rose from his seat. 'But what we're doing now is pointless.' He walked out of the cabin.

In the silence, Ramiro felt his own confidence faltering. 'I don't know how to reason about this any more,' he said. 'If it's a meteor that could actually kill us, isn't that where our efforts should go? Forget what the messages say or don't say about it: if we do our best to build something useful, how can that fail to make a difference?'

Agata inclined her head, expressing some sympathy with the impulse. But she wasn't swayed. 'I was the one who tried to argue that there's no such thing as an undetectable meteor – but what do we have on board for tackling that problem? A single time-reversed camera, and no facilities for building new photonic chips or any kind of high-precision optics. Even if we came up with a glorious new design, how are we supposed to manufacture a whole network of surveillance cameras and get them deployed? They can't just be drifting around the mountain detecting hazards for their own amusement – if they find something, they have to be able to trigger either a coherer powerful enough to deflect the thing, or start up the engines and make the whole mountain swerve. Do you really think we'd be able to do that in secret?'

253

'Maybe the Council will finally exercise enough discipline to keep it all quiet,' Ramiro replied.

'If they're capable of that,' Agata countered, 'then they're capable of doing a vastly better job than we are with the entire project.'

Ramiro gave up. He desperately wanted everything to work in the old way, when he could wrap his mind around a self-contained problem and take it apart without having to think about the entire history and politics of the mountain. But wishing for those days wasn't going to bring them back. 'Then we should go ahead with the star-occulters for our hypothetical saboteurs,' he said. 'Find a way to build them, and a way to keep them secret, and then hope that the cosmos takes us up on the offer to explain away the disruption with one simple, harmless conspiracy.'

26

Agata took hold of one end of the slab of calmstone, Ramiro the other, then they lifted it onto their shoulders and stood facing each other, some four strides apart.

'Are you ready?' Tarquinia asked.

'I'm not sure how steady this will be,' Agata replied.

'That doesn't matter. I just want you to be able to keep your grip when there's a force applied from below.'

Agata put a second hand on the slab. 'All right. Go ahead.' The improvised test rig looked alarmingly amateurish, but the ceiling of the cabin was made of the wrong material, and in any case they didn't want to leave it covered with incriminating marks. They'd hunted through the storeroom for something to serve as a trestle, but there'd been nothing ready-made, so in the end their bodies had seemed like the most expeditious substitute.

Tarquinia pushed a button on the remote control and the occulter rose from the floor. The core of the tiny craft was a dodecahedron about a span wide, with air nozzles fixed in the centres of eleven of its pentagonal faces. Attached to the top, twelfth face was a linear assembly, a pair of arms three or four spans long, as densely packed with gears and linkages as anything from the age of clockwork.

Staying low, the occulter steered its way across the cabin until it was hovering in front of Agata's feet; she could feel the spill of air against her skin. Then it ascended smoothly until it made contact with the calmstone slab – surrogate for the slopes of the *Peerless* itself. She gripped the slab tightly as four burred tips drilled obliquely into the stone. As Tarquinia had promised, the net force was purely vertical, so the weight of the slab bore most of it, and with the drills counter-rotating in matched pairs Agata felt no torque trying to twist the slab sideways.

After a few lapses the drills fell silent and the air jets cut off, leaving the device hanging.

'Try to shake it loose,' Tarquinia suggested. Ramiro ignored the invitation, but Agata slid her end gently from side to side, and when this had no effect she grew bolder and began rocking the slab back and forth. The linkage rattled alarmingly, but the four splayed drill bits remained lodged in place.

'That's reassuring, isn't it?' she said. 'The mountain is hardly going to sway like that.'

Ramiro wasn't so impressed. 'It doesn't tell us much about the real hazards. If there's a hole under the surface, or a powderstone inclusion—'

'If it comes loose that's not the end of the world,' Tarquinia stressed. 'It can always fly back and reattach itself.'

Agata said, 'Try the walking mode.'

Tarquinia tapped the remote. The four bits remained fixed in the stone, but the plate on which the drills were mounted began rotating on the end of its arm – or rather, the arm began rotating around the plate, swinging the entire occulter forward, carrying it from Agata's end of the slab towards Ramiro's.

When this repositioning was complete, the four drills at the end of the second arm pushed up against the stone and began biting into it. The new quartet managed to gain purchase with only the first set bracing them; there was no need to start up the air jets again. Then the first four went into reverse and disengaged from the stone, and the whole process began to repeat itself.

Agata watched anxiously as the machine whirred and clanked its way down the slope from her shoulder to Ramiro's. If the slab was unrealistically smooth, at least they'd made sure that it wasn't gravitationally level.

When the occulter had come within a span of Ramiro's body, Tarquinia used the remote again. The craft freed itself from the slab and flew away to alight on the cabin floor. Ramiro looked to Agata, and they carefully put the slab down together.

'Not bad,' Tarquinia declared.

Ramiro said, 'No. But we still need to decide what happens when the surface is uneven.'

Tarquinia had already reached her position on that. 'It should detour around the problem if it can, or drop away and fly past it if it can't. That makes it purely a question of navigation.'

'And a question of air,' Ramiro corrected her.

'Whatever we do,' Tarquinia replied, 'there'll always be a chance of the air running out. Letting the arms tilt so they can conform to the surface won't guarantee anything – and it's one more joint that can jam, two more actuators that can leak, plus six more sensors to make the idea work at all.'

Ramiro turned to Agata. 'It looks as if it's your vote.'

'Can we model the air use for different scenarios?' she wondered. 'Take a guess about the roughness of the mountainside, and see what the chances are that we can get these things from the dock to the antipode with air still in the tank, for each design?'

Ramiro said, 'I can try, if you want to help me with the model. "Roughness" isn't the easiest thing to quantify, but you're the expert on curvature.'

Agata sat beside him and they spent the next three bells working through the problem. In the end, with some plausible assumptions, there was a chance of about five in a gross that the current version of the occulter would run out of air before it had completed its task. With a new model where the arms could fold together or bend apart – allowing it to keep its grip in bumpier regions – that fell to three in a gross.

Ramiro said, 'That's for a single machine. But even if we build half a dozen spares, we can't afford too many failures.'

Tarquinia had been doing calculations of her own. 'You need to add in the chance of the modification itself leading to a failure. I get two in a gross for that.' Ramiro looked sceptical, but when he went through her numbers he couldn't fault them.

'Five in a gross . . . versus five in a gross.' Agata couldn't see how to break the tie. None of these numbers were precise, but without more information she couldn't make the uncertainties any clearer.

She looked across the cabin at the occulter. Their encounter with the Hurtler and their bomb-removal project offered plausible excuses for all sorts of items ending up in the void, or lost in the dust of Esilio – but she was already afraid that their depleted stores might attract suspicion. Ramiro's proposed changes would require dozens more proximity sensors – spares that ought to have been packed away neatly in a single large box. Why would they have taken that box out of the storeroom for safekeeping, but then never brought it back?

'I'm voting with Tarquinia,' she said. 'What we've got now is physically robust – and we'll already be hard pressed to build and test the whole swarm before we arrive. This isn't the time to start making things more complicated.'

For a moment Ramiro looked poised to respond with a further plea, but then he was silent.

Tarquinia said, 'It's good to have that settled. Everyone should get some sleep now, and tomorrow we'll go into production.'

'Do you want some fresh pictures for your wall?' Azelio asked, offering Agata a sheaf of papers.

She took them from him. The first drawing showed the mountain coming into view through the window of the *Surveyor*, with Luisa and Lorenzo standing on the summit waving, very much not to scale. In the second, they'd thrown out a docking rope to the craft and were reeling it in by hand. 'These are great,' she said. 'Thank you.'

Azelio lingered in the doorway. 'Come in for a while,' she suggested. He followed her into the cabin. There was only one chair, so she sat on the edge of the desk.

'I'm going mad,' Azelio said bluntly. 'I don't know what to think any more. I don't know what to do.'

'And I don't know what to tell you.' Agata had talked him through the situation a dozen times, but he was never satisfied with her account.

'Tell me that the mountain won't be destroyed,' he pleaded. 'Tell me that everyone will be safe.'

'The occulters aren't looking too bad,' she said. 'There are benign ways that the disruption might happen; I can promise you that.'

Azelio glanced down at the pile of notes on her desk. 'And doesn't everything that *could* happen, happen? Isn't that what your diagram calculus says?'

'No.' Agata nodded at the pile. 'For a start, you can only add up diagrams that begin and end in exactly the same way: they all take different paths, but their end points have to be identical. Getting to the disruption with benign sabotage leaves the mountain intact; getting there with a meteor strike hardly brings you to the same state. And even when the end points are identical, all the alternatives you draw for a process just help you find the probability that the process takes place. Those alternatives don't all get to happen, themselves.'

'Then what makes the choice?' Azelio pressed her. 'When a luxagen could end up in either of two places, how does just one get picked?'

'No one knows,' Agata confessed. 'In the years after wave mechanics was developed, there was a big debate about whether it was truly random, or whether there was some hidden structure beneath the randomness where all the results were certain. For a while, one group of physicists claimed to have proved that there couldn't be a deeper level. Their proof looked quite persuasive – until Leonia showed that it was tacitly assuming that information could never flow back in time.'

'Ah, the strange things people once believed,' Azelio observed dryly.

Agata said, 'No one believed it, even then, but they found it easier than we do to forget that it wasn't true.'

Azelio lifted a diagram from the stack. 'So what can this tell us about the disruption?'

'Nothing.' Agata wasn't sure how he'd ended up clutching at the diagram calculus as an answer to their plight, but if she'd been careless in describing her work to him in the past then what she owed him now was as much clarity as she could muster. 'Just because we don't know the cause of the disruption, that doesn't mean that every cause we can imagine will coexist. If you want history to unfold a certain way, forget about wave mechanics. What matters now are the usual things: who we are, what we do, and a certain amount of dumb luck.'

Azelio put the diagram down. 'So if there's a meteor coming, how do I stop it? Or avoid it?'

'You can't,' Agata replied. This was the sticking point they always reached. 'Not if the disruption is the proof that it hits us.'

'Then what difference does it make "who we are" and "what we do"?' Azelio asked bitterly. 'If I go through the motions of enacting something more benign . . . how will that help? If there's a murderer trying to kill your family, you don't protect them by moving your own tympanum to match the threats being shouted through the door. Or do you really believe in safety through reverse ventriloquism?'

Agata wrapped her arms around her head in frustration. 'We don't *know* that there's a murderer at the door! We don't *know* that there's a meteor on its way!'

'So we search the sky,' Azelio pleaded. 'We make better detectors. We try to peek through a crack in the door.'

'If we were going to find anything,' she said, 'we'd know that already. If we were going to spot a meteor and avoid it, then that's what the messages would be telling us.'

Azelio said, 'I can't accept that.'

Agata dropped her arms. 'I know.' There was nothing she could say that would change his mind, and nothing she could do that would bring him any comfort.

'We should fly over the antipode,' Tarquinia joked. 'Do a little reconnaissance.'

'Fly low enough and you could occult all the channels at once,' Ramiro suggested. 'Maybe there's a disruption earlier than everyone claimed, and all the later messages are just fakes.'

Agata said, 'I'd rather not test the defences.'

Through the window, the mountain cast a sharp silhouette against the star trails. It had been visible through external cameras for days, but they'd had to wait until they cut the main engines to rotate the *Surveyor* around for a naked-eye view.

'Ah, look at that!' Tarquinia gestured at her console, which was displaying a feed from the telescope. 'I think we've found a Councillor at home.' The grey hull that the instrument had picked up was lurking in the void, far from the *Peerless*. It wasn't quite identical to the *Surveyor*, but the overall design was eerily similar. Agata wasn't shocked that anyone with the means to do so had withdrawn to a safe distance from the mountain, but it was dismaying to see that Ramiro's guess had been right: even Verano had lost his powers of originality.

Azelio joined them, taking his seat and murmuring greetings. As subdued as he was, he seemed ready to make an effort to get through the formalities to come. Agata wished she could have assuaged his fears, but from a coldly pragmatic position she couldn't help thinking that his forlorn demeanour might serve as useful camouflage. No one observing the whole crew together could imagine them possessing even the shyest hope of influencing the fate of the *Peerless*.

Tarquinia brought the *Surveyor* spiralling in towards the docking point, and as the mountain finally hid the stars Agata felt a rush of pure joy. She wanted to burrow deep into these old, familiar rocks again, to drift along the core of an ancient stairwell, to gaze across a field of wheat that stretched beyond the ceiling's horizon. She glanced over at Azelio and he met her gaze with a look of shared relief, the sheer force of belonging overpowering his anxiety. How could they not feel safe here?

Tarquinia opened the link to the *Peerless*, and Verano appeared on her console. 'We've brought your creation back in one piece,' she said. 'But I suppose you always knew we would.'

'From the start,' Verano replied. 'No messages required.'

Agata knew she was off-camera herself, but when Ramiro's slight movements caught her attention she didn't dare turn to look at him directly. If she didn't see him start up the software that set the flock of occulters loose – before erasing itself from the communications system – the act wouldn't linger in her mind as they faced the scrutiny of the welcoming party. There was no predicting the full array of sensors and cameras aimed at them as they approached, but Tarquinia had lit up a docking beacon at the front of the *Surveyor*. As the occulters moved away from the literal blind spot directly behind the hull, the glare should be enough to allow the tiny devices to reach the slopes undetected.

Agata watched with a glorious ache in her chest as Tarquinia manoeuvred the *Surveyor* into the cradle of ropes that hung below the airlock. When the air jets cut out they were weightless for a flicker, then the net was holding them, swaying slightly.

She turned to Azelio. 'Can I tie my belt to yours when we go up?' she joked. 'You're the only one of us who's heard clear testimony of their safe arrival.'

Azelio buzzed. 'You're not counting Greta and Ramiro?'

Ramiro said, '*I'm* not counting Greta and Ramiro. I could fall into the void right now, and she would still have gloated about how miserable I was going to look at the reunion.'

They donned their helmets and attached the air tanks to their cooling bags. As they disembarked, the interior would remain pressurised for the sake of Azelio's plants.

'Agata's first,' Tarquinia decided.

Agata looked around the tilted cabin, wondering how much ill-behaved dust they'd brought back from the time-reversed world. She was wearing a pouch full of papers under her bag, and all her formal notes had been transmitted to Lila long ago, but she hesitated, afraid that she might have left something important in her cabin that the decommissioning team would discard as waste. But she'd returned all of Azelio's drawings to him, and her photograph of Medoro was with her, next to her skin.

She clambered up the guide rope and entered the airlock. When she closed the door behind her and started pumping down the pressure, she felt her hands shaking; for all her nostalgia, she wasn't sure that she was ready to face a whole crowd of non-crew-mates in the flesh.

She steadied herself and opened the outer door. The rope ladder was dangling against the hull; when she gazed straight up she could see the lights of Verano's workshop through the portal above. She resisted an urge to peer out across the slopes; if she had any chance of discerning one of the occulters clinging to the rock from this distance, the whole scheme really was doomed.

Agata climbed through the portal and ascended into the clearstone chamber from which she'd departed twelve years before. She could see a small crowd gathered in the workshop; they seemed to be chatting among themselves, though no sound reached her in the evacuated chamber. A few people turned to stare towards her with expressions of mild interest. She spotted Gineto, Vala and Serena with a young girl who had to be Arianna. None of them waved to her, and for a moment Agata wondered if she'd aged beyond recognition, but then she realised that between her helmet and her cooling bag she was effectively disguised – assuming that no one would bother to mention in their messages that she'd been the first to arrive.

Azelio came up the ladder, then stood for a while surveying the scene. 'I don't see any Councillors here to greet us,' he said. 'Five stints until the disruption, and they're still too afraid to visit the mountain.'

'Are you sure there are none? We might not recognise the new ones.' There'd been an election not long after the *Surveyor* had departed.

'There are no new ones,' Azelio replied. 'Girardo told me that the incumbents all kept their seats.'

Ramiro climbed through the portal. 'I suppose it's too late for me to make a run for freedom now.'

'They're not going to put you back in prison,' Agata scoffed.

Ramiro was amused. 'You mean, seeing as the whole sabotage thing is no longer an issue?'

'Someone would have mentioned it,' Agata suggested. 'Greta might have lied, but someone would have told you the truth.'

'I didn't call anyone who would have told me the truth,' Ramiro replied. 'If I'd wanted to know my future, I would have been on your side from the start.'

Tarquinia joined them, closing the portal behind her and sealing the rim. She spent a moment assessing the gathered crowd. 'And I thought we were the ones who'd look half dead. Let's get this over with.'

Ramiro pulled the lever to repressurise the chamber. Agata felt her cooling bag sagging against her skin. Azelio was closest to the door; he struggled with the crank, leaning down with all his weight to apply enough force to break the seal. Agata followed him out but then hung back, struggling to adjust to the vastness of the room, the hubbub of voices, the strange, sharp smell of the air.

Azelio took off his helmet and placed it on the ground, then strode towards his family. Agata watched the odd expression on the children's faces: as happy as they were to be reunited with their uncle, they looked bored and fidgety as well. It was as if he'd been playing this game with them for the last three years, the returning adventurer coming through the same door again and again. They'd seen the video message that Azelio would soon make with them, and however fresh it might have appeared at the first viewing, by now their parts in it would be mere recitations.

Agata removed her own helmet and started walking towards Medoro's family.

'Agata!' Serena finally recognised her and ran forward to embrace her. 'How are you?'

'Old. Don't squeeze me too hard.'

'If that's loose skin, you'll need medical attention urgently,' Serena joked, bumping up against Agata's papers. Vala joined them, followed by Gineto carrying Arianna. As they exchanged hugs and greetings with her, chirping with pleasure, Agata wondered if the adults were simply humouring her. But Azelio had been so intent on reassuring Luisa and Lorenzo throughout his long absence that he'd robbed them of any real joy at his arrival. So long as none of her own friends sent back every detail of this encounter, it need not be devoid of all spontaneity.

Serena said, 'You'll have to forgive me if I seem jealous.'

Agata was bewildered. 'Of what?'

'You did more or less meet the ancestors,' Vala interjected – gently teasing her daughter with the hyperbole.

'So everyone's seen the pictures of the inscription?' Agata had never been sure how people would respond; a part of her had been afraid that the find would be written off as a crude fake by an ancestor-worshipper. 'They're taking it seriously?'

'Of course!' Serena replied. 'That was the biggest news at the start-up, apart from the . . . other thing.' She glanced over at Arianna, making it clear that they weren't discussing the disruption in front of her.

Gineto said, 'It's the only reason I voted to keep the system running after the trial: we needed a piece of good news like that.'

'You changed your vote?' Agata was surprised, and a little disturbed. This sounded like a rationalisation for putting himself on the winning side.

'It would have been hypocritical to claim that I wished I hadn't heard about the inscription,' Gineto insisted.

'But if the majority vote had been to shut down the system—?'

'As I said, the inscription was my only reason,' Gineto replied.

'What was the vote?' she asked him. 'Do you remember?'

'Less than one in a gross against.'

Agata fell silent. If the system had stretched on unbroken all the way to the reunion, as she'd once imagined – endorsed at referenda again and again – would its persistence have been a true measure of its virtues, or just a self-affirming stasis, as pathological as the innovation block?

She glanced across the room and saw Ramiro talking to his sister; he did look shockingly old beside her, and her children seemed impatient to be somewhere else.

An archivist with a camera separated herself from the crowd and called to everyone to move into position. 'What position?' Agata asked. Then she understood.

Serena said, 'Don't worry, it's not as if you can get it wrong.' But as the group squeezed together to fit into the shot, she seemed to be looking around for reference points herself, anxious to conform to her own recollection. What happened, Agata wondered, to the woman or man whose nature demanded of them that they find a different spot or adopt a different posture than the one recorded in the famous image of the *Surveyor*'s return? That urge would have to have been beaten out of them somehow, or they would have been absent from the picture all along.

Agata turned to face the camera. In her rear gaze she could see people trying out their expressions, as if their imitations could fail to be perfect. As the archivist raised her camera, Agata struggled to hide the shame she could feel beginning to show on her own face. Perhaps it was the proper response to the plight that she'd helped to foist on the mountain, but she didn't want the whole of the *Peerless* seeing her reach that conclusion, three years before she'd reached it herself.

'I'm here to see my brother, Pio,' Agata told the guard.

The woman held out a photonic patch, connected to the wall by a cable. 'Form your signature.' Agata brought the squiggle onto her palm and pressed it against the patch.

'Valuables?'

Agata handed over the key to her apartment.

'Do you still have any pockets?'

'No.'

'Please resorb all your limbs.'

Agata hesitated, wondering what would happen if she argued, but then she released the guide rope and complied. Her torso drifted slowly towards the floor of the entrance chamber; the guard intervened and caught hold of her with four hands, then she began prodding Agata's skin with her fingertips, searching for any concealed folds. Agata closed her rear eyes and turned her front gaze towards the ceiling, wondering if the guards had access in advance to the outcomes of these searches. Why should they look too hard, if they knew they'd find nothing? But if there was well-hidden contraband, a tip-off might enable them to find it more easily. Or would that be yet another unlikely loop, self-consistent but hugely improbable?

When it was over, the guard let Agata fall, leaving her to reshape herself and catch the rope again. 'This is your pass,' the woman explained, handing her a red disc. 'Please don't lose it.'

'Do I lose it?' Agata asked.

'Of course you don't,' the guard replied. 'Because I asked you not to.'

'Right.' Agata suppressed a shiver.

'Visiting room three. Go through.'

Agata pushed open the swinging doors and followed the corridor into the prison complex. It was quieter than she'd expected, given the number of people still interned; all she could make out were some faint scraping noises in the distance, barely audible over the twang of the guide rope as she advanced. The two visiting rooms she passed were empty; she entered the third and harnessed herself to the desk. As she waited, she forced herself to glance around the room – she didn't want to be seen searching obsessively for the cameras, but to have stared at a fixed spot on the wall and shown no curiosity about her surroundings would have been equally suspicious.

She struggled to keep the possibilities straight in her mind: if the authorities were going to catch her conspiring with saboteurs then they would have known that for the last three years – but they couldn't arrest her until she'd had a chance to do whatever deed revealed her guilt. Once she'd been arrested, though, even if they kept that from becoming public knowledge, surely Lila or Serena would notice her absence and send her a message about it? Or better yet, send a message to their earlier selves to be passed on to her in person; that would be less likely to be detected and intercepted.

So was the lack of any warning a proof that she wouldn't be caught? Or did the fact that she'd received no messages at all from her future self mean that everything would turn bad very quickly?

Agata heard a door creak open in the distance, then the clank of hardstone links, an almost rhythmic sound as the prisoner approached. When the guard escorting Pio reached the doorway, Agata loosened the harness and pulled herself closer, but she still couldn't see her brother.

'Please stay back,' the guard instructed her. The woman held a loop of chain in one hand. She dragged herself over to the wall and attached it to a clamp, then turned and said, 'Come.'

Pio pulled himself into the room along the guide rope, moving nimbly despite the stone bar that transected his torso. 'Hello Agata,' he said.

'Hello.' For a moment she was numb, then the sight of Pio's gaunt frame became too much and she started humming softly. She was far from convinced of his innocence, but no one had come close to establishing his guilt. If he had murdered Medoro and the others then he deserved to be locked up until he died – but what did she know for sure? Only that he'd viewed the messaging system with the same degree of alarm and revulsion from the start as she now felt for it herself.

The guard watched as Pio climbed into the harness on his side of the desk. 'You have three chimes,' she told Agata. Then she withdrew into the corridor.

Agata composed herself, but she reached over and squeezed her brother's shoulder while the gesture still had a chance of seeming innocent and spontaneous. In the flicker before her palm touched his skin, she formed the words: **On your side. Tell me how to help.** She tried not to worry about how long it would take him to read the message if he hadn't been expecting it; the action had a natural timescale of its own, and if she over-thought it that would show.

Pio leant back and examined her appraisingly. 'Detours really do work the way they taught us in school,' he marvelled. 'Twelve years in that box. How did you stay sane?'

'The time passed quickly,' she said. 'After the first year.'

'I can't say the same, though maybe with the ratios it almost evens out.' He buzzed suddenly. 'Cira told me about your big discovery. The ancestors don't burn, we don't wipe ourselves out – what could be better than that?'

'People acting on it,' Agata replied. 'I thought I'd come back to find that everyone had buried their differences.'

'Not yet.'

Agata didn't want to start interrogating him about his views on the disruption, but it would seem strange if they didn't discuss it at all. 'Do you think the Councillors are going to pull the plug?'

'Why would they do that?'

'They've seen the problems that the system's created,' she said. 'We can't spend the next six generations stuck with the same technology.'

'But how would they explain the shutdown afterwards, without admitting that they'd planned it all along?' Pio wondered.

'They could claim that there'd been some kind of minor impact,' Agata suggested. 'With just the right size and trajectory to take out all twelve channels at once, but do no real damage elsewhere.'

'All of which they'd more or less guessed, of course. But lacking proof, they couldn't announce it officially.' Pio inclined his head. 'It's possible, I suppose. We'll know soon enough.'

'Yes.'

Pio changed the subject. 'Are you going to see Cira?'

'I don't think so.' Agata supposed it might sound suspicious that she was prepared to reconcile with Pio but not her mother. But she wasn't a good enough actor to pull off that encounter, and Cira would have much less motivation to play along. 'If she's stood by you, that's admirable, but I think she and I reached the point a long time ago where we'll be happier if we stay out of each other's way.'

'I understand.'

'Can I bring you anything?' she asked. 'They let you have books, don't they?'

'I can always use more paper and dye,' Pio said. 'I'm writing a book of my own.'

'What kind of book?' Agata couldn't help mocking him a little. 'Surely there's no need for a migrationist manifesto now?'

'It's a history of women and men,' he replied.

'You mean the discovery of shedding – that kind of thing?'

'More or less. You can read it when it's finished, if you like.'

Agata couldn't imagine what he thought he could add to the version in the archives, but if he had a project to help him pass the time that could only be a good thing.

When the guard returned to fetch him, Pio leant across the desk and executed an awkward hug. As he drew back, Agata was still trying to memorise the sensation of his palm on her shoulder.

'Will I see you again?' he asked.

'Of course,' she replied. The guard looked amused; apparently not in the next five stints.

Agata sat at the desk for a while, self-consciously pensive, her palms resting on her thighs as she passed copies of Pio's tightly scrawled instructions back and forth between the two hidden patches of skin.

The food hall was close to the rim of the *Peerless*, and even at the second bell it was crowded. Agata entered and queued at the counter, trying to remain unfazed as she noticed people looking her way twice, probably recognising her from the archival image of the *Surveyor*'s return. At least their faces showed a flicker of surprise, proving that they wouldn't make so much of the encounter that they let themselves know about it in advance.

She'd barely slept the night before, and then as she'd prepared to leave her apartment her console had beeped and offered up a message from her future self:

I still don't agree.

It would be sent three stints before the disruption; that didn't quite prove that she'd be walking free right to the end, but it was more reassuring than absolute silence. And if the meaning was opaque to her at present, she could only hope that anyone spying on her would find the lack of context unremarkable. There was no reason for anyone's private messages to spell out every detail of the dilemmas they were intended to resolve. The bandwidth quotas weren't infinite: gnomic brevity would generally be a virtue, not a sign that the sender had something to hide.

When her turn came at the counter she asked for two plain loaves; she'd discovered after the welcoming party that her gut no longer appreciated fresh spices. She carried the food to the corner farthest from the entrance, where an awkwardly placed cooling vent discouraged most diners. The present crowd left few enough alternatives for her choice not to seem too perverse.

She sat on the floor and ate slowly, her front eyes on her food, her rear gaze to the wall.

She was halfway through the second loaf when a man addressed her. 'Did you drop these?' Agata looked up. There were three coins on his outstretched palm; she squinted at them, memorised their value, then said, 'No, they're not mine.'

'Sorry to have troubled you.'

Pio hadn't told her how long she should wait, so as soon as she'd finished eating she left the hall and headed for the address indexed by the coins' denominations. The area wasn't familiar to her, but as she ascended the stairs towards the axis and then dragged herself along the corridor towards her destination, the smooth texture of the rock beneath her feet and the red tunnel of the moss-lit walls were enough to induce an ache of recognition. The death of every traveller save a handful of evacuees was beyond her power to imagine, but she'd come as close as anyone alive to feeling the absence of the mountain itself. If she needed a vision of the loss she was fighting to prevent, she could think of the *Peerless* retreating into the distance, shrinking to a dark speck against the stars and then vanishing.

Outside the door, she hesitated, but she'd have to trust Pio's comrades to have chosen an appropriate level of precautions, and the innovation block to have kept the Council from automatically tracking everyone, everywhere. She knocked firmly, and after a few pauses the door swung open and a man invited her into the apartment.

'My name's Giacomo,' he said.

'I'm Agata.' She closed the door behind her. 'Can we talk freely?'

'Absolutely,' Giacomo assured her.

There was no point in prevaricating. 'I want to help shut down the messaging system,' she said. 'We have a dozen and six small machines out on the slopes, capable of moving along the rock and flying for short distances. If you can tell us exactly where to send them, we can use them to occult the orthogonal stars for all of the channels.'

Giacomo hesitated before replying, but only as much as politeness required. He must have had years to consider her offer.

'The system uses light from the entire orthogonal cluster,' he said. 'It's not a matter of one star per channel. To shut it down, you'd need to blot out half the sky from twelve different vantage points.'

'The entire cluster?' Agata had always pictured a single star as the light source. When Medoro had first raised the idea with her, he'd started with a thought experiment where a distant object passed in front of a time-reversed star – and if the object had to be remote enough for the time the light spent in transit to be significant, it could hardly block out anything larger. But once you folded up the light path with mirrors, the same constraints no longer applied.

'The optics gathers light from all directions visible from the base of the mountain,' Giacomo explained. 'Or sends it out, if you want to talk in terms of our arrow, but it's easier for me to imagine the whole thing working backwards. All that each channel needs is a reliable light source that it can block or reveal with a shutter. Combining all the light from across the cluster makes the source brighter and more dependable.'

'And less vulnerable to sabotage,' Agata conceded. She'd convinced herself that the Councillors would be relying on secrecy, each one guarding the coordinates of their chosen star. Instead, they'd adopted a robust solution that could not be undermined merely by the revelation of a couple of numbers.

'But your machines will still be very useful,' Giacomo said encouragingly. 'I can promise you that.'

'How?'

'They've been part of our plan for years. They won't be able to block the channels with their presence alone, but they can still carry explosives to the sites where they're needed.'

27

'We're not doing it!' Agata declared angrily. 'We're not going to be accomplices to these murderers. We'll have to find another way.'

Ramiro said, 'There might not be another way.'

'So now you're happy to kill people?' Agata stared at him in disgust.

'We don't know that there'll be casualties.' Ramiro paused, dismayed by the weakness of this disclaimer. But he pressed on. 'If Giacomo's group sets off a blast beside each light collector that's just large enough to shatter it, that need not do a whole lot of damage further down.'

Agata was unmoved. 'So you'll trust the same fanatics who killed seven people in the camera workshop to be scrupulous now about sparing lives?'

Ramiro spoke bluntly. 'Whoever attacked the workshop intended to kill those instrument builders – they were targeting people's skills as much as the machinery. We shouldn't assume that Giacomo's group have any other goal beyond damaging the system itself.'

'Why would a single technician even be down there, when they all know the disruption's coming?' Tarquinia added. 'Whether they're expecting a bomb or a meteor, it's an obvious place to avoid.'

'And what if the damage goes deeper?' Agata argued. 'What if the hull is breached?'

'Most of that area's taken up with the cooling system for the engines,' Tarquinia said. 'That's self-contained: if it's damaged, it's not going to vent any of our own air to the void.'

'The light paths run all the way along the axis,' Agata replied. 'Blow up the optics on the outside, and there's no guarantee that you won't be connecting every channel straight to the void.'

'But they'll be sealed, for sure,' Ramiro protested. 'To keep contaminants out of the beams.'

'Sealed along the whole length of the mountain, well enough to hold against a vacuum?' Agata's tone was scathing. 'All twelve, with no chance of failure?'

Tarquinia said, 'If the Councillors want to impress voters with the value of foresight, they'll have spent all their resources for the last three years reinforcing every scant of those tubes.'

Agata buzzed sardonically. 'You mean the resources left once every Councillor had ensured that they could personally survive a meteor turning the mountain into rubble?'

Ramiro glanced at his console. Since he'd been back in his apartment he'd been wondering if his resolve to shun the system would ever falter, but now he felt an almost physical craving for the very thing he'd always reviled.

'What does Giacomo say?' he asked Agata. 'Is he expecting us to cooperate?' The answer to that might not settle things as clearly as a message from his future self – but even if it rang false and he concluded that Giacomo was lying, he would still have arrived at a prediction of sorts.

'I thought you didn't want to know the future,' Agata replied.

'If Giacomo knew for sure that we wouldn't go along with this . . .' Ramiro struggled to classify the consistent possibilities. 'He'd still have to put the proposal to us, wouldn't he? Or how could he know that we'd refuse?'

Agata said, 'He claims that his people do use the occulters. Make of that what you like.'

Ramiro waited for this revelation to bring him clarity, but it was no help at all. He could believe that, in the end, he would decide that the bombing was the lesser of two evils compared with a meteor strike. But if he'd heard the opposite claim he would have concluded that he'd convince himself that with the saboteurs left weaponless, the Council would step in and do the deed themselves. Neither answer would have rung so false as to convince him that it couldn't be true.

'What do you think we should do?' he asked Agata.

She said, 'I'm going to find a way to shut down the system without blowing anything up.'

'How?'

Agata hummed disdainfully. 'Do you seriously expect me to have the answer already?'

Tarquinia said, 'Not how to shut it down, but how to find a way.'

'The innovation block isn't an absolute principle.' Agata was defiant. 'Maybe in the long term it's impossible to keep anything secret – but the closer we get to the disruption, the easier it should be to keep my ideas to myself until it's impossible for them to leak into the past.'

Ramiro said, 'And the closer you get to the disruption, the less time you'll have to come up with something workable and put it into practice. That's a slender thread on which to hang the fate of the mountain.'

'Perhaps,' Agata conceded. 'But why did the ancestors send me that message, if not to give me the courage to try? They couldn't tell me what the method would be, but they could strengthen my resolve to find one.'

'You think the ancestors were speaking to you personally?' Ramiro glanced at Tarquinia, wondering if she'd finally break her silence and admit to the forgery.

'When the rock face was exposed,' Agata replied, 'I didn't think the message was for me at all. I didn't think I needed it. But the ancestors won't choose that site lightly. They'll know our whole history, they'll know how all the pieces of it fit together. They'll know exactly how and why we came through this unscathed. If the disruption had a natural cause, why wouldn't they simply tell us that? It's the fact that they *can't* reveal the details that reveals the nature of the event.'

Ramiro wasn't sure how much his own face was revealing. 'Go ahead, then,' he urged her. 'See what you can come up with.' It couldn't do any harm.

'That's not enough,' Agata said. 'I'm going to need something from you, or I'll be wasting my time.'

'What do you need?'

'If you join up with Giacomo,' she said, 'you have to keep a power of veto for yourselves, right to the end. A day before the disruption – a bell before, a chime before – if I can find a better way, you need to be able to cancel the bombing, or it will all have been for nothing.'

Ramiro didn't ask her why the ancestors would have gone to so much trouble to motivate her if her struggle would be in vain. 'We'll try,' he said. It was impossible to promise her more than that.

'Thank you.' Agata tipped her head in farewell and started towards the door.

'So what will you do now?' Tarquinia asked her.

'Sit in my room and think,' Agata replied. 'With the messaging system switched off.'

Giacomo had told Agata that he'd find Ramiro himself for the next stage of the negotiations – but having chosen to know the outcome in advance, their partners seemed to be in no hurry to go through the motions of resolving the matter. Ramiro looked for ways to pass the time without making his restlessness apparent. When he visited Rosita he could usually empty his mind and play games with the children for a while, but then she'd put them to bed and she and Vincenzo would start arguing about the disruption.

'The Council will do it.' Vincenzo was confident; he'd worked it all out. 'The evacuation is a sham; they know they're not in any danger. In the end, they'll use those craft for the obvious purpose: sending the malcontents off to Esilio.'

Ramiro said, 'So after the disruption, there'll still be malcontents? The Council will switch the system back on?'

'Of course.'

'Then why are they switching it off in the first place?'

'To force the saboteurs to show their hands,' Vincenzo explained. 'They'll think they're responsible for the disruption, so they'll trip over themselves trying to make it happen. What better way to lure them out?'

Except for the part about restarting the system, Ramiro wanted to believe this story. If it were true, he and Tarquinia could simply refuse Giacomo's request – proving that the occulters had never really been part of the saboteurs' plans – and then wait for the Council's game to play itself out.

Rosita wanted to believe it too, but she couldn't. 'It's a collision,' she insisted glumly. 'The only question is the size of it.'

'What makes you so sure?' Ramiro asked her.

'It's not saboteurs; saboteurs would get caught. No one could pull this off with all their movements known three years in advance.'

Vincenzo interjected, 'I never said they'd succeed. But that doesn't mean they're not stupid enough to try.'

'The Council won't switch off the system,' Rosita continued. 'A hoax like that would be political suicide, however many would-be bombers they catch. Do you think people would forgive them for three years of wondering if their family was going to survive?'

Vincenzo said, 'I'll forgive them, because I haven't been wondering that at all. Everything they're doing is going to leave us safer in the end. Why would I punish them for that?'

When he wasn't out visiting, Ramiro sat in his apartment tweaking the software on his console – mostly for the sake of killing time, though all his digging around had the advantage of reassuring him that the device wasn't being used to spy on him. He'd tried looking for work, but no one in the mountain was embarking on any new projects. One way or another, most people had learnt that they would do nothing about the disruption, and now they'd settled into a state of compliance with their own reported paralysis.

On his eighth day back Tarquinia dropped by again. It was the first time he'd been alone with her since they'd returned, but neither of them were in the mood to resume where they'd left off on the *Surveyor*.

'Have you told anyone?' he asked her. 'About us?'

Tarquinia was bemused. 'Who would I tell?'

'Your family.'

'Why would it be any of their business?'

Ramiro hadn't said a word to Rosita; he was sure she would find the relationship repellent. 'Are you ashamed of it?'

'Not at all.' Tarquinia sounded defensive. 'But why does anyone else need to know how we spend our time?'

On the *Surveyor* they'd had no choice in the matter; their secret had lasted about a day, and Azelio and Agata had taken it in their stride.

Ramiro said, 'I grew up being told that even thinking about fission was tantamount to murder. Why do we do that to people? It's a lie, and it's a cruel one.'

Tarquinia scowled. 'Do you really expect every boy to learn in school that he can abandon his duties to his sister and go chasing after less demanding pleasures?'

'But you'd heard about the whole thing years before, hadn't you?' Ramiro protested. 'Your own choices didn't come as any big surprise to you.'

'Is it my fault if women talk to each other about these things, and

277

men don't?' Tarquinia regarded him with a mixture of fondness and pity that made his skin crawl.

'Forget it,' he said. There were more important things to worry about. 'Do you think the occulters are still in place?' They had no way to make contact with the devices; Ramiro was hoping that their allies would be able to provide the necessary hardware.

'Maybe a few ended up on porous rock,' Tarquinia conceded. 'And of those that fell loose, maybe one or two failed to reattach. But that's why we made spares.'

'Would we be part of Giacomo's plan at all, if we weren't going to have at least twelve survivors to offer him?' It wasn't a rhetorical question; Ramiro was never confident about the possibilities until he'd talked them over with someone else.

'He wouldn't hear the bad news unless he stayed in touch,' Tarquinia reasoned. 'So even if the occulters have all disappeared into the void, he couldn't simply shun us before we'd worked that out together. But I can't see why he'd claim that all his hopes were resting on us if it wasn't true. I think the plan must keep holding together – at least for as long as ordinary people can keep sending back news.'

They had both heard from friends that, three days before the disruption, official communications would start taking up so much bandwidth that no private messages would be able to get through. If the occulters did fail, the failure lay somewhere beyond that horizon.

Ramiro was heading home from the food hall when a man bumped into him in the corridor, breaking his hold on the guide rope. As etiquette demanded they both reached out to steady each other, trying to kill the motion that the collision had imparted before they sent each other crashing into opposite walls. The manoeuvre succeeded, and they both muttered embarrassed apologies, but as they separated the man passed a slip of paper into Ramiro's hand.

Ramiro waited until he was back in his apartment before inspecting the message. The paper was covered in numbers, far too many to be an address. He stared at it for a while, then went to his console and confirmed his hunch. It had been encrypted with his public key, and the plain text did look like an address.

There was no time specified, but he was loath to delay the meeting or attract attention by trying to get hold of Tarquinia. He tore up the message and erased the plain text from his screen, then set out on his own.

When he knocked on the door, it opened immediately.

'Are you Giacomo?' he asked.

'Yes.' The man invited him in.

'Do you think I'm being watched?' Ramiro had counted at least five cameras along the way.

'Of course you are,' Giacomo replied cheerfully, 'but right now, someone resembling you is being watched in your place.'

'You sent a *decoy* into this corridor . . . to be spotted at the next intersection, as if I just carried on walking?' Ramiro was astonished, though matching the timing to his actual movements would not have been a problem at all.

'Let's not talk about the details,' Giacomo suggested. He'd had three years to think through the strategy; why would he be interested in debating it with someone who'd had three pauses?

'All right.' Ramiro clung to the guide rope in what he guessed was someone else's living room. If the group had gone to so much trouble to bring him here, what did that imply about the end point of their discussions? But he had to stop thinking that way, or his decisions would all be shaped by the presumption that it was impossible for anyone armed with foresight to waste their time.

'The occulters weren't designed to carry anything,' he began.

Giacomo tipped his head, acknowledging the fact without making an unseemly boast that he'd been aware of this before the occulters had even existed. 'We put suitable hooks on the caches,' he explained. 'Spring-loaded to secure them. All your machines will need to do is visit the right locations along the way to the base, and the cargo will more or less attach itself. Our devices have been stuck in place with resin, but a lateral tug will loosen the bond with far less force than it would take to break it vertically.'

'So you've managed to build a dozen of these things and smuggle them outside?'

'A dozen and a half,' Giacomo corrected him. 'Including spares. In the end it was just a matter of stealth and patience. Everything was based on pre-existing designs; it's only the delivery mechanism that would have been beyond us.'

Ramiro said, 'Tell me about the bombs.'

'They'll do the job,' Giacomo promised him.

'I don't doubt that. But what's the size of each charge? The blast radius?'

'In vacuum, they'll fracture clearstone within six strides of the detonation point.'

'That's all?'

'That's enough,' Giacomo insisted. 'Once the light collector's damaged, the channel will be dead.'

'And do you know how well protected the internal light path is?'

Giacomo said, 'There are three clearstone seals below the collector: at four strides deep, eight strides, and one stretch. Once you go past those three seals, the main tube itself is continuous – they don't put anything between the mirrors, because that would cut into the light with every bounce. But there's no chance of us breaching the tubes: the first seal alone will take most of the energy out of the blast.'

'You're certain of that?' Ramiro wished Agata hadn't given up on the plan before she'd heard these details.

'That's what the explosives experts tell me,' Giacomo replied carefully. 'Running a test on a mock-up would have been the best way to answer that, but there's a limit to what we can slip past surveillance.'

Three seals, with the last at double the blast radius. The saboteurs had no need to damage anything so deep. And even if something went awry in the delivery, that would lead to less harm to these structures, not more.

'What about the defences?' Ramiro asked. 'They won't have left the collectors sitting there unguarded.'

'All the original defences at the base were designed to protect the engines from micrometeors – arriving from out of the void at high speed without changing course.' Giacomo spread his arms. 'We believe they've tried to improve the system since they learnt about the disruption, but anything coming in low above the rocks and moving unpredictably will be a completely different kind of target.'

'So we have a chance.' Ramiro was beginning to feel optimistic.

'I believe so.' Giacomo had had three years to mull over the same facts; if there was no thrill of delight in his verdict, at least he'd earned the right to issue it.

'This next request is a little delicate,' Ramiro admitted. 'Though I don't suppose it will shock you.'

'Go ahead.'

'I'll need to talk everything over with Tarquinia,' he said, 'but even if she agrees, we'll have one more proviso: we'll want to hold onto the codes for the occulters ourselves. You provide the coordinates, we operate the devices.'

'I understand.' Giacomo was completely unperturbed.

Ramiro understood that his collaborator could hardly need more time to weigh up the proposal, but he was still taken aback by this placid response. 'Agata is hoping to find a safer way to cause the disruption,' he said. It felt incumbent on him to provide a full justification for Giacomo's ease; he couldn't drop the discussion just because they'd agreed. 'I don't know what her chances are, but this way it will be clear that we can still change the plan at the last moment if she comes up with something better.'

Giacomo said, 'We've always known that that was part of the deal, and we have no problem with it at all.' He reached across from his rope and clasped Ramiro's shoulder. 'To the end of the system, brother.'

'To the end of the system,' Ramiro echoed. This strangely dispassionate rebel could not have achieved much without his own knowledge of the future. But then nothing could have been more apt than their enemies' machine enabling its own destruction.

'Why do I feel that I have no choice in this?' Tarquinia complained.

'Because everything feels that way,' Ramiro replied. 'Just ignore it and do what you want.'

She slid away from him beneath the tarpaulin of his sand bed, a silhouette against the red moss-light coming through the fabric from the wall behind her. 'The codes remain in our hands to the end,' she said. 'What is there I could possibly object to?' She made this sound like a bad thing.

'It's strange being trusted by strangers,' Ramiro conceded. 'But they know we won't betray them for at least the next four stints, and we know we won't have any reason to regret the deal ourselves or we would have sent back a warning. This is what life is like without surprises. I wouldn't want it to last for ever, but at a time like this I can't honestly claim a need for even more uncertainty.'

Tarquinia said, 'What I'm afraid of is being certain, without being right.'

'About what, exactly?' he pressed her.

'If I knew that there wouldn't be a problem.'

Ramiro drew the tarpaulin away from his face and looked out across the room. 'What's the worst that can happen – short of a meteor strike? Vincenzo's right and it's all a set-up. Giacomo is secretly working for the Council. We'll end up in prison, but with a clear conscience: nothing we were planning would have harmed anyone, while the Councillors lied to the whole mountain for years. Come the next election we'll probably be pardoned, and the system will never be turned on again. Does any of that sound so bad to you?'

'No.' Tarquinia shifted uneasily.

'So . . . ?'

'We'll go ahead,' she said. 'Nothing else makes sense. Maybe I'm just not accustomed to things slotting into place so perfectly. It used to be that anyone who knew from the start what to say to win you over was setting an ambush. These days, maybe all it proves is that they bother to read their messages.'

Giacomo handed over the data link, a shiny black slab of photonics about five scants across.

Ramiro inspected it. 'That's perfect,' he said. He'd had no hope of getting hold of anything like this himself. 'How do you get past the inventory checks?'

'You can swap an inert mock-up for the real thing,' Giacomo explained. 'If you do it the right way no one will notice for years.'

Ramiro formed a pocket and hid the link. 'Do you have the coordinates for me?'

'Yes, but we should get the other business out of the way first.' Giacomo paused expectantly.

'Of course.' Ramiro had sat down with Tarquinia for a bell the night before, refining the sketches from memory. They'd kept no records of the occulters' design on paper or in photonics, and not merely to avoid discovery; they hadn't actually anticipated any need for it.

He summoned the final drawing onto the skin of his chest, with all the details and dimensions that Giacomo had requested. The explosives caches would need to have been carefully designed if they were to grab the occulters and ride them – without jamming the mechanism or fatally unbalancing their hosts. Still, Ramiro's first impulse when asked for the plans had been to challenge his accomplice, jokingly, to display them first. But the information would still need to pass between them in the conventional direction at some point, and Ramiro hadn't really wished to be confronted with an unarguable proof that he would agree to the transaction eventually.

Giacomo dragged himself closer along the guide rope. 'Do you mind if we do this by touch? My visual memory isn't so strong, and cameras are a security risk.'

'All right.' Ramiro hadn't been expecting this, but he had no reason to object. He moved forward and let Giacomo embrace him, and as their skin made contact the gentle pressure rendered the ridges of the drawing palpable to both of them.

'When will you send it?' Ramiro asked.

'Tonight.' Giacomo separated from him. 'In three pieces, hidden in pictures of my children.'

'Why not just encrypt it?' Ramiro hoped nothing had shown on his face as he heard the phrase *my children*. He would never have picked the man for a Starver, but then, once their children were born they had no reason to starve.

Giacomo said, 'The authorities can tell from the size of the message that it's unlikely to be text, and encrypting an image attracts more suspicion.'

'Right.'

'I'll give you the coordinates now.'

Ramiro waited for him to hand over the paper, but then he understood that this exchange was to be conducted the same way.

As they embraced again, Ramiro concentrated on the numbers, committing the pattern of ridges to memory. As a child, he'd passed messages to male friends this way, making a joke out of the harmless intimacy's mimicry of the forbidden act. But the skin that was pressed against his own now hadn't mimicked it, it had triggered the real thing.

'Do you have them all clearly?' Giacomo asked.

'I think so.' Ramiro pulled away, averting his gaze, unsure what he was feeling. *Envy?* If Tarquinia had ever really died in his arms, it would have been unbearable. Why should he envy a man who'd lost his co?

Giacomo said, 'The angle of approach and the orientation are crucial. We've made sure that the hooks are compatible with the dimensions of the arms, but if your machine comes in too steeply or the arms are turned the wrong way, it won't engage the hooks at all.'

'I understand.'

'And the retreat's just as important,' Giacomo stressed. 'If you pull away vertically, the resin won't give. The rope will snap, or something else will break.'

'We'll follow the whole flight plan as closely as we can.' Ramiro reviewed the list, bringing the figures back onto his skin as he checked them. 'What are those last sets of numbers?'

'The coordinates of the light collectors.'

Ramiro hadn't expected to be given the targets themselves until he'd reported back on the first stage of the process. 'So that's it? We just fly the occulters there . . . and then what?'

'The bombs are all controlled by timers,' Giacomo explained. 'All you need to do is get them to the right place.'

'What do we do if something goes wrong? How can we contact you?' Ramiro was prepared to accept responsibility for the occulters, but if anything else malfunctioned he'd have no idea what the options might be.

'Nothing goes wrong,' Giacomo assured him.

'You can't know that,' Ramiro protested. 'Not after the private messages are squeezed out—'

'That late?' Giacomo paused, struggling to frame an answer, as if he'd lost the habit of imagining anything beyond the reach of his foresight. 'The disruption is ours,' he said finally. 'We've been planning it for longer than the system's been in existence. We know that it happens – and we know that we're trying harder to make it happen than anyone else. So how can we possibly fail?'

Ramiro moved away from the console and let Tarquinia check the alignment of the link against her own calculations. They'd set the beam to be as narrow as they dared, to minimise the chance of anyone detecting it on its way out to the slopes. But if they failed to aim it at the precise location where they'd left the first occulter clinging to the rock they'd be risking discovery for nothing.

'This looks right to me,' Tarquinia said.

'Are you sure?'

'In the end it's just arithmetic and geometry,' she replied. 'If I do it a dozen more times I'll still get the same answer.'

Ramiro had already entered the coordinates of the nearest cache into the software. He tapped a key on the console and a tight burst of UV erupted from the link. The confirmation came back immediately:

the occulter had received the message and was proceeding to act on it.

'Perfect!' Tarquinia declared.

'So far.' It would take the occulter three days to crawl across the mountain to its first rendezvous. Ramiro pictured the prototype clanking down the plank towards him, back on the *Surveyor*. They'd made allowances for the machines losing their footing and needing to recover, but the complex manoeuvres required to pick up the cargo would cut into the air supply, and the extra mass being lugged around would shrink the margin for error even further.

Tarquinia said, 'Next target.'

Their run of luck continued for a while, but the fifth occulter failed to reply. Ramiro rechecked the direction of the link, then broadened the transmission, but it made no difference.

When they'd released the occulters from the *Surveyor* each one had been given preassigned coordinates, but if the composition of the rock proved unsuitable they were to try again at a number of adjacent sites. A pseudo-random algorithm varied the coordinates; knowing the seed for it they could match the sequence exactly.

After a dozen steps, Ramiro gave up. If the occulter hadn't found a secure purchase by then, it would not have had enough air left to be of any use to them even if they could locate it.

'One in five,' Tarquinia said. 'We can live with that.'

By the end of the day they'd set a dozen and three occulters in motion and given up on three.

'If Giacomo had stayed in touch with us,' Tarquinia mused, 'he could have spared his people the trouble of planting three of those caches.'

Ramiro said, 'Maybe. Or maybe we'll fumble the pick-ups on three of the others and have to go back and use the ones that seemed superfluous.'

'That's true.' Tarquinia reached across and squeezed his shoulder. 'We're doing well.'

Ramiro was exhausted. He stared across the room and tried not to think of the machines scuttling along the slopes; the more he visualised them, the harder it became to avoid picturing a cog jamming or a drill bit coming loose. 'At the turnaround, all our biggest problems had been solved,' he said. 'Every traveller before us had put up with far more hardship and uncertainty than we were facing then. So how did it come to this? Why are we the idiots who could lose it all?'

'Stop thinking about it.' Tarquinia took him by the arm and led him through into the bedroom.

When they'd finished, Ramiro clung to her body angrily. He'd wasted half his life on this imitation of fatherhood. If he hadn't wanted the real thing, why did he keep chasing this shadow? He was as much a slave now as if he'd meekly followed his uncle's commands.

Tarquinia eased herself out of his embrace.

'What happens afterwards?' he asked her. 'After the disruption.'

'After the disruption,' she said, 'life goes back to normal.'

28

Agata ascended the stairs slowly, her gaze cast down at the moss-lit rock, hoping that if anyone was watching her she'd appear suitably distracted: a moody theorist wandering the mountain, oblivious to her surroundings. Though every ordinary resident of the *Peerless* surely knew the size of the excluded zone around the axis, she hadn't been able to bring herself to ask Serena or Gineto to tell her. There was no way to phrase the question innocently: whoever she consulted, however obliquely, would be instantly burdened with the knowledge that she was contemplating sabotage. Which might have led nowhere, or might have taken her rapidly to a place she didn't want to be: finding a way to reassure an alarmed friend that she hadn't gone over to the side of Medoro's killers, but was actually striving to undermine them.

To make any progress on that task, she needed a rough idea of the dimensions of the messaging system. It was safe to assume that the designers had made every channel as long as possible, running close to the full height of the mountain, so once she knew how close to the axis the public were permitted to travel she'd have some sense of the mirrors' width and the volume of each enclosed light path.

As Agata's weight diminished, she continued upwards, using the guide rope beside her. The ancestors couldn't tell her how to halt the system, but they must have chosen her for a reason – and the only hint they could give her had to be encoded in that choice itself. She had measured the bending of light by Esilio's sun, hadn't she? There was no prospect of using gravity to distort the light paths in the messaging system, but gravity wasn't the only way to modify light's passage.

A woman passed her, descending, murmuring a casual greeting. Agata had chosen the stairwell at random; she had no reason to believe that she was heading for an entrance to the facility itself. The usual tiers of apartments here should simply come to an end a little sooner than they had before the system was built.

Above her, less than a saunter away, the twelve long tubes would run from mirror to distant mirror, carrying messages from the future in beams of densely modulated time-reversed starlight. The tubes would be sealed against contamination – against dust or smoke that might scatter the light – and perhaps the Council had made an effort to render them vacuum-safe, in case the ends were breached and they were opened to the void. But that would be a matter of structural reinforcement to limit the damage from a sudden pressure difference, not a matter of impermeability. There was no such thing as a hermetic seal on a container of that size. At the very least, particles of air would be constantly diffusing in and out of the tubes.

For most purposes, air was air. So long as it was chemically inert and dense enough to serve the crucial role of carrying heat away from bodies and machinery, any finer details were of secondary importance. When the cooling system had switched from using the old engines' exhaust to the gas produced by cold decomposition of sunstone, no one would have much cared that the range of particle sizes was different. But there were countless variations on the basic theme of a stable ball of luxagens, and different mixtures had different properties. The speed of each frequency of light was slightly different in air than in a vacuum, and the precise value depended on the precise composition of the air.

Agata reached the top of the stairs. A sign right in front of her spelt it out: LAST EXIT. She left the stairwell and dragged herself along the corridor, past the doors of the apartments. The Council would have left a large enough buffer above this unrestricted area so that a bomb planted here could not have breached the nearest of the tubes. But she had a number now, good enough to feed into an order-of-magnitude estimate: how fast could she expect a change in the air to diffuse through a resin seal into the tubes that contained the light paths?

Air was air, no one would feel a thing. But if she could make it happen, there'd be no need to damage a single component of the messaging system. The exquisitely calibrated timing of the data fed into each tube would include allowances for ordinary variations in the 'delay' created by the light bouncing from mirror to mirror, but once it drifted beyond that range and the signal was scrambled beyond recovery, there'd be nothing that the system could do about it – least of all send a message into the past to warn the operators of the nature of the problem.

Back in her apartment, Agata sat at her desk and worked through the calculations. If she could add a component to the air that was significantly lighter than the smallest particles in the present mixture, it would naturally rise towards the axis and diffuse into the imperfectly sealed tubes. Though a particle of air in isolation had almost no external field, each light wave that passed over it distorted its shape sufficiently to spoil the usual cancellation between the luxagens, and the secondary wave generated by that process combined with the first to slow it down.

Generations of scientists had uncovered the details she needed to quantify the effect: she was mining the entire intellectual legacy of the *Peerless*. Agata hadn't used half of these results since she was a student, but though her memory of some of the formulas was hazy – and she was afraid to consult the photonic library lest she alert someone in authority to her sudden change of interests – she discovered that she still had all her old paper textbooks at the bottom of a cupboard, not yet so insect-damaged as to be indecipherable.

Without access to the tubes themselves she couldn't hope for a precise answer, but she could sketch the limits of what was physically possible. In the worst case, time had already run out: if the tubes were large enough and the seals sufficiently tight, it could take half a year to infuse enough modified air into them to corrupt the signals.

In the best case, it would take close to three stints. So she had, at most, two stints to alter the composition of the mountain's atmosphere sufficiently to get the process started.

Agata rechecked the numbers, but they did not improve. She sat at her desk with her tattered books around her, bewildered but refusing to be cowed. The ancestors had spoken to her; she was joined to them across the disruption, across the generations yet to be born. The cosmos had no choice but to find a sequence of events that filled the gap and completed that connection, and it could not come out of nowhere. The right plan had to lie within her, just waiting to unfurl.

29

Ramiro was beginning to wish that they'd put cameras on the occulters. The extra transmissions needed to send back the images might have increased the chance of detection, but it would have been worth it just to have an objective version of the rendezvous with the cache in front of him, to take the place of the pictures in his head.

First, the occulter had to release itself from the rock, unwinding the drills and letting itself fall into the void. Then the air jets had to catch it and send it swooping back towards the slopes, approaching the cache with just the right speed at just the right angle. Two hooks on strings hung down from the cache, each one an open half-circle crossed by a vertical trigger about a third of the way in; the arms of the occulter needed to enter those half-circles and strike the triggers to send the second, spring-loaded halves sliding around to enclose them. Then the occulter had to move away, dragging the cache almost horizontally across the rock, unrolling the adhesive resin that was holding it in place against the vertical tug of its centrifugal weight.

Tarquinia interrupted his brooding. 'Relax,' she said. 'Or add up the navigational tolerances again, if you want reassurance. We can hit the hooks, I'm sure of it.'

Ramiro checked the clock on his console. 'Maybe we can, if the occulter turns up. It's already three lapses late.'

'Three days crossing the slopes, and you want it to be punctual to the flicker?'

'These things move like clockwork, literally. If not to the flicker, they ought to be punctual to the lapse.'

Tarquinia said, 'If this turns out badly, I'll drop my anti-messaging principles and let you know . . .' She glanced at the clock. 'One lapse from now.'

Ramiro buzzed dismissively. 'How would that help?'

'It wouldn't,' she admitted. 'But if you can convince yourself that I'm telling the truth, you can relax and assume that silence means success.'

A row of numbers appeared on the console – a transmission from the occulter, not from Tarquinia's future self. Ramiro waited, refusing to interpret the numbers in isolation. Then the second brief report followed.

The occulter was stable, well clear now of the cache site . . . and measurably more massive than before, as revealed by its response to the thrust of the air jets. It had picked up its cargo and held on to it, and as the bomb swung down from above the arms, the occulter had successfully compensated for the spin that would otherwise have been imparted.

A moment later a third report announced that the occulter had managed to drill itself into the rock again.

'One more,' Ramiro pleaded. To catch the hooks and stay balanced was miracle enough, but the occulter needed to be able to keep moving down the slopes towards the base. If the strings had become tangled around the arms, they'd either end up breaking and freeing the cargo, or the whole mechanism would grind to a halt.

'And there it is.' Tarquinia read all the numbers aloud, and worked through the meaning of the torques. The occulter was moving in the normal way, and it was still carrying the bomb. Nothing had jammed, nothing had broken.

'There it is.' Ramiro bent forward, willing the tension out of his shoulders, but only a fraction of the pain departed. A dozen and two equally finicky and precarious encounters remained.

Tarquinia said, 'The mass is less than I was expecting.'

'The mass of the cargo? You think we lost something? Dropped some component—?'

'No!' Tarquinia hesitated. 'I suppose I'm just admitting that Giacomo seems to have been honest with us. I was afraid he might have downplayed the size of the bombs.'

'But he didn't.' Ramiro was pleased. 'We'll need to get every one of them exactly on target, though. A few strides away and we might not even shatter the collector.'

Tarquinia was amused. 'We just threaded a needle on the slopes, and you're talking about missing by strides?'

'We had no time window with the cache,' Ramiro pointed out. 'There's no comparison with the base. In fact, if I was working for the Council I would have told them to build decoys: dozens of structures mimicking the light collectors, with exactly the same optics protruding from the surface. Who's to know which ones really feed into the tubes?'

Tarquinia said, 'Giacomo's group has had three years to think about all that. If they'd had any doubts about the coordinates they could have gone for a different strategy. If we start trying to second-guess them now, we'll go out of our minds.'

'Yeah.' Ramiro turned back to the console and read through the last report again, until he'd convinced himself that the numbers could not mean anything but success.

The next two encounters went as flawlessly as the first, but as the time for the fourth pickup came and went there was silence from the link. It stretched on for more than half a bell, until the fifth occulter began reporting.

Three bells later, the same thing happened again. They'd lost two machines.

At the second last scheduled rendezvous, the occulter missed the hooks and flew right past the cargo, its mass unchanged. Tarquinia stepped in, sending it looping back to try again – not at the same coordinates, but a progression of slightly shifted locations. Ramiro stood aside and watched her work, wishing more than ever for a camera as she swept the occulter over the slopes, trying to engage with a cache that had either slipped a little out of place or simply fallen away into the void.

After the fifth attempt she stopped the occulter and had it drill back into the rock.

'Can we send it to another cache?' she wondered.

Ramiro checked the positions of the three caches for which they'd had no occulters. This one would have to double back to reach any of the three – depleting its air tank to the point where it would not be able to make it to the base.

'It's as good as lost,' he said. 'We now have no spares.'

The last pickup was still almost a bell away. Tarquinia said, 'Do you want to get some loaves? I'll stay here in case there are any surprises.'

*

As Ramiro stood in the queue in the food hall, he noticed a group of diners stealing glances in his direction then turning away with pained expressions, as if his presence were mildly embarrassing. Perhaps he'd become a figure of pity for wasting half his life on the expedition, to so little avail. But if all the real action had been back on the mountain, what exactly had anyone here done to earn the right to look down on him this way?

'I trust you're keeping out of trouble.'

Ramiro turned to see the woman who'd addressed him, three places behind him in the queue.

'You're brave, showing your face in the mountain,' he told Greta.

'I've never left,' she replied. 'I never will. I'm staying through whatever comes.'

' "Whatever comes"?' Ramiro felt his anger rising. 'You talk about it as if it's some uncontrollable mystery, but I know you could persuade the Councillors to switch off the system, if you really wanted to. Once they'd made the plan and automated the shutdown, that would be it – there'd be nothing to fear.' He called out to the diners, 'This woman could set your minds at ease in an instant! Why aren't you demanding it?'

Greta said, 'So if we shut down the system deliberately – just close our eyes to danger – the danger will go away? That's a child's way of thinking.'

'Our eyes will be closed whatever we do,' Ramiro replied. 'There's nothing to lose by closing them voluntarily. After the disruption we'll find out soon enough if there was any other cause.' He tried again to rouse the spectators. 'Isn't that fair?' he shouted. 'Isn't it worth trying? You should be demanding it!'

But no one was being stirred into action; they just stared down at their food. What had they told themselves in their messages? 'Man from expedition made fool of himself in the food hall today, yelling at government adviser.' They already knew that they wouldn't take his proposal seriously enough to make any kind of fuss. And having told themselves as much, even if it made them feel a little weak and ashamed there was nothing they could do about it.

Ramiro collected his loaves from the counter and walked out. As his anger subsided slightly, he wondered if he'd been unfair to Greta. Not even the great fixer could sway the Councillors into acting entirely against their nature. Having chosen their own defining qualities, they wouldn't surrender power or deny themselves information – even when it was certain that events would soon relieve them of both.

Back in the apartment, Ramiro watched Tarquinia eating but he had no appetite himself. 'If this last one fails,' he said, 'don't break your principles and send back a message.'

Tarquinia said, 'I have a better idea: I solemnly promise that if it does fail, I'll send a message to you to be delivered yesterday.'

The first report from the final occulter came in: it had reached the location where the cache was meant to be.

The second report showed the occulter still stable, weighed down with its expected cargo.

The third report declared that the machine had reattached to the surface.

And the fourth report demonstrated that it had retained its powers of locomotion.

They had twelve targets, twelve bombs, and twelve machines with which to deliver them.

Tarquinia said, 'It looks as if we're the disruption after all.'

Ramiro wasn't so confident, but if the Council was intent on declining the role he was happy to match their stubbornness. It was his nature to oppose the messaging system, and history had finally offered him a route to its destruction just a few stints long. Until a meteor fell from the sky to show him up as an irrelevant trespasser, all he could do was keep following that path, and hope that the footprints in the dust ahead really were his own.

30

'I knew you'd want your old job back,' Celia declared.

Agata wasn't sure if she should take this claim literally. She was surprised that Celia remembered her at all, though they had been on duty together when the bomb went off. In the four years since she'd been here the ramshackle office hadn't changed, but the new construction along the axis had made it much harder to reach.

'I mean, now that you can't do cosmology,' Celia clarified, holding out the patch for Agata to sign.

'Exactly,' Agata agreed, forming her mark and accepting the tool belt from her supervisor. 'I thought I'd better make myself useful somehow.'

'Do you think it's a meteor coming?' Celia asked phlegmatically.

'No one can rule that out,' Agata replied. 'But I'm still hoping that it's just a glitch in the system.'

Celia looked sceptical, but she didn't press Agata for a detailed hypothesis. 'Don't take offence,' she said, 'but some of the older workers find it helpful to rehearse their resorptions and extrusions before going in.'

'I'll try that,' Agata promised.

She made her way towards the entrance to the cooling system, trying to appear mildly dejected for the surveillance cameras: the woman who'd travelled across the cosmos to confirm Lila's great theory, reduced to menial labour – and this time with no zealous strike-breaker's pride. In truth, she was ecstatic that she'd been allowed to take the job. The automated employment system, bless it, had had no idea how far from 'current' her experience really was, and more to the point she had clearly not been flagged as any kind of security risk.

Agata dutifully shortened and stretched her legs half a dozen times before fitting her access key to the hatch. As she descended into the cool air of the tunnel she felt a twinge of claustrophobia and her memories of the blast came rushing back. She would never stop mourning Medoro, but she let the grief move through her mind like a familiar presence, with no need for elaborate rituals or acknowledgements.

She made her way up-axis as swiftly as she could, advancing through the blackness, searching the walls for patches of red. Whoever had worked this section before her had been diligent; she saw only the tiny specks of new growth, easily disposed of with a quick flash from her coherer. As far as she knew no one else would be coming here now, but she'd resolved to do a passable job every shift in case there was an unannounced inspection. If her rushed work wasn't quite as thorough as that of her younger colleagues she could always blame her failing eyesight, but there could be no excuse for great glowing colonies of moss.

She reached the end of her allotted segment of the tunnel with almost a bell to spare, then she turned and raced back towards the start. The hard part was doing it quietly, keeping her feet low and lengthening her strides instead of breaking into a run. People were used to hearing workers in the tunnels, but the sound of outright sprinting might attract attention.

Light from the open hatch marked her entry point, but when she arrived at the ladder she slid the hatch closed above her and waited for her eyes to readapt to the dark. A couple of strides down-axis from the hatch, a hardstone grille covered the width of the tunnel. Peering between the bars she saw nothing: no flashes from the coherer of another tunnel worker burning off moss. Agata hadn't quizzed Celia about anyone else's shifts, but she'd chosen the latest of the time slots on offer. It was possible that right now there was no one at all between her and the cooling chamber.

She lay on the floor of the tunnel and rearranged herself so that she could reach down her throat and retrieve the small bundle of tools she'd swallowed. The rags they were wrapped in were covered with clumps of food and digestive resin; she shuddered but managed to avoid emitting a hum of revulsion as she flicked her hand clean.

By touch, Agata confirmed what she'd guessed by sight when the grille had been illuminated: the bars really were embedded in the wall, continuing right into the surrounding stone. The masons must have drilled one hole straight, but created a whole triangular cavity at the opposite point, allowing a rod that was too long to fit directly across the tunnel to be inserted at an angle and then made true. They would have packed the cavity with sand and adhesive, and over time it would have set into something almost as strong as the surrounding calmstone. But though the bars themselves were close to unbreakable, calmstone was just calmstone. Agata put the point of her hand drill against the wall beside the longest of the bars and set to work enlarging the hole that contained it.

By the end of her shift she'd made slots that allowed her to remove and replace three of the bars at will. Two more, and she'd be able to squeeze through.

Agata packed up her tools and forced herself to swallow them again. Beyond the half-disassembled grille and the last segment of the tunnel, there'd be another grille just like it guarding the outlet from the chamber itself. She'd need more time to transit that segment, but the task no longer seemed impossible.

Agata ground the roots with the mortar and pestle she normally used for spices, feeling like some kind of demented kitchen alchemist. The flowers she'd cut up were all decorative species that had been planted around the beds of travellers for generations, in a relic of the old folk belief that their petals' light had health-giving properties. She had never gone in for the custom herself, but at the garden no one had questioned her. The assistant had invited her to pick whatever she liked.

Every plant root contained substances that bound to a range of minerals. Over the generations, chemists had painstakingly tabulated their properties, species by species, and the appendices to Agata's school chemistry textbooks were full of such quaint pre-photonic compendia.

The effect she was hoping for was not dramatic; she didn't need a liberator to set the sunstone in the cooling chamber on fire. All she had to do was 'poison' a large enough portion of the surface of the rock. The size of the air particles that the sunstone produced was sensitive to the amount of time the decomposing agent spent in contact with it; if she could weaken the agent's binding, some lighter air than normal would be produced. The total volume didn't have to be enormous; the giant centrifuge of the *Peerless* itself would separate out the less massive component, concentrating it preferentially around the axis.

If she could get enough disruptor into the cooling chamber, the next step would be verification. She would need to be able to quantify the effect of her intervention on the refractive index of the air near the axis, not least to be able to convince Ramiro and Tarquinia to abandon their own efforts. The shift ought to be measurable in principle, but it would require specialised, high-precision instruments. Agata had no idea how she could get her hands on equipment like that without attracting attention – but she was sure that, like every other aspect of the plan, if she remained resolute it would fall into place.

'You get keener every day,' Celia observed. 'I can move you to an earlier shift if you like.'

'No, this is perfect.' Agata wasn't sure how much explanation her early starts required. 'I just have trouble planning the journey sometimes; if I'm not as energetic it can take me a few more lapses to get here, but if there's any doubt I'd rather make sure I won't be late.'

'Hmm.' Celia didn't care. 'Any new thoughts about the disruption?'

'I'm still optimistic,' Agata replied cautiously.

'You've seen the ancestors' writing,' Celia acknowledged. 'Of course that makes you hopeful. But they didn't tell you how many of us survive.'

'But nor did they mention a great tragedy,' Agata replied. 'They just offered their thanks. If the mountain had been shattered, you'd think they would have aimed for a higher level of solemnity.'

Celia was amused. 'Six generations on? It will all be ancient history by then. They'll carve their memorial on Esilio and some politician will make an empty speech.' She handed Agata her tool belt and access key. 'No one will know what our lives were really like, and no one will care.'

Agata said, 'Perhaps.'

Agata forced herself to complete a full sweep of the tunnel, burning off every visible speck of moss. But as she raced back towards the site of her real work, when she noticed one faint red smudge that she'd missed she did not stop to pull her coherer from her belt.

She paused to disassemble the centre of the first grille, then she slipped through and continued down the tunnel. Her fellow worker who came here on an earlier shift had left a few mossy smudges of her own; no one was perfect. Agata reached the second grille with almost a bell to spare. She reached into her gut and pulled out her tools. The package was tied by a string to her first canister of disruptor.

Working on the grille in utter blackness was pure instinct for her now; her fingers gauged the narrow trench left by her previous assault and guided the drill to the right location with no intervening thought. Between bars, she only stopped to check the clock on her belt.

When she'd eased the fifth bar out and laid it on the floor of the tunnel beside her, she hesitated. Maybe there were invisible defences around the outlet – vibration sensors and high-powered coherers. Before the bombing that would have been unlikely, but anything was possible now.

Agata reached through the grille and sent one of the bars skidding towards the outlet. No weapon's flash broke the darkness. She only had a few chimes left in her shift, and four days before her most optimistic deadline for starting the diffusion. If there ever was a time to take courage and tell herself she was untouchable, wrapped in the arms of the ancestors, this was it. She crawled through the broken grille.

She'd thought she'd grown accustomed to the blasts of chilly air, but as she crossed the last few strides each wave of pressure felt like a physical assault. She switched on her coherer at the lowest possible brightness and squinted into the machinery where the tunnel began.

In the chamber below her, the pressure of the newly formed gas was increasing, forcing the piston up along the outlet shaft. She could see the great polished stone cylinder rising now, the side of it completely blocking the tunnel, its motion only visible from flaws and scratches rushing by.

Then it cleared the mouth of the tunnel, and the cold air from the chamber came rushing out. Agata felt every hardened patch of wizened skin on her body forced into the flesh beneath, with the chill only sharpening the sensation.

As the pressure driving it plummeted, the piston stopped ascending and came hurtling down. Agata had known the rhythm of the full cycle from the first day she'd crawled into the tunnel, but what mattered now was the exact time the outlet shaft was exposed. She crouched before the piston, utterly attentive, letting the process imprint itself on her, binding every visual and tactile cue into a single act of perception.

She closed her eyes, waited for the moment, opened them: and there it was, the bottom of the piston rising up. She couldn't lose it now, she couldn't get it wrong.

Agata drew the canister of disruptor out of her tool belt, and unscrewed the lid to the point where one more quarter-turn would free it. A single knock would spill the contents, but mere passage through the air would not; she'd tested that a dozen times.

She closed her eyes, waited, then opened them. She hadn't lost the rhythm. Every muscle in her body knew what to do, and when.

The piston plunged, the pressure rose. Agata waited. The piston ascended.

As the piston rose above the mouth of the tunnel, she threw the canister. It entered the shaft and disappeared. She heard no sound from the impact, but she hadn't expected one; the bottom of the chamber would be far below, and the canister might yet be spinning in mid-air, still caught in the updraught.

The piston crashed down again, closing the mouth of the tunnel. Agata closed her eyes, overcome with relief. She had four more days; she could prepare and deliver at least four more doses. All her numbers were approximations and guesswork, but unless she had wildly miscalculated, that total would at least give her a chance.

The air burst out from the chamber once more; Agata opened her eyes to welcome it. A trace of fine grit stung her eyes, then something clattered loudly across the tunnel floor.

The canister came to a halt beside her. She stared down at the rejected gift. If it had travelled all the way into the expanse of the chamber, it was very unlikely to have entered the shaft again.

There had to be a grille or baffle of some kind at the bottom of the shaft – below the piston's lowest point, or the canister would have been crushed into powder. Some of the disruptor would surely have ended up inside the chamber, but the grit blown back at her must have been the rest.

Agata touched the clock on her belt; she needed to start moving immediately, or she'd be so late for her end of shift that Celia would send in a search party. She gathered up her tools and the lidless canister and forced them back into their hiding place.

She had four days left, and a barrier at the bottom of a giant, pounding piston that would reject most of what she threw into the shaft.

But as she retreated along the tunnel, she finally understood where the plan was leading her. She could dive under the piston, survive the landing on the barrier, and – if the low point of the piston's motion was high enough – remain there unharmed long enough to deliver the disruptor into the chamber by hand. That much was possible.

But once she was down there, there would be no way out.

31

'Have you checked the horizon lately?' Tarquinia asked Ramiro, following him into the apartment.

'I think it's still about a bell away,' he said. There was no official cut-off point, but there was a public site where people had posted the times of origin of all the messages they'd received from the last few days before the disruption. Ramiro harnessed himself to the desk beside his console and brought up the file.

'No change,' he reported. 'Do you want to try out the system while you still have a chance?'

Tarquinia hummed with mock regret. 'Too late. Let the messagers who want the bandwidth have it; I'm not going to steal it from them for a cheap thrill.'

'Then why do you care about the timing?'

'This is the start of freedom,' she said. 'The Councillors might know everything they're going to do for the next three days, but most people will have nothing proscribing their actions.'

Ramiro wasn't expecting an uprising. 'It's going to take more than three days for the effects of the last three years to fade. And if there was going to be public unrest, I think the Council's own bulletins would have mentioned it.' Censoring bad news wouldn't change anything, and once the omission came to light it would only undermine the government's credibility.

He took the link from its hiding place under the desk and plugged it into the console.

The occulters were approaching the bottom of the mountain. Having them crawl over the sharp edge that divided the slopes from the base would have been insanely ambitious, so the machines had been instructed to fly from one surface to the other, keeping as low as possible but sparing themselves the most difficult terrain.

Centrifugal gravity turned the base of the mountain into a sheer vertical wall. The cargo hooked to the occulters' arms would hang down over them, applying a torque that would try to peel them off the rock, and increasing the risk of the connecting strings becoming tangled in the clockwork. Ramiro had programmed adjustments to the depth and angle of the drills that he hoped would minimise the problems, but it was all untested; there'd been no reason back on the *Surveyor* to rehearse for this strange asymmetric loading. He found it hard not to resent Giacomo's group for failing to devise a better solution when they'd had three years' warning, but then the innovation block wasn't an imaginary disease that people invoked just to excuse their laziness. Agata's long silence since she'd set out to overcome it proved just how pernicious it must be.

A short burst of data appeared on the console. Tarquinia chirped. 'Number one's made the jump!'

Ramiro waited for the next report, then scrutinised the figures. 'It's clinging on, and it hasn't jammed.' He wasn't satisfied yet; it was still possible that the strings would become progressively twisted. The occulter rotated its body in opposite directions with each step, so all things being equal it ought to unwind as much it entwined, but he could imagine some configurations of the strings interfering with the process and favouring one direction.

But in the third report the torques were unchanged, and the fourth confirmed that nothing was escalating. The occulter was cycling its way up the rock face towards its target, tenaciously regaining the same equilibrium with every step.

Ramiro sagged across the desk. 'I think I just aged another six years.'

Tarquinia said, 'Better here than back on the *Surveyor*.'

'That's true.' Ramiro had never thanked her for the lengths to which she'd gone to spare him that fate. He sat and watched her for a moment, wondering what she'd say if he raised it after all this time. But he suspected that it would only annoy and embarrass her if he told her that he knew what she'd done for him.

The second occulter flew over the edge, and recovered as well as the first. Ramiro was wary of becoming complacent — but it made no sense to reason about the machines' fate without taking account of everything he knew of both the past and the future. The disruption would happen, that was close to a certainty, and the occulters'

306

behaviour had to be consistent with that. The cosmos was indifferent as to whether the solution of its governing equations described the *Peerless* obliterated by a meteor, or just a few conspirators managing to shatter a few mirrors. But even the most dispassionate mathematician who'd been told that twelve clockwork insects carrying explosives were crawling across the mountain towards the light collectors would have to accept that the second solution now appeared at least as viable as the first.

The third occulter reported success. The fourth, the fifth. Ramiro said, 'When this stage is over, we should go and tell Agata and Azelio. They deserve to have their minds put at ease.'

Tarquinia was sympathetic, but not so sure that it would help. 'Do you think Azelio would get any comfort from this?'

'Once he's confronted with the sheer improbability of a meteor arriving at exactly the same time as the occulters, it might change his perspective.'

The sixth occulter landed safely and commenced its upwards crawl. Tarquinia said, 'After Agata and Azelio, we should break the news to the Councillors.'

'Really?'

'Just to taunt them,' she stressed. 'No details.'

Ramiro said, 'Where's the fun in that? They've known for three years that they were going to be defeated.'

'I'm not sure that's true,' Tarquinia replied. 'I think they convinced themselves that it would be a meteor. No defeat, no surrender, just an act of nature.'

The seventh occulter sent its report. Ramiro squinted at the numbers, confused. 'What . . . ?'

Tarquinia leant closer to the screen. 'It's gone into the void. It fired the air jets to leave the slope, but then something jammed and it couldn't get back.'

A second report arrived; the accelerometer showed the occulter in free fall.

Ramiro was numb. 'That's impossible. How can we lose one when we have no spares?'

Tarquinia said, 'What if we change some of the targeting? Maybe we can take out two light collectors with one bomb – or three with two.'

Ramiro brought the target coordinates onto the screen. 'How do we model this? Do we add the pressures from each shock wave?'

'That will do, for an estimate.'

The estimate told them that the strategy wouldn't work. The light collectors were spread too far apart, and the blast radius of each bomb was too small.

Ramiro was lost. 'What is it that we don't understand? Could one channel survive?'

Tarquinia considered this. 'So one Councillor already knows what comes after the disruption? It's hard to believe that they could keep that a secret from the others, and I don't see how the politics would work: in the aftermath they'd just be despised by everyone for withholding the information.'

'It's not impossible, though.'

'It's not impossible, but I'm not going to rely on it.'

'So what do we do?'

Tarquinia hesitated, then came to a decision. 'I'll go out and repair the occulter – clean the jets, change the air tank. It's in free fall and we know the trajectory; it shouldn't be too difficult to intercept.'

Ramiro fought down an impulse to volunteer himself; she'd have a far better chance of success than he would, if she could get out into the void at all. 'Won't the airlocks be guarded?'

'I know a way out through the observatory,' she said.

'A way out that isn't an airlock?'

'It's a chamber with two airtight doors,' Tarquinia conceded, 'but no one ever uses it to come and go. There are some small instruments that we operate in the void, and we slide them in and out on tracks to avoid all the rigmarole of going outside to tend to them.'

'But a person can squeeze through?'

'Yes. Just barely.'

Ramiro said, 'We don't know that it won't be guarded, or monitored somehow.'

'No. But we can be sure that every other airlock will be.'

'How will you get access?'

'I think I can talk my way into an observing session – and there are tools, cooling bags and air tanks there already, I won't need to drag a lot of suspicious paraphernalia with me. All I need is a bell or two alone in the main dome, exploring some hunch about the disruption.'

'A hunch that your colleagues will know must come to nothing, or the Council would have sent the results back three years.'

Tarquinia scowled. 'No, it must come to nothing that's recognised as vital in the next three days – but that doesn't prove that the observations won't be valuable later. I can invent some wild theory on my way to the summit. Believe me, I've seen the observing program – no one has any idea where to point the telescopes right now. The chief astronomer will be grateful for anything that looks even half plausible.'

'So the instrument will be doing some automated sweep . . . while you're out in the void fixing the occulter?' Every part of this sounded desperate, but Ramiro had no better ideas. 'Won't you be tracked?'

'If I go straight up from the summit and then arc around towards the plane of the base I can stay out of range of the systems tuned for accidental egress – and I certainly won't have the signature to be mistaken for an incoming Hurtler.' Tarquinia reached across the desk and took the link. 'I'm going to need this to reprogram the occulter. We should have made it possible to talk to the things with a corset alone, but it's no use complaining about a lack of foresight.' She formed a pocket for the link then started dragging herself towards the door, then she saw the expression on Ramiro's face.

'We've both survived tougher jobs than this,' she said. 'I'm not going to die out there.'

'I know, but—'

'If I get arrested, just pretend to be shocked. Maybe there'll still be something you can do – don't assume that the whole plan's dead just because they've grabbed me.'

'All right.'

Tarquinia drew herself towards Ramiro and embraced him. 'This is just a glitch,' she said. 'In a few bells I'll be back here and we'll be joking about it.'

'Yeah.'

Ramiro watched her leave, then he sat by the console. Without the link he couldn't even check what was happening with the other occulters. He didn't doubt Tarquinia's skill or resolve, but if they lost one more machine she could hardly repeat the same ruse. The whole plan was on the verge of collapsing, and he had no idea how to salvage it.

*

Ramiro pounded on Agata's door until his hand ached, but there was no response. So much for her sitting in her room and thinking. Who would she visit? Lila? Azelio?

He looked up Lila's address on a public console, but he hadn't gone far when he ran into Agata coming the other way, carrying a box full of books.

Ramiro greeted her casually and restrained himself from blurting out anything compromising. 'That's a lot of reading,' he said.

'They're Medoro's books,' Agata explained. 'His family had no use for them, so I thought I'd take them.'

Ramiro gave a quiet chirp of approval, as if he were acknowledging a respectful gesture of remembrance. 'It'd be good to catch up with you,' he said. 'If you're not too busy.'

'I'd like that,' Agata replied. 'My apartment's a mess, though – it's not fit for company.' They'd never checked it for listening devices.

'You could drop off the books and come to my place, if you like.'

'All right. I'll see you in a chime.'

They parted at the next intersection.

When Agata arrived, Ramiro invited her in and closed the door. 'If you have another plan,' he said, 'now's the time to tell us.'

Agata's composure shattered as if he'd struck her. 'I couldn't do it,' she confessed. She started humming and shivering. 'I wasn't strong enough.'

Ramiro was horrified. 'It's all right, calm down! I was just asking.' In all their time together he'd never seen her so wretched. 'No one else could break the innovation block – and so far you've had about three bells without it.'

'You don't understand,' she said. 'I already had a plan three stints ago – no innovations, it was all gleaned from textbooks. But I couldn't go through with it.'

Ramiro led her over to the couch and sat beside her. 'What happened?' he asked gently.

Agata explained between bouts of shivering. 'I had everything worked out so that Celia would think I'd done a final shift and then quit. No one would have been searching the tunnels for my body. I'd even found a way to repair the grilles behind me so that the other workers wouldn't notice the damage. I was going to schedule a message to you and Tarquinia, telling you the threshold that the refractive index of the air near the axis would need to cross for you to know that you could cancel the bombs. But after I sent a message to myself to hold fast against Giacomo, I lost all my courage.'

Ramiro squeezed her shoulder. 'I'm glad you didn't do it.'

'Why?' she asked miserably. 'If your own plan's gone bad, all that's left to explain the disruption is a meteor—'

'We're not there yet,' he protested. He described what had happened to the occulter, and Tarquinia's scheme to get out and fix it. 'But if you have any non-suicidal alternatives, don't keep them to yourself.' Ramiro suspected that the three of them working together might have found a way to get Agata's chemical into the cooling chamber, but it was too late for that now.

'I have no more ideas,' Agata said forlornly. 'That's why I asked Serena and Gineto for the books. The Council has all of Medoro's notes on the time-reversed camera, but his design didn't come out of nowhere. If I can retrace the steps of his education myself, there's a chance I might see something that I missed.'

Ramiro pictured the bulging container she'd been lugging down the corridor; he couldn't read that much in a year. But if Tarquinia couldn't repair the occulter, they'd have three days to mine Medoro's textbooks and come up with a new way to shut down the system.

'I shouldn't keep you from your study, then,' he said. 'Just promise me you won't try anything like the last plan.'

'Why couldn't they have spoken more clearly?' Agata asked, bewildered. 'I thought they were giving me the courage I needed to go down that shaft . . .' She began shivering again. 'How can I fail them, when they know my whole future? How is that possible?'

Ramiro said, 'There was no message from the ancestors.' The stupid hoax had gone on far too long, and it had almost killed her. 'Tarquinia carved those words into the rock, before we left Esilio. You and Azelio were sick, bedridden in your cabins, so it was easy for her to slip away to the blast site while she was packing up the tents.'

Agata was stunned. 'Why would she do that?'

'To make the messaging system look redundant, so no one would have to scratch out a living on Esilio.'

Agata drew away from him. 'So the two of you lied to me for six years?' She thought for a moment. 'Because you wanted me to sell it on the mountain? You thought people might believe my testimony, so long as I didn't know the truth.'

'That was the plan,' Ramiro admitted. There was no point going into the whole convoluted history of the thing, explaining his failed attempt to make the inscription his own.

'We don't know anything now.' Agata seemed more wounded by this revelation than by the personal betrayal. 'If the mountain's wiped out, the Councillors might not make it to Esilio. We don't even have that comfort any more – we don't know that there'll be any survivors at all, that the home world won't burn.'

Ramiro said, 'I'm sorry.' He'd only meant to spare her the burden of imagining herself chosen by history, pinned to this impossible task by the ancestors' gaze. But there was no way to do that without stripping away the whole lie.

Agata rose from the couch and dragged herself towards the door. She said, 'When Tarquinia gets back, tell her I'm dead to both of you. I don't care any more. Let the cosmos work it out.'

Six bells after she'd left for the observatory, Tarquinia had still not returned.

Ramiro knew that if she'd been arrested she wouldn't tell her captors anything – but the mere fact of her transgression would mean that the two of them would have been under observation from the moment they'd left the *Surveyor*. If the authorities had found the link on her, they would have been searching for its signal all along, so they could have picked up the transmissions to the occulters. Even without decoding any of the content, they would have been able to deduce the machines' locations from the direction of the beam.

But he didn't know any of that with certainty. All he could do now was gamble on the chance that the plan could still be salvaged. If he could get outside and fix the occulter himself, everything might yet come together.

Ramiro checked the records on the console and committed the occulter's trajectory to memory. Heading straight for the nearest airlock would be futile; he might as well turn himself in. But anyone who could get more than a dozen caches of explosives onto the slopes would have to know a safe way out. His allies had been wise to limit their contact with him, and they'd managed to convince themselves that having set the plan in motion there'd be nothing more they'd need to do. But if they hadn't yet realised how wrong they'd been, it would be up to him to disillusion them.

'I don't know anyone called Giacomo,' the man protested irritably.

'I met him here a few stints ago,' Ramiro explained. 'I think he borrowed your apartment, because it wasn't convenient to use his own.'

'You must be confused about the address.' The man closed the door.

Ramiro supposed it was possible that the apartment's tenant had had no knowledge of the meeting, but he couldn't think of any other way to attract the group's attention. Perhaps they'd been monitoring the whole project independently and already knew what had happened to the occulter, but he couldn't take that for granted and rely on them to intervene.

Back in his apartment, he sat and waited for contact. Greta's people might be watching him, but that had always been true; either Giacomo's group had ways around that, or everything they'd done would have been spotted long ago.

After six bells, Ramiro lost patience. He knew he'd have no hope of sleeping, so he went out hoping to be found.

By most people's schedules it was night-time, and the corridors were lit with nothing but red moss-light, but the precinct was as busy as he'd seen it. Ramiro passed dozens of restless neighbours, crowding the guide ropes, moving as briskly and aimlessly as he was. When he met their eyes they turned away, confused. In two days the mountain might be gone, and any sane person would want to play a part in protecting it. But after three years of complying with the flawless predictions of their own private messages – or their friends' messages, or whatever impinged on their lives in the public news – what could they do when they'd been told that they'd do nothing?

Two young men approached on the adjacent rope, avoiding his gaze like everyone else, but to Ramiro they seemed more self-conscious about it than any stranger ought to be. As they drew nearer he waited for one of them to bump him and pass him a note, and he readied himself to play his part and make the collision look plausible. Then he saw the edge of a blade sliding out from its hiding place in the first man's hand.

He grabbed the assailant's wrist and stared straight at his

approaching accomplice. 'If I'm not back in my apartment in three chimes,' he said, 'every detail goes to the Council automatically.'

'Nothing stops us,' the man informed him solemnly. 'We already know how this ends.'

'So why this?' Ramiro bent the knife-wielder's hand – then crossed ropes to let a woman move past, positioning his body to hide the blade from her.

'It ends well because you take this as a warning and stop bringing attention to yourself,' the man replied.

Ramiro said, 'I think you might be confusing foresight and wishful thinking. I say it ends well because I have a meeting with Giacomo, immediately.'

The accomplice's expression of certainty was wavering. He must have grown so accustomed to his plans unfolding perfectly that he'd lost the ability to rethink them on the fly.

Ramiro said, 'I know it's hard for people to organise their calendar these days, but the only way I'll stop being a problem for your boss is by talking to him face to face.'

Giacomo sat on the floor of the food hall, chatting amiably with a dozen companions, but the gathering was large enough that he didn't need to be contributing constantly to appear to be engaged. Ramiro sat two strides away with his back to the group, straining to hear the whispers directed his way, while trying to look like a lone diner brooding sadly on the fate of his friend.

'We'll take care of the machine,' Giacomo said. 'There's nothing for you to worry about.' His rear eyes moved aimlessly, his gaze passing over Ramiro without registering his presence.

Save Giacomo's friends, there was no one else close enough to have any chance of hearing them, and Ramiro could only assume that his allies knew the location of every listening device in the room. But it was still a struggle to speak as if they had real privacy.

'If you can fix this,' he said, 'you should have told us earlier, and then my friend wouldn't be in trouble.'

'That won't last long,' Giacomo promised. 'Even if they've taken her, in a matter of days every prisoner will be free.'

Ramiro had no idea how he thought he could guarantee that; the whole government was hardly going to resign in shame. 'And what about the occulter? You can perform the repairs yourself?'

'Absolutely,' Giacomo assured him.

Ramiro gave him the communications codes that would be needed to instruct the navigation system and get the machine back on course.

'You should lie low now,' Giacomo said. 'I'm sorry about the incident before, but that wasn't my decision. Someone saw you as a risk and took things into their own hands.'

Ramiro chewed his loaf slowly. His trust in this man was disintegrating, but if the conspiracy was a sham and Giacomo had been working for the Council all along, why would anyone go through the motions of trying to warn him off?

'You don't need to make repairs,' Ramiro realised. 'You've got replacements. You've built your own.' They'd had the plans for three years. Why limit themselves to making accessories when they could copy the whole design?

Giacomo took his time replying, inserting a raucous joke into his friends' End of the Mountain celebration.

'We've built our own,' he agreed reluctantly. 'That was only prudent – and it's turned out to be essential.'

'You couldn't tell us?'

'The less you knew, the better,' Giacomo replied.

Ramiro suspected that it was Agata's position that would have been the sticking point; this made a mockery of the idea that the *Surveyor*'s crew had held a veto over the final deployment. 'How many spares did you make?'

'Enough.' There was a note of irritation creeping into Giacomo's voice.

'A dozen? A gross?'

Giacomo said, 'You don't need those details. We've been planning this for years, we know exactly what we're doing. Just go back to your apartment and wait.'

Ramiro stared down at the plate in front of him. These people knew him far better than he knew them – at the very least through Pio, and Ramiro had told Pio that he'd oppose him if he ever tried to use violence. Giacomo would have been forewarned not to expect Ramiro to cooperate with anything of the kind.

That was why they'd been so coy about the scale of their own resources: they were going to try to breach the tubes. They had as many occulters as they'd need, carrying whatever quantity of explosives it would take. The occulters from the *Surveyor* were just decoys; it had never mattered whether or not they reached their targets.

Ramiro said, 'I need some proof from you that the attack won't be excessive – that it will shatter the light collectors, nothing more.'

Giacomo's rear gaze turned on him briefly, before sliding away. 'How could I prove that? Do you want to come and observe all our communications? What would that tell you? If we showed you the data from the one machine that's replaced your runaway, you could always convince yourself that there were more.'

Ramiro was silent; he had nothing to bargain with. If he went to the Council and helped them mount a defence against the occulters, he'd only be risking a far greater loss of life from a meteor strike.

'Why?' he asked, dropping any pretence that there was still some doubt about Giacomo's plans. 'The disruption is enough. The Council will be humiliated, they'll fall at the next election. The system will never be restarted. What more could you want?'

Giacomo embarked on a long, loud story about someone's feud with someone else in their student days. Ramiro began to think that the meeting was over; he finished his meal and began picking up crumbs from the plate.

But then the story ended and Giacomo spoke.

'This is the fulcrum,' he whispered. 'This is our one chance. Or how many generations will be forced to bear the same ruthless people holding power? Prisoners locked up without trial? Men treated as lesser beings, made for one purpose alone? The disruption is not enough; there needs to be damage and chaos. The Council needs to fail the people so badly that they don't dare set foot on the mountain again. Let them run away to Esilio or die in their private fortresses. In two days everything will change for ever. There's nothing to lament in that. But if we want our time to come, there has to be a price.'

Ramiro lay sleepless in his sand bed, staring out into the moss-lit room. If the messaging system's tubes were breached, their walls might still hold against the pressure. The Council would have known all along that this kind of damage was possible; they must have taken steps to minimise the consequences.

But all the earlier construction along the axis had been carried out with no conception that it would ever be exposed to the void. Walls could be strengthened after the fact, seals could be laid down. But nothing would ever render the resulting patchwork the same as the solid rock of the hull that had been kept intact for that purpose from the start.

If the tubes gave way, whole precincts would crumble. People would be battered by the winds and debris, even if they didn't end up out in the void. Before the breach could be repaired there would be all the damage and chaos that Giacomo could desire.

But what other possibilities remained? Ramiro could still summon up a slender hope that if he went to the Council promising to reveal the details of the attack, they would agree to a voluntary shutdown. Maybe all the stubbornness Greta had displayed in public had only been for show.

Was that what he wanted, though: the Council triumphant? Could he really have half of Vincenzo's version – the disruption as a bluff to expose the saboteurs – without the messaging system starting up again and the same dismal paralysis descending across the mountain for six more generations? With his rash confession to Agata he'd destroyed any chance of Tarquinia's hoax convincing anyone that the system was redundant. And if he was sentencing people to the dust and darkness of Esilio, how many more would die there than would fall victim to Giacomo's plan?

He wanted change. He wanted the Council crushed. He wanted the men who came after him to be more than timid appeasers like his uncle, who'd clutched at their prescribed role with pathetic gratitude then done their best to instil the same subservient mentality in the next generation.

Whatever choice he made, whatever side he took, some lives would be endangered and some people would die. All he could do was look beyond that to the fate of the survivors. One path would lead, at best, to a miserable exile for the dissenters and generations of tyranny for everyone who remained on the mountain. The other would bring turmoil and grief for a while, but it would also bring a chance of enduring freedom.

32

Agata flipped over a dozen pages before realising that her concentration had deserted her and she had no idea what she'd been looking at.

She pushed the book away across her desk. Even if she stumbled on some crucial insight that had informed Medoro's design, what could she do with it in a day and a half? She wasn't going to build a magical machine that could reach through solid rock and turn the messaging system to dust.

There was knocking from outside. Agata dragged herself to the door.

'Are you busy?' Serena asked.

'Not really.' Agata invited her in.

Medoro's books were arranged around the room, stacked by subject and ordered by hastily assigned priorities.

'You're sorting through everything already,' Serena observed. She glanced at the desk, at the open book.

'I got caught up in *Principles of Photonics*,' Agata explained. 'Once you've read the first page it's impossible to put down.'

'We should go for a walk,' Serena suggested. 'Give yourself a break.'

'All right.' Agata wasn't sure what this would be in aid of, but she followed Serena out into the corridor.

They moved along the guide rope in silence for a while, single file with Agata in front. Then Serena said quietly, 'I've been talking to some friends about the disruption.'

'Yeah?'

'We all agreed that we have to do something.' Serena met Agata's rear gaze. 'So if you have any plans of your own, maybe we can work together.'

Agata said, 'Now you tell me.'

'You have no idea what it's been like here,' Serena replied bluntly. 'They switched on the system, and suddenly we had three years of our lives laid out in front of us: three years' worth of messages telling us exactly who we'd be. A few people were dragged kicking and screaming into whole new ways of thinking – but after the initial jolt they were just as incapable of change as the rest of us. That's what the system does: it turns you into the kind of person who knows nothing more each day than you knew the day before.'

'But now the feed's gone silent, and the spell is broken?'

'Half broken,' Serena replied. 'There are a lot of us who want to act, but the paralysis lingers. Some people think we should march on the messaging stations and smash whatever we can – but there's still a mindset that declares it's impossible, because if the Council have said we won't . . . we won't.'

Agata's spirits were rising, but she wasn't clear herself where this new force could be applied.

'There's already a plan to sabotage the channels,' she said. 'But I don't trust the people who set it up.' She scanned the corridor, then waited until she was certain that no passer-by could hear her before explaining Giacomo's scheme. 'I don't think they care if they break open the tubes. They're not going to err on the side of caution.' Agata stopped short of accusing the group of Medoro's murder; she didn't know that for sure.

Serena took a few lapses to come to terms with these revelations. She'd probably come to Agata hoping for nothing more than a technical opinion on the best place to attack the system.

'So what are you searching for in my brother's books?' she asked finally.

'Another way to cause the shutdown.'

'And if you find one, will the saboteurs call off their plans?'

'Probably not,' Agata admitted. 'Even if I could persuade Ramiro and Tarquinia, I doubt they're in control any more.'

Serena said, 'So you're saying that these saboteurs might be the greatest threat. But what would happen if we managed to stop them?'

'Something still has to cause the disruption,' Agata replied. 'A meteor, or a mob.'

'There are dozens of us ready to protect the mountain,' Serena avowed. 'But we might not be enough to cause the disruption by sheer force of numbers, let alone stage some second action against the saboteurs as well.'

They'd almost come full circle back to the apartment, but Agata couldn't face the piles of unread books again. She wasn't going to transform herself into Medoro in the next few bells. 'We had a time-reversed camera on the *Surveyor* for years,' she lamented. 'I could have spent all my free time experimenting on it, if I'd known how useful that would be.'

Serena was amused. 'The rest of the crew might not have been too happy if you'd destroyed it.'

'After we'd left Esilio it wouldn't have mattered. But we certainly took care of it until then.' Agata stopped and stood clutching the guide rope, thinking about the landing. 'Protecting it from too much exposure.'

'You mean not pointing it at Esilio's sun?' Serena frowned. 'Though wouldn't that have . . . brought it back to normal, if it had arrived burnt out?'

'Protecting it from too much ordinary light as well,' Agata said. 'Intense light would have damaged it: scatter from our engines, say.'

'So you want to steal the *Surveyor* and aim its engines at the base of the mountain?' Serena joked.

Agata said, 'No. But a big enough explosion above the base should have the same effect . . . or twelve smaller ones might do it.'

Serena understood. 'You want to repurpose the saboteurs' bombs? Use the flash but not the bang?'

'Why not? The collectors gather light from all directions – and they can't discriminate between ordinary light and time-reversed light. If we can shift the explosions far enough away from the surface that there's no risk of them breaching the tubes, they could still be the cause of the disruption. They don't even need to damage the cameras permanently – they just have to overwhelm the photonics long enough for the time-reversed light that's in transit to be lost.' The original plan for the occulters had been to blind each channel to a single star, but the design that made that impossible rendered this new plan far less demanding: it didn't matter where in the sky the explosions appeared. The collectors would funnel all the photons in and dazzle the cameras, regardless.

Serena said, 'What if there's a sensor that can bring down a shutter if the ambient light gets too bright? I mean, the light that's meant to do this damage will be bouncing back and forth between the mirrors before it gets to the camera. There'll be plenty of time for news of the danger to reach the camera by a shorter route.'

She was right, Agata realised. But it might not matter. 'They can bring down a shutter to protect the camera from permanent damage . . . but that shutter will block the time-reversed light, too. So it will all come down to the timing: whether the flash from the explosions forces the shutter to close for so long that the signal is lost.'

Serena was quiet for a moment. 'So how do we divert the saboteurs' bombs? Go out there and physically move them?'

'Maybe,' Agata replied. 'But I don't know how we can get out undetected.'

Serena was incredulous. 'You think the Council will try to stop us *protecting the mountain*?'

'Not as such – but if we're going to tell them our plan, they'll have known about it for the last three years. So why wouldn't they have modified their own defences at the base to take account of what we tell them about the occulters and the explosives?'

Serena said, 'Because we don't tell them. Because we're afraid that they'd find a way to prevent the explosions from causing the disruption – which would bring us back to a meteor as the cause.' She put a hand over her eyes and massaged her temples. 'Just when I'd stopped getting messages from myself, the future finds a new way to order me around.'

'Has it told you how to get into the void unseen? Or do some of your army of waking sleepers happen to be airlock guards?'

'No airlock guards,' Serena replied, 'but we have technicians capable of splicing photonic cables and disabling sensors.'

'That's not enough,' Agata said ruefully. 'There'll be people at all the airlocks, from now to the disruption.'

Serena hummed angrily. 'So do you believe we're going to do this, or do you think we're going to cower in our rooms and wait for whatever unfolds?'

'I don't know.' Agata hadn't been able to bring herself to reveal what Ramiro had told her about the inscription. The only certainty they had now was the disruption; there was no promise of any kind of triumph to follow.

'Are you still working in the cooling tunnels?' Serena asked.

'No.'

'But you're familiar with the whole system?'

'I've done the induction – it was fairly detailed. Why?'

Serena said, 'Cooling air *leaves the mountain* – and there won't be people guarding every vent. If my technician friends can disable the sensors, we can go out with the air and start looking for these bombs.'

Agata began buzzing softly. 'You think they'll let a mob of sabo-teurs congregate at an air vent? There are cameras in every corridor, there are people watching every move we make.'

'Maybe your moves,' Serena conceded. 'The mere fact that you were on the *Surveyor* with the anti-messenger Ramiro taints you a little. But who am I? Who are my friends? There aren't enough people in the entire security department to watch everyone, and the software never got smart enough to take over the job. We're not saboteurs, we're not known dissidents. While they're watching the usual suspects, all we have to do is avoid setting off the kind of alarms that can't be ignored.'

In Gineto's apartment, Vala spent a chime scrupulously copying Agata's posture and learning to mimic her gait.

'No one would mistake our faces,' Vala admitted, 'but if I hold this box of books on my shoulder to obscure my face from the camera . . .' She demonstrated.

Agata had carried Medoro's real books home in more or less the same way; a second instalment need not attract suspicion. She handed Vala the key to her apartment. 'Happy reading.'

She waited with Serena and Gineto, practising her imitation of Vala but hoping that no one would even be watching the camera feeds. Let them all be busy following Ramiro and Tarquinia.

Serena checked the clock on her belt. 'Time to go.'

Gineto said, 'Good luck.'

Agata followed Serena out of the apartment, trying to appear suit-ably motherly: mildly affectionate but mostly aloof. Vala had always seemed bemused that two lumps of flesh shed from her body had grown into fully functioning creatures, with no further intervention on her part. The corridor wasn't too busy, so Serena took the adjoin-ing rope, never concealing Agata entirely from the cameras they passed, but often obscuring part of the view. Anyone with access to the feeds would be able to reconstruct every party's true movements easily enough, in retrospect – or long before the event, if the information was recognised as important enough to send back – so their not being caught out now would be largely contingent on their not being caught out later. From their position of ignorance, success and failure seemed balanced on a knife edge, but from a cosmic point of view the two slabs of self-consistent events had been utterly distinct for at least the last three years.

As they drew nearer to the utility shaft, Agata could see a camera gazing straight down at the entrance portal. They hung back, and Serena glanced at her clock. 'Where are they?' she muttered. A moment later Agata heard a group of people approaching, talking and buzzing.

'Now,' Serena whispered. They advanced together. There were a dozen people coming the other way, spread out between the two guide ropes. Some of them, politely, tried to shift ropes to let Serena and Agata pass, but they were packed too close together along both ropes for them to all fit on either one. As the impasse clumsily sorted itself out, two women who looked like mother and daughter managed to break out of the throng and move away. Agata followed Serena down into the shaft and pulled the portal cover closed behind her. If the security sensors here hadn't been dealt with, they wouldn't be the first ones to trigger them: the portal's lock had been snapped a few bells before, and most of the team was meant to have come through before them.

As they descended the ladder in the red-tinged gloom, Agata could hear the muffled hiss of gas in the tunnel beside them. No one came here on regular cleaning shifts; the warm air was inimical to moss.

When they arrived at the bottom of the shaft the darkness was impenetrable. Serena said quietly, 'It's us,' and someone switched on a coherer. Agata squinted into the glare and counted two dozen and nine figures squeezed around them, already wearing their corsets, cooling bags and jetpacks. Many of them had never used the jetpacks; they should all have had one-on-one briefings earlier from their more experienced friends, but it was Agata's job now to go through the safety checks and remind them of everything they'd forgotten.

'If you get into trouble,' she began, climbing two steps back up the ladder to make herself visible to everyone, 'just draw a stop line: a straight horizontal line across your chest.' She demonstrated. 'The rock will still be moving below you, but don't let that confuse you:

the pack will bring you to a halt relative to the mountain's axis, so you won't go flying off into the void.'

There was no time for more than the basics, but if they could retain it, it ought to keep them alive. Agata put on her own equipment.

'Does everyone understand what we need to do with the occulters?' The protocol she'd written had been copied discreetly from skin to skin, and some of the volunteers would not have received it until they'd reached this assembly point. In a perfect world they would have rehearsed the manoeuvre daily for a stint or two, but at least the jetpacks would handle most of the navigation.

'Can the machines drill into our bodies?' a young man asked anxiously.

'Not intentionally,' Agata assured him. 'They're not that sophisticated; they have no defensive strategies as such. The only danger is if they're so confused that they mistake you for rock, but if you get out of their way they won't pursue you.'

Serena passed Agata a helmet. They were aiming not to use the links; this would probably be their last chance to talk until they were back in the mountain again.

'Happy Travellers' Day,' Serena said.

'Happy Travellers' Day,' Agata replied. She put on her helmet and turned towards the maintenance hatch.

A succession of shutters sealed off portions of the final length of the cooling tunnel, opening in sequence to allow air to pass from chamber to chamber at ever lower pressures until it was expelled into the void. The maintenance hatch wasn't meant to open unless the whole cycle had been stopped and all the chambers had reached the ambient pressure of the mountain's interior, but Serena's technician friends had managed to fake the sensor data to convince the hatch that it was safe to operate. The only catch was that it had been too complicated to try to lock it against any real part of the cycle. It would be up to each person exiting to synchronise their access with a time when the shutter below them wasn't open to the void.

Agata pressed her helmet to the hatch and listened to the sequence of clanks and hisses until the rhythm was embedded in her mind. The last time she'd dealt with machinery in the tunnels it hadn't ended well, but at least she'd had the timing right.

She slid the hatch open. Air blew in from behind her, but it only took a flicker for the pressure to equalise. She climbed into the tunnel and braced herself against the walls with her hands and feet. Serena closed the hatch behind her.

Agata waited in the dark, mentally composed but still viscerally terrified: there was absolutely nothing about the situation that her body found acceptable. She heard the creaking of the shutters above her and the sibilance of expanding gas drawing nearer.

A span from her head, the rotating disc of the shutter above her finally swung its aperture around to coincide with the tunnel. Agata felt the air rising up across her cooling bag, moving the opposite way to the usual cycle now that she'd wrecked the pressure gradient. But the sensors had been numbed – the anomaly would pass unnoticed.

When the shutter closed there was nothing to feel, and in the perfect darkness no way to be sure that it had happened. But then the exiting wind rustled the fabric on her limbs and starlight entered the tunnel from below. Agata didn't look down for confirmation; she just brought her limbs together and let herself fall.

Half a dozen strides from the outlet she drew a circle on her chest and the jetpack eased her to a halt, supporting her as she followed the rotation of the *Peerless*. She sketched an upwards arrow and ascended, until a safety handle set into the rock for maintenance workers came within reach. Wide-field cameras on the slopes monitored the space around the mountain, with their feeds analysed automatically to detect anyone in trouble falling away into the void, but as long as the team remained close to the hull they'd be out of view.

Agata waited for Serena to emerge, and for two more of their companions to join them. They couldn't stay to watch the whole team exit; there were only four handles, and hovering would waste too much air. Agata gestured to the others and they set off for the base.

The starlit slopes turned beneath them, the pale brown calmstone sliding past ever faster as they moved further from the axis, making their straight-line trajectories seem like giddy spirals. Agata kept watch for sudden changes in the topography ahead; the jetpacks knew the basic shape and motion of the *Peerless*, but they carried neither detailed surface maps nor proximity sensors. No one had ever intended the wearers to skim the slopes at high speeds, so if she slammed into an unexpected rise she'd only have her failing eyesight to blame.

The jetpack overshot the rim of the base, and the rock below her fell away to be replaced by black emptiness then a sudden, shocking dawn. She could see the blazing lights of the half of the transition circle that the mountain had been blocking, just peeking above the distant horizon. Agata sketched a down-arrow and the jetpack brought her closer to the rock; the dawn ahead vanished, but she still had the other half of the circle behind her. The base was slightly convex, so, however low she dropped, the *Peerless* wouldn't hide the entire transition circle, plunging her into complete darkness.

She looked around for the others; she could just make out Serena away to her left and another anti-saboteur to her right. The jetpacks had been programmed to take the volunteers to equally spaced points above the rim, but from here it was up to each of them to choose their path on a sweep in towards the axis.

The rock below her was a blur, moving past at more than a saunter every pause, but if she tried to match its velocity she'd be constantly using her jets to provide the necessary centripetal force – which would empty her air tank long before she got halfway to the axis. In all her training exercises with Tarquinia, in all the manoeuvres she'd performed around the *Surveyor*, she'd never faced anything like this.

The occulters could be waiting almost anywhere; in their final flight they could cover a lot of distance quickly. She couldn't assume that they'd all crawled close to their targets. So she had to find a compromise: she had to slow the relative motion of the rock just enough so she'd be sure to notice one of the machines sweeping by, and then try to move closer to the axis as quickly as she could, lessening the drain on the jets.

Agata turned herself around so she was facing the surface at an angle where she caught the reflection of the stars. The grey blur shimmered with colour now, the texture visible if still mysterious. She sketched a double arrow to begin reducing her relative motion; the jetpack complied, though it sent a warning message through her corset, alerting her to the cost.

She waited anxiously, afraid that this unrehearsed strategy would get her nowhere, but then the transition came in an instant: suddenly, the shimmer from the rock was comprehensible. Agata could see the small bumps and concavities, the fine crevices, an endless parade of details rushing by beneath her. The occulters had been clad well enough to blend in with the stone around them from a distance, but she was only a couple of strides from the surface. If she kept her concentration, the machines ought to be unmissable.

The mountain completed each rotation in less than seven lapses; her motion was stretching that out threefold, but rather than hanging back to witness a full turn at every radius she had to trust her companions to cover their own portions of the territory. Agata wished she could have made it a mathematical certainty that no square scant would go unsearched, but before she'd been out here and seen the conditions she'd been in no position to make binding plans. All she could do now was hope that most of the team found their own workable strategies, and between the symmetry of their initial placement and the shared conditions that prompted their individual actions they'd end up executing a combined sweep without too many gaps.

She began moving steadily in towards the axis.

The change below her was so stark and it came so abruptly that Agata almost began chasing it, but she caught herself in time. The smooth black expanse of the engine's rebounders was unmistakable, and the visual jolt of entering it was followed by near-perfect homogeneity. The idea of the occulters drilling into this precious lode was shocking – and it would also be the place where their camouflage was the least effective – but Agata decided not to speed past the region. However strong the argument for the machines avoiding it, she couldn't trust her adversaries not to exploit that presumption.

The surface became rough and grey again. Agata forced herself to readjust her expectations: her prey would show much less contrast now. The temptation to look around for her companions was growing, as much out of a longing for the support of their presence as any real fear for their safety. But with her front eyes fixed on the rock below, her rear gaze couldn't reach beyond the blackness of the orthogonal cluster. She tried to assuage the pangs by rekindling her anger with Ramiro and Tarquinia; at least that made her feel stronger and more focused. But as the pits and cracks in the stone swept by, she thought of Azelio, who believed that all their efforts were in vain. If a meteor had always been on its way, this charade would not deflect it.

A shape with hints of regular borders passed below her and was gone. Agata raised a triangle on her chest, the preprogrammed symbol to send the jetpack in pursuit. She waited anxiously for the rock to slow, but when it halted there was nothing below her. She edged sideways, stride by stride, and then there it was fixed to the rock: an occulter with a small package dangling from it, held in place by nothing but hooks and strings.

Ramiro had given her no details, but she'd been expecting some far more robust form of attachment. She took the knife from her tool belt, grabbed hold of the package and cut the strings.

The bombs would be driven by timers alone; any kind of trigger based on location would be too unreliable to take out all twelve channels simultaneously, and navigation was the occulters' job. Still, Agata kept the centrifugal weight on her cargo constant as she ascended from the rock, following a helix that kept the surface motionless beneath her. If everything she'd surmised was mistaken and some accelerometer was ready to cry foul, better not to take a piece of the mountain with her.

When she'd reached a decent altitude she let the jetpack kill her circular motion and spare itself the costly countervailing force. Nothing exploded. Agata was tempted, briefly, to try to prise open the stone box and take a look at the mechanism inside, but the risk of a booby trap seemed to outweigh any prospect of learning something useful.

She was still ascending slowly, in free fall now. She released her hold on the bomb, then instructed the jetpack to return her to the point where she'd left off. As she watched the package shrink into the darkness, a glorious ache of hope came to her unbidden. There were only a dozen bombs: the volunteers outnumbered them more than two-to-one. If even half the other searchers were as lucky as she'd been, the job would soon be done.

Back above the rock face, Agata fought to maintain her concentration. Twice she chased features in the stone that turned out to be nothing – perceptual illusions, or wishful thinking. It was better to pursue false alarms that to miss a single bomb, but her air supply wasn't infinite.

Looking back towards the rim she caught a glimpse of another searcher, a lonely silhouette against the blaze of the transition circle. By now there was no way of guessing who it was, but the figure looked safe and busy. It was tempting to exchange a few words, to compare counts, to share strategies . . . but even in its tightest directional mode the link was only for emergencies, so Agata did nothing to stop their drift apart.

The next find was so clear that Agata cursed her stupidity as she formed the triangle; the phantoms on which she'd wasted so much air seemed inexcusable now. As the rock halted, the occulter appeared almost directly below her, but she was surprised to see how different the package looked from the last one.

She moved closer. There were no strings; the bomb was secured to two posts that rose from the occulter's arms, lifting the rigid assembly clear of the dodecahedral core that held the air jets. But how had these posts been attached, out on the slopes? Was this the occulter that Tarquinia had repaired – and she'd had to perform some strange modifications in the void?

Agata was baffled, but she didn't have time to make sense of it. She took a wrench from her tool belt and set to work; the jetpack braced her with yet more expenditure of air. She tried to turn the post itself, but it was too smooth and she could get no purchase on it. She groped around the attachment point on the arms, but there was no bolt head. The posts seemed to be glued in place.

She closed one hand around the occulter's arm then shut off her jetpack's airflow completely, letting herself hang down across the vertical rock face. She took a flat bar and inserted it between the machine's arm and the rock, then began trying to prise the splayed drill bits out of the holes they'd made. But however hard she strained there was no perceivable effect; the drills were mounted too securely and the rock itself wasn't going to crack.

If she'd had more air she could have tried taking the drill assembly apart; she'd put half of them together herself, so she should have been able to reach in and unscrew all the same bolts by touch alone. But not while she was clinging to this sheer drop. She took a high-powered coherer in her free hand and began carving through the posts that held the bomb in place.

Every few lapses she had to stop and wait for the occulter to cool down; it wasn't smart enough to use its own air to deal with this unexpected contingency, and the heat was slow to dissipate into the rock. At least her own need to be able to hold onto the frame gave her a clear signal to act; it was unlikely that any temperature she could tolerate on her skin would be high enough to trigger the explosive.

When the second post was all but severed, she started up her jetpack to support her and then snapped the post by hand.

Agata moved quickly into a disposal trajectory, cancelling her motion around the axis as she ascended – rising a little faster than before, now that her cargo would have less time to reach a safe distance. She released the bomb and resumed the search. She was exhausted, but she still had enough air to go farther.

More experienced now, she dared to let the rock below her blur a little, trading off perfect clarity for less costly centripetal force. Agata didn't want to grow complacent, but the numbers were already better than she'd dared hope. While the majority of the team had barely been into the void before, five people had done maintenance work out on the hull. If those five alone had dealt with two bombs each, as she had, the job would already be completed.

The amorphous blur below her was broken by a sharp edge spinning by. Agata went in pursuit, astonished by her luck. She was beginning to pity all the searchers who must have come just as far with no result; everyone would understand that that might happen to them, but three times now she'd seen the signs that their collective effort was heading for victory, while others would still be wondering if the whole endeavour had been misconceived.

The third occulter came into view. The cargo was attached in exactly the same manner as it had been on the last one. Agata didn't delay her assault; she grabbed one of the posts, shut off the jetpack and began applying her coherer. But as she worked, she sifted through the possibilities.

Tarquinia had not repaired the lost occulter with stone and glue. This one and the last had not picked up their cargo in any manoeuvre out on the slopes; the bombs had been glued into place in a workshop somewhere. But how and why would Giacomo's people have retrieved occulters from the slopes in order to do that? The answer was that they hadn't. They'd built occulters for themselves, and affixed the bombs before sending them out.

Agata moved her grip and began cutting through the second post. Three bombs diverted out of a dozen had seemed glorious. Three out of an unknown swarm could mean anything.

Before she severed the second post completely, she stopped to think through her choices. If she spent air carrying the bomb onto the same kind of path as the others, that would be the end of her contribution; she'd have too little air left to intervene in any other way. But if there were already enough bombs waiting above the light collectors to cause the disruption, there was no need for this one to be carefully positioned. She could simply let it fall away into the void.

Agata looked up across the rock face; she could see a glimmer from the transition circle reflected in the dome of one of the light collectors. How many other bombs had been grabbed and slowed and sent to play their part in the pyrotechnics? She should trust her fellow searchers to have caught at least half a dozen by now – all the more so, given how plentiful they'd turned out to be.

She had one hand around the arm of the occulter, which remained firmly attached to the mountain. She snapped the second post and tossed the freed bomb over her shoulder, watching with her rear gaze as it tumbled down and disappeared.

But how many remained, clinging to the rock, waiting to make a final dash towards the collectors? A dozen? A gross? Agata closed her eyes and thought of letting go, falling clear of everything and losing herself in the stars.

She'd wanted a glimpse of the reunion before she died, but in the end the only thing that the future had ever promised her was the cosmos meeting up with itself: every particle, every field, every wrinkle in space matching perfectly as they came full circle. The geometry that achieved that had no need to please her; it was what it was, and she'd never been more than a tiny part of it. The miracle was that she'd lived to understand its nature as well as she had. But if a meteor struck or the bombs blew the axis open, she did not want to stay and witness the carnage.

Agata opened her eyes. Her right arm was aching; she pulled herself up and managed to grab the occulter with her left hand as well, but it was too awkward maintaining both holds so she let her right arm rest completely. She checked the clock on her belt by touch; less than two chimes remained to the disruption. She wasn't going to flee. She had no hope of finding another occulter on the rock face, but the time was approaching when the bombs could come to her.

She stared down into the transition circle, but then she caught herself and turned her gaze to the side, trying to adjust for her own rotation and the arc that her adversary would need to follow as it fought to cancel its greater sideways velocity and spiral in on the target.

She waited; the stars moved by serenely.

A dark speck interrupted the blaze of the colour trails. Agata didn't wait to guess its nature; she pushed away and let herself fall. As she plummeted beside the rock face she hunted for the occulter and found it again. It was almost level with her, hewing close to the rock just a saunter away. She started her jetpack and began arresting her fall, just in time – the thing was above her now. She drew an arrow on her chest, angled in anticipation, and rose to meet the machine.

She collided with it, her arms outstretched, grabbed it and held it fast. They tumbled together and struck the rock; the mountain scraped at her shoulder, shredding fabric and skin. Agata shouted from the pain and tried to form an arrow that would lift her clear, but nothing happened. Her jetpack was gone, smashed and torn away.

The half-circle of dawning stars wheeled around her. Agata looked directly at the thing in her embrace; she could feel its feeble puffs of air trying to get it back on course. All she could do was apply whatever muscular force she had left and hope that would be enough to propel it out of range.

Her left arm was useless after the blow from the mountain, but she managed to bring her legs up and brace her feet against the stone box. She watched the stars spinning, and thought her way into their cycle. Then she pushed her legs out and drove the occulter away.

The recoil slammed her against the rock. She closed her eyes as the mountain tore into her body.

A light appeared, penetrating her eyelids, filling her skull. Agata embraced the radiance and vanished.

33

'One day there'll be a whole set of synthetic influences that we can administer with a photonic device,' Maddalena predicted. 'There'll be tools for every occasion, but the best will be the one that forces the recipient to tell the truth.'

'That's your vision of the future, is it? That's what you've taken away from all this?' Ramiro stopped himself; whether she was goading him deliberately or not, he was wasting his energy. 'Just sign the release form and I'll get out of your way.'

'There'll still be a trial,' Maddalena insisted stubbornly. 'You know we can implicate her in the sabotage.'

'Whatever you say.'

Maddalena sprinkled dye on her palm and signed the form. Having released the longest-serving untried prisoners, the Council, even in its death throes, was still fighting every smaller concession. Nobody in the mountain was quite sure what Tarquinia had or hadn't done, but compared to four years without trial, four stints did not evoke quite so much passion. Ramiro had had the money for a bond himself, but it had taken all his time to collect the requisite eight dozen signatures from disinterested travellers willing to attest that her ongoing imprisonment offended their sense of justice.

He left Maddalena's office and headed for the jail.

At the guard post there was more bureaucracy to deal with. Ramiro tried to stay calm as all the paperwork he'd lodged was scrutinised and complained about and the associated photonic records summoned, peered at and misunderstood.

After half a bell of this idiocy, the guard told him, 'Just wait now. We're bringing her out.'

Ramiro watched her gait as she emerged. If she'd been shackled, she showed no sign of it now. He dragged himself forward and embraced her.

'Are you all right?'

'You know what they say,' Tarquinia replied. 'There's no greater honour than following Yalda, mother of all prisoners.'

Ramiro wasn't sure if she was being sarcastic.

'What did you hear about the disruption?' he asked, as they moved away down the corridor, side by side on the guide ropes.

'Explosions at the base. People coming and going from the void. The confused version everyone got in the aftermath – that's all, no details.'

Ramiro said, 'Two of the tubes were breached at the base, but they were resealed in time. Giacomo's group had their own occulters; they would have torn open the axis if they could.'

Tarquinia had thought things over for too long to be surprised by the betrayal. 'What stopped them?'

'Agata,' Ramiro replied. 'With a couple of dozen friends. They went out onto the base and tossed the bombs into the sky. Only three light collectors were physically damaged. It was the flash from the explosions that caused the disruption.'

Tarquinia absorbed that in silence.

'They saved the *Peerless*,' Ramiro said. His gratitude was sincere, but he still felt like a hypocrite.

'Was anyone hurt?'

'Agata lost a lot of flesh. For a couple of stints no one thought she'd survive, but she's finally recovering.'

Tarquinia hummed softly. 'Can we visit her?'

'Of course.'

As they dragged themselves towards the nearest stairwell, Tarquinia recounted her own misadventure. 'They let me have the observing time, and everything was looking perfect, but then the most officious busybody among my colleagues decided to check in on me just when I was inspecting the jetpack from the emergency kit. She decided that was suspicious enough to execute a citizen's arrest; most of the other staff thought she was an idiot, but she had an ally. I was afraid that if I was released, the two of them would be disgruntled enough to make a real effort to get the attention of someone with the power to mention the incident in an official message.'

'And then the Council would have known from the start.' The

whole crew would have been under close surveillance from the moment the *Surveyor* arrived.

'Exactly.' Tarquinia buzzed. 'So I ended up having to let myself be detained in a room at the observatory, with the idiots kept busy watching over me and arguing with my colleagues who wanted me released. It was only after the disruption that they managed to get the security department involved.'

They'd reached the level of the hospital; it was just a short walk up-axis now. Ramiro said, 'Before we see Agata, there's something I need to tell you.' He explained his debunking of the hoax. 'Don't be angry with me,' he pleaded. 'The whole thing about the ancestors was making her crazy.'

Tarquinia said, 'I'm not angry, but you shouldn't have told her that.'

'Why not?'

'I didn't make the inscription,' Tarquinia declared. 'I went out there to try, but nothing happened: no shards of stone rose from the ground to meet the chisel. I tried different tools, different movements . . . but I couldn't unwrite those symbols. If anything, when I left they were sharper than I'd found them – as if all I'd done was make the message less clear for Agata and Azelio than if I'd stayed away completely. I wasn't the author of those words. Someone else must be responsible for them.'

Ramiro didn't know if she was telling the truth or just trying to hold on to the benefits of the hoax, but he wasn't going to start questioning her version of events now. If this was her story, there was nothing he'd seen with his own eyes that contradicted it.

When they entered the hospital ward, Agata caught sight of Tarquinia and called out excitedly, 'Ah, you're free! Congratulations! Come and hear some great news!'

As they approached the sand bed, Ramiro could see that Agata had gained some flesh since his last visit, but she was still limbless. The doctors had told him that she would need every scrag of tissue to support her recovering digestive tract.

'What's the news?' Tarquinia asked her.

'I just had a visit from Lila and her student Pelagia,' Agata replied. 'The innovation block is well and truly over!'

'Yeah?' Tarquinia had probably been expecting to spend the whole visit trying to put the record straight about the inscription, but Agata's mind was on something else entirely.

'Pelagia's settled the topology question,' Agata proclaimed. 'The cosmos is a four-dimensional sphere. It's not a torus – it can't be!'

'This is from your work?' Ramiro asked. 'Pelagia found a way to complete the calculations?'

'Not so much complete them as see into my blind spot,' Agata explained. 'Listen, it's simple. A luxagen is described by a wave that changes sign when you rotate it by a full turn. That has no effect on any probability you calculate – so long as you apply the same rotation to everything in sight – because the probability comes from squaring the value of the wave. Minus one squared is one, so the change of sign makes no difference. It only shows up in more complicated experiments where you rotate some things and leave others unaltered.'

Tarquinia said, 'I follow that much.'

'Pelagia's idea just replaces rotations with trips around the cosmos. Suppose the cosmos were a four-dimensional torus, and you carried a luxagen all the way around it in a giant loop. What happens to the sign of its wave? Does it come back unchanged, or does it come back reversed?'

Ramiro frowned. 'I can tell that you want us to say "reversed" by analogy, but I thought there had to be perfect agreement around a loop.'

Agata buzzed. 'I didn't want you to give either answer. There could be perfect agreement, or the sign could be reversed: nothing rules out either possibility. If the sign's reversed, that will be undetectable: everything you can measure locally will still be in perfect agreement.'

Tarquinia said, 'Hang on, if the sign changes . . . where exactly does it change? What's this special place on the torus where it flips over?'

'There is no special place,' Agata insisted. 'It's like cutting open a band and rejoining the ends with a twist: once you've glued them together, there's really nothing special going on at the join. The twist isn't located there – or anywhere. It's a property of the whole band.'

Agata began to form a sketch, but Ramiro saw that she was having trouble so he drew what she'd described on his own chest.

'So you're talking about the cosmos being some kind of . . . twisted torus?' Tarquinia asked.

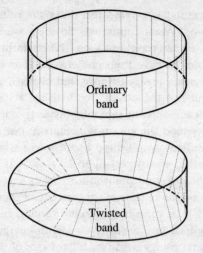

'No, not the cosmos,' Agata replied. 'The two bands, twisted or not, both have identical circles as their midlines—'

Ramiro added the midlines to his diagram.

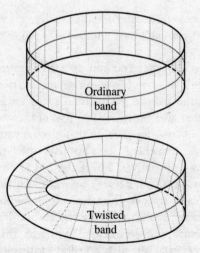

'—and you should think of *those circles* as the cosmos. What happens with the bands is an additional structure that the topology of the cosmos doesn't fix, one way or the other. It's all about the luxagens, not space itself.'

Tarquinia said, 'All right. I think I've got it.'

'Then the next step is to remember that we're talking about a *four-dimensional* torus,' Agata continued. 'So there are four completely different ways you can travel in a loop. There's nothing that compels those four routes to have the same effect – it would be perfectly consistent to have a luxagen whose sign changed around some of those loops but not the others. So there are sixteen possibilities altogether: for each loop, the sign might change or it might not.'

Ramiro understood the counting argument, but he couldn't see where it was leading. 'Aren't these distinctions all invisible, though? They have no effect on any probabilities.'

'They have no effect on probabilities,' Agata agreed. 'But if there were sixteen times more choices for the state of every luxagen, that would multiply their contribution to the vacuum energy by a factor of sixteen. Photons give a positive vacuum energy, but luxagens make the vacuum energy negative, and a factor of sixteen would be enough to guarantee that the total energy density in the cosmos was negative, *absolutely everywhere.*'

Ramiro struggled to recall the implications of this, but Tarquinia beat him to it.

'A negative energy density means positive curvature,' she said tentatively. 'But you can't have a torus that's positively curved everywhere.'

Agata chirped. 'Exactly! You end up with a contradiction. So the cosmos can't be a torus. But in a four-sphere, every route you might travel can be shrunk down gradually to a tiny circle, and then to a point: a path that goes nowhere. The sign of the wave can't change along a path that goes nowhere, so there are no extra modes for the luxagens. The vacuum energy stays positive, which means the curvature will mostly be negative – but it also has to change from place to place, because you can't have uniform negative curvature on a sphere. And because the curvature depends on the entropy of matter, that has to change too. That's why the cosmos isn't in a state of equally high entropy everywhere. That's why there's a gradient. That's why we exist at all: with a history, with memories, with an arrow of time.'

Watching her as she spoke, Ramiro couldn't help sharing her joy. Perhaps the discovery changed nothing tangible, but it vindicated all her years of effort – and it proved that the *Peerless* was back on course. New ideas were possible again. The paralysis was over.

'And that settles everything?' he asked. 'Cosmology is complete now?'

'Not at all!' Agata replied gleefully. 'There are still dozens of open questions. People will be working on this until the reunion, and beyond.'

Tarquinia said, 'I have some news of my own that you should hear.'

Ramiro had been afraid that the change of subject would go down badly, but Agata listened to the revised version of the last day on Esilio with no sign of hostility.

When Tarquinia was finished, Agata said mildly, 'I'm glad you weren't lying to me, after all.' She glanced over at Ramiro. 'And I'm glad you weren't either, even if you meant to.' It was an infinitely gentler barb than he'd expected.

A doctor approached and suggested that they let Agata rest. Agata glanced down at her shrivelled torso, as if she'd forgotten the state of it while they'd been talking. 'Not one person has said that I look like I've shed twice,' she complained. 'I've been ready to tell them the names of the children, but the joke's just not happening.'

Tarquinia placed a hand gently against her cheek. 'Get strong. We'll see you again soon.'

Ramiro shared a meal with Tarquinia in the food hall, then they retired to his apartment.

'What is it that's troubling you?' Tarquinia asked. 'I thought it was the inscription, but Agata was fine about that.'

Ramiro didn't reply. Better to offer no denials or explanations, and she'd come to her own conclusions about the cause.

'We survived,' she said. 'We might have been fools to go along with Giacomo . . . but if we hadn't, what would have caused the disruption?'

'So whatever we did was just the way it had to be?' Ramiro had meant to sound sarcastic, but the words ended up more like a plea.

Tarquinia said, 'I wouldn't put it like that. But with everyone clinging stubbornly to their own agendas, it's a miracle that it ended without a single death. It's physics that makes us free – binding our actions to our intentions – but in a tight enough corner with enough people refusing to act against their nature, it's not hard to imagine that the only route to consistency might involve killing them all.'

Ramiro couldn't keep silent. 'Giacomo told me what he'd planned,' he said.

Tarquinia was confused. 'When?'

'After you disappeared. I went looking for him, to see if he could get me out into the void.'

'But he couldn't.'

Ramiro said, 'He told me there was no need. He told me that they had more than enough occulters of their own to do the job – and that the job was much more than we'd asked for.'

'So what could you have done?' Tarquinia still wanted to smooth it over. 'It's not your fault that you didn't have Agata's idea, and you couldn't risk going to the Council.'

Ramiro said bluntly, 'I wanted it. For a while. I wanted exactly what he wanted.'

'Why?' she asked.

'Because the way things are makes me angry,' he said. 'I'm not afraid that men will be wiped off the mountain – I'm afraid that nothing will ever change for us. We'll keep on being made for the one remaining purpose where we can't be replaced, and if we try to do anything else with our lives we'll be treated like mistakes.'

Tarquinia was silent for a while. Ramiro had expected her to be enraged and disgusted, but even if that had been her first impulse she seemed to be searching for another response.

'Do something,' she said.

'I'm sorry?'

'If you want things to change, you're going to have to do something.'

'Like Pio? Like Giacomo?'

Tarquinia hummed impatiently. 'No. Tamara didn't blow anything up. Carlo didn't blow anything up.'

Ramiro said, 'I'm not a biologist. I don't know how to fix the problem that way.'

'What do you want for the men who come after you?'

'I want them to have easier choices than I had.'

'That's a little vague,' Tarquinia complained. 'But I'm sure we can work on it. There's an election coming up, and we haven't had a single male Councillor for far too long.'

Ramiro drew away from her. 'No. Find another punishment.'

'You want change,' she said. 'It's Giacomo's way, or it's politics.'

'I'm not too old to study biology.'

'I think you might be.' Tarquinia became serious. 'If even a fraction of the men on the *Peerless* feel that there's nothing left to do but plant a bomb somewhere, we're never going to have peace. If you've shared that rage, if you understand it, it's your responsibility to help find a better way.'

Ramiro replied irritably, 'And the women who run things have nothing to do with it?'

'I didn't say that. We're still insecure, because we know exactly how bad it would be for us if everything unwound. But do you really think the only voice for men on the Council should come from women?'

'Not at all. I've voted for male candidates, but they never get a seat.'

Tarquinia said, 'Consider it. That's all I'm asking.'

They shared Ramiro's bed, but lay apart. Ramiro watched Tarquinia sleeping in the moss-light. He didn't know if she was telling the truth about the inscription, but he didn't care; he'd had enough of trying to fit his own life around some supposed future certainty.

Whatever had been written in the rocks on Esilio, in six generations the travellers had discovered everything they needed to return in safety and protect the home world. The hardest task now would be to find a way to live in peace for six more, and reach the end of the journey without throwing everything away.

34

Valeria woke in darkness to shouts of panic from the street below. She clambered out of bed and looked down from her window. Everyone was staring into the eastern sky.

'Was it a Hurtler?' she called out. She could see nothing unusual herself now, but a fast-moving near miss might have unsettled people.

'It's the sun, you fool!' a woman replied.

Valeria could make no sense of this. Had another planet been ignited – had Pio gone the way of Gemma? Pio might well have risen by now, but she could see no evidence that the world had gained a third sun while she slept.

'Where?' she demanded.

The woman pointed towards an unremarkable patch of sky. If it did contain Pio, the planet was too dim to discern without some concerted staring. Valeria wondered if the crowd had succumbed to a kind of collective hallucination. She'd imagined fires out in the desert herself, when she'd been tired enough, but right now her lack of sleep seemed merely to have left her bleary-eyed, struggling to focus on the stars right ahead of her, as if she'd developed a blind spot—

In fact there was a small black absence in her vision, but when she moved her eyes it stayed fixed in the sky. She ducked back into her room and checked the clock beside her bed, by touch. She'd slept far later than she'd realised: it was a bell after dawn.

The black disc in the east was the sun.

Eusebio said, 'I don't see how a Hurtler could do this. Gemma made perfect sense, but how could an impact put out the fire across a whole star?'

Valeria sat in a corner of the meeting room with her dye and paper, listening to the twelve men of Zeugma's Fire Watch Committee who'd assembled on this lamp-lit afternoon. The Committee had made plans long ago for every imaginable crisis, but no one had anticipated this eerie extended night.

'A large enough shock to the surface might disrupt the reaction,' Cornelio proposed. 'We have no experience of the interaction between combustion and extreme seismic events, but if a pressure wave altered the structure of the sunstone, even temporarily, it's conceivable that the flame might be extinguished.'

'Across the entire surface?' Eusebio was sceptical. 'I could believe a Hurtler inducing a dark patch at the point of impact, a flameless region that survived for a bell or two. But not this.'

Giorgio gestured towards the window. 'The result's not in dispute. And if a Hurtler wasn't the culprit, what alternative is there?'

Valeria raised his words on her chest and looked around the room, poised to squeeze one more contribution onto the page, but no one had an answer for Giorgio so she took the opportunity to dust her skin with dye and commit the discussion so far to paper.

'At least the agricultural effects might be positive,' Eusebio suggested hopefully. 'If the uncovered crops finally get something close to the old cycle of illumination, that ought to lead to higher yields.'

He looked to Adelmo, but the agronomist spread his hands in a gesture of uncertainty. 'Gemma's bright enough to ruin the night, but it might not be bright enough to count as a signal for day.'

Silvio entered the room and spoke privately with Eusebio. Valeria heard a snatch of the conversation, as Eusebio's voice rose in incredulity. 'She told them it would happen?'

When the exchange was over, Eusebio looked agitated. 'The meeting's adjourned until tomorrow,' he said. Valeria began gathering her papers, preparing to leave Eusebio huddling with his confidants to discuss Silvio's news, but to her surprise he walked straight up to her.

'Could you come with me to the prison?' he asked.

'Why?'

Valeria's look of panic seemed to dispel his disquiet. 'No one's arresting you,' he joked. 'I just want you to come and talk to someone.'

'You want me to keep a record?' She fumbled with her box of dyes.

'That wouldn't hurt,' Eusebio decided. 'But actually, she asked for you by name.'

'I'm not the only person in Zeugma with that name.' Valeria trusted Eusebio not to form unwarranted conclusions, but she didn't want to be known as having criminal associates.

Eusebio said, 'She asked for Yalda's adopted daughter. And she said something about Nereo's force that the jailers were incapable of conveying precisely. So I'm fairly sure that she did mean you.'

There was nothing unusual about the sight of Zeugma lit by Gemma alone, but Valeria's body had its own reckoning of the time and the disjunction rendered the streets hallucinatory. She followed Eusebio across the dark cobblestones towards an encounter with a mad-woman.

'She gave her name as Clara,' Eusebio explained as they walked into the entrance hall. 'I know everything else has to be nonsense. The guards probably half-remembered what she'd said, and when this bizarre thing happened they reinterpreted her words in the light of it.'

Valeria said nothing; she had no theories.

They sat in an interview room, waiting for Clara to be brought up from the cells. When the guard led her in, a chain looped around her melded arms, Valeria's skin tingled all over. She'd never set eyes on the woman before, but the prisoner was beaming as if she'd just walked into the presence of two long-lost friends.

Eusebio gestured to Clara that she should take a seat. She complied, and the guard left them.

'Can you understand my speech?' Clara asked. She spoke with a heavy accent that Valeria couldn't place.

Eusebio said, 'Yes.'

'I hope I've got the grammar and vocabulary correct. We have written sources, but no sound recordings.'

'Sound recordings?' Eusebio buzzed appreciatively. 'That's an inventive embellishment, I'll give you that.'

Clara said, 'I gave the city police the location of my rocket. If they'd sent someone to look at it, that would have saved us all this con-fusion.'

Eusebio replied bluntly, 'The *Peerless* isn't due to return for three years. And when it does, I think we'll manage to spot the engines in the sky.'

Clara tipped her head, amused. 'Some people did argue for a light show to help set the scene . . . but then, I was in the other camp who thought that *putting out the sun* really ought to be more than enough to establish our credentials.'

Valeria watched Eusebio. He said, 'Conjurors have made an art out of convincing people that they've foretold the future. The jailers here must have made a good audience.'

'The *Peerless* did travel three full years into your future.' Clara sketched a portion of the mountain's proposed trajectory on her chest, but every educated person in Zeugma was aware of that. 'At the turnaround our plan was to follow a straight line back home and then decelerate for a year. But eventually we realised that it would be perfectly safe to arrive earlier. So we executed a big loop, going a few years into the future then curving around and travelling a few years into the past.' She added these unlikely adornments to her diagram. 'All of that happened before I was born, though. For most of my life, the *Peerless* was travelling homewards through the void at a time, by your reckoning, when it was yet to leave the ground. And I saw the old mountain through a telescope when we passed it! It was still accelerating, burning sunstone. We weren't so visible: our engines work very differently – they don't consume fuel at all.'

Valeria said, 'Why did you ask for me?'

Clara turned to her with an expression of terrifying joy. 'When I was a girl, I read Yalda's biography, and there was a story she'd told one of her friends about you. You gave her a gift before she left Zeugma: a diagram showing Nereo's force for spherical shells.'

'There were a lot of people at that party,' Valeria pointed out, trying not to be rattled. Eusebio's point about conjurors was an apt one. 'A lot of people could know that.'

Clara tried to gesture with her arms; she'd forgotten that they were melded behind her back. 'Is this really going to be so hard? If there's nothing I can say that could convince you, can't we ride out to the place where I arrived?'

Eusebio said, 'So the *Peerless* itself is still out in the void, and the other travellers just let you come down here alone?'

'There was a lottery for the privilege,' Clara replied. 'I walked empty-handed into Zeugma because that seemed like the right spirit in which to come: no showy artefacts, certainly no weapons. I thought I'd end up engaged in some spirited debates at the university for a couple of days, outraging the physicists with my claims about luxagen waves until astronomical events finally proved my credentials.'

'Arrest for trespass wasn't part of your plan.'

Clara said, 'I hold no grudges against anyone for my own mistakes. But I would be lying to you if I didn't admit to some disillusionment. If you have no thanks for me, I can promise you that you owe them to my forebears. When I tell you their history, you'll understand your debt.'

Eusebio began shivering. Before Valeria's eyes, his composure disintegrated.

'Forgive me,' he pleaded. 'Let me deal with your chains, then we'll find a place for you to rest. If you'll accept my hospitality—'

Valeria was confused. 'Why do you believe her now?'

Clara turned to Valeria. 'You still need to see the rocket?'

'I'm afraid so.' The woman had managed to prick Eusebio's conscience, but his guilt over the travellers' ordeal had no bearing at all on her story's credibility.

'Then let's go for a ride.'

Silvio drove the three of them out into the desert. Gemma was setting, but four long Hurtlers lit the sky.

'Why would anyone want to put the sun out?' Valeria demanded.

'We're planning to turn half the surface into an engine.' Eusebio had had Clara's hands separated; she gestured as if she were cupping a globe. 'Moving the sun is the safest way to move the world. There'll still be some seismic activity as it tugs you along, but not as much as if we put the engines here on the ground.'

'Tugs us along?'

'You have heard of gravity?' Clara joked. 'And we'll be bringing Gemma as well, for light. It will end up closer when the new orbits settle, so it will do a better job than it does now.'

'But where would we be going?' Valeria was furious that she had to conduct the whole interrogation herself. Eusebio was huddled beside them in silence, apparently too ashamed to speak. He'd wanted to get Clara ensconced in the largest guest room of his father's mansion immediately, but she'd insisted on making the trip first.

'This planet needs to match velocities with the Hurtlers,' Clara explained.

'Which would just turn everything else around us into Hurtlers!'

Valeria protested. 'You didn't research this fraud well enough. The *Peerless* went into a dust-free corridor, but it doesn't stretch on for ever. If we followed the mountain's route, what would we do at the end?'

Clara said, 'Actually, you could zigzag up and down the corridor on a trajectory that would last for eons, but we settled on a better solution than that. If you shadow a world in the orthogonal cluster, we can read the future density of dust in the region by inspecting its surface. That's the helpful thing about a time-reversed planet: it gives you a forecast that can't be wrong.'

Valeria couldn't fault the woman's imagination. At the very least, she must have gone to one of Yalda and Eusebio's recruiting lectures when they were trying to assemble the crew for the *Peerless*. Maybe she'd even signed up, but then lost her courage at the last moment.

'Here we are,' Clara announced.

Valeria had been expecting some kind of conical structure adorned with parachutes, contrived to resemble one of the test rockets that had made short flights and returned, but perhaps Clara hadn't been close to the real project after all. The object sitting on the sand, a few saunters from the road, looked like a small stone cabin on stilts, with the upper parts of each wall tilted outwards so that the windows they bore faced down at an angle. Just getting the bizarre construction here must have involved quite an investment – but what advantage did the woman hope to garner?

The four of them trudged across the desert together. Silvio looked even more contemptuous of the whole farce than Valeria, but he said nothing.

'Where are the engines?' Valeria asked.

'Underneath, of course.' Clara gestured to the bottom of the floor, about a stride above the ground. Valeria ducked down between the stilts.

'There's nothing here but a kind of . . . black mirrorstone,' she reported. It was hard to see much by starlight, but the surface looked utterly smooth and unbroken. 'Where does the exhaust come out?'

'There is no exhaust. Just light.'

'Light? Your rocket runs on light, but no one spotted you descending?'

'Ultraviolet light,' Clara persisted. 'The faster the light a rocket uses, the less heat it generates in the process.'

Valeria emerged and straightened up. 'Let me guess: your vehicle suffered some damage in the landing, but with sufficient funds you could get it working again. Your backers will be rewarded, of course, with new inventions that will put them so far beyond their rivals—'

Eusebio said angrily, 'Enough! Whatever you believe, this woman is my guest, and I won't allow you to talk to her that way.'

Clara said, 'Scepticism is an admirable trait, and we seem to have confused everyone by arriving early.' She turned to Valeria. 'My vehicle suffered no damage. And I promised you a ride.'

Valeria stared at her. 'You want to . . . ?' She pointed upwards.

'Yes. Eusebio? Will you come with us?'

He said, 'If you're sure you're not too tired.'

'I'm not a pilot; the photonics – the machines – will do everything for us. Silvio?'

Silvio said, 'Thanks, but I should watch the truck.'

Clara led Valeria and Eusebio up the short flight of stairs and through the doorway. Valeria's gut was squirming: she didn't know what she believed any more, but just letting the woman take charge felt dangerous.

A little starlight entered through the cabin's thick windows; Valeria could make out four couches and what looked like a tank of compressed air. Clara said, 'Lights,' and three large panels in the ceiling immediately began to glow. Valeria reached up and pressed her fingers to the illuminated surfaces; she could feel no heat, and the light was impossibly steady for any kind of lamp.

'How . . . ?' she pleaded.

Clara said, 'Nothing I say would make any sense to you until you've learnt about the energy levels in a solid. But don't worry, I'm sure I could bring you up to speed in about a stint.' She gestured at the couches. 'It shouldn't be bumpy at all, but the protocol is to strap in during take-off.'

Valeria lay down on one of the couches and Clara helped her with the harness before attending to Eusebio.

'There should be a reception at the university tomorrow, or the Council chambers,' he babbled.

'I'll be happy to talk to anyone, anywhere,' Clara assured him. 'Anyone but jailers.'

She climbed onto her own couch. 'Pilot?' A diagram appeared on the wall, as self-luminous as the ceiling panels. After a moment,

Valeria thought she recognised it as a topographical map of Zeugma's environs.

Conjurors could do all kinds of things with lenses and hidden lamps. But they were getting close to the moment of truth, and if this woman had secreted a few hefts of sunstone above the smooth black panel in the floor with the hope of actually making this cabin fly, the only effect it was likely to produce would be to incinerate them all.

'Pilot: plan a vertical ascent to an altitude of five slogs, followed by a return to our starting point, with a maximum deviation of one part in six from standard gravity.'

The topographical map *tilted* and became something like an artist's rendering of the landscape. Then the viewpoint ascended to take in an ever wider portion of the desert, while a dashed red line rose up from the ground, sprouting strange annotations.

Valeria said hurriedly, 'I believe you! We don't have to do this!' In truth she still doubted the woman's story, but she did not want to be proven right and consumed by flames.

Clara buzzed mischievously. 'Don't be a killjoy. Pilot: execute the plan.'

Valeria felt a gentle pressure pushing her into the couch, as if someone had placed a young child on her belly. She looked to the window; they really were ascending, albeit with an impossible grace. No one could have done this but a traveller returned.

Clara dimmed the lights so that they could see out more easily, but once the hills by the roadside had dropped from view there was nothing in sight from their present vantage but the unchanging sky.

'You can get up now if you like,' Clara announced, unstrapping herself and rising to her feet. Eusebio did the same, then Valeria joined them by the window. The dark ground was receding rapidly; she could already see the lights of the city. But their motion was so smooth that it felt more like the product of ropes and pulleys than any kind of rocket.

Valeria said, 'I'm sorry I doubted you. I'm sorry for what we've put you through.'

'It's all right,' Clara assured her. The traveller put an arm around her shoulders.

'Yalda's really dead,' Valeria said. 'Years ago. Generations ago.'

'Yes. But she had four wonderful children in the flesh, and in spirit you could call her the mother of us all.'

Eusebio leant against the window, covering his eyes.

Valeria composed herself. 'When can we meet everyone? When are they coming to Zeugma?'

Clara said, 'There'll be other emissaries soon. Once I've reported back.'

'But the *Peerless*—?'

'The mountain itself won't come down to the surface. People will be welcome to visit it, but most of the travellers won't be settling on the home world.'

Valeria was astonished. 'They're going to stay inside?'

'Some will,' Clara replied. 'It's what they're used to. Some might settle on the sun, opposite the engines, if it proves safe there.'

Valeria gazed down at the crevasse that divided Zeugma; from this height, in the starlight, it looked like a faint scratch.

'Tell me about your family,' she begged Clara. 'Your father, your brother and sister, your co.'

Clara hesitated. 'I don't have that kind of family.'

'They all died?' Valeria was horrified.

'No, no! Of course not.'

'So . . . you're a solo?' With no father, so her mother must have fissioned spontaneously, like Valeria's mother Tullia. 'But you didn't even have a brother and sister?'

Clara said, 'Most of us have just one child. My mother shed me; I shed my daughter.'

Valeria understood. She felt a slight giddiness at the implications, then it gave way to a glorious sense of a new world spreading out beneath her gaze.

Eusebio turned from the window. 'And who has the sons?'

Clara thought for a moment. 'I said mother and daughter, but they're not the right words. We tried very hard to live as men and women, but we couldn't make that work, so we folded the two into one. My "mother" raised me as a father would, as I raised my own "daughter".'

'So you've wiped out all the men?' Eusebio asked numbly.

'No more than all the women,' Clara insisted. 'If I can promise myself to a child, how am I a woman? If my flesh can become that child, how am I a man?'

Eusebio looked sickened, but he fought to maintain decorum.

'These are your choices,' he said. 'If we're to accept your help, we should respect your culture.'

Valeria buzzed. 'Could I be the father of my own child – and live to see her do the same?'

Clara said, 'Yes.'

'But what about my co?'

'Between you, you'll have to decide. He could be the father of your child, if you both wanted that.'

'And I could still live? He could trigger me, and I could survive?'

'Yes.'

Valeria looked down at the speck of light that had been her city. 'Who did all these things? We have to know their stories.'

'You will,' Clara promised. 'We had some good archivists, but I think the translations will need to be a collaborative project.'

'How many generations was the voyage?' Eusebio asked.

'About a dozen.'

'A dozen,' he repeated. 'An era.'

All of this had grown out of Eusebio's endeavours – and in one year from the launch, not four. Valeria thought it must feel as if he'd stepped out of his house for a day and returned to find his children replaced by a whole vast swarm of descendants, all of them with strange ideas of their own.

Valeria said, 'And how many people lived and died in the mountain, without seeing the end?'

Clara squeezed her shoulder. 'A lot.'

Valeria pictured them, generation after generation, lined up across the years. Farmers and physicists, inventors and instrument builders, maintenance workers, millers and cleaners, biologists and astronomers. Hidden behind her outstretched thumb, for ever out of reach. 'I wish I could talk to them,' she said. 'I wish I could thank them. I wish I could tell them that it wasn't for nothing, that it ended well.'

Clara said, 'If that's what you want, then I believe you'll find a way.'

Appendix 1:
Units and measurements

Distance		*In strides*
1 scant		1/144
1 span	= 12 scants	1/12
1 stride	= 12 spans	1
1 stretch	= 12 strides	12
1 saunter	= 12 stretches	144
1 stroll	= 12 saunters	1,728
1 slog	= 12 strolls	20,736
1 separation	= 12 slogs	248,832
1 severance	= 12 separations	2,985,984

Home world's equator = 7.42 severances		22,156,000
Distance from *Peerless*		
to the Object = 193 severances		576,294,912
Home world's orbital radius = 16,323 severances		48,740,217,000

Time		*In pauses*
1 flicker		1/12
1 pause	= 12 flickers	1
1 lapse	= 12 pauses	12
1 chime	= 12 lapses	144
1 bell	= 12 chimes	1,728
1 day	= 12 bells	20,736
1 stint	= 12 days	248,832

Peerless's rotational period = 6.8 lapses	82

In years

1 year	= 43.1 stints	1
1 generation	= 12 years	12
1 era	= 12 generations	144
1 age	= 12 eras	1,728
1 epoch	= 12 ages	20,736
1 eon	= 12 epochs	248,832

Angles   *In revolutions*

1 arc-flicker		1/248,832
1 arc-pause	= 12 arc-flickers	1/20,736
1 arc-lapse	= 12 arc-pauses	1/1,728
1 arc-chime	= 12 arc-lapses	1/144
1 arc-bell	= 12 arc-chimes	1/12
1 revolution	= 12 arc-bells	1

Mass   *In hefts*

1 scrag		1/144
1 scrood	= 12 scrags	1/12
1 heft	= 12 scroods	1
1 haul	= 12 hefts	12
1 burden	= 12 hauls	144

Prefixes for multiples

ampio-	$= 12^3$	= 1,728
lauto-	$= 12^6$	= 2,985,984
vasto-	$= 12^9$	= 5,159,780,352
generoso-	$= 12^{12}$	= 8,916,100,448,256
gravido-	$= 12^{15}$	= 15,407,021,574,586,368

Prefixes for fractions

scarso-	$= 1/12^3$	= 1/1,728
piccolo-	$= 1/12^6$	= 1/2,985,984
piccino-	$= 1/12^9$	= 1/5,159,780,352
minuto-	$= 1/12^{12}$	= 1/8,916,100,448,256
minuscolo-	$= 1/12^{15}$	= 1/15,407,021,574,586,368

Appendix 2:
Light and colours

The names of colours are translated so that the progression from 'red' to 'violet' implies shorter wavelengths. In the *Orthogonal* universe this progression is accompanied by a decrease in the light's frequency in time. In our own universe the opposite holds: shorter wavelengths correspond to higher frequencies.

Colour	IR Limit	Red	Green	Blue	Violet	UV limit
Wavelength, λ (piccolo-scants)	∞	494	391	327	289	231
Spatial frequency, κ (gross cycles per scant)	0	42	53	63	72	90
Time frequency, ν (generoso-cycles per pause)	49	43	39	34	29	0
Period, τ (minuscolo-pauses)	36	40	44	50	59	∞
Velocity, v (severances per pause)	0	41	57	78	104	∞
(dimensionless)	0	0.53	0.73	1.0	1.33	∞

The smallest possible wavelength of light, λ_{min}, is about 231 piccolo-scants; this is for light with an infinite velocity, at the 'ultraviolet limit'. The highest possible time frequency of light, ν_{max}, is about 49 generoso-cycles per pause; this is for stationary light, at the 'infrared limit'.

Afterword

Gravitation and cosmology in the *Orthogonal* universe are governed by essentially the same equation that governs the geometry of our own universe: the relationship between the curvature of space-time and the density and flow of matter and energy that was proposed by Einstein in 1916. The solutions of Einstein's equation that describe our universe have three dimensions of space and one of time, but the equation itself can easily accommodate four space-like dimensions.

As in our own universe, Newtonian gravity with its inverse-square law of attraction serves as a good approximation to the effects of mass on curvature. The only departures on the scale of planetary systems are in the very same subtle effects that were ultimately understood through general relativity in our own history – but here they are reversed. The precession of close orbits goes backwards in the *Orthogonal* universe, compared with the precession of Mercury's orbit that Einstein's theory explained. And where Einstein predicted twice as much deflection of starlight by the sun than would be expected under Newtonian gravity, the degree to which light is bent is *less* in Lila's relativistic theory than in the classical version attributed here to Vittorio.

In cosmology, the solutions with and without a time dimension have much more radical differences. For example, there is no equivalent in our own universe of the kind of high-entropy state where the world lines of star clusters are equally likely to be pointing along any direction in all four dimensions, and the arguments in the novel over the inevitability or otherwise of the entropy gradient are very different from arguments over possible explanations for the low entropy of our own universe at the Big Bang.

But it's the necessity for the *Orthogonal* universe to be finite in all directions that has the most striking consequences, requiring the entire history of the universe to return eventually to its initial state – wherever one starts from, and whichever direction in four-space is treated as 'time'.

Supplementary material for this novel can be found at www.gregegan.net.